The Woman
at Otowi Crossing

OTHER BOOKS BY FRANK WATERS

The Woman at Otowi Crossing

a novel by

FRANK WATERS

SAGE BOOKS

SWALLOW PRESS
ATHENS, OHIO • CHICAGO

First Edition

Second Printing 1970

*Reprinted in 1981 by
Ohio University Press*

Sage/Swallow Press Books
are published by
Ohio University Press
Athens, Ohio 45701

LIBRARY OF CONGRESS CATALOG NUMBER 66-25961
ISBN 0-8040-0415-3

NOTE

Much has been published about the actual woman who lived at Otowi Crossing, including her recipe for chocolate cake corrected for every change in altitude. Despite the homely facts known of her simple life, there gathered about her an air of mystery no one could dispel. Today her life has grown into a myth composited by the legends and folklore of three races, Indian, Spanish, and Anglo. This novel is a narrative of the growth and meaning of that myth.

F.W.

PROLOGUE

Excerpt from the *Secret Journal* of Helen Chalmers, now so widely known as the "Woman at Otowi Crossing."

There is no such thing as time as we know it. The entire contents of all space and time co-exist in every infinite and eternal moment. It is an illusion that we experience them in a chronological sequence of "time."

As you know, Jack, I didn't learn this gradually during all my lonely years running this obscure tea room at a remote river crossing. I was trying to escape a miserable past, suffering the makeshifts of the day, dreading the future. Then suddenly it all spun before me like a wheel turning full circle. Everything I had known and would ever know congealed into one rounded, complete whole. And it's been that way more or less ever since.

Perhaps none of us really ever learn anything by degrees. We just keep on absorbing things unconsciously without realizing what they mean. Till suddenly, for no apparent reason, it all comes into focus with a blinding flash. Civilizations like people must evolve the same way. Not continuously. But by steps. Sudden unfoldments and blossomings like the Renaissance and the Atomic Age, followed by another dormant period of darkness and ignorance. So too do planetary systems form and re-form in bursts of fiery nebulae, solely to conform with our own expanded realizations. For they are all within ourselves—the continents, worlds and stars. We contain the contents of all space as well as of time.

What determines when we are ready for these mysterious up-surges and Emergences? I don't know, Jack. I don't know why this happened to me when it did. All I know is that it started late that afternoon when we were waiting for the last run on the Chile Line. We heard her whistle as she came around the bend. I was thinking then in terms of time. That this was the last lonely screech from my darling little narrow-gauge and a life going from me forever—and with it my livelihood from a tea room here. I didn't know that it was whistling in a new life, a whole new era. But these, I found, were illusions too. There are no beginnings, no ends, nothing new. Everything has always been within us, just waiting to be recognized.

It happend like this . . .

THE WOMAN AT OTOWI CROSSING

Part One

1.

The woman at Otowi Crossing heard it now for the last time as she had heard it day after day for years on end: that long-drawn, half-screech, half-wail of No. 425 whistling round the bend—to her the most mysteriously exciting, excessively romantic, and poignantly haunting sound in the world. Sitting on a weathered bench in front of the narrow-gauge siding, she peered eagerly forward through the blood-reddening New Mexican dusk.

"Take it easy, Helen." The man beside her laid his hand lightly but warningly on her shoulder. She reached up her own hand to grasp his without swerving her gaze from the jutting mountain slope ahead.

Even before the train rounded the bend, the woman could see the smoke rolling up the blackened face of the redrock cliff, hear the flanges of the wheels squealing on the curve, feel the earth trembling with a nervous and joyous expectancy. And now she was coming round the mountain as she had always come, impacted with all the mystery of the far off and unreal, of mountain, mesa and mushroom butte, the mournful beauty of the timeless river that kept its pace, and all the aching loneliness of the ancient and eternal earth it threaded; coming round the mountain with a last loud whistle from her quill echoing up the dark canyon like the scream of a cougar.

The locomotive snorted in, spitting steam. One of the little Mikado eight-wheelers, with a polished brass number plate, a big square headlight box, a straight stack spouting hot cinders, and a brass bell tinkling behind it. A squat tender. A mail-express car followed by a single coach.

Helen caught her breath. There were no fishing rods protruding from its bay windows, no childish faces glued to dirty panes. The proud red plush seats were empty; the car was dark. Where were

11

the Spanish *paisanos* come from visiting *primos* forty miles upriver for the first time in their lives? An Indian sitting stiffly upright in his blanket, his enigmatic face turned a bilious green by the smoke, the jolting, and the dizzy fifteen miles an hour speed with which he was whirled around hairpin turns and over high trestles? The hunters standing in the vestibule with their rifles? No! There wasn't even a lady tourist and a city Anglo crowding the tiny observation platform in back.

It slid in slowly now. A locomotive and two cars. A ridiculously small train for all the noise and smoke it made, really. So ominously dark, so heartsickenly empty!

"Oh Jack!" She rose in disappointment as well as in welcome.

"You can't possibly expect her yet. Her letter didn't say when she was coming." The man's warm soothing voice lacked any trace of exasperation.

"It isn't that. It's — "

"But you knew the last passenger run was made a week ago."

"Yes, but to meet an empty train—"

The wheels screeched to a stop in front of the adobe squatting on the high bank of the Rio Grande, and the woman and man standing on the weeded siding before it. The warm, poignant smell of steam and coal smoke, cinders and clinkers—that cloying, irrepressible smell which for years had seeped into her tight adobe, her clothes closets and cooking pots, her very blood stream—choked Helen like a shawl. She threw it off to greet the crew.

The engineer was the first to climb down from the cab: a white-haired, portly Kewpie doll swaddled in starched, faded blue denim jumper and overalls, and wearing a red bandana around his throat.

"Uncle John!"

"Miss Chalmers, I do declare! Why, the minute we come round the bend and I seen the lamp in the window I knew you hadn't gone." Red-faced and grinning like a schoolboy, he shook hands formally, then permitted himself the paternal familiarity of patting her clumsily on the shoulder. "Howdy Jack."

"Did you hear that last whistle? It was just for you, Miss Chalmers. Strictly against regulations," added the scrawny fireman who had come up behind. Winter or summer, she had observed, Andy

Hawkins was always wiping sweat from his narrow, bony forehead with a grimy blue rag.

"For that she'll probably give you a second piece of cake, Andy," said Turner.

The brakie's last name Helen could never remember. He always seemed to be hunting it for her with a lantern. She watched him amble up, a lanky, loose-jointed Tennessee hill-billy who as a boy had heard, miles away, his first train whistle, and had followed its echo ever since.

"Hello Bill."

"Howdy, Ma'am. Mighty nice to find you here, Ma'am. To pass by a dark station on our last run would of broke our hearts."

"And Mr. Jackson." She stuck out her hand toward the conductor, patiently waiting for him to stow away his sheaf of onion-skin orders in a worn leather case, and to remove his gold rimmed spectacles. You would have thought he carried in the pockets of his thin, black alpaca jacket all the operating responsibilities of the whole Denver and Rio Grande Railroad, to say nothing of this inconsequential branch Chile Line.

"Yes indeed, Miss Chalmers. The wrecking crews are behind us, tearing up the rails. It's a sad business."

"I've got a bite for you," she said resolutely. "It's on the table now. Come in, all of you."

The chocolate-mud adobe seemed dwarfed by the huge cottonwoods around it, the patches of alfalfa glimpsed across the swollen Rio Grande, and the blue Sangre de Cristos rising beyond.

"Ready, Maria? Let's go."

She walked through the tiny entrance room, turned left into the dining room, and pulled back the chairs from the table. In a moment they were all seated: herself at the head, Jack Turner at the foot, two members of the crew on each side.

"Miss Chalmers' posole," sniffed Uncle John bending down.

The Indian woman shuffled in with an earthenware platter of brown-crusted bread toasted with butter, garlic and grated cheese.

"Miss Chalmers' bread." The brakie took two chunks.

"And Miss Chalmers' chocolate cake to come, I hope," laughed Turner. "The three things that have made your reputation, Helen—and that have outlasted the Chile Line itself. Ponder that please."

13

"Indeed, indeed." Mr. Jackson glanced at his watch, a perpetual recurring gesture. "When was it you came, Miss Chalmers?"

"So many years ago!" She clapped her hands softly for Maria to bring in the meat and green chiles. How she loved the taste of the roasted green pods in late summer; their aroma in winter as she ground them into red powder; the sight of them each fall, scarlet necklaces hung to dry from the roof tops up and down the whole valley! No wonder this little narrow-gauge which hauled them out to market had been nicknamed the Chile Line.

Uncle John wiped his hands on the red bandana knotted round his throat, and looked around the room. He did not have an eye to read the details of its beauty: the creamy adobe walls rubbed smooth with sheepskin, the fluid lines of the Indian corner fireplace, the tin reflectors behind the oil lamps. Only the effect of its gracious simplicity soothed him.

"By golly, you sure fixed the place up!" he declared with vehemence. "Takin' out that old counter and puttin' in a table or two makes it look real nice. You got yourself some new curtains, too!"

The memory of her early years came suddenly back to her. The appalling loneliness of an adobe lunchroom on a weedy siding of a remote baby-railroad line running from nowhere to nowhere. The strangely dressed Indians from the pueblo across river watching her with their dark inscrutable faces. The simple heart-rending fear of not making a dollar stretch to the next day. And the haunting fear of what she had left back East . . . Suddenly, unaccountably, a new premonition gripped her.

"What are you going to do now, Miss Chalmers?" the brakie asked forthrightly.

"She's going to stay right here," answered Turner calmly, "Chile Line or no Chile Line. Automobile tourists, picnickers, and visitors to the Frijoles ruins will keep her busy. I'm going to run a big ad in the paper that'll make Miss Chalmers' Tea Room known from Santa Fe to Antonito."

"I thought that little one-horse paper of yours was in worse shape than the Chile Line, Turner," said Uncle John somberly.

"It was, but it won't be long," he said sharply. "A rich Philadelphian has bought it and hired me to help spend his money on it."

"It's not that bad, Jack," Helen remonstrated. "You'll still be editor and can build it up as you've always wanted to. But anyway we're both going to get along fine. It's you we're worried about."

Uncle John opened his mouth in a wide yawn. "Time for me to retire. Albuquerque. A little house and chicken yard. Not too far for me and the Missus to keep an eye on you, Miss Chalmers."

"Andy and Bill are being reassigned to new runs in western Colorado," Mr. Jackson announced officially. "The System takes care of its employees."

"And you, Mr. Jackson?"

"I report back to Denver."

"Let me have the details on all of you. It's news, you know." Turner scribbled his notes on a piece of scratchpaper. "Tell me, Jackson, is it true the rails are being shipped to Burma? With war spreading—"

He was interrupted by a prolonged and impatient automobile horn sounding below at the narrow suspension bridge. A moment later the light of the car swung in upon the window. There sounded another impatient horning.

"Hey!" Turner shouted angrily.

"I'll go!" Helen walked to the door and opened it to a noisy pounding.

"This is Otowi Crossing, isn't it? Where's the sign?"

"What sign?"

"I was told there was a sign at the crossing pointing the road to the Los Alamos Ranch School For Boys."

The questioner was surveying the room over Helen's shoulder. He was in Army uniform, with shined boots, and wearing an eagle on his collar. She noticed that the two officers with him had stepped back respectfully in the dusk outside.

"There's never been a sign," she answered quietly, "but the road goes due west up the canyon. Keep to the right at the fork. The one to the left leads to the Frijoles cliff-dwellings."

"Thank you." He turned quickly and let his aides close the door behind him.

When Helen re-entered the dining room, Turner was still standing at the window, peering out between cupped hands. "A Colonel and a limousine Cadillac. What's the U. S. Army doing way up here in these God-forsaken mountains? Have the schoolboys up at

15

Los Alamos revolted against learning Greek and Latin? Maybe I ought to run up there."

Everybody laughed. "The Colonel probably has a son up there," said Helen lightly. "It's a very exclusive and expensive school, you know."

An uneasy silence moved into the room. Uncle John gathered up from the cloth the last crumbs of his chocolate cake. Mr. Jackson glanced at his watch. The moment which she had dreaded had come. She stood up to meet it.

"It's time for you to go, boys. You'll all come back to see me. Let's don't say good-bye."

Each member of the crew said it in his awkward way, none quite believing it, as they moved to the door. Long ago she had first stood there to confirm the rumors of a woman at Otowi Crossing—a scrawny young woman with hair skinned back over her ears, scared as a rabbit, offering coffee, sandwiches and cake. In the lamplight now she seemed a different woman: full-formed and mature, with a gracious ease and quiet assurance. Yet strangely it was the younger woman they remembered and would always remember. It seemed impossible that they would never be back, that the very tracks they came on were being torn from the earth to which they were rooted.

Maria shuffled out from the kitchen in her high, white deerskin boots, offering a jocular escape.

"We're giving the land back to the Indians, Maria. Be sure and get your share." . . . "Good-bye Maria! Take good care of Miss Chalmers" . . . "So long, Jack." . . .

They were gone . . . A whole era was gone. She stood in the doorway, watching the last sparks fly into the darkness from the blur of the receding train. There was a single last whistle—the voice of one of America's last baby railroads confiding its history to memory.

"That's that!" She felt Turner's arm around her, pulling her inside.

2.

A young Indian had come in the back door. He was standing

16

in the kitchen, pigeon-toed in his muddy moccasins, wolfing the remains of the chocolate cake. When he finished, he ran his long, graceful fingers down his hair braids.

"Pretty good all time."

Maria shoved an empty bucket toward him from the sink.

"When you go to the well-house look at that rope, Luis," said Helen. "It's beginning to unravel."

"It good."

"No, it isn't good! It's liable to break and drop the bucket. Then you'll have to climb down a spruce pole and fish it out like you did the last time."

"I fix." Luis lit a candle and went out.

Maria continued washing dishes.

"I'll help wipe," offered Turner.

"No. Go in and smoke your pipe. Here." She poured him a cup of coffee. "We'll be through in a minute."

He went into the long room behind the kitchen, put some piñon on the fire, and settled down with his coffee. Helen had a knack of fixing up a room, he thought restfully. A Navajo rug or two on the bare floor, a Chimayo blanket flung on the bed, a few doodads set around, and the place somehow seemed home. Well, it had and it hadn't been for him, he thought, but he ought to be used to it by now. Why wasn't he? A little perturbed without knowing why, he rose and stood warming his back at the fire.

Luis came in, taking a package of Wheatstraws out of his Levis. Turner offered him tobacco and watched him deftly roll a cigarette.

"Did you splice that rope for Miss Chalmers?"

"I fix."

They smoked in silence. Then Luis asked quietly, "That train gone. She no come again?"

"No Luis. War is coming to the world, and our train is going away to meet it."

"Miss Chalmer, she go too?"

"No, she's staying here."

"I take care of him same."

"I know you will, Luis. And so will I, same as always."

The Indian flipped the edge of his flimsy cotton blanket over his shoulder with what seemed a gesture of finality and stood staring out the window. Years ago, as a small boy, he had started doing chores for the incomprehensible white woman who had obtained permission to build this adobe at the Crossing on the edge of the Reservation. At periodic intervals he left to do his ceremonial duties, to plant and harvest his corn, to fish in the river or hunt in the mountains above. But eventually he showed up again with a wagon load of piñon and resumed his chores as if nothing had intervened. Only once had he explained his absence—the morning that he had brought a girl with him.

"My wife, this Maria. She do the dishes good."

Helen had shrugged a helpless and inevitable welcome. "What was I to do?" she had asked Jack later. "You know what they are—just plain fixtures!"

Fixtures she could never have done without, he thought now, watching Helen come in. What a strange woman, really! Dressed in a soft flowered print but wearing a pair of moccasins. A close-knit bundle of contradictions he had never tried to unravel.

Maria appeared in the doorway behind her. She had taken off her showy, clay-whitened boots and put on a pair of Luis' sloppy moccasins. A blue rebozo was wrapped about her head and shoulders. She was carrying a brown paper bag.

Luis turned around as if he had sensed her appearance without hearing her noiseless shuffle.

"Did you lock up, Maria?" asked Helen.

"No lock. You here," stated Luis flatly, looking at Turner with his black expressionless eyes.

If his remark carried an insinuation, neither the man nor the woman noticed nor resented it. "Tomorrow," said Helen, dropping into the big chair by the fireplace.

The couple vanished as quietly as if blotted out by night.

"Now what's the trouble?" asked Turner, sitting down cross-legged on the floor beside the big chair.

A tiny frown creased Helen's forehead as if the reason for her vague uneasiness was an enigmatic puzzle. "This terrible war that keeps spreading over the world like a horrible disease—"

"I know."

"And the Chile Line. It's the end of everything we know, and have lived with, and—"

18

"And you'll keep right on here just like Luis and Maria. Change doesn't come overnight, you know."

She jumped up, determined to unearth that secret, invisible root of premonition. From the mantel she took down a letter that had come two weeks ago and reread it to him aloud again. When he did not answer she exclaimed irritably, "Can't you understand what it means? A daughter coming whom I haven't seen since she was less than a year old! Why, she must be over twenty now! What does she look like? What does she think of me—a mother who abandoned her? What is she coming here for—if she ever does come!"

"Come, come, Helen," Turner said kindly, knocking out his pipe. "You're trying to work yourself up into a literary dilemma. There isn't any real problem. You walked out on your husband because he was a hopeless, shiftless drunk. His family was glad to grab and pamper the child. They never liked you anyway. All that was over twenty years ago. You've established your own life. The girl has grown up without you. Mark my words, Helen. There is no problem. She's just coming as a tourist on a short vacation."

"You think I have no feeling for my own daughter?"

He looked at her quizzically from a rugged, homely face that suddenly grew almost beautiful with a smile. "Not a bit or you wouldn't have stayed here for all these years! Now stop worrying. She'll show up eventually."

Helen folded the letter back into its worn envelope, and let her hands drop loosely into her lap. She looked so prim, like an old lady in a sentimental print dress, he thought, that he reached up and grasped her hands.

"Trouble, trouble. On the double. We've all got enough without imagining more. Well, you should have married me long ago."

"Oh, Jack! I'm forty years old!" she cried plaintively and illogically.

He reached up quietly and pulled her down upon him in a heap. The action was impelled by a loose and relaxed mood of tenderness and intimate comradeship. But the result was born, in an electrifying instant, from his first touch of her warm and pliant body. It always came like that to them, instantaneously and without warning. A quick surge of passion that enveloped them like a sheet of flame. He felt an odd flurry in the pit of his stomach, a tremor rippling up his

19

legs and arms. Almost instantly it was gone, and he felt solidified by a strong but curiously patient desire.

The woman relaxed at once, stretching out across his lap, her face turned toward the darkness to escape the heat of the fireplace. He ran his hands lightly and possessively over her breasts. Without haste he bent down to kiss her opened lips, aware as if for the first time of the distinctive, intimate fragrance of her breath. For minutes they lay quietly together.

"And I just pressed my dress," she murmured without protest.

He got up, kicked the crumbling logs back into the fireplace, and threw the iron catches on both doors. When he turned back she was already in the bed, her clothes flung limply over an arm of the big chair.

He undressed and got in beside her. Neither of them was under the compulsion of nervous haste; they had been lovers for several years. She turned on her side to face him, and again he felt the miracle of holding so intimately close all the ripeness of her rich maturity.

"Listen to the leaves fall," she murmured haltingly. And then again, "The wind must be coming up."

The remarks meant nothing. They seemed to come not so much from her fading awareness of their factual location in space and time, but from a heightened consciousness of every sensory perception— the rasp of a brittle cottonwood leaf settling upon a flagstone outside, the faint odor of the pine slopes above, the flicker of the dying flames.

He was holding her now in a stronger, more demanding embrace that forced her breath in short gasps. It was she who broke the mounting tension with an uncontrollable surrender that was impelled not only by a natural and intense desire, but by the strange nervous tension she had suffered all day.

The man was dimly aware of this supplemental force to her passion. A quick moment of personal tenderness, of the considerate love he felt for her, halted his instant response. But with this imperative summons which could not be denied, he too plunged into the fulfillment of that desire which so long had cemented the intangible bond between them.

For minutes after consummation they still lay locked in arms before parting. Then she turned on her side away from him, drawing his hand across to her moist, limp breast. "Maybe this is the best moment of all—maybe," she murmured. "Don't go too soon, Jack."

It was the first time he felt her nervousness gone. He brushed back the damp hair from her forehead, kissed her lightly on the cheek. "Go to sleep now. I won't leave."

The wind was still up. The brittle cottonwood leaves were still rasping across the flagstones outside. The coals were still red . . .

Suddenly he was aware that daybreak was near, and that he must go. He got up quietly so as not to disturb her, dressing stealthily in the dark. But as he tiptoed across the room he heard her quiet voice. "Wait, Jack! You can't start out without a cup of coffee."

She jumped up, and ran into the kitchen to stir up the coals banked in the stove. Finding her old blue robe, he went out to join her. She was bent over the stove, her bare body full and pliant in the lamplight. His glance curved lightly and lovingly around it, then came suddenly to rest on the sun-browned, collar-like ring around her neck showing underneath her brown hair. With a shock he noticed the wrinkles for the first time. Like cuniform characters of a language made suddenly comprehensible, they revealed to him the story of her lonely years. Abruptly he flung the robe about her, kissed the flesh-writing below her ear.

"The floor's cold. What did you do with your slippers? Don't you ever take care of yourself?"

She looked up and smiled. "Don't you want some bacon and eggs before that long ride, Jack?"

He shook his head, poured his coffee.

"Don't let that new publisher get you down," she said. "And if Emily does show up there first"—

"She will and I will. Leave it to me. Now jump back into bed."

He kissed her again and went out the door.

3.

Helen watched the lights of his car fade northward, then turned back to bed.

21

The coals still glowed. She stretched out relaxed and comfortable. But once again there returned to plague her all the interwoven ramifications of that vague uneasiness she could not long escape.

Day after day for years she had regulated her life by the whistle of the Chile Line. Now there was nothing to get up for, she realized suddenly. For a naturally active woman the prospect of indolence was frightening, to say nothing of her meager finances. The enforced alternative of relying upon casual picnickers and stray tourists was not encouraging. With war coming on, she might be forced to give up. After all these years? Unthinkable! Whatever happened, she had cast the die of her existence upon this remote New Mexican shore.

Why didn't she marry Turner after all? Why hadn't she long ago? She recalled his small, book-cluttered adobe on the outskirts of La Oreja, his perpetual struggle with a small country weekly whose dilapidated machinery kept putting him in debt for repairs. Yet now it wasn't because his house wasn't more than adequate, nor his income to keep them. Perhaps it was the town, she thought. La Oreja was essentially little different from all the other old towns throughout the Rio Grande valley which constituted the *tierra madre* to which she owed her allegiance. But for some reason or other, probably its scenery, perhaps its aristocratic heritage, La Oreja had drawn a colony of artists and pseudo-artists, escapists, and screwpots that secretly offended her fastidious shyness.

"I'm just not comfortable up here, Jack," she had told him during one of her visits. "I feel I'd never really belong. These people just aren't real."

"They're just one small group of many. And people are people wherever you go. Why try to escape them?"

"I don't try to escape. I just want to be left alone."

He shrugged and dropped the subject. But just the same she was glad to get back to the lonely mouth of her remote canyon. And not until now had she questioned the craving for solitude that had become so fixed in her character.

Places, houses, people! What did they matter to a woman who loved a man? She flung over on one side, acutely conscious of the absence of his sturdy body beside her. With an intense physical ache, she could imaginatively reconstruct every curve and hollow

22

of his body and how her own fitted them. That was what had happened the first time they slept together.

She remembered the picnic supper along the river they had had soon after their first meeting. They had built a fire on a narrow, sandy spit close to a clump of old cottonwoods. It was a warm night in early June. She remembered how palely silver the moon looked as it rose over the black rock wall, how tepid the river felt to her fingers when she knelt to splash him with water. He did not stir, not even to shake the water from his face. He kept grinning like a broad-shouldered, lazy boy.

At that instant the feeling swept over her that she could trust him as she had never trusted a man before in her life. "It's warm, Jack! Warm enough to go swimming!" Without hesitation she stripped off her blouse and pants and moccasins.

"Too shallow. You'll snag yourself on a rock," he answered without stirring.

She waded offshore to where the water rushed over her knees, then stretched out, head upstream, belly down, and let the river run ripplingly, caressingly, over her back. A river silvered by moonlight, thick as quicksilver, warm with June, and washing her with a strange contentment, a quickening and sweetening of life. She ducked her head as if in baptism, and when she raised it Turner lay stretched out beside her.

They had waded farther out then, hand in hand, to deeper, swifter water which carried them downstream. Still hand in hand, they walked back to stand drying their backs before the fire. The breeze felt chill, but it was not that which made her turn around and step within his embrace. She had no thought of his nakedness save for the comforting warmth and smoothness of his big chest and the strength of his arms around her. It was something within him, perhaps the solidity of his character and his essential goodness, to which her loneliness and aching for intimacy responded.

"I'm cold and hungry, and we're naked as jaybirds!" he shouted suddenly, releasing her.

She let out a peal of laughter. "Well, go get my clothes!"

When had she laughed like that—before or since?

So they had dressed and broiled their steaks on the coals, and sat talking while the white June light of the rising moon quenched

23

the warm red flicker of the fire. She could not let him go!—and that night she had kept him with her. That miraculous sense of their utter unity, and even more mysterious, the feeling of her own physical completeness for the first time. How wonderful it was, even after all this time, that magic illusion which comes but once to every woman, which may be broken, betrayed or outgrown, but can never be forgotten in the depths where the spirit dwells.

Concomitant with the physical was the intimacy of their casual companionship. A simple woman, she detected in him as sharper mind than he liked to show. Practical, down-to-earth as the small-town newspaper publisher he was, he was without pretensions, sensitive to people, and ruthlessly honest. Yet at the same time he could be flagrantly idealistic as a hopeless daydreamer. It was this irrational streak in him which he seldom indulged that she liked best.

"Why haven't you gone to New York or California where you'd be appreciated?" she asked him once.

"Why didn't you become a Fred Harvey waitress? By now you'd be the hostess of El Alvarado's dining room!"

So she had come to accept him as a friend and a lover in a relationship that permitted a close intimacy while still preserving their separate independence. Yet it was a relationship that allowed her to escape her ultimate responsibility to him, and with it the annoying daily friction of constant companionship. A solitary woman by nature, Helen was not consciously aware of these deeper limits to their relationship. But she felt a lack, and knew now that through outward circumstance things might have to change. How? She was not selfish enough to marry him simply because her livelihood was threatened. Yet neither was she unselfish enough, nor aware enough of her deeper need, to enter marriage without misgivings.

So she continued to roll and toss in bed in an agony of indecision. The faint light of a car swung and held upon the west window. Jack! she thought instantly, jumping out of bed and rushing across the floor. Or Emily! But even as she peered out the window, the car rolled past. It was the big Cadillac with the Army Colonel who had inquired the way up the canyon. She watched its headlights turn slowly upon the struts of the suspension bridge, then light up the big cottonwoods across river. A queer nocturnal visit! But her momentary conjectures were instantly replaced by the growing doubts of what she would have done or said if it had been Emily.

The whole problem of her daughter's impending arrival was upsetting. What was she coming for? How would she accept her own mother? What would she think of Jack? All these pent-up questions not only connected Helen's present and the impending future, but they dredged up events and issues she had submerged long ago.

It had never been a marriage, really. Merely a youthful infatuation with a Yale sweater, a coonskin coat, and a cardinal-red Marmon runabout. And then a bride's repugnance to bathtub gin and noisy dinner parties. All these combined in her one predominating memory of Gerald Chalmers: a tall, handsome young man stepping into his car with a bottle of gin protruding from the pocket of his coat. She could see herself, pregnant and sulking, watching him from the window.

The birth of Emily did not help matters. It intensified them. For now came "Pater" and "Mater" Chalmers. Pater signing checks and proudly harrumping, "Boys will be boys!" Mater dominatingly spoiling the child, step by step, with a restraining pat on Helen's shoulder. "But Helen, darling, you're so inexperienced!"

It all happened with the smoothness of the inevitable. Gerald absent from home for days, then weeks at a time. Pater calling home from his brokerage office with patent excuses of out-of-town clients Gerald had to see. Mater insisting that Helen and Emily move into her own home.

"It's so huge, darling. A barn, really. Why, we have a whole separate apartment already prepared for you. A surprise! Now we'll just have Nurse take Baby, and you grab your hat. No! Don't embarrass us. After all, you're both Chalmers too, especially Baby!"

Within a month after moving, Helen felt like a second maid. Mater dominated the household with an implacable sweetness. Nurse monopolized Baby. Pater and Gerald faded away into the nebulous remoteness of the brokerage office.

For a few weeks Helen sat with folded hands, staring in desperation at the specter of an impossible future. One afternoon she unfolded her hands, got up and put on her hat. It was a beaver toque lined with brown satin. As she walked through the hall, Mater called out from the living room where she was having tea. "Are you really going out, dear—this time of day?"

"To send a telegram," she replied tersely, slamming the door.

At the railroad station she sent her telegram. It was to her older sister, and it read simply, "Arriving tonight. Helen."

She never went back. Nor did she ever write, even when a divorce waiver finally reached her for signature.

Now, some twenty years later, it all came back with a vividness of feeling which she thought had been completely obliterated—as if anything truly felt could ever be erased from man's undying memory. No! Everything—past, present, future—could not heap itself upon her now, all at once! It wasn't fair! She flung over in bed and buried her face in the pillow. Unable to weep, she wearily dragged out of bed. Perhaps a hot bath would help. Putting on her old blue robe, Helen trudged out for an armful of kindling. By the time the water was hot, the first flush of sunrise colored the sky above the Sangre de Cristos.

Helen loved these early mornings when the world emerged with a pristine clarity and freshness that was ever new. She poured the hot water into a big wash basin set on the floor in front of the stove. Over a small cane chair drawn up beside it she draped a large yellow Turkish towel, laid out a bar of perfumed soap. Waiting for the water to cool off a bit, she stood staring out the window. The night wind had died. The huge cottonwoods, not yet stripped of leaves, puffed out like yellow balloons. Across the river winged a large black-and-white magpie screaming raucously. Listening intently, she imagined she heard the Cacique at the pueblo yelling his morning announcements from the roof-top.

Leisurely she sipped a cup of coffee, disrobed, and sat down to her bath. Long ago these makeshift sponge baths had irked her. Every week she drove to town and indulged in the luxury of a tub in the scrubby hotel. But it became too much of a chore, and she had come to enjoy the peaceful procedure of scrubbing a leg and an arm at a time in her own big kitchen before Luis and Maria came.

The water was hot enough to turn her skin pink. The scented soap—one of her few extravagances—smelled rich and spicy. She stood up, wrapping herself in one of the huge towels Turner had given her for Christmas, and looked at herself in the tin-framed mirror with some assurance. The puffiness under her sleepless eyes was gone. A faint flush filled out her cheeks.

But as she patted her neck and breasts dry, her hand was suddenly arrested by a faint swelling in the hollow between her left breast and shoulder blade. Almost concurrently, so swift was her mindless reaction, she felt as if something had struck her in the pit of the stomach. The towel dropped to her feet. Petrified by a swift obsessing fear, she stood staring into the mirror. It gave back the image of her wide, horror-struck eyes, her half-opened mouth with its faintly trembling lips, her smooth paling cheeks. The woman saw nothing of these. Her stare was transfixed to that fatal spot on which was written the ineluctable dictate of a destiny beyond her comprehension.

She stumbled on trembling legs back to bed. Lying on her back, both hands protectively folded over her breast as if to hide it from a world of health and life, she gave in completely to its meaning.

This was what her body had been trying to tell her for days through a vague uneasiness and an inescapable premonition. Beside it nothing else mattered—the removal of the Chile Line, the coming of Emily, nothing! It was as if, in one instant, she had been moved to a plane upon which all the activities and values of life had no substance nor meaning at all.

In a new and terrible loneliness she cried soundlessly for the one link she treasured most. Jack! Oh, Jack! But now it was too late. Too late to drive to town and telephone him. Too late to give their life the deepest meaning of love.

She was aroused by a faint noise. An old Indian was standing outside, tossing pebbles against the pane: old Facundo, Luis' ceremonial "uncle" who had obtained the Council's permission for her to build her home on the edge of pueblo land, and who for years had tended her vegetable garden. In the wan light she could distinguish the red headband around his straggly, graying hair; his dark seamed face, carven by all the passion and the patience of the elements into the timeless visage of his race; the sharp steady stare of his fathomless black eyes. His look steadied her for an instant. She waved at him; he went on.

She lay back down again, staring fixedly at the spruce *vigas*

27

overhead like a woman who had received a summons that could not remain unanswered.

4.

All that day and night she stayed in the shut up house, withdrawn from life. Then anaesthetized by fear, she rose at sunup, drank a cup of tea, and drove her battered old Ford to Espanola. Dr. Arnold's office was not yet open. She slumped down on the doorstep like a lump of clay.

Eventually he came walking toward her briskly, a little man squinting through bifocals, his thin black overcoat flapping above his worn-down heels. "Not under the weather on a day like this, Miss Chalmers? Well, come in."

He unlocked the door, opened a window, switched on the light. Once in his office, Helen was calm and resolute. Without hesitation she unbuttoned her blouse. "That's it there," she pointed. "I thought you'd better have a look."

Dr. Arnold was a little too old, and practicing in too small a country town, to keep his interest ahead of the great demands made upon him. But he had been reliable enough for years to sew up fiesta knife wounds, deliver babies against the threats and wails of native midwives in nearby villages, and cure all ordinary ills that resisted the effects of native herbs. Also he was honest enough, on difficult cases, to send his patients to specialists in Sanat Fe or Albuquerque. All these courageous, commonplace ministrations paraded through Helen's mind as he began his examination.

"All right. Both arms over your head now. Let's see if there's any relative fixation of that left breast . . . Now, hands on hips" . . . He held her right hand, placed his left in her armpit. . . . Then he went behind her, placing his hands on her neck to examine the supraclavicular lymph node areas. "Any other members of your family have mammary carcinomas?"

She shrugged without answering and he continued his examination. Finally he straightened and wiped his glasses. "I don't believe there's anything to worry about, Miss Chalmers. I really don't. I've

known several women to have similar swellings that disappeared in a short time. Let's give this one a few days."

Helen stared at him with a long, level look of almost indignant disbelief as she put on her blouse. How could she believe him against that secret intuitive self which had soundlessly foretold her fate with incontrovertible conviction?

Dr. Arnold had known her a long time. "Look here, Miss Chalmers," he said quietly. "You've had quite a scare. I can see that. But you're too sensible a woman to panic at a slightly swollen gland that'll probably go down in a few days. If it doesn't, go see a top man. Here." He scribbled out the name and address of a diagnostician specializing in carcinomas and thrust the paper into her pocket. "It could be a small, benign lesion of no significance whatever. But even if it does happen to be malignant there's nothing to be frightened about at this early stage. For goodness sake!"

Without a word, she put down a five-dollar bill on the table and walked out to her jalopy. It wouldn't start. Without annoyance or hurry she went to the garage for a new battery and a Spanish boy to install it. Sitting on the curb while he worked, she took out from her pocket the slip of paper Dr. Arnold had given her, stared at it a long time, then tore it up. It was almost noon when she reached home.

A strange feeling possessed her. It was as if she had gone a long, long distance away, and had been gone a long, long time. Only to come back and find that the calendar pages had not turned, and that everything appeared outwardly as before. The house . . . The ripples breaking against the sand bar . . . The raucous cries of the magpies, and the silent sweep of a hawk. Yet she seemed somehow disassociated from them. As if she had gone so far and stayed so long from the world she lived in that she was no longer attuned to its meanings.

Listlessly she sat down in a rocker by the window, and thumbed through a stack of newspapers and magazines that seemingly had accumulated during her long absence. Every newspaper screeched the war news in big, black heads. Blood and guts and whining steel. . . . She leafed through the slick-paper, fashionable magazines that came from New York. Their over-ripe, ultra-sophisticated advertisements whispered seductively to her with blasé clichés and aphrodisiacal suggestiveness of a worse death-in-life; whispered of diamond and sapphire pendants, matched furs, lace negligees, and creative headgear for the five o'clock hour . . . Still she sat rocking, unable to escape the mounting pressure of a frantic world being driven to a verge.

Nor could she escape the pressure of her own immediate worries and behind these, still more anxieties: guilt about the Chalmers she had forsaken, the betrayal of her love for Turner, worries about old friends ignored and forgotten till now, and the secret foibles of a youth and childhood she had long repressed. Everything she had done and said and neglected to do or say—her whole life pressed in upon her with an overwhelming conviction of its utter uselessness.

This was the meaning, she felt now, of that swelling over her breast. What did it matter whether it was a malignant growth or merely a swollen gland? It had thrown her life into true perspective. She did not fear death. It was that nullity of not being, of having never really been. That waste of time, of life, that horrible futility. It kept squeezing her. Her breasts ached from the pressure, her back and ribs hurt. She thought she'd choke.

Then suddenly it happened.

A cataclysmic explosion that burst asunder the shell of the world around her, revealing its inner reality with its brilliant flash. In its blinding brightness all mortal appearances dissolved into eternal meanings, great shimmering waves of pure feeling which had no other expression than this, and these were so closely entwined and harmonized they formed one indivisible unity. A selfhood that embraced her, the totality of the universe, and all space and all time in one immortal existence that had never had a beginning nor would ever have an end.

Her instantaneous perception of it was at once terrifying and ecstatic, for it was as if she had always known it and yet was comprehending it for the first time. Like a mote of earthly dust decalmed in the still, dead center of an actual explosion, she continued to sit there long after the blinding glare broke into gradations of color too infinite and subtle to define, and slowly faded and died. Within her now she could feel a strange fusion of body, mind and spirit into a new and integrated entity that seemed apart from the gross elements from which it sprang. Slowly she came to herself enough to realize that it all had happened within her.

Had she died? Suffered an epileptic seizure? A paralytic stroke? Gingerly she moved a hand, a foot. Sensations rushed back into her as into a vacuum. The hammering beat of a clock was deafening. She went into the kitchen and stopped it. A pan of cold tortillas sat on top of the stove; mechanically she broke off a piece. The taste evoked the whole shape, texture and life-cycle of the corn. It was that way with everything she saw and touched: it set off a chain of associations whose ramifications had no end.

Dazedly she wandered outside. The sun was setting in a glow that made her dizzy. Face down, she lay on the little bluff above the river only to feel herself merging into the earth. Like a piece of decomposed granite, whose every grain and particle was separate but which still maintained a curious entity, she sank through the porous, wet sand into the river. Now she knew how a drop of water felt when it dashed against a stone with a queer, cushioned shock and rubbery bounce. How it bubbled up on top; the fun of tossing on the surface; of being lifted up and riding in a cloud! There seemed nothing she did not know and feel—the slow pulse in a stone, the song of the river, the wisdom of the mountains. For the first time she glimpsed the complete pattern of the universe, and knew that everything within it, to a blade of grass, was significant and alive.

It was too much for her. She returned to the house and lay down on the couch without undressing. But she could not sleep for the joy that seemed now to bubble up within her and burst into a fountain at the top of her head, flooding every crack and cranny in the mortal body that held her. All her fears, worries and anxieties were gone. She felt freed of the past: not only from her personal, remembered life, but detached from that pattern of repetitive human passion which long before her time had begot at last her own faulty personal self. It was as if she had just been reborn with all the freshness, purity and innocence of one entering the world for the first time. But one so different—so wonderful and frightening, so joyous and overwhelming—she could hardly comprehend it. A world that was a complete and rounded moment in which she would never die. She was content to lie at its core, watching it revolve about her.

She was still lying there next morning when old Facundo came and tossed his gravel against the window pane. Helen was too engrossed to notice him. In a little while he came back; she saw him standing outside the window with a grave look of compassionate concern on his weathered face. She looked up, and something passed between them. It was as if all that she had experienced was absorbed, understood, and reflected back from the pupils of his dark eyes. Facundo knew. He knew!

"Sun good. Dark no good!"

Helen obeyed him and went out to sit on the ground. In a little while he brought her a cup of tea. It had too much sugar in it, but it gave her a surge of strength.

"*Vegetáble* gone. Berries come now. Pretty soon we catch them pine cones for fire, no?" The old Indian moved off, slowly raking the garden.

The sense of his presence, and of his complete awareness of the moment and all the things that composed it, brought her back to the familiar. She felt the warmth of the sunshine, caught the smell of pine needles, heard the wind in the cottonwoods. Facundo was right. There would be a bumper crop of juniper berries; the grosbeaks were moving in. A pair of blue herons stood motionless in the shallow lagoon at the curve of the river, reflected in the water . . . A huge pattern that kept spreading illimitably.

She was still not quite herself and kept wondering what had happened to her. It was something strange, indescribable and yet familiar; something that Facundo seemed to understand without being told.

5.

Early that morning after leaving Otowi Crossing, Turner drove home to La Oreja. It lay about fifty miles north, on a high windswept plateau that stretched almost unbroken from the deep gorge of the Rio Grande to the curving wall of the Sange de Cristos. The horizontal plane of sage-gray desert structurally counterbalanced by the vertical mass of spruce-blue mountains rising abruptly into the turquoise sky, the constant subtle shifting of light and color, the miraculous clarity of the air—all these composed a landscape incomparably beautiful and justly famous. The only break in the vast expanse of sagebrush was a solitary mesa shaped into the crude semblance of a human ear. It was this that gave the name of La Oreja to the adobe town squatting at its foot.

For centuries it had kept attuned to the three races which now comprised its small population: the Indians who still lived in a prehistoric pueblo not far away, the preponderant Spanish villagers tilling their little corn *milpas,* and a thin scatter of newer Anglos who seemed to live on mere scenery. The town's last vestiges of almost Biblical serenity, however, were beginning to be erased by a long delayed commercialism. This Turner fought with his little weekly, *El Porvenir.* It dispensed the local news—its admitted function. Yet Turner was more concerned with the feature articles reflecting his interest in history and folklore. Printed in both English and Spanish, with fiesta-issue splurges into phonetic Tiwa Indian, its homely and yet poetic flavor was undeniable. *El Porvenir,* in short, was a country weekly for a retired journalist, a novelist, or a pseudo-literary effete to play with as a hobby. Its subscribers could not understand how Turner kept it alive year after year, and were sorry to learn that he now had agreed to sell it.

Everyone in town suspected the reason: Helen Chalmers. They knew he was sleeping with her and expected the affair to blow over any day. Both of them were too mature and set in their ways to be harnessed as a working team. Helen Chalmers had spent a couple of weekends with him in La Oreja, but hadn't come back. Obviously she didn't like the cozy familiarity of the town where everyone knew everyone else's business, the perpetual gossip, the squabbles, the cliques. Compared to bluff and out-going Turner, she was too withdrawn, too introverted. But Turner was hooked, really in love with her and dead set on marrying her, Hell or High Water.

He had never been married and his neighbors could not envision him as a house-broken husband; but his impassioned intensity of purpose impressed them with its maturity. They did not detect in it the same romantic streak that ran through his pursuit of Western Americana. Anyway he had sold *El Porvenir* to gain money and

33

freedom to start a new life with Helen Chalmers. Where and when? The whole town awaited the outcome.

Eating breakfast on the plaza, Turner went directly to *El Porvenir*. It was housed in a dilapidated adobe divided into halves by a rickety wooden partition. The back shop, which he entered, was crammed with an old flat-bed press, Linotype, type cases, and a casting outfit. The floor was littered with last week's page and galley proofs, the grimy walls hung with pin-up calendar girls. Turner went into the front office. It too was a hodge-podge of old furniture, files, and a broken glass case full of stationery supplies. His own battered roll-top desk was in back, set against the partition where he could hear the frequent breaking down of machinery in the back shop. Here in the early morning calm he settled down to lay out the week's issue.

A farewell editorial to the readers who had supported him claimed precedence over everything else. It had to be worded carefully, for Turner had not yet met the new owner, and *El Porvenir's* readers would have to draw their own conclusions about him when they read his biographical sketch. Pecking away at his typewriter, Turner tried to add up the facts into a presentable whole. But Cyril Throckmorton III didn't jell. Age forty-four, scion of the well-known and wealthy Throckmorton family of Philadelphia, Main Line, he had nothing that could be pinned on him except a Dun and Bradstreet rating. No high school graduation year, no college degree, no political positions, no jobs identified him. No hobbies to indicate a leaning to art, sports, wine, women, or song. My God! thought Turner, he couldn't be a vacuum. Or could he?

At eight o'clock the editor of the Spanish section came in and sat down primly at his desk up front. No one in town ever dreamed of addressing him other than Don Jorge. Small and impeccably dressed in a black serge suit with white facing on the vest, he seemed to have just stepped from the pages of Becquer. For years he had written birth and death notices, rosarios and requiem masses, with a Castillian flourish that made him locally famous; he was a fixture as old-fashioned and necessary as his own roll-top desk.

Jimmie came in, standing patiently at his desk until Turner's gaze climbed from his red socks to his tousled hair. Just graduated from high school, he served somewhat inadequately as reporter and

34

more adequately as errand boy. "Hi, Mr. Turner!" he said blithely. "Can you loan me a dime for a cup of coffee?"

"There's a dime in the cash register. Be sure and leave an I.O.U. But before you go, listen. I've two assignments for you. Go to the library and get everything you can on Cyril Throckmorton I, II, and III. Where they came from and why. One of them must have rung the Liberty Bell or left his footprints on Plymouth Rock. What was his shoe size? Savvy? And get back here by four o'clock to meet your new publisher."

Jimmie grinned. "What's the other one? You said they waꙅ two."

"There were two," Turner answered patiently without looking up. "Your memory is improving, but not your grammar. Well, the second one I've mentioned before. For God's sake learn to spell— by this afternoon at four. If you misspell a branch on the Throck-morton tree, you're going to be hanged from it."

When Mrs. Weston came in, Turner put her to work on the morgue. "We're losing our Chile Line at last, Mrs. Weston. One of the most famous narrow-gauge lines in American railroading. I want to give it a fine obituary. Remember, up until a few years ago every person who came to La Oreja rode her to the junction and was hauled from there in Jenkin's stagecoach. And don't forget to add any amusing details."

Mrs. Weston's plain face lighted up with a smile. Quiet as a mouse, she kept books and posted subscriptions. But her main value lay in her extensive knowledge of people—not the Spanish people whom Don Jorge knew, nor the small elite group of artists and name-visitors, but the most important of all to any newspaper—the average, small-town, working people who comprised La Oreja's growing population.

By this time the boys in the back shop were yelling for copy, demanding mats and a dummy. Absorbed in the homely, trying duties of a job that to most men would have been too nerve-wracking and ill-paid, Turner forgot himself until almost four o'clock. Then, with a start, he came to. It was a momentous day and hour for *El Porvenir*. For promptly on the hour walked in the new publisher and his wife.

What first struck Turner was that the man strode in ahead of

35

his wife. For a Philadelphia socialite, the incident seemed unusual. The second thing that caught Turner's attention as Cyril Throckmorton III entered the room was the extreme pallor of his face. Even through the moments when Turner got up and introduced the couple to the members of the staff in the front office, he was fascinated by that pallid skin. It was not that of a man who was or had been ill. Indeed, Throckmorton's small plumpish body showed him to be in the best of condition. The pallor of his face was like that of unpainted porcelain; it seemed to penetrate far into the fine-grained flesh; and to have been bred into him by a lifetime or even generations of indoor life. One could not imagine it ever momentarily infused with a flash of anger, embarrassment or excitement. For to balance the pallor of his complexion was the dead-pan expression of his fine, regular features. They were set like concrete in an immobile look of disinterested pleasantry; a perfect expression of the frigid, inhibited, Puritan inheritance of his controlled breeding.

Only in Throckmorton's delicate, long-fingered and nervous hands did Turner detect his unstable character. But the pleasant, aimless greetings to Don Jorge, Jimmie, and Mrs. Weston were over.

"Now come out and meet your boys in the back shop," said Turner, opening the door.

"Do I shake hands with these—employees?" asked Mrs. Throckmorton, a stout, toothy woman hiding under a large and elaborate hat.

"Certainly," answered Throckmorton. "Shake hands when you meet them. Once and never again. The same as house servants." He smiled at Turner.

The "boys" were all Spanish, likewise imbued with a tradition of courtesy, but embarrassed by their ink-stained hands. To cut short their fumbling and fustian welcomes, Turner paraded the new owners around the littered room, showing them the Linotype and flat-bed press.

"But a new press is on the way," announced Mrs. Throckmorton. "We ordered it in New York from the nicest person."

"What kind is it?" asked Turner.

"Ah, the best," said Throckmorton. "We must have the best for expansion of facilities."

"Yes, he was the nicest person!" added Mrs. Thorckmorton. "A traveling representative of a well-known firm specializing in just such machinery. But very intelligent, really. He told us that a newspaper was the best outlet for releasing one's creative ability."

Turner was annoyed by Throckmorton's exhorbitant foolishness in buying a new press before he knew if one were needed, and shipping such a heavy item all the way from the East when a second-hand one could have been bought in Albuquerque or Denver. He began to wonder if Mrs. Throckmorton had been responsible.

"Why did you ever decide to buy a little paper way out here?" he asked.

"Precedent, Mr. Turner!" she answered quickly.

"Ahem! Precedent. Yes indeed," said Mr. Throckmorton.

"You see, Mr. Turner," she explained, "we have friends in Washington with eyes toward the future who are negotiating the purchase of an influential newspaper Out West. We shall share with them the great responsibility of dispensing proper news of world affairs and advising the people in this far frontier region where their best interests are. Our dear little weekly, small as it is, will give us an equal opportunity to expand our own interests."

"It is not a family habit to spend money for nothing. Not at all, sir!" said Throckmorton. "Is it, Josephine?"

"The odor in here is trying," she said quickly. "Besides, it's growing late and we all need a cocktail. You'll join us of course, Mr. Turner, and stay for dinner?"

"Of course, of course," echoed Throckmorton.

The Throckmortons had taken a suite in the hotel, pending the purchase of a house suitable for their needs. Drinks and dinner were ordered served in their sitting room, which allowed them some privacy in which to get acquainted. When they arrived, Throckmorton excused himself to wash his hands again.

"His hands are so delicate and sensitive!" commented Mrs. Throckmorton. "I've seen him thread a needle instantly, after the maid had been struggling with it for half an hour. He loves to sew, you know." Downing her cocktail with a gulp and pouring herself another, she said abruptly, "Mr. Turner, you don't know what it means to be Mrs. Cyril Throckmorton III! The terrible, overwhelming responsibility. The feel of the world's eyes upon one—"

"You haven't been married long?"

"Two years. But the responsibility grows more heavily each year. Why, the mere pensioning of the family's old butler was a task itself, to say nothing of selecting and shipping five van loads of furniture for our eventual use here. Two grand pianos. I love duets!"

"You have given up the house in Philadelphia?"

"Yes. Not the one in Washington. You see, we don't need too many houses, especially since we're establishing ourselves in a new milieu—the spacious freedom of the West!"

"Exactly!" Throckmorton entered the room and sat down stiffly in a corner chair.

"Cyril, I have been telling Mr. Turner we must all be friends as well as business associates in this tremendous undertaking."

"Precisely."

"A newspaper. A vehicle for self-expression and guidance of the people! Why, when I think of the power in our hands . . . The power we have to form public opinion . . . To make or break careers . . . The absolute power we have over everyone frightens me!"

Turner frowned. "A small, remote, weekly newspaper doesn't give anyone quite so much power as all that, Mrs. Throckmorton. People out West are pretty independent. And right here in La Oreja are three diverse groups—Anglo, Spanish and Indian—with different traditions and languages, and a good many cliques. We don't try to knock their heads together and force our opinions down their throats. *El Porvenir* simply gives them the news, from which they can make up their own minds."

"We don't want to change a thing! Do we, Cyril?"

"No indeed, no indeed," he assented.

Dinner was brought in at last. When they had finished, Throckmorton took out from his pocket two folded pieces of paper, handing them to Turner. "For this week's paper perhaps," he said stiffly.

"But you must sit down in this comfortable chair by the light to read it!" ordered Mrs. Throckmorton, rising. "I'll have the table cleared and coffee brought."

Turner unfolded the two sheets of paper. They were written

in a tortuous penciled scrawl like that of a ten-year-old child. A poem, he decided. Bending closer, he read its title:

Thoughts While Treading the Trail That Kit Carson
Trod in Previous Days Long Gone By and other
Famous Pioneers.

A queer uneasiness gripped Turner.

"You like it, you think it will do?" asked Mrs. Throckmorton with a pitiless smile. "Cyril hasn't let me read it yet. He's given it to his editor first!"

Turner hesitated, then handed the poem to Mrs. Throckmorton without looking at the author. "It's obviously a quick, first draft that needs considerable editorial revision. Don't you think so?"

She skimmed through it rapidly. "A little polishing, of course, and I shall be glad to do it . . . Cyril! Your first published poem, under your own name, in the first issue of your own press! Mr. Turner, you don't realize how tremendous—tremendous," she repeated in her high nasal voice, "a thing like this is! It calls for a drink. A Napoleon brandy. Nothing else will do!"

As Turner reached out to take his small glass off the silver tray, he glanced at Throckmorton. His delicate hand was also outstretched; it was trembling slightly. But his pallid face was immobile save that his thin, unfriendly lips were pressed together in a short, straight line.

"Ahem! I instructed my lawyers to send your bank a draft for the sales price agreed upon."

"I was informed that it had been deposited to my account," answered Turner calmly. It was the greatest amount of money he had ever owned in his life; and deposited in an account that was always threadbare and often overdrawn, it had provoked considerable joshing at the small bank. He said abruptly, "According to the terms of the sale, I was to remain as editor until you could assume full management. But wouldn't you rather that I abdicate now?"

"Not at all, not at all," answered Throckmorton hastily.

"I only mentioned it because an editor has got to edit the paper. Everybody can't do it. Someone has to take the responsibility, and with it he has to have the authority. I'll stay on that condition."

"Of course, of course!" echoed Throckmorton.

Mrs. Throckmorton tucked back a few wisps of her frowsy hair.

Her eyes shone with the glassy hardness of obsidian. "But you have no objections, I presume, to the publisher publishing his own views in his own paper?"

Turner braced himself against the prospect of an unending barrage of poems. "Certainly not. But all copy, whoever turns it in, should be edited thoroughly, don't you think?"

"We shall naturally cooperate in every manner possible to insure the success of our venture," she snapped, rising.

"Indeed, indeed!" Throckmorton stood up, rubbing his hands together.

Turner walked out into the chill fall night feeling he had met only the caricature rather than the living image of a man.

6.

By Thursday *El Porvenir* had recovered from its first shock of Throckmorton's arrival, but it was still perplexed and amused.

Turner had set a desk for Throckmorton in the center of the front office where he could watch everything that went on. Promptly at nine o'clock—an hour after the office opened—he entered the room and neatly hung up his black Homburg, white muffler, and black topcoat. It was his custom not to speak to anyone until he was greeted first. Clearing his throat with a resounding "Ahem!" he began opening the day's mail with a silver blade on which was engraved the Throckmorton crest. As Don Jorge gave Turner the most expedient-looking letters, the large stack on Throckmorton's desk consisted of advertising circulars, canned releases, syndicated mats, political diatribes, and free handouts of every kind. Throckmorton, after perusing them carefully, stacked them on his desk in a heap that kept mounting day by day; he seemed incapable of throwing anything away. The task took him all day.

But with press day making its demands, Turner was too busy to pay his new publisher much attention: checking inside page proofs against galley proofs, making up the front page, and laying out an advertisement for Helen's tea room.

As he was finishing this, the first press run of the page containing Throckmorton's revised poem was brought in to him. Set under a two-column head, the poem took a good twelve inches. Turner carried the page over to Throckmorton, pointing it out with an ink-smudged finger. A few moments after he had returned to his desk, he happened to look up. What he saw flooded him with a warm wave of compassion almost instantly chilled by a premonition containing an element of fear and disgust.

Throckmorton's arms were outspread, his hands gripping the edges of the sheet with a frenzied clutch. Over his tense, white porcelain face spread a look of inordinate pride and achievement. As Turner watched him, he drew his legs up on the chair under his pudgy body in the posture of a seated Buddha, put the sheet down on the desk, and began softly clapping his delicate hands in front of his breast. Turner stared at him as if transfixed. Throckmorton acted like a child just presented with a new Christmas toy. It was pathetic and unbelievable. Yet at the same time his look of monstrous pride and power, betrayed by his clenched lips and jutting jaw, rang a warning in Turner's mind. Mrs. Throckmorton's phrase, "the power of the press" echoed in his ears. With the guilty feeling of looking through a keyhole at something no man had the right to see, Turner tore his gaze away and returned to work.

Early that morning he had casually noticed a strange girl sitting at the morgue, taking notes. At noon, after a quick lunch with Mrs. Weston, she was still there. She was rather attractive. Medium height, a compact body with plenty of curves, an open face whose rounded pinkish cheeks indicated great vitality. But her whole-hearted intentness on whatever it was she was doing made Turner feel she was strictly bookish. Also, he noticed, her clothes were simple but expensive: a pleated Scotch plaid skirt, cashmere sweater and a smartly tailored jacket.

There was no time to wonder who she was. The Linotype was squirting lead, delaying copy for the front page. All afternoon the boys shouted and swore, and did not bother to wash up for a hurried supper. It was ten o'clock when the operator began to set the remaining copy; after midnight when Turner OK'd the proof of the front page.

"It's a little light on the bottom corner, but let it go," he said wearily. "Run off a couple of hundred or so for the drugstore the

41

first thing in the morning, and then knock off. One of you can come in early and finish the run." He went out scowling. Issue number one of *El Porvenir* under the new management had been put to bed.

Next morning he went late to work. The last press run had been finished. The papers had been addressed and were being taken to the Post Office. Everybody was relaxed and cheerful. It was always a good feeling, this queer sense of heroic achievement at having got out only another issue of a small, unimportant weekly—the feeling that is the greatest reward of newspaperdom.

Turner lackadaisically cleared the hooks of old copy, straightened his battered desk, and settled back comfortably in his chair. As he lit his pipe, the girl who had been combing through the morgue the day before came in. She walked directly to his desk.

"Hello," he said abruptly. "Getting everything you want?"

"Almost," she replied. "I didn't bother you yesterday but I want to introduce myself now."

"Sure. Go ahead," he said pleasantly.

"I'm Emily Chalmers."

So that's why she had postponed announcing herself! Giving herself a few days to get the lay of the land and snoop around!

When he did not answer, she said quickly, "I would very much like to ride down with you when you visit my mother, if you are going this weekend by any chance. I prefer not to go down alone, it might be a little awkward. Besides, I don't have a car."

Turner stood up. "O. K. Let's go. I've been expecting you."

She followed him out to his car.

"I'll drop by the house first if you don't mind," he said, driving a mile out of town to his old adobe at the edge of the Reservation. "I'll only be a minute."

Yet when he stepped inside the house, Emily was right behind him inspecting the room with undisguised curiosity. It was the original room of what had been a large one-room adobe. The solid walls were nearly two feet thick, washed on the inside with *tierra blanca*. The dirt floor was packed hard and soaked with linseed oil and turpentine until its surface was as smooth as hard rubber. There was a conical, Indian-made, corner fireplace blackened with smoke. Yet this simplicity of form was choked with a careless content of furnishings and decorations: Navajo rugs, Chimayo blankets, a hand-hewn pine table and a rare Spanish chest, a Fechin portrait and a Dasburg landscape, a litter of books, Apache baskets, Pueblo pottery, beaded buckskins, peyote fans, *bultos* and *Santos*, native handicrafts of all kinds. It was the room of a man who knew and appreciated his environment. But also, as Helen often told him, it was the trap of a man who loved it too much to leave it even for the further development of himself and his talent.

Turner strode into the adjoining bedroom and began packing a small handbag. Emily stood watching him, noting the big, carved, four-poster bed, and the goatskins on the warped pine floor. Suddenly he looked up to see a flush spreading over her face, and followed her fixed gaze to a photograph of Helen on the dresser.

He snapped his bag shut, and walked into the kitchen piled with unwashed dishes. Turning around to Emily behind him, he said abruptly, "Now! If you'd like to see the bathroom, the color of my toothbrush——"

She smiled faintly. "You know, I followed you in here purposely to see your house. I had looked over the back issues of your paper—for specific information I wanted, of course. I have also learned a great deal about you in the two days I've been in town. But the house you live in, the daily articles you use, the books you read, the pictures you look at day after day—all this tells the real story. That is, to a professional," she added primly.

Turner stared at her, trying to fathom her unbounded gall. "Professional what? Snooper?"

"I'm an anthropologist. You know, one who tries to recreate the living character of a vanished people from the material remains they leave behind them. One can use the same technique in evaluating the character of a living but yet unknown person, I've found."

"I'm a newspaperman, myself, as you've deduced," grunted Turner. "I deal with the living today, not the dead yesterday."

"Oh, I don't know," Emily said pleasantly. "I understand you're considered something of an authority on Western Americana. Indian culture is my own special field for research. But we'll get to that later."

"I see. You haven't forgotten you are going to drop in and say hello to your mother after a brief separation of twenty years? Did it occur to you she has been expecting you for three weeks?"

The girl pivoted on a high heel and walked swiftly out. They drove in silence to the plaza, where Emily asked him to stop in front of her hotel. "Good!" said Turner. "I'll go right up to your room with you. You see as a professional I would like to report the color of your nightgown, the brand of tooth-paste you use, the—"

Emily slammed the car door and ran into the hotel. Turner laughed. But his amusement vanished when she returned with a porter carrying two heavy suitcases, a hatbox, brief case, and a box of books. He had supposed she was going down to spend only a day or two with Helen, not to move in with her. Emily dispelled this latter notion as they drove out of town. *"El Mirasol* it's called. The map shows it to be not far from her, and the folder describes it as a comfortable guest ranch."

"It's all right. But not cheap."

"Nothing is nowadays, is it? After all, I can't walk right in on a woman I don't know, even if she is my mother. I thought I'd go right there and register first, so there wouldn't be any question about it," went on Emily. "Then you could take me over to meet my mother. After all, you're her best friend."

"I am that," he said quietly.

The road dropped swiftly into the dark, basaltic gorge, twisting along the course of the turbulent river. Farther down the white-water rapids disappeared; the river deepened and widened between the black volcanic cliffs on each side. Turner pointed out where the little narrow-gauge had puffed along the opposite bank. "Look! There's a bridge left, and a stretch of rails!" There had been a folksy intimacy about the Chile Line, an unhurried air of careless indifference, he continued, that a mainline never achieved. The old wagon road winding through the little Spanish villages, the fields and orchards, was like that too. The new paved highway would never replace either of them. It was merely a way for strangers to get from one place to another; it never touched the quick of this ancient, slow-pulsed valley.

Perhaps it was the nostalgia in his voice that drew out the girl beside him. She talked a little about herself, condensing her autobiography into a few terse sentences. The Chalmers family had kept track of her mother for a few years, until her father had obtained an uncontested divorce. He finally had drunk himself to death, if that's what cirrhosis of the liver really meant. To escape the benevolent tyranny of her grandparents, Emily stayed away at school every winter; and majoring in anthropology and ethnology, spent her summers taking field trips. A large allowance provided her with ample means and freedom.

"So that's why you're here in New Mexico?"

"Yes. Research and field study. Bandelier wrote that the key to the aboriginal history of Mexico and Central America lies between the City of Mexico and the southwestern part of Colorado. That's what I want to find! A race, a country, you know, has to assimilate its past before it can evolve into the future."

This bookish assertion, expressed in anthropological terms as she believed, suddenly revealed to Turner an unhappy, talented, and wealthy child continually escaping into school, books, and the racial past of forgotten peoples, driven by an unconscious compulsion to seek out her own individual beginnings.

"But I wanted to see my mother, too," added Emily. "The older I got, the more necessary it seemed. So I finally found out where she was. Do you think she'll like me?"

El Mirasol did not quite justify its name. Formerly an old sprawling *hacienda,* it was surrounded by large cottonwoods that shut off the sun. But two wings had been added, one on each side with an open patio between, to convert it into a fairly modern guest ranch. The rooms were comfortable and cheerful. Emily chose one looking east over a corral of weathered aspen poles toward the Sangre de Cristos. Then she returned to the lobby where Turner was waiting.

"All settled?"

She nodded, a look of anxiety on her face.

He took her by the arm. "Let's go!"

7.

"I was so young then! How could I ever have suspected that my mother would be the object of so much attention, and that I'd be plagued with these interminable questions about my first impressions of her?"

45

Emily, looking not much older but curiously harder, frowned slightly over her cluttered desk. It was difficult to reconcile her with the young and naive, but rather spoiled and willful girl she seemed when she first came to New Mexico. Between them there seemed one of those great gaps noticeable in so many persons after even a short passage of time. No such gap exists, of course. At every moment in our lives we are all that we have been and will be; a seed whose growth unfolds in a pattern predestined to it from germination. Our failure to perceive any continuity only betrays how shallowly we ever know anyone, especially ourselves.

"No, I was too excited seeing her for the first time to notice anything striking about her." She drummed nervously on the table with her fingers, then resumed in a voice that became musingly slower. "Mr. Turner stopped the car on top of the hill, as I recall, to let me see the Crossing full perspective. There was the sluggish Rio Grande crawling southward past the straggle of giant cottonwoods. A narrow, rickety suspension bridge. And beyond it the canyon winding up to the flat top of the forested plateau and the *pichachos* of the Jemez Mountains above. A massive, top-heavy landscape in which I didn't notice at first the small adobe squatting on the bank just above the bridge.

"What attracted my attention was a woman emerging from the well-house with a filled bucket. She was bent over by its weight, her left arm upstretched as if trying to grasp the rim of the mountain for support. A woman alone and dwarfed by the magnitude and solitude of her setting. That was Helen.

"She must have seen or heard us crossing the bridge. When we stopped the car and got out, she was standing at the doorway. You might have supposed she'd have run out to welcome me, a daughter she had abandoned in infancy. But no. I had come two thousand miles and I had to take even those last few steps up to her.

"An unearthly light didn't radiate from her; she emphatically was not flaming like a celestial torch! But I was greatly relieved at her appearance just the same. She had come from a middleclass family distinctly commonplace compared to the Chalmers, and she had had no advantages and little education; and while my grandparents never disparaged her in front of me, I rather expected to find a drab waitress in a dirty apron and thick-soled shoes. But she

46

was neatly dressed in a silk print, old but in good taste, and there was a sense of quality about her. I remember though that she was wearing a pair of sloppy Indian moccasins instead of shoes.

"I was almost up to her by then, and still she made no move. I could distinguish her creamy oval face beneath her carefully parted wings of dark brown hair. Her lips were trembling slightly; she was emotionally disturbed as I was. Then just as she moved her head and I braced myself to look full into her soft brown eyes, I glimpsed a feather stuck in her hair. It was a woodpecker's feather with a streak of salmon-pink from the underside of the wing.

"These printed assertions that the 'Woman at Otowi Crossing' could speak the language of the birds are ridiculous, of course! It was just that she had something about birds. Every feather she found she regarded as a message or an omen left especially for her, and she never did anything or went anyplace without looking around for one. This one, as a matter of fact, she had picked up just before we got there. Charming and innocent, but not significant. I don't know why it struck me as odd, this feather in her hair. And before I got my mind off it, her arms were around me and I was looking into her warm brown eyes. My mother was flesh and blood all right, odd as she was.

" 'You've met before, I take it!' grumbled Mr. Turner. 'I thought I was going to have the pleasure of introducing you!'

"That broke the ice. We went inside. The new tea room with its few tables and some bright chintz looked pitifully inadequate, not at all up to Mr. Turner's ad. The place was still just a mud hut with a pine-slab privvy outside.

"Maria and Luis came in, and Helen introduced me as her daughter. Maria clasped me to her big bosom without a word.

" 'Huh. You marry all time,' Luis said.

"It was that simple, really.

"There just wasn't anything to talk about, but we had a good, all-New Mexican dinner as only she could cook it: lamb from Luis' small flock garnished with wild horsemint, *chicos*, green chiles, and Maria's paper-thin blue-corn *tortillas*, all topped off with Helen's own chocolate cake. Mr. Turner had brought some wine for the occasion, which she didn't touch. Luis and Maria ate with us. Mr. Turner decided we'd go on a picnic next day—so Helen could rest up from the pangs of sudden motherhood, he said. We left early, Mr. Turner dropping me off at the guest ranch and going to a hotel in town, so we could make an early start in the morning. And that was all.

"My mother was relaxed and untalkative the whole time, though I could see the quick response in her extraordinarily expressive eyes. There was a warmth about her, and yet a curious aloofness and objectivity. This is an Indian characteristic I have commented upon in my *Inquiry*." She tapped the large volume on her desk. "Helen had lived around them so long there's no reason to suppose she hadn't taken on some of their qualities. Undoubtedly she had just suffered the first shock of that mystical experience or strange malady that possessed her from then on. But I detected no sign of it."

After leaving Emily at El Mirasol that evening, Turner hesitated before driving back to the Crossing. He really had intended to go to the small hotel in Espanola. It didn't seem quite proper to stay with Helen on the night of Emily's arrival; she might be embarrassed. Then a deeper honesty rejected this surface cowardice. Why the hell should Emily's arrival change his feeling for Helen or their relationship?

The lamp was still lit, turned low, when he arrived, and Helen was in bed, lying back toward him. He undressed and lay down beside her. Putting his arm around her, he felt how inert and unresponsive she was. "Asleep?"

"No, Jack."

"Did she upset you?"

"Emily? No, it was all right."

For a moment they lay quietly together, then she turned over to face him, putting her hand against his breast to hold him almost imperceptibly away. "It was good of you to come back. There's a pot of hot coffee waiting for you on the table, and I made up the couch for you."

He flung over to throw a look of disbelief at the prepared couch which he had not noticed in the dim light when he came in, then straightened stiffly beside her. "I knew damned well she would!"

"You mustn't blame Emily. Or anyone, Jack. It's just that I want to be alone."

He sat up on the edge of the bed and poured himself a cup of coffee. "What's got into you?" he asked with a worried frown.

"I don't know, but we'll talk about it later," she said with a tender smile. Yet even her smile had the quality of an impersonal love and a strange withdrawnness.

He lay down beside her again. She rolled back over, away from him. She did not talk and he forebore questioning her. After awhile he got up and went to the sofa across the room. Still she said nothing to bridge the gap that so suddenly had opened between them. For a long time he lay awake, hurt and puzzled at the subtle and indefinable change that had come over her.

Early next morning, *bolsas* and baskets packed, they chugged up the canyon. Within an hour the car had climbed so high up the narrow, winding road that on getting out to let the radiator cool they could see the valley spread out below them: village, pueblo, orchards, fields and pastures, all flanked by the opposite blue-ribbed Sangre de Cristos.

"Look right down at your feet," said Turner. "That bare spot on the ridge where the two canyons open. That's the site of the prehistoric pueblo of Otowi. For it have been named the post office at the ranch above, Otowi Crossing and Otowi Bridge across the river at Helen's place, and Otowi Station, the Chile Line's old mail depot for the Ranch."

"Please! Let's have our lunch there," begged Emily. "You promised."

"I promised sometime to show you a ruin. But Otowi down there since the researchers, schoolboys, and pot-hunters have got to it, is nothing but a heap of sand sifted through a sieve."

"Tsankawi may be the place for her to see first, Jack. Then Tchirege, Puye, Tyuonyi. Let her work up to them gradually."

Emily listened carefully, scanning the wild and remote plateau gashed by deep canyons, walled with yellow and pink cliffs, and shadowed by dark forests of juniper and piñon.

Turner, it seemed now, had something else on his mind besides her interest in ruins and their own picnic. He drove on up the plateau to a scatter of log buildings on an isolated mesa cut off on two sides by deep canyons from the surrounding forest of spruce and pine. In its pristine setting Los Alamos Ranch School looked

49

to Emily as picturesque as a postcard. The buildings ranged in size from small cabins to large three-story structures. No two were alike, and they might have been dropped at random on the meadow so perfectly were they placed. The timber work, even to her eyes, was exquisite. Each huge log in the larger buildings had cost the life of a pine; they were hand-hewn, perfectly jointed, and their interstices sealed with slim, straight aspen poles.

Turner named them off quickly. Edward Fuller Lodge with the big portal and a two-story dining room inside . . . The Big House, containing faculty offices, classrooms, dormitory for masters and younger boys . . . Spruce Cottage, quarters for older boys . . . The Trading Post, school store and post office . . . The Pack House, home of the first settler up here, where gear for pack trips was now stored . . . The Carpenter Shop, cabins and cottages for the help.

"All just for boys?" broke in Emily.

Turner snorted. "For forty very rich boys. Greek, Latin and the classics—a secondary and college preparatory course. Dietetically balanced with the traditions of the American Out West. Look at those grain-fed horses out there! One for every boy. The first mounted troop of Boy Scouts in America. Pack trips in the mountains, hunting, fishing, camping. Ashley Pond back there for swimming and skating. The boys are grouped by size and age, and named for the march of trees up from below: Piñon, Juniper, Fir and Spruce, the last timber on the mountains. All perched up here in the mountain wilderness of northern New Mexico. A few mountain ranches off toward Jemez Pueblo, and an open range occasionally crossed by a Forest Ranger. Nothing else. What more do you want for a pallid city boy choking from soot and grime and boarding-house hash?"

"Write your feature article for *El Porvenir* after your interview," chided Helen. "Run along now. We'll meet you later."

8.

The director, A. J. Connell, received Turner cordially in the Big House, and gave him all the brochures and photographs he needed.

The Ranch School, he reminded Turner, was the most distinctive school of its kind in the United States. It had been in existence, under trying conditions, for twenty-four years. Staff and students were proud of it . . .

Turner had difficulty seeing his face. Like an erring boy called up for reprimand, he was seated in front of Connell's desk so that the light from the sunny window would glare on his own face. To escape it, he turned sideways and stared vacantly out of the small side window while he listened to Connell.

Yes, it looked like a good year. Forty-two boys were enrolled. All with good family backgrounds and high scholastic standings . . .

Why, then, wondered Turner, did he sound so unenthusiastic, almost discouraged? A group of men at the corral outside caught his attention. They were throwing hitches on two pack horses; three other horses stood saddled, with reins hanging. One man was a Ranch School wrangler in dirty blue Levis, one was obviously a Forest Ranger in his green whipcord, but the other two were Army officers.

"How's hunting?" he asked casually.

"There's always a lot of deer around. Turkey are still plentiful, and the bear are coming down. I believe we had a scare the other night."

"The season hasn't opened yet," Turner reminded him quietly, nodding toward the window. "Don't tell me they're going hunting, our representatives of lawful government."

Connell looked out the window and frowned. Indian-file, the two pack horses and three mounted riders, scabbarded rifles slung across their saddles, were slowly plodding toward the mountains.

"Just looking around, I suspect, Mr. Turner."

"Just tourists—United States Forest Service and United States Army tourists on vacation. No hunting. No fishing. Damn cold camping out these nights at this altitude. But excellent scenery, so new to a Forest Ranger."

The director's frown grew deeper.

"What's going on up here, anyway?" Turner asked bluntly.

"I wish you would withdraw that question, and not indulge in any press conjectures," Connell said slowly. "Nothing may come of their looking around, but I am not free to talk."

51

They looked at each other steadily.

"Sure. Forget it," said Turner. "But if they turn anything up, let me have it instead of Santa Fe or Albuquerque. I'll pass it along if you wish."

"This war. It keeps getting bigger and more frightful—and more close." His irrelevant statement seemed somehow relevant to the conversation, but he did not develop it.

"Well, I hope the School can hang on," said Turner rising. "You've got a nice set-up, and I'm going to give it a spread in *El Porvenir.*"

"A good little paper; we're one of your subscribers. I hope you can hang on, too, if the worst comes."

"I sold out a month ago. But I got out while the getting was good. Still running the place, though."

Connell looked discouraged. "Lunch?"

"No thanks. I'm on a picnic. But don't forget to call me."

Turner walked slowly out, sniffing the sharp air. Something was up. It had the smell of war . . .

The two women soon returned to meet him. Helen had driven Emily up to Water Canyon, so full of wild flowers: fringed gentians, red paint-brushes, delicate columbines, and blue and yellow asters. "If we could only go on up to Valle Grande, that big volcanic crater!" she murmured. "I've just been telling Emily about the lavender mariposas up there!"

Instead, mindful of their promise to Emily, they drove down the hill and up a side canyon so that she could see Tsankawi. At the base of the mesa Turner found a small spring. Here he set down their *bolsas* and baskets. "As good a place as any, what?"

When finally the basket was emptied and Turner put the blackened coffee pot on the fire, Helen stretched out on a blanket underneath a pine. This continual talk! It wore her out. Ever since that strange break-through she wanted only to be alone; to keep grasping at that vision of reality already fading away, but whose indistinct outline of meaning still was too precious to be forgotten. Emily jumped up with the inexhaustible curiosity of youth. "Come on! Let's go to Tsankawi. Jack promised!"

"I'm just too tired, Emily. Do you mind?" Helen rolled over and closed her eyes.

52

Turner groaned, stretched, and strode off with Emily.

A foot trail led up the slope of juniper and piñon to a protruding rocky ledge of gray volcanic ash that ages ago had congealed into a soft, porous rock blanketing the whole upper slope of the mesa. Gently winding upward through this led a smooth groove perhaps a foot wide and deep, that Turner said teasingly always looked like a small water ditch.

Emily bent down and excitingly ran her hands over its worn surface. "It's the ancient trail itself! Worn into the rock by the bare feet of the people trudging back and forth from the pueblo on top to their springs and corn patches down below. Look at it! Think of the centuries it must have taken for bare feet to cut so deep! Oh, how beautiful!"

She raced ahead like a goat, putting one foot in front of the other in the ancient groove. It wound steeply upward between huge fragments eroded from the cliff, and on up to a series of hand-and-toe holds cut through a rocky defile. When Turner caught up with her, Emily was standing in front of a maze of pictographs and petroglyphs on the smooth face of the cliff.

"Look, Jack! Stylized birds. The terraced zigzag lightning design you see on old pottery. And these human figures with the funny things on top of the head. Either corn husks as they are worn today by the *Koshare* in the corn ceremonials, or parrot feathers brought up from Mexico. It shows there *was* a contact."

Before he could answer she had bounded away again. They finally reached the top of the long mesa; and threading the growth of pine and juniper, came to the high eastern promontory overlooking the tangled canyons below, the valley, and the majestic Sangre de Cristos beyond. Emily did not pause for the immense panorama. She stood staring quietly at the crumbled ruins of yet unexcavated Tsankawi.

The tumbled stones formed a large, rude rectangle scarcely knee-high and in many places overgrown with salt brush, chamisa and gramma grass. To Turner it had never looked very imposing.

"On the contrary," Emily said quietly. "It's a major ruin that will prove most important when it's finally excavated. Look here. Every one of these big stones has been hewn to fit." She lifted one to show him. "Tufa—light, easy to work. Like our own pumice blocks."

Swiftly she built up the whole structure before him. Three terraces of small rooms: those on the inside, facing the inner court, one story in height; the second terrace two stories high; and the third, outside terrace three stories high, providing a high, solid wall for protection. Possibly as many as three hundred rooms. "And here were the entrance passage ways," she said, showing him the areas free of debris on the northwest and southeast corners.

"I suppose these two big round depressions were tin-can dumps," he muttered teasingly again.

"Kivas. Big ones, round and subterranean, of course." She knelt and heaved up stones to reveal a portion of the sunken wall. "Big flat tufa blocks with little stones stuck in the mud between the layers. There's roof timbers down there that can be dated, I'll bet."

"What's your guess?"

"Not very old, according to the best authorities. Probably built by people migrating from the Mesa Verde and Chaco regions during the long drought late in the thirteenth century."

Clambering over the crumbled walls, she began scooping out dirt from a shallow runoff. With a sure instinct, she soon brought up a handful of potsherds. "The rains always bring these to the surface," she explained casually. "You could collect a bushel of them in five minutes."

"You're pretty good at this old stuff, aren't you?" he said gruffly.

She smiled, then suddenly throwing her arms around him, kissed him ligthtly on the cheek. "Not as good as you, Jack, for bringing me here. Thank you so much. I'll never forget it! Now I want to see Tyuonyi, Tchirege, and Puye—every one! It's so exciting!"

"Not today. It'll take you a month of prowling around. But on the way back I'll take you around the south face of the mesa. You can see the caves where cliff-dwellers lived before they built the pueblo up here. Some of the pink walls are still blackened with soot. But it's tough going. There's only little hand-and-toe holds cut in the rock. Think you can make it?"

"I'm not fat and forty, lazy and cautious!" she cried. With a flip of her skirt she vanished over the edge of the cliff.

What a curiously intellectual and emotionally immature girl she was, he thought, carefully climbing down behind her.

9.

With the end of Indian Summer the river cleared and slowed; little patches of paper ice formed over puddles along its banks where loose stock and an occasional deer came to drink. Every morning the fields of stubble glistened with frost. A small impetus in business kept the tea room going. Artists stopped for tea and cinnamon toast. Santa Fe tourists drove up for Sunday dinner. Even a few valley folk came over regularly. Helen found no encouragement in it. Her transcendent peace was being worn off by the stresses and strains engendered by Emily's arrival.

They were so wary of each other! What manner of mother is this who had abandoned her child in infancy, forsaken her home, and come to live in this lonely wilderness without a backward look? This was the question implicit in Emily's manner. Helen's only answer was the question posed by her own attitude. What idle curiosity or inner compulsion had driven this girl, so independent and well-provided for, to seek out a mother after all these years?

Each brought back to the other with agonizing clarity the memory of Gerald Chalmers. For days they avoided mentioning him. Then gradually, with careful casualness, they talked of him.

"Of course I loved your father—at first," Helen said. "He was such fun! And we were so young, just children really. But—"

"Oh, I know! Why, even when he was sick and had a couple of drinks, he put us all in stitches. Right up to the end."

Helen had seen the terrible beginning, Emily the terrible end. But what of the man between? That was the question uppermost in both their minds. Who was the father, the husband that they had really never known? So Emily sought him in Helen, and Helen sought him in Emily, without finding out. A secret strangeness, wariness and hostility created an intangible barrier between them neither could break.

Nor could Helen close the distance that opened between her

55

and Turner. Self-conscious of their relationship around Emily, he no longer came down to stay the night with her; and this sudden termination of their physical intimacy was making him more and more irritable. Yet if she could not assure him the fault was not Emily's, neither could she bring herself to explain to him the reason for her own change in feeling.

Every night she got into bed alone and worried. Then slowly the effect of her suddenly expanded awareness reasserted itself. Once more her soul stood in the plenitude of its nameless origin. She realized the imperfect and haunted dimensions through which she had moved all day. She could catch glimpses of herself as of a strange person playing familiar roles. Yes! The emotions she had believed she felt belonged not to her, but to the role she had been playing. Her marriage with Gerald Chalmers had not hurt her as she had imagined for so many years afterward. It had hurt only the woman who had persisted in identifying herself as a tragically disillusioned young bride. So it was with the remorse and guilt that had followed her after abandoning Emily, and her present faulty relationship with Emily and Turner. They all belonged to the worldly roles she played. Not to the essential selfhood that had been revealed to her that afternoon. She wanted desperately to recapture and hold on to it constantly in peaceful solitude. But how could she? Every morning Emily came, demanding to be taken to the pueblo.

San Ildefonso, a few miles from the Crossing, was an E-shaped cluster of ancient adobes surrounding two plazas. There was nothing showy about it; it had the same soft aliveness and withdrawn remoteness Helen felt in the Indians themselves. A place to be felt, not seen. Driving Emily to it, she felt a sense of irritation at her daughter's rambling account of her long and compulsive search for its apparent secret.

Emily first had gone to the ruined cities of the Maya in Yucatan. Their gargoyle symbolism had been too elaborate to hold her. Yet there, for the first time, she felt a rhythm wholly and distinctly American. It ruined Boston for her forever.

Next summer on another archaeological tour she went to the Valley of Mexico. A strange, bookish little monster burrowing into the continent's past. There it began to come alive. Ignoring her fellow-students she trudged to one pyramid after another.

"Emily!" the class remonstrated when it caught up with her. "Your're not having any fun! Don't be a grind!"

She shrugged off their Sunday boat rides at Xochimilco, politely dismissed their handsome Mexican boy friends. Even the accompanying professors let her alone, regarding her, erratic and spoiled as she was, as a student of originality who had the bug.

Whatever it was, it kept biting Emily deeper. The following summer she had gone to the great Casas Grandes ruins in Chihuahua and worked north to the ruins in Chaco Canon, New Mexico, the greatest ruins north of Mexico. "Of course I wanted to see you," she added, "and since I was so close, I came."

Helen let her talk on, realizing that if there was a personal element in her compulsive search for a motherland Emily was not aware of it. But her compulsion had kept increasing with her loneliness, emotional insecurity, and growing alienation from the aging Chalmers. And when her grandparents died, leaving her with ample funds, Emily had committed all her resources to the search.

"But just what do you expect to find here, Emily?" Helen asked finally.

"I've been telling you all the way from the house, Mother! There's a direct racial link or migration route between all these northern pueblos and those to the south! Where did it all begin? What were its roots—this vast prehistoric motherland of America?"

Leaving the car parked on the outskirts of the pueblo, they walked across the plaza. Luis and Maria lived in two rooms with dirt floors. Maria did all her cooking over the fireplace, carried her water from the stream, and seemed content to do without all the gadgets provided her at the tea room. She poured out some of the coffee made from the used grounds she had carried home from Helen's the night before, and set the earthenware cups on the table.

"Why don't you bring over that extra coffee pot instead of using this old iron kettle?" asked Emily. "Boiled coffee's bitter."

"This Indian way!"

Luis was just as noncommittal. His fields were a long walk away. To work them he had a scrawny team, a rusty plow, and innumerable traditions to observe—certain days to begin planting and harvesting, special ways of selecting his ears of seed corn, a vast ritual procedure from beginning to end.

57

"Now Luis," began Emily. "If you'd team up with several others—"

"This Indian way!" He flipped the corner of his blanket over his face and disappeared into silence like an ostrich burying its head in the sand.

No. Neither one of them, nor anyone else Emily talked to, knew the history of the pueblo, who their ancestors were, where they had come from—nothing! It ended as it always ended. Emily walked out in a huff. "They're your friends and they won't talk. You've been here for years and won't talk either! What's the matter?"

Helen frowned. "It doesn't do any good to ask these people such direct questions. They just don't look at things like we do," she said at last. "Maybe because they don't have our sense of time as a linear movement. You know, a horizontal stream flowing out of the past into the future, leaving on its banks deserted ruins, pots, and skulls that can be dated and classified. Indian time's different. There aren't any clocks and calendars to chop it into segments, ever smaller and faster. I can't explain it very well, Emily, but to Indians time has depth instead of movement. Like a great, still pool with a life and meaning of its own. As if it were an organic element which helps to fashion our own shape and growth in its unique design of being. Indians aren't in any hurry; they have all the time there is."

"Nonsense! That's unscientific! There's always a chronological development, and I mean to trace it back to its beginning!"

Emily was still in a huff when she got into the car, and Helen was glad to get in beside her. She wanted only to go home, to get away from these irritating distractions of a world to which she no longer owed her full allegiance.

Despite a twinge of conscience, she was relieved a week later when Emily impulsively bought a second-hand car and announced at dinner that Saturday she was going off on a trip.

"Now! The beginning of December! Where the hell you going?" demanded Turner. The anger in his voice had been a long time breaking through. He was irked because Emily was so extravagant and selfish, living in style at El Mirasol with no thought for her mother's obvious struggle to make both ends meet. He also had been getting more and more jealous of the time and attention Helen

58

showed her. And now her purchase of a car—a convertible at that!
—for a foolish pleasure trip seemed the last straw.

"If it's any of your business, I'm driving over to Zuni to see
the masked Shalako dance!"

This added still more fuel to Turner's fire. Helen had always
wanted to see this particular ceremony. Now he was embarrassed
because he hadn't taken her, and angry because Emily didn't invite
her to go along. "Rats! You're always going off half-cocked and—"

"Stop it!" interrupted Helen. "Emily's going to do just what
she wants to do, as she always has! If she's going anywhere, now's
the time to go before winter does set in."

Her face had paled. All this wrangling, even their continual
company, had got on her nerves until she could have screamed.
Fortunately neither Turner nor Emily stayed long. She watched
Emily prance out to her ridiculously jaunty convertible, young,
vital and carelessly indifferent, followed by Turner stiffly walking
out behind her, still resentful.

With great relief she got into bed and lay wondering what was
wrong with her. How could she have had the great awakening she
had experienced, and yet be so distressed by these trivial strains in
her few personal relationships? It seemed to her now that she was
caught between two worlds, belonging to neither. Somehow, sometime, she had to make a choice between them. But how?

Late next morning Turner came back; he had stayed overnight
at El Mirasol and watched Emily drive off after breakfast. Helen
could feel his unbounded relief as he sat down in front of the fire.
It was a quiet Sunday morning; Emily was gone; Maria and Luis
would not come until afternoon. Now was the time for him to get
off his chest everything that had been troubling him.

"The deal for the paper has finally been settled," he said abruptly, "but I don't think I can stand editing the sheet for Throckmorton any longer."

"There's no need for you to stay and stagnate from frustration,
Jack. Why don't you get out and do something more creative?"

"Creative writing? God Almighty! I'm sick of the phrase!"
he exploded. "Every pansy and half-assed poet, every rich mother's
pip-squeak rents a 'studio' for the summer to do some 'creative writing'! And all their drivel put together isn't worth a single inch

59

of the commonest straight reportage in the most stinking newspaper!"

Helen was not intimidated. "But even the best reportage restricts itself to what journalism considers facts. Post-mortem facts! Dead the instant the headlines hit the street!"

"Wait a minute!"

She was suddenly conscious again of existing at the hub of that circle ever wheeling slowly around her. In a segment of its perimeter she saw him as she had never seen him before: a man imprisoned within a superficial and fallacious time-span limited only to those events looming highest on its surface horizon, his whole being keyed to the reportorial realm of the ephemeral present. It was at once the secret of his boyish charm and a weakness hidden from her till now.

"Don't you see it, Jack? You're obsessed with keeping up with time, with meeting 'dead'—lines! Your whole life is dedicated to writing obituaries of events and people!"

If Turner was surprised at her tone, he was more shocked by such heresy. "That sounds literary as hell and I don't want any of it!"

"You want some coffee though," she said quietly.

He followed her out to the kitchen and thrust some crumpled sheets of paper at her.

They were so badly penciled in a childish scrawl that Helen could hardly read the top lines on the first page:

> "Arch Traitor F.D.R. Sits in President's Chair
> Smoking That Cigarette, Jumping Taxes, and
> Scheming for War"

"That's creative writing!" Turner said caustically. "At least I've never seen quite so many words in a head for an editorial!"

"Mr. Throckmorton?"

"Cyril Throckmorton III."

Helen slowly read through the bitter, vindicative pages. "Look, Jack. Here's a small boy in a wealthy, historic family of the highest social standing. He can't learn to spell, he can't do his arithmetic. He is given tutors, put in obscure private schools. He never does graduate from a college nor learn a profession. The family dies, leaving its immense wealth and name to an undeveloped, thwarted, grown-up child. And now—look! He owns a newspaper. Here are his grade school papers!" She gave the sheets back to Turner. "There isn't any family to be ashamed of them. No teacher will flunk or expel him because of them. He can give full vent to all his feelings."

"No he can't!" Turner threw the pages into the fire.

"In his own newspaper—that he has bought outright?" Helen sighed. "Jack, get out of this unhealthy situation. Leave La Oreja and do something constructive. Marry a lovely young girl and lead a normal life, for goodness sake!"

There. It had jumped out of her suddenly and unbidden. She could see him staring at it with a frightened, hurt look in his eyes.

"I intend to take you with me," he said quietly.

"No, Jack. We can't go on together any longer. I just can't."

"Why?"

"Something's happened inside me. I can't explain it because I don't understand it. But it's changed my whole life—the way I see us, everything! If I could only explain how it suddenly shook me awake and made everything clear!"

He made a quick turn around the room and returned to face her with a calm, set face. "I understand these emotional upsets. All women have them. Let's don't worry about it. We'll talk about it later when you're rested up—when I come down again."

"But this isn't a mood. Let me explain. It's—"

"No!" he exclaimed stubbornly. "I don't want to hear anything about it! Nothing inside you or out is going to come between us— ever!"

He angrily switched on the radio.

It was blasting out the news that Pearl Harbor was being bombed by Japanese planes, catapulting the country into World War II.

10.

Even at Otowi Crossing, Helen could see its swift effects. Emily returned East to continue school or take a war job. Spanish and Pueblo neighbor boys left for Bataan. Other Anglos deserted the

61

valley for lucrative jobs in the California war plants. Gasoline rationing cut down Turner's frequent trips and reduced the tea room's customers. Even sugar became difficult to obtain.

Yet she welcomed the solitude enforced upon her. The long days and empty nights gave her time to brood upon the inner world she had glimpsed, and during the weeks and months that slid past she weeded out almost all her casual Anglo acquaintances. There was a cruelty in her refutation of them she could not help for they appeared to her now as etiolated dream-projections in a world that was itself one great mirage; at best merely receptacles of fatuous thoughts and desires stuffed into them by newspapers and radios which they evacuated like undigested ejecta in superficial prattle and malicious gossip. In her desperate search to establish her own identity she felt drawn more and more to the simple Spanish villagers and Indians who became her sole friends. She would sit looking at their austere, mindless and almost primeval faces; at the loose flowing lines of their sturdy bodies which might have been sculptured from the earth itself. A dark eye lighted up like a pool catching a ray of moonlight. A work-hardened hand raised in poetic gesture. How difficult it was for them to talk! They were receptacles too; but of passions and desires engendered by remote ancestors and derived from the forces of nature which fed them. Their very impersonality took on the strength of a vast anonymity, their silence was eloquent, for somehow they expressed an intuitive awareness of the mystery of which she too was a part.

With old Desideria and her three invariable companions she became close friends. They were *parteras, cuanderas, brujas*—native midwives, herb doctors, and witches—who often passed by on their way up into the mountains to gather herbs for their cures and charms: *topalquin* to break a fever, *cota* for rheumatism, *yerba buena* for pregnant brides; horsemint, mushrooms, the droppings of a hawk. On the way home they always stopped to see her. Waiting respectfully at the door until Helen invited them in. Then sitting stiffly, black *rebozos* over head and shoulders, teaching her what powers of the earth and sky to invoke with each of the herbs they gave her.

"*Ay de mi, Señora!* What power they have granted you, yourself! That is plain to see!" And they would make the sign of the cross over her upon leaving.

What strange old women they were! They knew so much without knowing they frightened her a little. She did not question the deep bond that drew them together.

"Yes, Goddamn it!" Turner always maintained. "It was these old Mexican crones—excuse me, Spanish-Americans they are nowadays!—who probably started the preposterous myth about her. At least I first heard of it from them. Looking in her open door one afternoon, they saw Helen lying on the couch, hands crossed over her breast, eyes open but not seeing them. In the middle of a trance, they said.

"Helen always enjoyed having them stop in and they often did so, regarding her as being a little fey herself. You know, 'An earth woman. A sky woman. *Una Señora que no ha pecado.*' Another *bruja*! Seeing Helen like that only confirmed their belief. Yes, Goddamn it! It must have been a baling wire testimonial to their wildest imaginations, to hear them relate it. One of them was old Desideria from Cundiyo, a horny old witch of a woman if there ever was one. She had a wart on her nose with four black hairs sticking out from it—the antennae of her acute perceptions, no doubt. She swore to me she could see light between Helen and the couch; that she was lying suspended between earth and sky, communing with the devils and spirits of both. 'An earth woman. A sky woman. *Una Señora que no ha pecado.*'

"This was the myth they began spreading through the little Spanish villages and the Indian pueblos, and that has now grown out of all proportions. To it I have nothing to contribute. All discussions that smack of the metaphysical make me sick. I've never leaned toward the spooky side of life. I believe in people, not ghosts. And Helen was a woman. I'll be damned if I'll ever believe she flew on a broomstick to consort with Indian *kachinas* and Mexican *brujas* on Black Mesa at midnight. She never stayed up that late."

Turner hated anything mysterious or secret, and early that fall he was nettled by the huge loaded trucks pounding up the mesa to Los Alamos Ranch School. "It's preposterous! All this truckage!" he stormed after driving up to see what was going on. "Supplies and machinery all over the place. If the Army intended to activate a training camp or something, why was the Chile Line abandoned?"

"Did you see Mr. Connell?" Helen asked.

"Yes. He's giving up the school after Christmas. Crowding a full year's work into this semester, so the graduates will have their college entrance credits."

"After twenty-four years? It's a pity. Why?"

"The Under-Secretary of War has directed acquisition of the whole plateau—school property, homesteads and grazing land, even the wilderness area supervised by the Forest Service. That much is public news. There isn't any more."

He was stung by the secrecy surrounding these goings-on. Yet Helen detected in him also a trace of pleasurable excitement. War, secret projects, red tape—they appealed to the capacity for childish make-believe hidden in all men however much they denied it. Still irritated, he left without waiting to be asked for supper.

That evening she saw a mounted security patrol ride by, fully armed and with a walky-talky outfit on a pack horse. A shiver of apprehension shook her. What was going on up there on the Hill?

Yet if a new world was being shaped by catastrophic war, her inner new world continued to engross her more. For now to her who had seldom dreamed, there came dream after dream in quick succession. Whatever they meant, if they had a meaning, they revealed her increasing receptivity to influences beyond her mental ken. Something was untying the hard knot inside her; trying to break through the shell of the rational, materialistic world about her; to illiterate Desideria and wordless Facundo, the mute river and mountains, to all that archaic world to which she still owed allegiance.

One night she had a dream so complete and vivid she could not keep it to herself. So fretting with impatience until Facundo came next morning, she cornered him in the kitchen the moment he walked in the door.

"I had another dream, Facundo! It—"

Facundo raised his hairless eyebrows at her impatience, then slumped down stolidly on a chair at the table. "No coffee? I cold!"

Helen accepted the rebuke, set a cup of coffee in front of him and squirmed as she watched him pour in rationed sugar. Sitting down across from him, she waited patiently to begin. Facundo was

64

in no hurry. He sipped his coffee, smacked his lips. Finally he fixed on her a sharp, inquiring look.

"The dream, Facundo."

"I listenin'."

"It was like this," she began slowly. "I was standing on the floor of a strange world, like the bottom of a well. The walls were of rock, cylindrical like this water glass, Facundo. They rose steep and high around me, so high I could hardly see their top. Just below me was a deep, dark hole or canyon, round too. The light was dim. Where it came from I couldn't tell. Maybe from a big red disk high above the cliff walls. Peeking down into the gaping hole below me I glimpsed another just like it, or maybe its reflection. Then I drew back quickly.

"Out of that deep chasm something was coming. A whole procession of shadowy figures. Queer animals whose shapes I couldn't see very well, except that of a deer, a big deer with spreading horns. Then half-human figures, brutish looking monsters with heads bent over, their long arms swinging. One of them wore a stovepipe hat. Another carried a lace-trimmed parasol. They gave me the creeps, I can tell you!

"As I drew back to let them pass, the procession started climbing up the rock walls in great spirals. There were four of these spirals; I could count them as the procession went round and round, higher and higher, till they were out of sight. Then I noticed that the big red sun above was gone. In its place was a patch of sky, and in the middle of this stood the deer. His head was up and with one forefoot raised, he was jabbing toward me as if to say, 'Well, why didn't you come on up too?'"

She paused. "Facundo, do you know what I was waiting for?"

He bent forward slightly with a look of respect and admiration.

"I'll tell you," Helen said solemnly. "I was waiting for a taxi to arrive and drive me up that spiralling ascent. It didn't come, and the next thing I knew I was awake in bed!!"

She leaned back and burst into a peal of laughter. She couldn't help it. The dream had been so vivid and intense that this preposterous climax now opened the only safety valve to her nervous tension. "A New York taxicab, Facundo! With a little yellow light on top and a meter clicking away inside to count the cost of the ride.

That's what I was waiting for!" She kept laughing till the tears ran down her cheeks.

Facundo sat staring at her with stern disapproval. He had no sense of humor. Abruptly he got up and strode out the door to do his chores.

For several days he avoided her and neither of them ever mentioned her dream, although she occasionally caught him looking at her with his sharp, probing look. Late one afternoon a few weeks later she happened to meet him at the pueblo. Facundo was strolling leisurely across the plaza. In the crook of his left arm was a prayer bowl of corn meal. In his right hand he carried an eagle feather.

"I'm going home, Facundo. Do you want a ride?"

The old Indian gave her a placid look. "I go kiva."

Helen was about to turn away when he lightly brushed the feather across her breast. "You come. *Cómo no?*"

The casual invitation struck her with curious force. During all her years here she had never been in the kiva; women and white people were not allowed. Reluctant as she was to break this taboo, her curiosity impelled her to follow him.

The massive kiva stood in the center of the empty plaza. It was simply a cylindrical, thick-walled adobe perhaps eight feet high, with an inset flight of terraced steps ascending to the ladder entrance on its flat top. This of course was only its surface structure; the ceremonial chamber itself extended underground.

Facundo stopped in front of it, urging her to the steps. Halfway up she stopped. People were stirring across the plaza, aroused by the sight of a white woman about to enter the kiva. Facundo ignored them. From his bowl of corn meal he was laying on the ground a protective line to seal off the kiva behind him. This done, he climbed slowly up the steps past Helen. At the top he glanced back at her, beckoning with an impatient little whisk of his eagle feather. Timidly Helen followed him to the roof, then climbed down the ladder behind him.

She had picked up during her many years here the usual smattering of pueblo ceremonialism. Although she never discussed it with Facundo for fear of endangering their friendship, it had led her to anticipate in the kiva all the paraphernalia of a vast and complex ritualism. Now as she stepped off the ladder and stood in the kiva for the first time, she was disappointed by its appalling barrenness. There were no furniture nor rugs on the bare dirt floor, no paintings frescoed on the bare adobe walls, no window openings. It was simply an empty, cylindrical room unlit save for the pale light from the ladder-opening above.

Off to the side in the floor, however, she detected a small round hole. "That the *sipapu* where everybody come from," said Facundo casually. "You see him in your dream." He moved closer and with his elbow pointed to her crotch. "That place where Mother Earth borns us."

The first underworld, the Place of Beginning, the womb of all life. Yes, it was like her dream. Next to the *sipapu* was a small sunken firepit containing a few sticks of piñon which Facundo lit and blew into flame. Its small sunken glow reminded her of the faint red sun she had seen in the chasm of her dream. And the spiral trail upward she had seen. It was there too. Across the circular floor Facundo was sprinkling a faint trail with pinches of corn-meal; the second mythical world into which man had emerged. The raised seating ledge around the wall she saw as the third world. From it the ladder, serving as another *sipapu* or umbilical cord, in turn led up to the present fourth world of man's successive existences. How simply and profoundly it was all symbolized by this one underground chamber, the whole multi-world universe of Pueblo mythology.

Facundo was busy at his duties: opening a wooden door in the seating ledge and taking out painted panels of cottonwood which he set up as a rude altar; placing on it a bowl of sand, of water, of eagle feathers, and four ears of corn of different colors; and tying small hawk feathers and tufts of eagle down to the ladder. Helen hardly noticed him. Not only had the vivid memory of her dream returned to her, but something of the vast and blinding experience she had had so many months ago. In a flash she saw it all. The kiva, the whole multi-world universe, was at the same time the body of man. The whole of Creation already existed in him, and what he called an Emergence or a round of evolution was but his own expanded awareness of it. Once again with ecstatic intuition she glimpsed what she really was. Constellations ringed her head and waist; planets and stars gleamed on her fingers; the womb-worlds of all life pulsed within her.

How clear everything seemed to her now! Nothing unusual nor fearful had happened to her. She was but breaking through into that hidden reality through her dreams, intuitions, and the symbols long known to these ancient, illiterate Indians.

Facundo brought her back to size. The fire was almost out, and in its dying glow she could hardly see him as he loomed up before her in his Montgomery-Ward blanket, rolling a cigarette in a wrinkled cornhusk. "This old kiva cold and dirty. Lots of work gettin' ready for them big doin's."

Watching him blow smoke to the six directions, Helen glanced upward to follow his last puff. In the patch of sky above she saw the faint twinkle of a star.

"Too early," said Facundo. "The Deer not up yet. But comin' sure."

Helen realized that by the Deer he meant the Pleiades. She followed him up the ladder and climbed down the steps outside. It was dusk. People were crossing the plaza as if nothing had happened. It all seemed drab and familiar as always.

Facundo paused beside her, looking around. "I don't see no taxi."

11.

Emily wrote that she was returning to New Mexico to write her dissertation; the war was creating a shortage of qualified teachers and she had been advised to take her doctorate.

Turner took Helen to meet her the day before Christmas. Main-line passenger trains had never entered Santa Fe, and it was necessary to drive to Lamy, some fifteen miles southeast in the rolling piñon hills. The junction comprised only a few ramshackle houses and a general store, the squat wooden depot, and what to Helen was one of the most charming of all the Fred Harvey railroad hotels, *El Ortiz*. Spanish-Colonial in style, its rooms opened on an inside patio flanked by a horseshoe lunch counter of green marble.

"This is what I always wanted at the Crossing," said Helen as they sat down for a cup of Fred Harvey's famous coffee. "Isn't it a beautiful place!"

Turner shrugged. "It's going to be abandoned and torn down."

"No! They can't! Oh, what's happening to the world?"

They had come early, of course. For to them as to all people of the region, Lamy was a rare experience to be savored slowly and fully. When the Train Came In!—that was the event for which *El Ortiz,* all Lamy was expressly planned. They wandered down to the little depot to see If the Train Was On Time. Trainmen in fresh-washed denims were fingering heavy watches. The telegraph operator was bent over his clattering keys. Already baggagemen were wheeling out trucks piled high with trunks and boxes. The little waiting room was beginning to empty.

"It's been so long since I've heard a train whistle and smelled the smoke and all. Jack, you don't know how much I've missed it!"

Now they stood on the long brick platform that stretched between the low, snowy hills. It was crowded with old Spanish *señoras* wrapped in their rusty black *rebozos,* dark faced *paisanos* softly clapping their cold hands, wealthy townspeople shivering in mink. coats, businessmen importantly puffing cigars, a Pueblo Indian stolidly wrapped in a bright red blanket, and a huddle of Indian women squatting with a litter of pottery, baskets, and corn necklaces spread out on a blanket. Behind them stood a few wagons with their scarecrow teams, a row of shiny automobiles, sleek station wagons emblazoned with the crests of dude ranches, and a mud-spattered bus. And everywhere, somehow conspicuously out of place in this immemorial setting for the Lamy drama of Waiting For the Train to Come In, somber groups of draftees and uniformed GIs...

"Jack!" Helen gripped his arm; her accustomed ear had heard it.

A moment later the train was in the block. And now they heard it beyond the frosty-white hills—that long-drawn, half-screech, half-wail which would always be to Helen the most poignantly haunting sound of her old world. Black and brutal, flaunting a dark weather in the wind, the train swept round the bend. A double-header with a sinuous line of Pullmans, immeasurably long and bearing with it all the mystery and the glory and the sadness of the far off, rushed past them, slowed smoothly, and screeched to a sudden stop. Immediately they were caught in a milling mob of people shouting "Merry Christmas!" and "Adios," "Adios," the immemorial and synonymous word of greeting and farewell. Then far down the platform they saw Emily beside a pile of luggage, books, and Christmas packages. Arm up, waving, she was sniffing the cold, thin air.

"Helen! Jack! I know I'm back in New Mexico! I can smell the piñons!" she shouted as they hurried toward her.

Helen was glad to see her and resolved that this time, now that she felt more secure, she would not let their relationship be marred by trivial happenings. Yet she was relieved when Emily moved back into El Mirasol, for there was still a strain between them however hard they tried to ignore it.

Soon after Christmas the Los Alamos Ranch School closed. All its staff and its forty-eight boys moved out. A carful of them stopped at the tea room for a good-bye snack when they came down the Hill. They reported that huge wire gates protected by machine gun emplacements had closed the road behind them; everyone who entered from now on was required to have a pass. "But we won't forget you, Miss Chalmers, or your chocolate cake either!"

Helen could not still a little ache in her heart as she watched them leave. The Ranch School, the Chile Line, and the old hotel at Lamy. What on the Hill could ever take their place?

But on San Ildefonso's feast day, towards the end of January, the ancient and eternal asserted itself again. The evening was bitterly cold when Emily drove her over to the pueblo. Snow had fallen all day, and now in pale moonlight it shone with a bluish tinge. "As blue as my nose feels!" muttered Emily, drawing her scarf closer.

The bonfires were already lit in the plaza when they arrived, and Maria was waiting for them with hot chile and coffee. "Where's Luis?" asked Helen, gratefully soaking up heat from the fireplace.

Maria shrugged. "That kiva business. He has his duties. You see him, maybe, dancing like a deer."

The formal Deer Dance would not be held until the morrow; tonight the dancers simply made their first public appearance. But Emily could not wait to see their masked figures. So bundling up again, the three of them trudged out into the plaza to stand miserably stamping feet and rubbing ears. The flickering glow of the scattered bonfires only accentuated the cold and the darkness and the everlasting mystery of man's existence in the illimitable universe that pressed upon them from all sides. Anonymous shapes shrouded in blankets moved quietly as shadows or stood patiently immune to the illusion of flowing time. A door in the pueblo opened, an oblong of yellow light fell on the snowbank. Far off on a hill a coyote yapped. Two small boys, their naked bodies painted above and below their breechclouts, fed more sticks to the fires. The blanketed shapes moved back from the smoke. The wait resumed anew.

There was a sudden stir. The mountain walls shook slightly. The stars flickered . . . The drums had begun to beat softly but powerfully. Helen could feel the vibrations running through the earth, creeping up her legs . . . Then abruptly she heard a loud jangle of bells.

"They're coming! Look!" Emily pointed.

Maria swiftly reached out from her blanket and dragged the girl's hand down. "Don't put your finger on them! Nobody!"

There they were, unlooked and uncalled for from the folds of the snow-blanketed mountains. A long line of dancing deer, elk, antelope and mountain sheep. With tossing antlers and pointed heads with sad, still eyes. With sharpened sticks for forelegs, and with human hind legs wearing straps of dangling bells, colored Hopi sashes, and a Paris garter. So they danced in crimson flamelight, their enormous, grotesque, black shadows keeping time on the wall behind them. Beautiful and barbaric, rooted in the archaic depths of time.

"Now I know how those Aztec temples and pyramids swarmed with masked figures in torch-light," murmured Emily.

Helen kept searching for the figure of Facundo in the deer, antelope, mountain sheep, and elk threading their way between the bonfires and the snowbanks to dance as men imbued with all the primal forces they represented. She could not recognize her old gardener, his humble role was so transformed by the power loaned him. Or was he so old and wise and powerful that he remained in the kiva to externalize and direct it in younger, lesser men? So she watched, as women always watched, elbows drawn in close, her mittened hands clasped tightly. While the snow began to fall again quietly on antler, horn, and mane. And the mystery deepened, so unutterably strange, as strange as America itself with its archaic hoariness forever masked by its seeming youth and newness.

But not to Maria who began to giggle. "You see him, that crazy husband of mine? In the skin of that deer he killed last week and had no time to cure properly? Not in the old, nice one. In the green one! And it smells. It smells!" She smothered another giggle in her blanket.

The dance ended suddenly as it had begun, the masked figures filing back into the kiva. Now Helen could see Facundo. He had come out in his faded store blanket and was drawing a thin line of cornmeal around the kiva to seal it for the night's secret ceremony against profane strangers and evil thoughts.

The red fires faded to pink. Silence rushed in over the earth. Only the mystery remained, the everlasting mystery of man's relationship to the ancient, eternal earth, intensified by the evocation of its invisible and invincible powers.

"Mother!" exclaimed Emily. "It's been so exciting I won't be able to sleep! Come back to El Mirasol and stay all night with me. It'll be fun. Please!"

Before Helen could answer a brilliant flash of light from the mesa above spurted high into the sky. An instant later came a sharp detonation, followed by a muffled rumble echoing across the snowy hills.

"What's that?" Emily grabbed her arm.

Helen tried to repress the shocked surprise in her own voice. "It's nothing. They're probably just blasting for a new road so the dust and loose rock will settle before morning."

"But I don't like it!" whined Maria.

"Who does?" snapped Helen, amazed at her own annoyance. How could this frighten her after she had been initiated, as it were, into the enduring wholeness that could withstand any such defiant force? Yet trembling a little, she turned shyly to Emily. "I think I will stay with you, Emily. It might be fun."

A windfall had come to El Mirasol. All winter it had been so empty that the manager, Mr. Saunders, had considered closing it until summer. Only Emily's lucrative and promptly paid account delayed him. Now suddenly it was beginning to fill with a curious type of men Helen had not seen before. Sitting in the dining room next evening with Emily, she could not place them. They all looked and acted alike, just as all cowmen and all bookkeepers somehow reflected the nature of their calling. Intelligent, studious-looking, very much aloof, and not accompanied by any women.

"Snooty!" said Emily. "They've come to work on that secret project on the Hill. Leaving every morning, returning every night for dinner. They keep to themselves. Too precious to speak to any outsider."

She threw up her head, glanced defiantly across the room, and blushed slightly.

Helen covertly studied the two men sitting at the table. One was a pleasant and rather pudgy middle-aged German with twinkling blue eyes and a hearty laugh. The other was a lean, long-legged young man with a sharp nose and crew-cut brown hair. Obviously listening with close attention to his older companion, he kept furtively eyeing Emily. The by-play embarrassed Helen. It was such bad taste! She saw too that the older man was aware of it as she.

Abruptly he laid down his fork and called loudly to the manager standing across the room. "Mr. Saunders!"

Obviously he was a person of some importance, for Saunders went quickly to his table.

The German's loud voice carried across the room. "Those charming women! The only ladies here. You have not introduced us!"

"I will sir, if"—

"Ja!"

The two men followed Saunders to Helen and Emily's table. "This is Mrs. Helen Chalmers, an old resident of the valley. Miss Emily here, her daughter. Dr. Hans Breslau and Dr. Edmund Gaylord."

Dr. Breslau bowed. When he straightened, his blue eyes had lost their twinkle and his voice was sharp as he faced Saunders. "Charming Miss Emily here. She is a guest? A Project member no doubt?"

"Yes sir. A charming girl. She's been with us some time."

"Was it your understanding, Mr. Saunders, that your guests were to be restricted to Project members from now on?"

Saunders began to flounder. "Yes, Dr. Breslau, but she's been here so long I figured it wouldn't hurt to let her stay a bit longer.

She's an anthropologist. Putters around the pueblo and those old ruins all day long. Minds her own business. Yes sir!"

Helen could see Emily's face flushing with anger and young Dr. Gaylord squirming with embarrassment. Still Dr. Breslau insisted, "But she's not a Project member?"

"As I told you, sir. But nobody has said—"

"It's not my say. I simply asked you what your understanding was when arrangements were made to take over your place."

Emily could stand no more. "Mother, we're interrupting a business conversation. Let's go!"

Dr. Breslau's whole manner changed as he grabbed her by the hand. His eyes twinkled, his voice broke into a hearty laugh. "You're not leaving now, my little anthropologist? Depriving us of your mother's company before we have had our coffee together? And my young friend here. What about him?"

No, he would not let them go until they had sat over a cup of coffee, listening to his amusing chatter.

But on the way out Emily gave vent to her anger. "Snobs! Spiteful snobs! I told you so. But I won't let them drive me out of here! Never!"

12.

"I think we all felt the same about Project Y or the Manhattan Project in those early first years," Gaylord often recalled. "Most of us were young. The work was new. The place was remote and primitive. We were all confused, but imbued with a strange sense of adventure, urgency and secrecy."

He seldom drank himself, but he enjoyed mixing cocktails for his guests. Stirring the shaker slowly, he looked curiously urbane and polished in his white dinner jacket and imported English flannels. Not at all like the tall, harassed Dr. Gaylord with one gray-filmed eye so often pictured in newsprint.

"Los Alamos always had about it an air of mystery. For a decade it conjured for the whole world a sense of the fantastic unreal. Even now when it seems so sedate there hovers about it a miasma of mythic import.

"It seems strange to me now that when I first arrived I was not conscious of the myth beginning to take form. Not only the myth of the Project on top the mesa, but the myth at its foot, at Otowi Crossing. Only now can one realize they were two sides of the same coin, neither of which could have existed without the other. Both growing, as all myths must grow, with agonizing slowness and in secrecy. Forming one myth as we know it now—perhaps the only true myth of these modern times.

"I first passed by the Crossing without even noticing it. As a boy I never had the time nor inclination to indulge in fairy tales, but a wood-block print in an old German edition of Grimm must have caught my eye sometime. And when I later noticed the small hut set back among the trees along the river, it recalled to me that old print of a woodcutter's hut in the Black Forest. Save that it was of adobe, it had the same dark air of mystery and abandon. For a long time I knew nothing about it. I was completely immured in the secrecy surrounding my own work—actually confined with the Project and that whole New World in a Post Office box.

"In New York I simply had been given a railroad ticket to Santa Fe, an address there to report to, and an order to tell no one where I was going. The address was a suite of office rooms at 109 Palace Avenue, a dilapidated old building housing curio shops just off the town plaza. Here a friendly woman named Mrs. McKibben checked me in and sent me in a car with an armed escort thirty-three miles up a steep mountain road, past machine gun emplacements, to Post Office Box 1663. It was a mammoth absurdity, of course! There was no semblance of a town; no laboratory, no library, no shop nor power plant; no hotel, no stores, no homes. Simply a scatter of old log cabins, new utility structures and Army barracks being thrown up by a construction crew. In the wan afternoon light everything looked forbiddingly wild, lonely and remote.

"At the Security Office I was given an identification card permitting me admission through the main gate, and a badge allowing me entrance into the Technical Area. Then I was given a Security lecture.

" 'Post Office Box 1663 is the only address you will give to anyone, even your family,' I was cautioned. "If it is necessary for you to obtain an auto registration, driver's license, income tax return, food and gasoline ration books, or an insurance policy, clear through this office. With the cooperation of national and state government officials, we will issue you a code number in order to avoid the disclosure of your name and address. In some cases eminent personnel will be assigned assumed names. You will be permitted to move within certain limits under certain conditions and with the special permission of the Director. We request that you never go to any nearby inhabited place alone, and suggest that you do not have any member of your family come within one hundred miles—except those immediate members who come to live with you.'

"For a few weeks, however, all staff members were quartered in nearby guest ranches like El Mirasol, rather than in Santa Fe hotels, for Security reasons. Then when our living accommodations were ready, we moved up to the Hill and the lid of Box 1663 closed upon me.

"No, even then I could not quite understand how I had got into it."

Despite his charming protestations of uncertainty, there was no doubt about the beginning of his career. It had begun precisely at twenty minutes after three o'clock on that afternoon of December 2 in an abandoned squash rackets court under the West Stands of Stagg Athletic Field in Chicago.

A secret scientific experiment was being performed by forty-two men. One of the minor participants was Edmund Gaylord, a young physics major who had just finished his Ph. D. work at Columbia University. Weeks before, he had pulled in his belt to undergo years of teaching and scrimping to pay off his debts when he had been offered a job at the Metallurgical Laboratory of the University of Chicago. Not until he arrived did he find out that the laboratory was but a code name assigned to a secret project to determine if a chain reaction could be initiated with uranium.

Now everything was ready: a huge cube or "pile," as they called it, of graphite blocks and uranium controlled from an instrument panel mounted on the balcony above. Around this Gaylord stood with most of the men listening to the steady click of a neutron counter, and watching the quivering pen of a recorder tracing the activity within the pile.

"There!" ordered Dr. Enrico Fermi, in charge of the experiment.

"Zip in. The reaction is self-sustaining. The curve is exponential."

The experiment was over. Man had initiated and stopped the world's first self-sustaining nuclear reaction.

Gaylord saw Hungarian-born Eugene Wigner step up and hand Italian-born Fermi a bottle of Chianti wine. Fermi uncorked the bottle while somebody brought in paper cups. Without a word, Fermi poured a bit of wine in the cups and passed them around. Gaylord drank his sip without a toast as did all the others. Then he wrote his name on the label of the empty bottle as it went around. As he left, Gaylord noticed Arthur Compton, in over-all charge of the project, at the telephone. He was calling President James B. Conant of Harvard.

"The Italian navigator has landed in the New World," announced Compton crypically.

"How were the natives?" asked Conant.

"Very friendly."

If a landing had been made in a New World, the old one knew nothing of it. Gaylord returned home to New York feeling little elation. The secret experiment had been a success, but it was purely scientific; he had no idea of its immediate and practical significance. The entrance of the United States into war, his own new Doctorate, and the problem of his immediate future were enough to worry him.

The months wore by. Living with his mother in a dreary brownstone flat on the upper West Side, he felt confined in a tawdry prison. He had no girl friends; his few male companions were in the Armed Services or away at work. Day after day he fumed and fretted, wondering when and where a teaching post would open up or if he should seek a technical job in a wartime industrial plant.

The evenings were worse. He stood at the window watching the street fill with neighbors returning home. One drab building after another lit up. Radios switched on. The smell of cooking filled the air. Garbage pails rattled. Everywhere sounded voices in Portuguese, Greek, German, Hebrew, Italian, Spanish and Manhattanese—the raucous, whining, multitudinous voice of this one vast, block-long tenement overflowing with one multiple-celled human organism whose gross appetite for food, sex, comfort and misery, sorrow and joy was unappeasable.

Gaylord had hated it since he was a boy. Everything about it was

77

so lustful, uninhibited and emotional that it frightened him with its monstrous vitality—squeezing hands and pinching breasts under the stairways, hurling bricks through a shop window, hoarding pennies, snoring, laughing, wailing, singing and cursing in seven languages. He had kept to his books, seeking solace in clean and frigid algebraic equations, in the cold precision of Euclidian geometry, in the abstract beauty of a rational world where everything was conducted with unassailable logic.

In a little while his mother returned from the candy shop on upper Broadway where she had worked ever since his father had died. Gaylord heard her taking off her rubbers on the stoop, saw how little and thin she looked when she took off her coat. Then she turned around. Her worn face under her bun of hair lighted up.

"My boy is here! You just don't know what it means to a body to come home and find somebody waiting! It just makes the day. It does so, Edmund!"

For an instant he saw it. Like an irridescent, brilliantly colored soap bubble. The complete, rounded and immortal moment detached from the milky spume of time, sufficient to itself with all its love and faith. Then it burst. With guilty annoyance he stood listening to her wracking little cough.

"My son's a Doctor!" she said, wiping her lips with a soiled hanky. "Prescribe for my cold, Dr. Edmund Gaylord!"

He handed her a peppermint drop from the table; she always brought home the broken pieces. "Take one of these pills once a day, Mama."

Mrs. Gaylord popped it into her mouth with an indulgent smile. Inordinately proud of his new Doctorate, this was her favorite daily joke.

"Come on. Let's eat out, Mama. I'll buy you a good dinner!"

"But I got a son home to cook for!" she protested. "Look at the chops I brought. Nice chops in wartime, Edmund. And two pieces of Maxie's cheesecake . . . Besides, you're not working, son. All outgo and no income ain't no way to make ends meet, like Papa used to say."

So again he settled down to resume his fuming and fretting, waiting for the letter that would open to the new Dr. Edmund Gaylord the tidy academic career of his long reasoned, carefully planned ambition; waiting for some means of escape from this dreary boredom, from the gloomy shadows of The City whose towers hung over him ready to topple, from this Old World so war-torn, stale and disillusioned.

Once before the air had hung heavy with doubt, despair and decay. Over an England impoverished by the Crusades and the Wars of the Roses. An Italy where Savaranola was preaching of an awful last Day of Judgment. Over Ottoman Turks marching through Greece to batter the gates of Vienna. Over a Spain where stalked the dread specter of an Inquisition expelling tens of thousands of Jews and Moors . . . Over all the impoverished, disease-ridden Old World of the Middle Ages, waiting for a new idea to renew the human spirit, the discovery of a New World to give it room to breathe.

The telephone rang. Gaylord picked up the receiver. With attentive ears and mind he listened to crisp and rational words. Yet to an intuition he did not believe in they spoke an old familiar message:

"Dr. Edmund Gaylord? This is Columbus . . . Yes, Don Cristobal! That New World we hit upon has turned out to be no little spice island at all. By San Fernando! It's a whole vast and unknown continent! We've got to explore it thoroughly. There's something in it that'll confound the imagination of man. I'm trying to sign on some able-bodied seamen now. What about a voyage?"

It was done. Gaylord submitted to a snarl of red tape involving a full F.B.I. background investigation, "Q" clearance, oaths of allegiance and secrecy. He committed himself to a project of such national importance and so Top-Secret that he was not told where he was going nor the work he would do. He packed his bags, put his arms around his mother for the last time.

"Going off not knowing where you're going don't seem reasonable! You're sure it's honest work, son?" she cried, clinging to him with hands of steel. "Oh I know it is or you wouldn't be going. But take care of yourself. And remember me, boy, and your father too." She shook his tall, rangy body with her sobs, then suddenly dragged down his face to meet her own. "I know how it always was with you and Papa. But he never objected to your getting educated, Edmund. He just wanted you should have a little fun like other boys. Don't hold that against Papa. Remember that, son!" she hissed through her tears. "Now we got a Doctor, and Papa would be right proud of him. Proud as all get out! He was a good man, Papa was. A first rate garage mechanic, and when he worked on the El people swore by Mr. Gaylord. Remember all he did for you!"

"I know all he did for me! I know all you've done for me too, Mama!" he burst forth with all the resentment born of his anguished memory of their years of sacrifice. "Why in the hell shouldn't I know, without having to say it!"

She had begun to cough again. He grabbed up his bags and leapt out the door only to be pursued by her last frantic cry from the stoop. "You look good in your new coat, son! Keep it buttoned so you won't catch cold . . . Write me, son!"

Neighbors were rushing to doors and windows as Gaylord fled down the street toward the subway entrance. All this frantic display of emotion rousing the whole block and creating a turbulent storm within him! But in the New World, wherever and whatever it was, things would be different. A world run by reason, man's only hope for the future.

THE WOMAN AT OTOWI CROSSING

Part Two

1.

With wartime costs, shortage of paper, and lack of experienced help in the back shop, Turner was having hard sledding with *El Porvenir*. The Throckmortons gave him no help nor encouragement; they had fled to Washington to spend the winter in more comfortable surroundings. Turner was tempted to shuck the whole business himself and take a war agency press job in Washington, but a queer loyalty to his subscribers held him back. So despite his difficulties, he slowly increased the weekly's pages, advertising, and circulation. Every month he meticulously sent detailed financial reports to the Throckmortons, calling attention to the encouraging fact that *El Porvenir* was now almost on a paying basis.

The Throckmortons never acknowledged them. Not a damned line in answer! Turner began to stew. He was losing his temper and his eyesight, and without even a raise in pay. Impulsively one morning he drove to Albuquerque and caught a train to Washington where he could confront Throckmorton in person.

Cyril Throckmorton III, as Turner should have known, was not a man to be bluntly confronted; he had learned the value of lawyers, financial advisors, and formidable Mrs. Throckmorton. So when Turner telephoned, it was Mrs. Throckmorton who answered. Her husband had been obliged to go to Philadelphia, but would Mr. Turner come for tea Sunday afternoon?

The Throckmorton home in Washington was a huge, twenty-room, gray stone mansion on Connecticut Avenue. Turner was conducted by a uniformed maid into a sitting room just off a mammoth drawing room whose ornate sumptuousness appalled him. Mrs. Throckmorton, larger than ever and seeming all teeth and frills, greeted him coldly and inquired about his health and the weather. In a few moments she barricaded herself behind an imposing silver service and an array of dainties that refuted the current myth of rationing. Then like a priestess officiating at a sacred shrine, she served tea.

Turner was not to be put off from his errand by her determined, casual talk. He launched into an explanation of his successful job in expanding *El Porvenir* so greatly under trying conditions. Mrs. Throckmorton remained silent during most of his laudatory tirade. But when he mentioned how he had reduced the weekly's running expenses, she raised her eyebrows and said cuttingly, "Mr. Throckmorton and I do not approve of your so-called economical management. Our acquisition of your little newspaper was not predicated upon the anticipation of a monetary return. Naturally! You should know that income taxes levied by That Man in the White House upon persons in our position are a national disgrace. If it weren't for our dear little *Porvenir's* expenses, which we can deduct, we would be really concerned."

Turner felt too deflated to answer.

"Have another one of these cakes, Mr. Turner. A French caterer makes them especially for Mr. Throckmorton," she said smoothly. To this she added sharply, "We will be returning to La Oreja late this spring. In the meanwhile let me caution you about being too diligent, shall we say, in reducing our deductible expenses."

This ended a miserable hour.

Turner returned home mouthing the only comment he could think of to sum up his futile trip. "The bitch!"

It was quite clear that something had to break soon. It did; unaccountably, after years of anonymity, *El Porvenir* suddenly became fashionable. It was listed among the top weeklies for its distinctive style and regional, tri-lingual news coverage. Libraries, museums, and journalism schools wrote for copies. Then Turner was invited to speak at the annual Western press association meeting that year in Salt Lake City.

The trip and the men he met were a welcome relief. One of them was E. C. Greenleaf, head of the Rocky Mountain Features Syndicate, in Denver. "You ought to be syndicating a column of your own," he told Turner. "Don't limit all that Western Americana to a few rural readers. The field's wide open now. Just find a peg to hang a column on, then write me."

When Turner returned home, he found that Throckmorton had been in a jealous rage all week because he too had not been invited to the meeting. He did not come over to congratulate Turner on the fine press given his talk and his own newspaper. Nor did Turner walk across the room to greet Throckmorton. Sitting at their desks without speaking all day, they had finally reached an impasse. Turner grabbed up his hat and went home.

Here he found a note from Helen Chalmers. "You haven't been down to see me for ages, Jack. Don't be angry. Let's be friends." With it she enclosed three sheets of paper written in her flowing hand and headed, "Christmas Greetings to My Friends." Pinned to them was a request. "I just don't write letters as I should. To make up for my neglect I've written this one long letter to all my friends and boys overseas telling them what's happened all year at this remote spot. Don't print it, Jack. Nothing so cold and formal. Just run off some copies with your mimeograph on any cheap paper. Will you, please?"

Already upset, Turner angrily threw the pages on the table. Goddamn it! Why didn't he wipe the slate clean, go out and get rip-roaring drunk, and then forget it! An affair damn well over with! She wouldn't sleep with him any more, she didn't want to marry him. But neither did she want to break things off with him. What the hell was the matter with her anyway?

Uncorking a bottle of Bourbon, he sat down to face it squarely. It was unnatural for a woman as warm-blooded as she to break off their relationship so abruptly and without reason. Yet there was a reason if he could only put his finger on it. He poured himself another stiff drink. Then another. There was no escaping it. She had always been a little fey, and now she was acting queerly. Having dreams, psychological fantasies or supernatural visions, by God! Being called a *bruja* like themselves by those old Spanish crones. Taken into the kiva by the pueblo *cacique,* himself. Hell, the news was spreading everywhere, ruining her reputation! And where would all this superstitious nonsense lead to if she persisted in her abnormal leanings?

He was too tight and wrought up now to think clearly. What he needed was a hot bath to put him to sleep. Unfortunately his bathtub drain was clogged somewhere; he had forgotten to call the plumber. Turner was in no mood to be balked. He put water to boil on the gas range for his second bathtub.

It stood in an alcove off the kitchen where it could be handily shown to visitors. Made of tin, shaped narrowly at the bottom to curve upward and outward with a seductive flourish, it somehow reminded everybody of an Egyptian sarcophagus. To add to this illusion one of the artists in La Oreja had painted it red with an overlay design of vari-colored hieroglyphics. A length of garden hose was attached at one end to drain it into the patio, and on this was still tied a faded Christmas ribbon that a party wag had attached some years before. The appearance of this contraption did not belie its historic importance. It was the first bathtub brought into La Oreja, transported from the Chile Line junction by stagecoach. In those early days before plumbing had intruded its comforts upon curiously resistant La Oreja, a surprising number of National Academicians and distinguished visitors were glad to avail themselves of its use with no thought of comedy. Of late years it had become simply another relic of the hundreds that cluttered Turner's adobe, yet occasionally someone wandered in to demand its use; one was not a true old-timer unless he had bathed in its historic, unstable confines.

Even Helen, when she first saw it, had broken out into laughter. Yet she herself had insisted on utilizing it because she still had no tub down at the Crossing, and she simply enjoyed a hot bath whenever she could get one.

By the time his own water had boiled and he had poured it into the tub, the memory of that first night Helen had spent here completely dominated his thoughts. Absent-mindedly he added a pitcher-full of cold spring water, then undressed and gingerly sat down in the tub.

How she had enjoyed her bath! From his desk in the other room he had heard her splashing with abandon. "Whooo-hoooo! I feel I'm in a swamped canoe!" she called. "You in there on the shore! Bring me the soap, please. I'm afraid I'll tip over."

He had brought it to her, dutifully scrubbing her back. How magnolia-creamy her skin looked in the yellow lamplight, how fine-grained and supple her flesh felt. Again he was washed with a wave of tenderness and desire as he remembered how he had slipped his hands under her arms and over her breasts, and bent her back to kiss her soapy face before fleeing into the other room again.

This acute reminder of the intimacy they had shared for so long only accentuated still more the abnormal streak in her that now

86

separated them. The hot water in the tub did not relax him. He suddenly, angrily and drunkenly lurched for his glass on the floor. What happened could have been predicted by anyone in town. The top-heavy, wide-brimmed tin sarcophagus promptly overturned, and Turner was spewed out on the floor in a flood of water. The ridiculousness of his mishap infuriated him. He got unsteadily to his feet, hurled the bar of soap across the room, and kicked the tub upright, injuring the big toe on his right foot.

The stab of pain for a moment sobered him. When it relaxed into a throbbing hurt, he contritely hopped about mopping the floor, having been too long a bachelor housekeeper to let the water, even now, destroy his hard-won glaze on the earthen floor. At last, naked and shivering, he went into the bedroom. Here again, as he entered the doorway, his memories of that night leapt at him.

Helen had been propped up in the four poster walnut bed, reading a newspaper. She had looked up casually. "Well! Where've you been, back-scrubber?"

"I didn't hear you finish your bath, I was so interested in that old account of Fray Ortega's. His description of the pueblo two hundred years ago sounds as if it had been written only yesterday. Let me read you a paragraph."

He returned to the other room, put on his pajamas, and came back with the book. Getting into bed beside her, he leafed through the pages and began to read. Abruptly she switched out the light and he found himself smothered by her soft body still warm and moist from her bath.

It was the peculiar, distinctive fragrance of her body—that individual, almost indefinable odor which is as distinctive to each one of us as our invisible aura of personality and which is most noticeable in times of high emotion—that Turner now recalled with almost preternatural intensity. How in the hell could such a passionate woman become so inhibited? But Goddamn it, it couldn't last! He would have to endure with tact and patience the platonic friendship she enforced upon him until her strange spell wore off.

Unable to sleep, he rose at daybreak and went down to the paper to confront again his two insoluble problems. He had to quit *El Portenir*. But what could he do in La Oreja if Helen refused to move with him somewhere else?

It was then, sitting with his feet propped up on his old-fashioned rolltop desk and his hat pulled low over his eyes, that the idea hit him with all the force of divine inspiration. It combined at once his own absorption in Western Americana, Greenleaf's suggestion he do a column for syndication, and his need for getting away from Throckmorton without leaving Helen and La Oreja.

He thrust back his hat, dropped his feet on the floor. There it was, one hell of an idea, perfect as a dream! He could see the extinct Chile Line forever tooting down valleys, climbing up mountain peaks, and leaping rivers throughout the whole West. With him as its sole passenger.

He had, of course, found the peg on which to hang a syndicated column. He was made and he knew it. Flipping a sheet of paper in his typewriter, he banged out his first column:

WHISTLE STOPS ON THE CHILE LINE
by
Jack Turner

The late Ralph Byers once rode the Chile Line down to Santa Fe with a party of excursionists from La Oreja.

The train was meandering along the Rio Grande when one of the lady picnickers suddenly yanked the emergency bell cord. With a whistle, grunt, and grinding of wheels, the toy train jerked to a stop. The engineer jumped out of his cab. Passengers poured from the coach. The conductor came running with anxious questions.

"I dropped my false teeth out the window," explained the lady. Whereupon everybody began searching the right-of-way.

The incident provided Byers with one of his characteristic stock phrases. Whenever there occurred a delay in life's schedule . . . a holiday halt in business . . . the death of a friend, he shrugged his shoulders. "A whistle stop on the Chile Line!"

*   *   *

The narrow-gauge branch line of the Denver and Rio Grande Railway which followed the Rio Grande river down from Antonito, Colorado, to Santa Fe, New Mexico, was one of the West's most famous Baby Railroads.

Your Old Timer knew it as the Chile Line. It freighted out all the chiles grown in the lush river bottoms and red-rock canyons.

There was no special place to get to, no hurry to get there, and plenty of scenery to keep you company on the way.

Strung out in sage and sunlight were water tanks and weed-grown sidings: Volcano, Tres Piedras, No Agua—names like that. Down the river gorge you glimpsed Indian pueblos: San Ildefonso, Santa Clara, San Juan.

To the east you stared out the window at the Sangre de Cristos. To the west rared up the Jemez range. You were caught between them.

But downriver was Santa Fe, the capital of all this Land of Mañana. Now you knew where you were traveling. Toward Tomorrow.

No wonder Byers called any delay "a whistle stop on the Chile Line."

*　　*　　*

2.

A few evenings later Turner drove down to the Crossing with mimeographed copies of Helen's belated Christmas Letter and his own momentous news. Emily was there when he arrived; it was evident she and Helen were in the midst of an argument.

"Yes, Emily," Helen was saying. "You live in the past too much. You just never have your wits about you. They're always way back beyond the Long Drought of 1276!"

"Naturally, when one's business is anthropology!" Emily snapped back.

Of course that was her trouble, Helen explained calmly. The prehistoric past of America was the only world in which she existed; she carried it with her, like a snail its shell, wherever she went. This general cult of the past was also subscribed to by Greek classicists, European art connoisseurs, archaeolgists, antiquarians, and scholars in every field. Their work was valuable, of course. But perhaps it clouded their own awareness that the living present contained all the past and the future too.

"That's nutty and you know it!" screamed Emily. "Why are you always trying to run me down?"

"Now Emily!" Helen put her arms around her. "Don't lose your temper. I'm just trying to tell you that the Road of Life is a one-way road. There's no going back. Aren't you finding that out in writing your thesis?"

"Oh, stop it!" interrupted Jack. "I've got real news for you!" He waved a sheaf of clippings at them. "Toot-toot, here comes the Chile Line again, and this is my favorite whistle-stop!" He began to dance a jig around them as they read his first columns.

Helen laughed, his enthusiasm was so infectious. He had been publishing and editing a paper for years, yet he was more proud of these columns than anything he had done.

"The contract's signed, we've had a fair reception, and now I'm off for more whistle-stops!"

"And now you can leave *El Porvenir?*"

Turner grinned. "Throckmorton beat me to the punch. Or rather Mrs. Throckmorton did. She left a note firing me early yesterday morning. Then they left town to avoid facing me."

"Did you make trouble, Jack?" Helen asked anxiously.

"It struck me as funny! I showed the note to everyone!" He rocked back on his heels and laughed.

"That was unkind of you, Jack. But now you're free!"

Turner caught the note of anxiety in her voice. "Yes, Helen. I'll be away often but only on short trips until I find a place that will suit us both."

When she did not answer, he turned to Emily. "Come on, let's celebrate! I'm going to take you both over to El Mirasol for dinner!"

"No! You can't come!" exclaimed Emily. "Outside guests aren't allowed there for dinner any more. The Project on the Hill's taken over the place." She strode toward the door.

"Then we'll drive down to Santa Fe! I've got gas!"

"No! I don't want to!" Emily was still irritated.

"Please stay here then, Emily," begged Helen. "Those meals at

El Mirasol are so expensive and my cooking is so much better. And it makes the evening so long for you alone."

Emily flung open the door. "But I've got to work on my dissertation!"

"Now Emily," cautioned Helen. "Don't ruin your eyes working too late!"

Emily flung out the door in nervous haste and drove swiftly home to El Mirasol through the spattering mud. In her room she bathed slowly, then stood powdering herself with talcum before the mirror. Her body, stripped of clothes, revealed more than her youth. She turned slowly to observe how her long slim legs swelled out at the thighs and curved into firm, rounded buttocks. Her hips were full and mature, though surmounted by a narrow, girlish waist. She powdered her breasts with care. The pointed pink nipples stuck out too boldly; she would have to blunt them with brassieres. But at least they were not flattened into big brown paps. On the whole, Emily decided, she had a good figure.

She dressed carefully. Heavy white silk panties and a French lace brassiere. Nylon stockings—so difficult to obtain these days! A loose white silk dress embroidered around the hem with colored flowers and caught at the waist with a wide, embroidered Hungarian belt. Sitting down at the dresser to do her hair, Emily began to get nervous again. Every two minutes she looked at her watch. He was so punctual for dinner every night!

Dr. Edmund Gaylord! He seemed so young in his baggy flannel trousers, unpressed jacket, and muddy sneakers. And that crew haircut! He looked as if he had been scalped by Comanches! But there was no denying his taut alertness and the incomprehensible warmth that rushed out to her whenever she walked into the dining room. The collar of his shirt was usually open. Emily could feel the flutter of butterflies inside her when she saw the tender white flesh of his throat below the line of sunburn.

Every night it was the same. A quick look, a smile, a greeting— nothing more. For Gaylord always sat with Dr. Breslau, in whose presence neither of them attempted to build on the embarrassing evening when they had been introduced. Emily would put on her

91

horn-rimmed glasses, hide behind a book during dinner, then flee back to her room.

For a while she would settle down to a long, massive table for her evening's work. It was cluttered with books and monographs, notebooks jammed with field observations and sketches, and neatly stacked pages of the thesis on which she was working. Thumbtacked to the wall were topographical maps, aerial photographs of the ground ruins of ancient pueblos, and drawings of excavated kivas.

But unable to keep her mind on her work, she would put on a new pink nightgown for which she had driven to Santa Fe on her scant ration of gas. Carefully she brushed her hair, securing it with a narrow pink ribbon to match. Then she propped up in bed and, like a cat awaiting a mouse, stared steadily at the thin crack between the floor and the door of the connecting room.

Eventually it appeared—a sheet of paper thrust under the door. Emily pounced upon it, holding it up to the desk lamp with trembling fingers.

"So he scared you away again tonight," she read. "You ran out like a frightened rabbit for shame. He is the kindest man alive and one of the smartest!"

Swiftly she scribbled a reply: "I wasn't scared! Of what? Dr. Breslau and you are perfectly free to come up to my table. Unless you're frightened. Of what?"

Giggling softly, she thrust it back under the door and settled back to reread his note. Gaylord's calligraphy told her a great deal about himself. The individual letters were small and finely formed, revealing his analytical nature, but the lines were loose and sprawly as his long legs. There was little punctuation. It was as if all of him, in one breath, rushed out to her even in his notes. She had kept them all, locked in her drawer, so she could read them over and over.

Especially the first one: "Dear Miss J: Don't you have a balcony?"

And a more embarrassing one: "Was that you scrubbing your teeth? Don't rake the enamel off. They're pretty."

And still another: "Pot hunter? What *do* you do?" To this she answered curtly with the subject of her dissertation: "*An Inquiry Into the Probable Origin in New Mexico of the Aztecan Tribes of Mexico, Based Upon the Parallelism of Aztec, Navajo and Pueblo Religious Ceremonialism.*"

This, she was sure, had floored him! Triumphantly she had followed it with a curt, "And what do *you* do, Mr. Scientist?" The answer came back immediately—a blank sheet of paper. Emily crumpled and hugged it to her breast. Good! He thought too much about his profession to joke about it. Later she smoothed it out, inscribed the date upon it, and added it to her stack.

Every night it was the same: a series of scribbled, childish notes exchanged under the door. And every morning or evening when they met in the lobby it was again the same: a brief and casual "Good morning, Miss Chalmers," "Good evening, Dr. Gaylord," as if they were casual acquaintances.

It could not go on like this forever, she thought irritably tonight as she slicked back her hair. If he were too bashful to come over to her table, she would go to his. Tonight! The prospect of confronting that nasty Dr. Breslau with him was another matter. Desperately she gritted her teeth and marched down to the dining room.

They weren't there, neither one of them! Nor did they come in during the hour she dawdled over her dinner. At last, with a sense of foreboding, she left the room.

"Miss Emily!"

It was Saunders, the manager, beckoning to her. "Miss Emily, I'm embarrassed but there's nothing I can do about it," he began apologetically.

"About what?" she asked tartly.

"You've been our one constant and loyal guest all winter, Miss Emily. But since the Project has taken over the place temporarily, it needs your room for a while."

"So that Dr. Breslau has succeeded in having me kicked out, just as he threatened?"

"Not Dr. Breslau! Really. Why, it was through his influence that you've been allowed to stay ever since he met you. But now—"

"I'll be out of here tomorrow morning!"

Angrily she rushed up to her room. It was all over, a dear friendship with a very intellectual man, just when something might have happened.

She was sure of this an hour later when she heard Gaylord come down the hall and go into his own room. For a long time she waited for him to begin their exchange of notes. When nothing slid under

93

the door, she yanked off her clothes and pitched them to a chair where they caught and hung in limbo as awry and unhappy as she. Then she strode to the closet, taking out the voluminous flannel nightgown that had hung unused for nights. It fit her like a shroud, she thought. Why not? Savagely she got out her curlers and bobby pins.

Her hair finally screwed up, Emily put on her glasses and bent over her table to reach for a textbook that might drive her to sleep. She was arrested in this jack-knife posture by a sudden draft that whipped up her legs. One arm still outstretched, she twisted her head around to peer unsteadily through her glasses at Dr. Edmund Gaylord standing quietly in the doorway between their adjoining rooms.

It was absurdly impossible that the maid had forgotten to lock it and that he had discovered and opened it without knocking. Yet there he stood, coat off, his shirt open at the throat, grinning with amusement. Emily was too petrified to speak or move. She simply stared at him with a hopeless acceptance of the unbelievable.

Gaylord's wide grin contracted; his lips trembled slightly. Without a word, he stepped forward, picked her up, and carried her to the bed where he laid her down and carefully drew the covers over her. Dropping to his knees, he clumsily put his arms around her and kissed her tremblingly on the mouth.

Emily felt the kiss run through her like a sip of wine. But even as she reached up her own arms to clasp him, and raised her mouth for a more satisfying draught, Gaylord dropped his head to her breast in a gesture of mute and humble adoration. Emily did not stir. She lay smilingly possessed by a new and strange feeling that she had never experienced before. The triumphant feeling of a woman who realizes for the first time her incomprehensible but complete power over a man.

3.

Every day now Helen's sense of its reality sharpened: that one great unity of all creation, imbued with one consciousness and enfused

94

with one power, of which everything in the universe was an embodied part. Before its irreducible reality her illusions of temporal time, of individual separateness, vanished. There was no "dead" matter. Everything was alive, differentiated not in kind but only in the degree of sentiency with which it reflected this all-pervading consciousness in the ascent from mineral to man. Each cell, each atom and solar system repeated in its constant movement the same great in-breathing and out-breathing rhythm of the whole, the pulse of life itself.

Her apperception of this came clearest in the early dawn when she stole out to await selflessly as the Indians on their rooftops across the river the mysterious daily manifestation of the invisible unity in visible diversity. All about her was a dark and formless void, an unlimited continuum, a tenuous and bodiless veil. Suddenly a ripple ran through it. Indistinct outlines of earthly shapes appeared, warped into separate selfhoods as was she by the same limited stresses in the limitless void. A star blinked above her, a tall pine stiffened, a mesa of volcanic stone stirred gently.

The first movement produced sound—a sound such as she heard at no other time, it was so like the one common expiration of their first breath. Then suddenly all was sound: the rustle of branches in the breeze, the rattle of a stone rolling down the steep escarpment, the ripple of the river, the call of birds . . . The multitudinous voices of the one primal sound whence came all ideas, the languages which expressed them, and the objects they designated. The Word itself, with which they Became.

The veil dropped; there was light; and now they stood apart from her in their own worlds of living matter, with their own transient forms and names, reflecting with their own degree of sentiency the one pervading consciousness that still held them in an invisible but living kinship. Facundo and the other old men on the rooftops of the pueblo were now standing, she knew, to cast their pinches of sacred cornmeal to the rising sun—that great deified luminary which was the source of all energy and all life for this one of many solar systems.

Every morning Helen experienced this genesis with an ever new sense of its sublime mystery. But by afternoon it wore off. She felt tired and discouraged. Fewer and fewer people came to the Tea Room. Her meager income shrank until she could hardly afford to keep enough supplies on hand to stir up a presentable dinner when someone did come. Yet traffic up the Hill kept increasing. Groaning trucks. Creaking buses. Shiny black Government cars. Military jeeps and half-tracks . . . Mysterious cars; one did not know what they were about.

One morning a Government car stopped. An Army officer got out and pretended to inspect Helen's little flower patch while a civilian strolled up to her door. Something about him was vaguely familiar. Several years ago a tall, lanky man with a crew haircut had stopped at her place while on a camping trip into the mountains. With him was his wife, Kitty, who had bought a chocolate cake. They had sat in the kitchen, talking of a small ranch he owned near Pecos and how wonderful it was to camp out in the mountains . . . Oppenheimer. Yes, that was his name.

"Yes, I do remember you!" she said quickly. "Won't you come in?"

Oppenheimer shook his head. He had to get back on the Hill, but he could not pass by without stopping to say hello and to inquire how she was getting along. Nervous and preoccupied, he shook hands warmly and rushed away.

A week later another car stopped and a Project officer came in for a cup of coffee and a brief chat. Her Tea Room, he said, was highly regarded by certain people on the Project. She did not serve liquor and was known to be discreet. It was possible that certain restrictions could be removed, allowing some of the personnel to come down for meals.

"Why not?" Helen answered at once. "I'll be glad to have them. Of course the place is small. I can't accommodate many, and those only for dinner."

"They won't give you any trouble, and they'll bring you a small, steady group of customers. You won't have to rely on out-siders. In fact, we would like to suggest that you don't take any others. They would only create gossip about the Project which we must avoid. Would that he agreeable to you?"

Everything flashed into focus for Helen. J. Robert Oppenheimer. Was it he who was now in charge of the work on the Hill? Who had made it possible for other Project workers to come down to dinner? One thing was certain, she thought with some amusement. She knew whose crew haircut young Gaylord had copied!

So now small groups of Xs, as she called them, began to come down to the Tea Room for dinner, replacing occasional tourists and valley folk whom she turned away with quiet apologies. Isolated on the Hill as the Xs were, they needed this slight change. Helen was grateful for the money it brought her and the creative energy it demanded.

Immediately she enlarged her vegetable garden and helped Facundo to plant it. "More peas, Facundo! We've got to put in more peas than this. They taste so good with lamb!"

She rushed into the house to answer the persistent ring of a new telephone, then rushed back out. "But we need more beans, Facundo! Fresh wax beans with butter. There's never enough!"

"Who eat all them things? Mebbe too much already. I say it."

"You heard that telephone ringing. More people calling for reservations. Tonight, tomorrow, five nights every week. We need a big garden. Big, Facundo!"

Patiently he wrapped his dirty cotton blanket closer about his waist. "I fix." She watched him squat back down, old, dark and wrinkled; a small heap of earth repeating in shape the great mountain of living flesh rising across the canyon, both of them timeless and indestructable as the force that made them.

When Maria came—late as usual—Helen put her to work preparing chile sauce from a heap of chile pods which she had detached from one of the big *ristras* hanging from the *vigas*.

Emily came in, listless and bored. "Can I do anything to help?"

"Why, set the tables if you'd like," answered Helen cheerfully. "Light the fire too. Just a small blaze to chase away the chill."

What had got into them? Maria, of course, was grumpy every spring. Her serpentine Indian blood always ran low in cold weather; it hadn't quite warmed up yet. Emily was a different problem. The Xs had moved out of El Mirasol, and Emily had moved back into her room from the little commercial hotel in Espanola. But she was still moping over that young Dr. Gaylord. Helen would have to ask Dr. Breslau about him; he had made reservations for three that evening.

They came into the kitchen a half hour later. "Miss Chalmers! We're a little early. You don't mind?" Recognizing his voice, Helen turned around to greet him and to meet his two companions: an

97

Italian whom he introduced as Mr. Farmer, and a Dane named Mr. Baker. Alert and interested, they examined the *ristras* of chile and the strings of garlic and onions hanging from the rafters above them, and then bent down to the bowl of thick, red sauce.

Dr. Breslau dipped in his finger, tasted it, and grinned. "Red hot!"

"All the heat of last summer is stored up in it, Dr. Breslau."

"And what do you call it, please?" asked Mr. Farmer.

"*Chile caribe.* Just like adobe, isn't it?"

The Dane touched it gingerly with the tip of his finger. "It's radiated. Yes. I feel the reaction," he said quietly, with a twinkle in his blue eyes.

The Italian laughed like a boy.

Maria ambled in with a huge platter of spareribs. Helen plastered each chunk with the thick *caribe* and replaced it on the platter. "*Costillas adobadas,*" she said lightly. "Plastered ribs."

"Good," said Mr. Baker. "I will have two helpings, please."

"I'm sorry," Helen answered swiftly. "That's for tomorrow. It has to soak all night so the flavor won't come out while it's cooking."

"Ah. The factor of time must be included in the equation of taste, my friend," added the Italian. "Is it not so?"

"But don't be disappointed," went on Helen, opening the oven door. "See, your roast is already brown. Now if you'll give me just a minute more . . . Emily! Light the candles now!"

There was no answer. Then Maria said grumpily from the doorway, "She outside watchin' that crazy horse. Hear him run!"

They could all hear it now, even before they walked outside to join Emily on the high bank of the river: a dull, resounding thunder of hoofbeats, silence, and then another prolonged reverberation.

"Him crazy!" snorted Maria.

It was too dark to see across the river, but they could hear the lone stallion racing wildly up and down the field.

"Poor thing!" murmured Helen. "Oh, I hope he doesn't go into the fence!" That tremendous, upswelling power forever seeking transformation and release! So frightening and beautiful too. She could feel the wonder and the mystery coming back upon her in a wave of compassion.

"You're shivering, Miss Chalmers. I think we go back inside

now." The quiet, heavy-set and middle-aged Dane took her arm. Something in his whispering voice, his vague eyes, steadied her. Was he another one who knew *it* too?

Candles and fire lit in the little dining room, Helen and Emily served dinner. The men ate leisurely and hungrily, then sat talking and smoking over their coffee for nearly an hour. How good it was to see them full and relaxed and cheerful. She left them and returned to the kitchen. The stallion was still pounding up and down the long field across the river. Emily kept staring out the window into the darkness.

Dr. Breslau roused her with a cheerful shout from the doorway. "My little anthropologist—who hasn't spoken to me all evening! Well! I am in disgrace. No?"

Emily turned around grumpily. "Oh, hello. I guess you were just too busy for me to interrupt."

"I am never too busy to be interrupted by such a pretty girl," he stated vehemently. "But tell me. You have been pursuing your studies in the ruins up the canyon, have you not?"

"No, I haven't. I've been too busy on other things."

"Ah, but you should go up there in this fine weather." He gave Helen a quick look. "The little birds are roosting for a while near their ancient nest. What a pleasant chapter in anthropology you might write up there . . . But I must pay now for two meals each because we ate to the power of two. Yes?"

"You pay for one now, Dr. Breslau, and the other when you come again," said Helen.

"Yes. We come back," said Mr. Farmer.

Mr. Baker gave her a look of quiet concern then followed his companions out. What strange men the project on the Hill was drawing, Helen thought. German, Italian, Danish, Hungarian, and those Englishmen who had come down to dinner a week ago.

The next day Mrs. Frey stopped by for a chat. She was another old-timer in the region, having operated the lodge in Frijoles Canyon for years. Fortunately for her, said Emily, it and the ruins were in the Bandelier National Monument which had not been included in the area taken over by the Los Alamos project.

"Well, I don't know," answered Mrs. Frey. "Things don't look so good for us this summer. That outfit on the Hill is going to take

99

us over for a while. At least they get some housing built, a bunch of Xs will be quartered at the lodge."

"You too now!" protested Emily. "First the Ranch School, then El Mirasol, mother's place here, and now the country's most precious prehistoric remains and a National Monument. The whole valley, everything, everybody, is being taken over! For what?"

"I don't mind it, honey," remonstrated Mrs. Frey. "They've got a right to a place to eat and sleep. Some of them are right nice young men too. But come on up before they take us over completely. There's a couple of ruins that ain't on the books that might give you something new."

When she had puttered away in her old Ford, Helen turned to Emily. "He was right, Emily. How quick he is!"

"Who?"

"Dr. Breslau. Remember what he said: 'The little birds are roosting for a while near their ancient nest."

"What's that got to do with what?"

"Don't be so dumb. The 'little birds' are 'Pajaritos,' the Xs on the Hill. And 'roosting near their ancient nest,' Tchirege, which means 'Place of the Bird People,' clearly told you that they were staying in Frijoles Lodge nearby." She began to laugh.

"What's so funny about that?"

"Well, I just have a hunch that young Dr. Gaylord you've been mooning about is staying with Mrs. Frey. Now if I were you, I'd go up there and see if your infatuation has worn off. You've got to get back to work some time, you know."

"Work? What else do you think I do all day and night?"

Yes. Heaped high on her desk were monographs, treatises, and transcripts. Over the floor spread maps, notebooks and histories. In the midst of this accumulated debris of centuries, as it were, she squatted for hours on end: a curious little owl blinking behind her horn-rimmed spectacles.

An Inquiry Into the Probable Origin in New Mexico of the Aztecan Tribes of Mexico, Based Upon the Parallelism of Aztec, Navajo, and Pueblo Religious Ceremonialism.

Of course! The mythical seven tribes and seven womb-caves of the Aztecs suggested immediately the seven clan kivas within the early pueblos. The plumed serpent Awanyu of the Pueblos corresponded to the Aztecs' Quetzalcoatl. The Sun Temple at Mesa Verde and the Pyramid of the Sun at San Juan Teotihuacan; the New Fire ceremony of the ancient Aztecs and the modern Hopis;—one parallel after another arranged themselves neatly in her mind. She did work long and well, for she was essentially a serious bookworm with an advantageous background of school and field work. Yet more and more often she was interrupted by a vague tremor that disturbed her like that stallion wildly racing up and down the field along the river. Even at night she was aroused by the same, sudden, and uncalled for hoofbeats of secret longing. She remembered the weight of his head on her breast, his bashful embrace, the look of humble adoration in his eyes . . .

"Go to see Mrs. Frey?" she now shouted back at Helen. "I'll be damned if I will! He knows where I am if he ever wants to see me!"

4.

Finishing his hasty dinner in the old ranch school's Fuller Lodge, Gaylord walked out on the large portal and leaned against one of its massive log pillars. His wrist watch in the June twilight showed that he had plenty of time for a cigarette. He lit it and stared unbelievably at the scene before him.

The nucleus of old log buildings and pine trees on the meadow that he had first seen a few months ago was now surrounded by a motley jumble of Army barracks, wooden utility buildings, dormitories, ramshackle huts, trailer courts and storage yards. Through this bulldozers were ploughing more haphazard streets down which roared a constant stream of trucks and jeeps. The dust was thick enough to cut with a knife. In its haze he saw people swarming everywhere. GIs crowding about an old log trading post, now the P.X. Mounted Security guards in big cowboy hats riding in from their perimeter duty stations. Hundreds of workmen arriving for the night shift. Long lines of men and women forming in front of the mess halls. Army officers. Technicians. Government officials. A woman in a silk dress hurrying toward Bath Tub Row. It seemed impossible that this isolated mesa-top high in the forest wilderness had been transformed so quickly into such a madhouse of activity.

101

To Gaylord it looked like a movie setting for a Western frontier town, a boom mining camp, an Army post. Whatever it was, the Project on the Hill had no precedent. For over it all hung an intangible miasma of mystery and secrecy. One didn't question it nor his own presence. One did his job and let it go at that.

"Ah, my young friend! You're going down to the meeting?"

He recognized Dr. Breslau's voice before he turned around. "Yes sir."

"Well let's be off. It will probably be crowded."

They dodged across the swarming road, exchanging remarks above the clatter.

"Got a day off tomorrow, I hear. A Sunday too. How do you rate that, Gaylord?"

"Perhaps because I haven't had one yet, Doctor!"

"That's the kind of place this is. What are you going to do?"

"Catch up on sleep!"

Dr. Breslau grinned. "A waste of time! You'll only dream of beautiful young ladies."

Gaylord could think of no reply. They came to a gaunt utility theater that served on Sunday for church services, and during the week for frequent colloquia and conferences for staff members. Showing their badges to a Security guard at the door, they walked inside.

"I hear you're getting along all right, Gaylord," said Breslau, walking down the aisle.

"Thank you, Doctor. Nice to have seen you."

Gaylord found a chair in back and sat down with proper modesty at being present in such distinguished company. Around him, almost anonymous in sweat-stained shirts and wrinkled trousers, there sat and lounged talking in the aisles physicists, chemists, metallurgists, mathematicians, engineers and technicians drawn from universities, laboratories, industrial plants and hospitals throughout the United States. Among them he recognized several men for whom he had worked on the Chicago pile including Enrico Fermi who travelled under the name of "Eugene Farmer," and Dr. Arthur Compton, known as "Mr. Comstock." Others had fled from Europe to escape Nazi persecution or capture. Sitting down next to Dr. Breslau was the great Danish physicist and pioneer explorer of the structure of the atom, Niels Bohr, whose pseudonym was "Nicholas Baker." Off

102

to the left sat a delegation from Great Britain headed by Sir James Chadwick. Still more whom Gaylord could not identify kept coming in. Undoubtedly he was looking at the most extraordinary galaxy of scientific stars ever gathered under one roof.

As he sat there waiting for the room to fill and quiet, Gaylord knew that he had been lucky from the day he had been picked to work on the Chicago pile. That brief preliminary landing on the New World already seemed remotely far behind him. The New World he had glimpsed then had been no more than an entrancing, deceptively inviting shore line. Now he saw it for what it was—a dark, unknown and forbidding continent which threw up unknown obstacles, unguessed problems to hinder every foot of advance.

Gaylord had prided himself on his new doctorate. Now, dwarfed by an imposing staff of Nobel Prize winners and world-famous scientists, he sweated night and day over problems that seemed insignificant when they were assigned to him, but which seemed hopeless when he confronted them. Yet he persisted with methodical thoroughness. Gaylord, in fact, was an extremely capable young physicist; and at this early period of his career it was precisely his lack of imagination and his meticulous attention to detail that made him valuable. He prided himself, with the little personal vanity he had, that he never let his emotions get the best of him—emotions that he did not yet know he possessed in the periodic table of his own elemental personality.

The room by now had filled and quieted. A subdued feeling of excitement washed over him when General Leslie R. Groves, in over-all charge of the Project for the Manhattan Engineer District, stood up for one of his infrequent appearances. Heavy-set, his impeccable uniform in odd contrast to the sloppy shirts and pants of the scientists, Groves seemed to Gaylord to have the air of a bulldog worrying a bone. Chewing away, he assured every one of the 100 university-employed scientists present that twelve men had been brought in to help him. There were now, he said, nearly 1200 military personnel, civilian Government employees, and construction workers who were doing their best to provide living accommodations. Housing was still short, however. Until more space was made available, he had taken over Frijoles Lodge in Bandelier National Monument fourteen miles south. He hoped that the men assigned there would understand why.

Gaylord groaned to himself; he already had been transferred and had to commune the exhorbitant distance over a lonely mountain road each day.

The next speaker was a Security officer whom Gaylord could not identify, but whom he resented instantly for his repetition of familiar facts. The speaker cautioned him not to give his address when writing letters. "Post Office Box 1663, Santa Fe, New Mexico, is all that is allowed. As you gentlemen know, it is the largest postoffice box in the world. To it is addressed box-cars of equipment, truck loads of supplies. Our children are born in it. We dwell in Box 1663." This was an old joke already. Nobody smiled.

Gaylord began to squirm uneasily in his seat. Despite the urgency, exhilaration and pervading air of excitement as the work got under way, he had felt irked from the start by the strict secrecy. Now he was shaken by a sense of alarm as the speaker commenced reading from a new handbook on Security:

"Do not establish or maintain social relations with residents of nearby communities. It is expected, as a condition of employment, that project employees will break normal social relations with the outside world.

"Do not arrange for visits with friends or relations in nearby communities without special permission from the Director."

To punctuate the importance of these restrictions, the speaker now read a new memorandum issued by the Security committee:

"Under no circumstances must any project employees go to parties or dances in nearby communities or maintain any other social relations except for quiet visits with their families.

"Make only very occasional visits with your families and get special permission in each case to do so."

Gaylord's resentment flared. He had no real cause for frustration, being without a family to visit, and detesting parties and dances for which he never had had time in school. Yet the memorandum touched the quick of his secret longing. There jumped at him the vision of Emily excitedly talking at a gay party, swirling away in a dance . . .

He pushed it away as a thin, shy and ascetic looking man with a crew haircut eased up on the platform. It was J. Robert Oppenheimer, the Director. As always, he commanded Gaylord's instant attention and complete admiration.

"Things are getting under way," the Director said simply. "The conferences on procedures began about the middle of April. On the 14th we began laying the bottom pole piece of the cyclotron magnet. Material is coming in. The cyclotron from Harvard, two Van de Graaff electrostatic accelerators from the University of Wisconsin, the Cockcroft-Walton from Illinois, chemical and cryogenic equipment from the University of California. New facilities are shaping up. Next month—early in July, the first experiment will be performed. I think you know all the work that lies ahead of us."

Experimental work of all kinds. Differential experiments for determining the cross section for fission of specific isotopes, and integral experiments for determining the average scattering of fission neutrons from actual tampers. Perfection of the use of the Van de Graaff. Measurements of nuclear constants of U-235, U-238 and plutonium over a wide range, and final purification of the enriched fissionable materials.

" . . . hard work, long hours, the utmost concentration," Oppenheimer was saying. "I do not have to remind you what it means to so many. But from one whom you all know, I have received this letter—"

And suddenly, almost miraculously, a great, laughing President wielding a long cigarette holder like a sword and a scepter began speaking directly to Gaylord in the rousing, resonant voice of all America, and with the invincible hope of the whole free world: . . .

"I know that you and your colleagues are working on a hazardous matter under unusual circumstances. The fact that the outcome of your labors is of such great significance to the Nation requires that this program be even more drastically guarded than other highly secret war developments. . . . You are fully aware of the reasons why your own endeavors and those of your associates must be circumscribed by very special restrictions. Nevertheless I wish you would express to the scientists assembled with you my deep appreciation of their willingness to undertake the tasks which lie before them in spite of the dangers and the personal sacri-

105

fices . . . Whatever the enemy may be planning, American science will be equal to the challenge. With this thought in mind, I send this note of confidence and appreciation. . . . While this letter is secret, the contents of it may be disclosed to your associates under a pledge of secrecy."

No, resolved Gaylord striding out from the meeting, nothing should swerve him from this task to which he had dedicated the highest hopes of his unspent youth. Nothing! This exaggerated exhilaration swept him to his car, carried him to the edge of the high mesa. Showing his pass, he was cleared through the guard gate, and dropped swiftly down the tortously winding canyon road. At the junction below he stopped and looked back. Up above, the Tech Area complex of laboratories and shops stood out on the edge of the sheer, high cliff. Flooded with spotlights, white and shining against dark sky and black mountain walls, it gleamed with all the romantic unreality of a medieval castle, an isolated monastery in mysterious Tibet. A queer tingle raced up his spine. For the first time he realized why it was beginning to be called "Shangri-La, the Forbidden City of Atomic Research."

He drove on now through the dark and untouched mountain wilderness. A deer bounded out of the piñons. A porcupine waddled across the road and stopped, blinded by the headlights. Soon the rough dirt road narrowed. Dizzy drops and horseshoe curves leapt at him from the darkness. His high mood ebbed; wearily he reached Frijoles and climbed into bed.

When he got up next morning he was merely a run-down machine, a fish out of water, a man with a day off and nothing to do. The isolated stone Lodge always acted on Gaylord like this. It cut him off psychologically as well as geographically from Los Alamos, marooning him in a world with which he had no contact. It sat in a deep, narrow valley flanked on each side by sheer, high cliffs of pink and buff tufa, down which trickled El Rito de Los Frijoles, the Little River of the Beans.

Unaccountably irritable, he strolled upstream to the excavated ruins of ancient Tyuoni, once a circular, walled city five stories high, with two great kivas sunk in the enclosed court. Allegedly famous, the dead jumbled masonry did not interest Gaylord. He continued walking up the canyon past the caves which the prehistoric cave-

and cliff-dwellers had pecked into the volcanic rock, and the crumbled walls of their rude, talus slope pueblos.

A mile farther, he glimpsed a huge cave high in the cliff wall. From its floor protruded the tip of a ladder leading down into another of those everpresent kivas. Another ladder led up to the cave itself. On a sudden impulse he climbed up it.

Here he saw her sitting on the rim of the kiva. It was as if she had been patiently waiting for him, staring dreamily out across the wide blue distance that stretched unheeded far below. Her little red beret lay in her lap. The wind touseled her soft brown hair.

She turned to see him, and smiling, lifted her hand in greeting. The gesture was so natural, casual and unaffected that it erased immediately the time and distance between them; dismissed as inconsequential the prehistoric past in which generations here had lived and bred and died forgotten, and all the nebulous hopes and fears of a future yet unborn. The time was now, complete and self-sufficient. Gaylord felt like a vacuum suddenly filled with a rush of life.

"Emily!"

He ran forward, caught her as she rose, and clung eagerly to her warm and living softness that bent and gave to something within him that he had never dreamed existed . . .

Their meetings on companionable procedure had begun in April. Now it was late June, and his first experiment in the simple mystery of living had begun—the only true science of mankind.

5.

Unusually late for Saturday, Helen awoke feeling utterly depleted. Maria was having another baby; for five nights in a row Helen had been obliged to stay up till midnight washing dishes after cooking all day and serving alone all evening. It was too much. Her arms were stiff, her legs ached. There was not even any wood left for the morning fire, she suddenly remembered.

This finally got her up. Putting on her old robe and moccasins, she went out with an axe to hack at some easily split cedar. The fall morning was swathed in a cheerless gray mist that veiled the mesas and trailed low and tenously in the canyons. On the only visible cottonwood a few leaves hung still and stiff and heavy as if hammered out of rusty iron and riveted to the stark branches. Even the song of the river was choked by the oppressive silence.

She came back into the house; built a fire with bark and shavings in the fireplace; put water to boil on the kitchen stove. Then, chilled and too tired to take her usual morning bath, she huddled forlornly in her robe, waiting for her tea.

No, she now admitted to herself, it was not the weather, the lack of help from Luis and Maria, nor her own work that depressed her. All summer, ever since Turner had left, she had been losing the deep inner security which assured her of her continuing emergence to that new world still beyond her full realization. For the first time she felt reduced again to a mere, lonely woman trying to earn a bare living by serving meals with inadequate, makeshift facilities. This unwarranted slip back into an existence limited to mere mortal expediency had stripped from her the joy, glory and staunch assurance of meaningful living. Helen was not only depressed, but a little frightened. She caught herself resenting the awakening that had promised so much, only to withdraw from her completely. Why? It wasn't fair! Somehow she had lost touch with herself, the only passport to the immortality of each living moment.

It was now almost nine o'clock. She hurried out to the highway to meet the mailman on his rural delivery route, a pleasure she looked forward to daily. She had missed him; another evidence of her negative state of mind. But he had left in the box a letter from Turner.

Fixing her tea, she came back to the fireplace. The cedar, as she should have known, was throwing sparks out over the floor and rugs; and in shaking down the sticks, she extinguished the blaze. By the time she settled down again, her tea was lukewarm.

Turner's letter was fat with clippings. She picked up the first random column that fell into her lap.

WHISTLE STOPS ON THE CHILE LINE
by
Jack Turner

This column believes in ghosts.

Our preferences are pale spectral shapes that creep up midnight stairs. Flit across dark arroyos. Haunt weedy courtyards, guarding buried Spanish gold. Respectable ghosts. Reliable family ghosts.

Old 60 is another kind of ghost. Squat, black, rusty iron, it clanks up and down in broad daylight. A ghost of Vanished Yesterday. Of the era of Romantic Railroading.

Old 60 is the last of the famous Consolidated 2-8-0 mountain-climbing locomotives of the Midland Terminal. A week ago it was cold and dead in the shops. Today it is tooting up and down the yards. Bringing to mind more memories of the Old Railroader. Like this one . . .

Preposterous! Helen thought, dazedly skimming through it. Who nowadays would know what a 2-8-0 type locomotive was, or care? But something in the column—a phrase, a sentence, a flashing picture it evoked, or even the feeling expressed between its lines—brought back to her all the sounds and smells, the leisureliness and high adventure of a trip on her old Chile Line.

Uncle John, portly and white-haired, waving to her from the engine cab. Andy ringing the bell for her to hurry. Mr. Jackson, the conductor, gallantly boosting her up the steps. Brakie giving the highball . . . She remembered the coarse texture and stale musty smell of the red-plush cushions as she settled down next to the window with her box lunch . . . The coal stove up front, and the washrooms marked *"Mujeres"* and *"Hombres"* . . . The sudden jolting and crashing of couplings as the train got under way.

Now she was off, all care and worry left behind! New mesas, new canyons and valleys opening at every curve as she chugged up-river. And accompanying these enchanting new vistas, the swelling symphony to whose crashing brass, high pizzicatos and subtle overtones her life had been pitched for years on end. The steady clickety-clack of the wheels on the rail joints beneath her. The squealing of the flanges on the sharp curves. The rise and fall of the main and side rods. Time and again her heart leapt at the mournful, lonesome, somehow gloriously triumphant and yet infinitely poignant wail of the whistle from the quill.

There came the treasured halts to let the wheels and brake shoes cool, when she could get out and watch Brakie stuff oiled rags in a smoking hot-box . . . The little sidings, the gaunt water tanks, tubercular Agent Wallace standing beside the turntable at Embudo, and the wonder and mystery of the far-off in the eyes of the simple Spanish people come to herald her arrival and departure.

Now she could hear the little straight-stacker talking as her drivers bit into the grade of Barranca Hill, the muffled thunder of the exhaust against the blackened cliffs. Andy was sweating on the apron now, she knew. Smoke was shooting high at every stroke of the pistons. Pressing her nose against the grimy window pane, she could see it rolling up the mountainside. Overhead she heard the gentle rain of cinders on the roof of the coach.

"Ten minutes late," Mr. Jackson said importantly, taking out his wagon-wheel watch as he stopped in the aisle to punch her ticket. "But we'll get you there on time, Miss Chalmers!"

"But I'm not going anywhere, really," she wailed.

On top the grade the three-footer gathered momentum as Uncle John let her out to the maximum speed of fifteen miles an hour. The country spread out. A vast, empty sea of sage beating against the far blue Colorado Rockies. Tres Piedras, Servileta Tank, No Agua. . . . And then, surfeited with new scenery after months of confinement at Otowi Crossing, her whole body rhythmically adjusted to the jolting and bucking of the coach, it was time to unwrap her chicken sandwiches and spill from her thermos a cup of hot tea . . .

It all came back to her now as she sat in her fireless room. Abruptly she broke out into tears. She wept because it was all gone and would never come again. She wept because she was lonely, because her tea was cold. But mostly because Turner, in a preposterous column, had evoked a love they had shared together.

Drying her eyes, she skimmed through his letter, her throat knotted with both anticipation and apprehension. His column had been picked up by one of the big Eastern wire services. Apparently it appealed to frenetic war-workers crowded in industrial centers and war installations throughout the country, and to homesick boys overseas.

"There'll be a big exodus west after the war, mark my words!" he wrote. "But what they're all going to do out here in these barren deserts of the West I don't know. But anyway I've been tooting right along. Now, before Christmas, listen for my whistle at Otowi Crossing. I can't bear being away from you any longer. When I

110

come back I've got a big surprise for you. Neither of us are young, and time is getting short."

Helen thrust the pages from her and covered her face with both hands. When she wept this time it was not an easy flow of sentimentality. The great dry sobs seemed to come from deep inside her, twisting and tearing every muscle as they broke forth. With them came the deep-rooted guilt she had hidden from herself. Yes! She had let him go without a clean break because she could not bear to give him up. So month after month she ate her cake and had it too. Forever looking forward to his return, and forever postponing her inevitable loss.

On no other day of her life had she wanted him so much, the things they could share together, and all the little comforts and joys deprived her for years. It seemed impossible to face alone the empty, aging years. And yet deep within her still unquenched desire for the old world to which she still clung, she knew that she had never been allowed to have what she believed she wanted. Some unseen power had driven her from a young husband and a child and a comfortable home years ago; driven her to a remote and lonely lunchroom at an unknown river crossing in a mountain wilderness. And now would it drive her, a middle-aged, lonely woman, from the last home and life-companion to be offered her?

Gripping her hands until the knuckles turned white, Helen fought to control her fright and resentment against this monstrous power. She didn't want to be different! She wasn't ready for an Emergence to a new world nebulous and unknown! And yet, having set her foot on the ladder, she could not resign herself to going back into a cramped material existence.

Why was it she couldn't have them both? Which did she want, really?

Sitting there in a chill room besieged by the somber gray mist of a fall morning, Helen felt herself torn by forces she could not understand. And against the torture of their struggle she could cry out, woman-like, only a weak and human lament. "And I've never had my morning tea!"

There was no time for it now. She was aroused by a shrill, metallic squeaking outside.

111

Peeking out the window, Helen saw that it came from an ungreased axle on Facundo's old box wagon approaching the narrow suspension bridge. By the time he had arrived at the door, she had hurriedly washed her face in cold well water and regained some measure of composure. Facundo seemed not to notice her wet hair and swollen eyes.

"Maria have that baby," he said casually. "Man-child. Big!"

"That's fine, Facundo. I'll go right over."

"Mebbe don't go," he said softly but positively. "She sleepin' all day. That the way it is." He looked quietly and unhurriedly at the cold, smoking fireplace and around the disordered room, then turned toward the door. "That noisy wheel. I grease him now. Then we go. Good day to get wood in the mountains!" He closed the door behind him.

"Why not?" she thought, dressing quickly in Levis and stout shoes, laying out mittens and a heavy coat. She was making some sandwiches when Facundo came in the kitchen door.

"Them cold sandwiches white peoples eat! No good! Fire and meat. They better in the mountains."

She found some chops, put bread and fruit in a paper sack, filled the coffee bag. Then they started up the canyon. The plodding broomtails in patched harness with ridiculous eye blinders. The springless Studebaker, with an axe bumping around in the empty wagon box. And Facundo and herself sitting on a plank seat covered with a tattered Navajo blanket against splinters.

The old Indian sat comfortably erect, the reins held loosely but without too much slack in his lap. There was a rent in the knee of his trousers, she noticed, and one ripped moccasin was held together with a greased string. Around his coarse graying hair he wore, Santo Domingo style, a brilliant red silk rag. His dark, wrinkled face looked solid as weathered mahogany. He did not talk. Soon she forgot him.

They were plodding steadily uphill now, the horses keeping the traces taut, their breaths spurting out like smoke. The canyon wall to the left was sheer, black basalt. To the right rose a steep slope thickly forested with spruce and pine. Over them both the mist still hung, silver-gray, wispy and tenuous as a cobweb. Suddenly she felt its cooling dampness, and smelled the moist fragrance of sage and pine. Summer had been so hot and dry, with dust over everything and swarms of grasshoppers, that Helen now welcomed the mist as a promise of winter snow. It was so good on her face, so fresh to breathe!

But it was chilling too. Facundo unfolded his shoulder blanket; she moved closer to him so he could wrap it around both their shoulders. In this enclosed proximity she became aware of his peculiar, spicy, Indian smell, so different from the rather sweetish odor of her own race. It was strong but not disagreeable, and soon she did not notice it.

When the canyon widened out, Facundo turned to follow the faint, rutted track of wagon wheels. These rough, almost indistinguishable "wood roads," long used only by those going after firewood, crept through the whole area. Soon Facundo stopped in a clearing in the forest. He unhitched, unharnessed and hobbled the horses to graze. The yellow gramma or bunch grass was short and dry, but Helen knew it was nutritious; down below in years gone by it had nourished immense herds of buffalo, and stock could still keep fat on it all year if it were not overgrazed.

Without a word, Facundo took his axe into the woods with Helen at his heels. He was not idly gathering dry sticks for a picnic fire now. He wanted stout logs that would throw up a bulwark of heat against a long winter's night. Helen watched him select a high pine, dead but still sound, and measure its length with a sharp eye. Then he set to work. It was amazing how much strength his thin, aging body still held, as his axe bit into the trunk. Perhaps it was life-long skill, rather than strength, for he wasted no strokes. Each bite of his blade deepened the previous cut; the scarf was smooth as if cut into butter. With a last stroke he stepped back; the lofty pine crashed neatly into an opening in the brush where there was room for him to trim off its branches. And now, without pause, he began to cut the trunk into wagon-lengths. A strange feeling crept over Helen as she watched him. For how many generations had a woman followed her man here, watching him gathering their winter's wood?

She wandered deeper into the forest to fill gunny sacks with pine cones. How dark and cold it was under these great pines whose lofty tops soughed with the wind! Years of fallen needles had built up underfoot a soft and springy mat upon which lay the cones. Each one, it seemed to her, was the skeleton tree in miniature; and deep in the heart of its seed she was sure there must be another microscopic pattern of a future tree to complete, in a century perhaps, the ceaseless cycle. Occasionally she froze to watch a bird flutter to a nearby branch, fluffing its feathers with a sharp beak, its tiny black eyes shining like glass. How many there were, if she held still: grosbeaks, towhees, juncos, even a bluebird.

Back in the clearing she built a small fire at which she could stand, her coat spread out like a blanket to catch the heat. "These white people's fires," she remembered Facundo complaining once. "They so big, people stand far away and freeze. Little fire under the blanket, Indian way. It warm."

When he came, they cooked their chops, ate bread-and-butter sandwiches and fruit, and sat drinking coffee. The food gave Helen strength; with the hot black coffee she felt life rising within her. Trouble and weather were never so bad when you got out into them. It was always fun to be out here gathering one's own wood. Once she had been taken down a coal mine near Raton. Never thereafter could she abide the thought of burning coal; the very smell of it reminded her of those black, sweating bodies toiling underground like slaves.

Facundo was too busy to talk. The minute he finished lunch, he began sharpening his axe with a rusty file. Helen was content to sit watching the precise movements of his delicate, dark hands. Finally he stood up and smiled.

"Now I cut piñon! Burn good, smell good, too!"

"I'll help!" she offered cheerfully.

His face quieted; he nodded vaguely toward the flat top of the forested mesa behind her.

"Mebbe you climb up there, find something."

"A pueblo ruin, Facundo? Oh, why haven't you told me about it before!"

"Mebbe *pueblito*," he corrected her. "Mebbe some old houses, mebbe all gone." But he could not diminish her quick excitement.

"Yes! What's it called, Facundo?"

"Mebbe no name. Mebbe forgot. Mebbe not tell." As always

he shut off her direct questioning. Nor would he point out its location and thus draw off its power. He merely nodded sideways at a rocky point, without looking at it. "Old spring by that rock. Mebbe you find trail close. Then walkin' easy."

She hurried off to the foot of the rocky point. A landslide had covered the spring, but she found where it oozed up through the brush and matted pine needles. The trail was too old to be clearly visible; with difficulty she traced its course up and across the steep slope. Soon she was above the pine tips; the canyon below, filled with mist, looked like a gray and turbulent sea. She kept climbing.

Near the top she could have let out a squeal of delight had she had a spare breath. To the right, a trail led up to the top of the mesa. Straight ahead she saw a wide, sandy passage overhung by the basaltic cap. And here at the fork she saw stuck in the rocks a weathered clump of prayer-sticks—the little feathered plumes, bound with colored yarn to a carved stick, that men had planted here for centuries when their hearts were right.

Without touching them, she hurried ahead on the sandy passage. There she saw it. A small group of cliff-houses clustered protectively under the overhanging ledge which had served as its roof. The front wall had fallen, its stones washing down the steep precipice. But the side walls still stood firm and smooth, like two outstretched arms holding between them the crumbling stone partitions of the tiny rooms. Inside, she dropped to her knees and let the ancient, talcum-like dust dribble through her fingers. As she had hoped, it contained a small piece of charcoal. It was then, suddenly, she felt her "radio" tuned in.

Years ago someone had asked her, "Why is it, Helen, that almost anyplace you go you can find sherds—edges, handles, all kinds of pieces of pottery? I go to the same place and hunt hours, and I can't even turn up an arrowhead!"

Helen had laughed a little self-consciously. "Why, I guess it's just my radio, or something like it in me, that seems to turn on. The farther I go in a certain direction, the more excited I get. Pretty soon I'm just so tingly all over I don't know where to turn or anything. Then I just stick out my hand—in a rock crevice, among a heap of stones, oh anyplace!—and whatever it is, it just seems to come right into my hand!"

That's the way it was now. A continually mounting excitement that led her like a radar beam to prod among the tumbled stone partitions, in the debris at the back of the ledge, and finally against the dark back wall. Feverishly now, conscious only of the excitement impelling her, Helen stuck her hand down into the choked mouth of a hollow in the floor.

It leapt to her fingers: a smooth round edge which carefully scooped out became the rim of a large perfectly formed bowl. Helen carried it out to the light with a sob of triumph hovering between laughter and tears. Brushed free of dirt, the bowl glowed reddish-brown in color, with a glazed black symbol of the plumed serpent moving in his sky-path around the rim, its smooth texture unblemished save for a thick blob of clay stuck to the rim. In this Helen now saw the clear imprint of a woman's thumb.

She was still standing on the ledge, tremblingly clutching her discovery, when she heard the faint, familiar honk of wild geese flying south. In a moment she could detect the undulating V sweeping toward her, high in the mist. Always she had believed the flocks followed the course of the river below. Now she knew that some of them used the plateau to mark their high road. That ancient Navawi'i woman, thumb pressing into the wet clay stuck to her cooking pot, must have watched their passage too, as she prepared for winter.

A muffled report from Los Alamos sounded over the ridge. The wild geese swerved, dipped toward her. Helen could see the sharp point of the V, the two trailing lines separating into distinguishable projectiles of lightning speed. Instinctively she braced herself against the airway shock of their hurtling passage.

At that instant it happened again: the strange sensation as of a cataclysmic faulting of her body, a fissioning of her spirit, and with it the instantaneous fusion of everything about her into one undivided, living whole. In unbroken continuity the microscopic life-patterns in the seeds of fallen cones unfolded into great pines. Her fingers closed over the splotch of clay on the bowl in her arms just as the Navawi'i woman released her own, without their separation of centuries. She could feel the enduring mist cooling and moistening a thousand dry summers. The mountain peaks stood firm against time. Eternity flowed in the river below . . . And all this jelling of life and time into a composite *now* took place in that single instant when the wedge of wild geese hurtled past her—hurtled so swiftly that centuries of southward migrations, generations of flocks, were condensed into a single plumed serpent with its flat reptilian head outstretched, feet drawn back up, and a solitary body feather displaced by the wind, which seemed to be hanging immobile above her against the gray palimpsest of the sky.

Nothing, she knew, could ever alter this immemorial and rhythmic order. Not the mysterious explosions on the Hill, nor the ever-increasing mechanism and materialism of successive civilizations. This was the unchanging essence to which the life of mankind was ultimately pitched. With this reassuring conviction, the fierce proudness and humble richness of her life at Otowi Crossing rushed back at her with new significance and challenge. A woman and a cooking pot! They could defy time, bring civilization to heel!

As if a switch had been turned on again, life resumed its movement. The wild geese swept past. The wind soughed through the pines. Her heart took up its beat. But as it had before, the wonder and the mystery and the beauty remained.

When she reached the wagon, Facundo had filled it with wood and lashed the load fast with rope. What could she say? It was all in her shining eyes, in the vibratory aura about her, in the pot in her arms. Facundo stepped back as she held it forth. He was no longer a ragged old man out cutting wood on a cold Saturday. He seemed again a living receptacle into which had been ceremonially instilled the esoteric wisdom of a tribal entity, handed down from a remote past in which mankind had survived only through its direct intuition of the living powers of earth and sky.

"That got the power," he said quietly. "I no touch!"

No. He would neither touch the old bowl nor sit in contact with her all the way home. Helen shivered without a blanket on the plank beside him. She felt too happy, a little too lightheaded, to care. Nor did she mind lighting lamps and fires in the cold, dark adobe while Facundo unloaded his wagon. He showed up quietly with a solemn face at the kitchen door.

"Come in, Facundo! I'll have some supper ready in just a few minutes."

"I go."

117

"All right. But wait till I fix a little package of nice things for you to take to Maria."

"I wait," he answered patiently.

When the package was tied and stuffed into a brown paper bag, Helen turned around to see him steadily staring at her with a look of grave concern.

"That Luis. No come no more," he said without preamble. "Workin' on that new road. Get rich, he say."

The information struck Helen queerly. Not that Luis had gone to work on the new road being blacktopped between Espanola and the Hill; the high wages were drawing many Indians as well as Spanish men from all the valley. Nor that after all these years of service to her, he had left her without so much as a word. But that Facundo had waited all day to tell her. Why?

"Mebbe that Maria no come too. That baby mebbe make too much work here. Mebbe she go work up there too."

Why hadn't she suspected that long ago? Helen had heard that due to the shortage of help and the makeshift living quarters, almost every woman up on the Hill was working at something on the Project. Maids were at a premium. Every morning busloads of Indian women were transported from San Ildefonso and Santa Clara, and taken home again at night without cost. "A free ride for nothing, and lots of money besides!" Maria had grumbled, watching the crowded busses rumble over the bridge. And now she was going too. Helen had no doubt of it.

"You no got man to chop wood, get water. You no got woman to cook, carry them plates to people. You got nobody mebbe." Facundo's voice was flat and expressionless.

If she had received the dire news this morning, Helen knew she would have been completely stricken; it was a blow even now. Where could she ever get competent, loyal help now, at the modest wages she could afford? But she felt instilled with a new courage.

"No, I haven't," she answered forthrightly. "But I know I'll make it somehow. Just like long ago."

Facundo looked at her a long time, then stated in the same flat voice, "I come. Livin' in that little house mebbe."

"That old adobe out in back? Why, you'll freeze to death!"

"Get new door. Mebbe stove. Me fix!"

"Move here from the pueblo, Facundo? Won't Luis and Maria miss you? And—"

"They goin'. I say."

It was all talk to gain time to catch her breath. For his suggestion had broken upon her immediately with the incontrovertible truth of something long written in invisible ink that she had suddenly learned to read. "All right, Facundo. Tomorrow we'll talk about getting a little stove from Montgomery Ward. I'm going to buy you some new clothes, too. You must be neat and clean to help me with lots of people around. You won't mind, Facundo?" she finished anxiously.

He smiled with a warmth that enveloped her wholly.

"I goin' now."

Alone again, Helen felt reclaimed by a destiny that somehow always overpowered her. She dropped off to sleep without questioning it.

7.

Turner, as the sole passenger on his imaginary Chile Line, was having an excellent time tooting through the mountains and deserts of the storied Southwest. Its hell-poppin' past and its lethargic present he mixed freely. Like prospectors of old, he sought specks of color, not statistics. He had an eye for the ignored significant; and this, with the practiced hand of a journalist, he translated into columns that were casually read with high interest and amusement, and also clipped for reference by the more wary.

Where he would stop next was always unpredictable. Near Uravan in southwestern Colorado an old abandoned processing mill snared his attention. Here he found that back toward the beginning of the century, carnotite ore had been mined and processed to extract radium for the experiments of the French scientists, Marie and Pierre Curie. For a decade this vast and rugged Colorado Plateau region had been the world's chief source of radium. Then richer deposits were discovered in the Belgian Congo, and mining had ceased. The abandoned mill was now but another relic of the past, forgotten in a heart-rendingly beautiful wilderness that—thank God!—would never be opened to exploitation and industrialization.

The great upland deserts of Nevada he found just as serenely remote from man's foibles. He ambled north from Las Vegas to a lonely valley just east of awesome Death Valley itself. A leathernecked old desert rat showed him a forgotten ghost-town called Wahmoni near Jackass Flat, a few miles out from the cottonwood oasis of Indian Springs. Turner listened appreciatively as the old prospector recalled a hilarious Saturday night during its brief boom. But it was the empty awesomeness of the valley itself that ate deeper into his feelings: its great Frenchman's Flat and Yucca Flat, separated only by a solitary, bare rock ridge. Standing on this he saw the desert, flat as a pancake, stretching away on both sides. The ancient lake bed rippled with heat waves; the wind whined through the weird cacti. Turner returned to town feeling that perhaps no other area in the country remained so inaccessibly remote.

Next day he headed south for California before highballing back home. A man long rooted to a houseful of relics and the local traditions they imbued, he had realized he could live with a handbag and a portable typewriter. But he could not live without Helen! Everywhere he went, he imagined her accompanying him. But the mountain would not come to Mohammed, so Mohammed was going back to the mountain of his desire.

Every night in his successive hotel rooms, he 'sketched out a plan for enlarging her little Tea Room: a big dining room here, a larger kitchen there, a pantry, perhaps a small bar and a new wing to live in. All modern, with the latest gadgets; no more drawing water from a well! For himself he would build a separate workroom, utilizing that old adobe in back. Thenceforth they would live together happily ever after, each doing his own work. Why not? How could they, at middle age, face dreary lives alone?

Still a strange uneasiness stealthily followed him into California, over Cajon Pass, and into Riverside where he checked into the Mission Inn. The hotel long had been one of his favorites. Built around three patios and surmounted by four towers, it was a cabalistic maze of flower gardens, shady walks, cloisters, balconies, fountains, turrets and domes, with several art galleries, a baronial hall, refectorio, and a complete chapel brought up from Mexico. Every square foot was so choked with antiques and relics that it reminded Turner more of a museum collector's nightmare than a mere hotel. Yet Turner loved the place; the Inn, although he did not realize it, was merely a monstrous exaggeration of his own cluttered adobe in La Oreja.

Following the bellboy upstairs to the room assigned him, Turner stopped dismayed at the damnable coincidence played upon him. There on the wall of the hallway hung the old oil of Guadalupe with the tiny rent in the canvas that Helen's quick eye had caught instantly. A few steps beyond was his—their—room, Number 39, designated in Spanish *La Sala de los Recuerdos Dulces*, The Room of Sweet Memories. With a grunt compounded of a curse and a groan, Turner flung it open and helplessly confronted the bittersweet memories it evoked.

A few years before, soon after he had met her, Turner had persuaded Helen to accompany him here on a business trip. Their constant and close intimacy, their joy in traveling together for the first and only time, their delight as California's orange groves and palm trees wrapped round their green-hungry hearts—it was enough. When they finally checked into the Mission Inn their high lark demanded a splurge: two rooms with a connecting bathroom. It seemed luxuriously intimate, the whole Inn enchanting, the warm winter sun a miracle.

Next morning Helen had shopped for a new dress, prowled through the hotel on a guided tour, and fed Napoleon, the parrot, in the garden. Turner made his business call, and brought back for lunch Dr. Maurice Gottman and his wife whom he had just met. What had happened while he had been gone, Turner did not know. But Helen was stiff and restrained, and said nothing. All afternoon she stayed in her own room, refusing to have dinner with him, and ordering a sandwich sent up to her.

Lying in his bed in the adjoining room that evening, he became worried. "Hey!" he called through the open bathroom door. "Have you gone to bed?"

There was no answer. He got up and peeked through the doorway. Helen was stretched out on the bed in her robe, hands crossed under her head, staring moodily before her. He went in and sat down on the foot of the bed.

"What's the matter? Just plumb tired out?"

After a time she said abruptly, "Look at that imitation Corot! You'd think a muddy oil like that would be self-conscious in Sunny California!"

After another long interval she said crossly, "You're sitting on my foot. I'd think you'd have felt it yourself!"

Good-naturedly he flung himself down, put his arm around her. Helen did not stir. Her body was stiff as a log. Her face was grim. Turner had never seen her so negative and sour. At last he stood up. "Call me if you need me. I'll leave the door open. You've probably got a touch of indigestion."

Back in his own room, he undressed and went to bed. He could not sleep. What had happened to change her mood so suddenly? Had she found out by chance the real nature of his "business" trip to Riverside? The suspicion terrified him.

He jumped up, went into the other room, and got into bed beside her. Helen neither acknowledged nor rejected his familiar presence. Desire built up between them. Inevitably it happened as it always happened. Yet even the impulse to sex did not break through her strange mood. No, it was no good. And afterward it was worse. She lay separated from him as if by interstellar space, sobbing into her clinched pillow. "Leave me alone! Get out! And close that door!"

All night Turner lay propped up on his pillow in the dark, seething with worry and anger. What the hell was wrong with her, anyway? Towards morning he must have dropped off to sleep for a moment, for he was suddenly aware of the wan gray light dimly etching the outline of a palm outside. Helen was up; he could hear water running in the bathroom. The door opened softly, then suddenly the covers were thrown back and Helen flung down beside him, both arms around him, in a tempestuous gust of remorse.

Later they lay together wordlessly united and at ease. How wonderful it was to make up after a quarrel and to make love in the gray, quiet dawn!

Yet as Turner now lay alone in the same bed, long afterward, that miserable night of resentful separation returned to haunt him. Helen had always been like that. An iceberg floating alone in a sea of loneliness. Let anyone come too close to her and he would run aground on that mysterious nine-tenths of her existing invisibly

122

below her surface consciousness. What was it? And what allowed him to believe it would ever permit her to marry him? For whatever her malady was, it was getting worse.

Oppressed by the certainty that she was suffering from a mental disorder, he made up his mind to drive into Los Angeles for a consultation with Dr. Maurice Gottman before returning to New Mexico.

Dr. Gottman, a Freudian psychologist on "Libido Lane," as North Roxbury Drive was popularly known in Beverly Hills, remembered Turner clearly. He was a big man with a head bald and brown as his walnut desk; and over him and his panelled office was spread the same varnish of indubitable success. The room was hung with the right pictures painted by the right artists, and was provided with a trick door out of which a patient could leave without being seen. His own manner was impeccable; he was constantly filling, lighting, and relighting a pipe which he never smoked in order to give the interview an air of cozy informality.

"How is it possible to diagnose a physical illness without examining the patient? Mental illness is still more difficult; sometimes a psychosis takes years of analysis. That is what I told Mr. Turner when he came to see me about Miss Chalmers."

Lighting his pipe, he continued. "I had seen him and Miss Chalmers once before. He had brought her to Riverside and my wife and I had lunch with them in the Mission Inn. We ourselves had been in America only a short time, and were living out there in the country until I could open an office in Los Angeles.

"The lunch was rather a strain on all of us, I must confess. Miss Chalmers and Mr. Turner were not the urban type, shall I say, that my wife and I had been accustomed to in Berlin. Coming from what we regarded as a wilderness populated by wild Indians, they seemed to us, I'm afraid, somewhat provincial and naive. Not that Miss Chalmers wasn't rather charmingly self-conscious of her new dress. But she talked very little and gave me only one clue to her character.

"My wife had ordered a fresh persimmon, and just as she was about to cut it open Miss Chalmers grabbed her wrist. 'Not cold steel to living fruit! Oh no!' Her face was pale. She was really quite upset . . . A trivial incident. But we were all surprised by the intensity of her reaction. How does one eat a ripe persimmon anyway!

"Mr. Turner did not quite seem himself, either. For one thing, it was obvious they were in love and having a little affair. The state, as you know, is not conducive to equanimity. For another thing, he was nervously afraid that by mischance I might give away the real reason for his 'business' trip to Riverside.

"It was his illegitimate daughter, of course—an interesting little child who had been sent to the government's Indian school there, Sherman Institute. For a bluff and open-hearted man like him, it seemed strange that he wanted to keep the child a secret. Still one could understand his reluctance in wanting Miss Chalmers to know of it so soon."

Dr. Gottman lit a match with a flourish and held it suspended over his pipe. "No, there was little to go on when Mr. Turner came here to see me later. Miss Chalmers had broken off physical relations with him, had been steadily growing more introverted, and had begun to see visions as he called them. Yet he was still in love with her, considering marriage. What could be done about her?"

His match burned out. He flipped it away and looked up again. "For a woman her age, and so introverted, the prognosis was unfavorable. I was busy; it was wartime; psychologists and psychiatrists were at a premium. Still I consented to take her for analysis if she would assent to come to me. What more could I say? After all, I had only seen the lady once. Miss Chalmers, however, never came. I never saw her again. Nor Mr. Turner."

He paused to refill his pipe. His voice grew sharper. "How then can I make any post-mortem statement now about her alleged mystical experiences? The literature throughout the world is full of such case histories. The introverted Eastern mind especially regards such an experience of 'enlightenment' as natural. But this introversion is generally felt here to be abnormal and morbid, what Freud called auto-erotic. Just as the East in turn regards our extraversion as an abnormal repression of spiritual forces.

"Still, human nature is the same everywhere. So possibly we can equate what the East—and Miss Chalmers—call 'mind' with what we call the 'unconscious.' If so, our 'collective unconscious' may be the equivalent of the 'enlightened' or universal mind. Because it is the root of all experience of oneness, the matrix of all thought-forms.

"You must understand, of course, that the term 'collective unconscious' is an expression of Jung's psychology. Freud rejects it, and I myself do not believe there is a God or a universal oneness. I agree with Anatole France who said that he loved the occult, but the occult did not reciprocate his love for it never showed itself in his presence!

"You follow me?" he asked sharply. "Persist in identifying yourself with this universal oneness and you lose all sense of individual reality. Or perhaps you connect with a greater reality. Who knows? Perhaps all the mystics, saints and sages of the past should have been in lunatic asylums. Perhaps all the inmates of our present mental institutions are mystics, saints and sages. Who knows?"

Dr. Gottman glanced at the clock and ran his hand over his head as if brushing back his non-visible hair—perhaps a gesture of the unconscious of which his conscious mind was not aware. The customary fifty-minute hour was over.

8.

Turner arrived home in La Oreja to find a note from Helen reminding him that he was expected for her usual gathering on Christmas Eve, and enclosing another Christmas Letter for him to have mimeographed.

Taking it to the back shop of *El Porvenir* for the boys to run off some copies, he looked through several issues of the paper. It had shrunk to its former eight pages. The make-up was crude and the ads poorly laid out. Worse than its appearance were its contents.

"My God!" he said profanely to Mrs. Weston who had come out to hug him to her tremendous bosom. "It looks like a political handout! No straight news. Everything's slanted to butter up the local *politicos.*"

"We're doing fine," whispered Mrs. Weston, thumbing at the front office.

Turner peeked through the door. Cyril Throckmorton III was

125

sitting at his desk, still a caricature. Around him in a cringing circle sat a dozen local *politicos:* small Anglo businessmen whose livelihood depended upon political contracts, Spanish political *jefes* who controlled the votes in rural precincts, men out of work, poor farmers after subsidies. To them all Throckmorton was declaiming on war, soil erosion, education, and highway paving. Frequently he passed out cigarettes which they accepted with humble gratitude. Then again he stopped to write out a check which one of them grabbed with rapacious eagerness. Meanwhile they all kept spitting into a big brass spittoon, Throckmorton carefully keeping his patent leather slippers out of the way.

"I get it!" said Turner. "He's going to have to start with the State legislature, of course. But isn't it a little early?"

"He's taking no chances," she said in a low voice. "He'll make it too."

Yes, thought Turner, if there ever had been any mystery about the reason for Throckmorton's purchase of *El Porvenir* it was dispelled now. He was glad to get out into the fresh air.

The day before Christmas the weather cleared after a deep snow. Turner left for Otowi Crossing just after lunch. On the seat of the car beside him was his stack of presents gaudily tied with a red ribbon.

Helen did not hear his car drive up. She was in the kitchen making too much of a clatter with pots and pans. Every one in the place was dirty, she thought joyfully. There were cool fine-bodied pumpkin pies and juicy hot mince pies; cream sauce and brandy sauce; wild raspberry jam, wild gooseberry preserves and cranberry sauce. The vegetables had been peeled and sliced; the biscuits made and ready for the oven; the turkey stuffed and ready. She looked in the ice-box to see again the chilling pickles, olives and celery, milk and cream and butter. She had even fancied she could afford a bottle of the Scotch Turner liked.

This last month she had worked so hard! Not only feeding groups of Xs five nights a week, but helping to fix up the old adobe in back for Facundo. He had brought a couple of Indian boys to replaster the walls, put a new door on it, and install a little wood stove. How proud of it he was ! Every day she caught him standing outside, admiring it. She had ordered him new clothes from Montgomery Ward too. A decent pair of trousers, some shirts and socks and underwear, and colored ribbons to tie his hair.

"Every afternoon before you come in to help me serve dinner I want you to put on a clean shirt, Facundo. And wash your hands and show them to me. Will you?" she had demanded. "We must be very clean and look nice to those people or they won't come again." At first it had looked odd to them, she knew; an old, dark, and wrinkled Indian stoically carrying in and out their platters with never a word. Soon they, as she herself, forgot him. His soft moccasins carried him across the floor noiselessly as a ghost. His strong, gentle hands never fumbled; he had not broken a dish yet. And when everyone had gone, and she was ready to collapse with fatigue, he cheerfully rolled up the sleeves of his cheap shirt and did all the dishes, the pots and pans as well, singing softly in his strange high-pitched Indian voice. No, without Facundo she would never have made it alone.

Happening to look out the window, she saw Turner. Facundo was proudly showing him the fixed-up hut. With a glad cry of welcome, Helen rushed out. "Jack! You're home!"

He did not fling his arms around her. He did not even greet her. He simply thrust the packages upon her and turned away.

"But Jack! You're coming back?"

Before Helen could move, he was in his car. She watched it hurtle across the narrow suspension bridge, heard the screech of tires as he whipped it around the turn on two wheels.

She walked slowly back into the kitchen and sat down at the table. The Christmas-wrapped presents for Emily, Facundo and herself she laid aside to be opened that evening. Spreading out a ribbon-tied roll of paper, she saw the scale-drawing he had made for remodelling her Tea Room. A wave of compassion engulfed her as she examined the plan. Facundo installed in the very adobe he had planned to reconstruct for himself! Now he knew how she had planned her life here without him.

As she contritely rolled up the drawing, an envelope dropped on the floor. She picked it up. It was imprinted with the name and address of a Dr. Maurice Gottman in Beverly Hills, and it was addressed to herself. Frowning slightly, she opened it. The typed message was professionally brief. Dr. Gottman, at Mr. Turner's request, would be pleased to take for a preliminary analysis. His schedule was heavy. Would she please let him know when she could come to Beverly Hills and how long she could stay? Financial arrangements would, of course, be made between Mr. Turner and himself.

Dr. Maurice Gottman . . . Who was he? Suddenly she remembered. That stuffy little German with whom she and Turner had lunched once at Riverside. A psychoanalyst, psychiatrist or something. She sat staring at his note, gripping the sheet with both hands, her face turning white.

Resentment came first—a sudden, uncontrollable gust of anger. Turner wanted to marry her, remodel and modernize her Tea Room, and move in with her. But not until he had sent her to a psychiatrist to make sure she was mentally sound. That was the price she had to pay!

Almost instantly her gust of anger burnt itself out and with it her last vestige of false pride. Now she faced without shame the image of herself she saw through his eyes. A neurotic recluse, now in danger of becoming a psychotic lost in a meaningless dream-state. He believed she was losing her mental balance and, unknown to her, had tried to commit her to a psychiatrist for treatment. Jack, yes Jack!

The realization hurt her too much to weep. She bent her head down on her clenched fists, staring open-eyed at that monstrous specter he had evoked in her image. Was it real? Could it possibly be true?

In the profundity of that bottomless well of pain into which his betrayal had cast her there was no surcease of anguish, no escape. But still farther into the blackness of her despair, still deeper into the rending pain, she could dimly sense that selfhood to which ignorantly or protestingly she always had been committed.

In that hour she made at last that irrevocable turn from which there was no retreat, ever, come what may. The darkness lessened. The pain stopped. It was over, all over. She had let him go at last. It was as if they stood, each on a different shore, slowly drifting apart. These two loved and loving strangers who had clasped each other and in that moment of their earthly embrace held fleetingly the evanescent mystery which had drawn them together.

Tears came now. Of intolerable regret. The break had come as she had known it must come since the day when she went to gather wood with Facundo. But it had not happened right. Not like this! Oh no, not like this! She had wanted to tell him quietly alone, with her arms around him, all those things she had never been able to explain and why this had to be. But now the squeal of his tires kept echoing in her ears. In this new fall of snow on already icy roads there was no telling what might happen to him when he was so upset.

Fear for him stung her into quick, decisive action. She doused her face in cold water, threw on her coat and galoshes. Calling in Facundo, she showed him how to keep basting the turkey and told him when to put on the potatoes. "I'm going out. I'll be back for dinner." Then she ran out to her old jalopy.

Where she was going to look for him Helen did not know. But as she topped the hill just above Santa Fe, a quick premonition told her she was on his track. At the bottom of the hill she saw tire marks in the snow where a car had skidded off the icy pavement, whipping across the road into a fence. Here the car had flung about, tail end to, and crashed into a telephone pole. She could see the dry, splintered timber, snapped off six feet above ground, still lying across the smashed top of the car. It was Turner's car.

Momentary fear froze her heart as she stopped and looked inside. He was gone. Without wasting time in useless telephone calls, Helen drove directly to the Police Station. The Desk Sergeant was Spanish; he told her that Turner had not been hurt, but had been picked up and brought here, suspected of being drunk. There had been a row, but Turner had patched it up by offering to buy them all a drink. "Of course, Señora, we do not drink on duty," he reminded her. Finally she wormed out of him the information that Turner and one of the officers ("off duty, of course, Señora!") had gone out together. The Sergeant did not say where.

The bars she went to were crowded with customers, but in one a bartender recalled them: a civilian who had bought the officer with him and himself each a bottle of Bourbon. Helen went outside and stood staring across the snowy plaza. Sidewalk and stores were jammed with last-minute shoppers. Even the Indian women squatting on the cold stone portal of the Palacio Reál were surrounded by avid buyers dickering for pottery and trinkets. Lights and streamers

129

splashed color against the snowy walls. A church bell tolled; chimes began another Christmas carol.

Where would a man go in Turner's emotional state and suffering from the nervous shock of a serious car accident? To a hospital, carrying a quart of whiskey? Not Jack!

With sure instinct Helen strode across the plaza to La Fonda Hotel. "Has Mr. Turner registered here within the last hour?" she asked the desk clerk sharply.

He gave her a brief look. "Room 322."

Helen went boldly upstairs without stopping at the room telephone. The door was unlocked. Opening it and snapping on the light, she saw Turner sprawled out on the bed with the open bottle beside him.

He raised his bruised face, blinking at the light. "Oh, iss chew, huh?"

"Yes, it's me, Jack," she said, walking up to him. "Are you hurt? Tell me!"

He looked up at her through puffed, squinting eyes without answering. Helen glanced at the bottle; he had been doing a hasty job of it. She calmly set it out of his reach and called room service to send up a pot of coffee. "Bring a salt shaker too!" she demanded. "Yes! A salt shaker!"

For a long time she sat beside him. His nervous trembling ceased. There came a knock on the door at last. Helen took the tray and in the bathroom stirred up a glass of strong, tepid salt water. Turner had rolled over, stertorously puffing whiskey fumes through his swollen lips. Quietly, insistently, she forced the brine down him. When he began to gag, she dragged him to the bathroom. "Get it out, Jack! Put your finger down your throat! Now! Again!"

Weak and sweaty, he crawled back to bed. Helen let him rest awhile, giving him sips of hot black coffee. Gradually his eyes cleared; he reared up with an angry look. "You double-crossed me!" When she did not answer, he broke out again. "I had it all fixed up. The house, the doctor, everything! I'll pull you out of it! I will!"

She let him talk. The retching and the coffee had done their work; his voice was clearing. Yet every word revealed how acutely he was suffering under the illusion of time rushing past; constricted to feelings and loves that must be grasped hurriedly and held tightly lest they be swept away and lost forever. How could she make him understand that the essence of her love would always be with him; an inalienable part of all that once deeply felt existed forever in timeless time? But now was no time to try. His face had broken out into a sweat and he was trembling as with cold.

There was nothing vague nor introspective about Helen now. Quickly she peeled off the clothes from his muscular, bruised body. Then stripping to her slip, she managed to get him to the shower. Steaming hot, then icy cold; she held him there cursing profanely in both English and Spanish, and wailing like a schoolboy. "*Sorda hija de tal!* . . . Mother of God! . . . Turn off that faucet!"

She laughed with relief, seeing him pulling out of it. Stepping back from his grasping hands, she ruthlessly thrust his head under the shower again and turned on the icy mountain water full tap. When he came out sputtering and howling, still a little wobbly, she flung a couple of towels around him and pushed him back into bed.

Dressing in the bathroom, Helen watched him through a crack in the door. He was sitting up, moaning, but vigorously drying his hair; he was quite all right. Her lips compressed. Now at last they must have it out, she decided ruthlessly.

She walked out, sat down on a chair beside the bed. Turner looked up and grinned sheepishly. She said abruptly, "Your emotional spree is over, Jack. So's mine. Let's face it squarely. I'm not ever going to marry you. I'm not going to be your mistress any more. If it'll be easier for you, go away and never come to see me again. But if you can and want to, let's be friends always and remember the love we still share."

Turner did not flinch, nor did she avert her steady gaze from his.

"I was weak and wrong, fixing up that hut for Facundo and not letting you know. You betrayed me too. Trying to commit me to that stuffy little psychologist. Dr. Maurice Gottman! As if I were irresponsible for my actions, going out of my mind. Why, you must be crazy yourself to think of paying $30 an hour for me to lie down on his couch every day for weeks!"

"Psychiatric treatment might help you. It might not," he said doggedly. "I think you ought to find out."

"Because I'm not social and want the things you want. Because

131

I'm abnormal. According to whose standards? Yours and Dr. Gott-man's?"

Struck again by the mammoth absurdity, Helen laughed ironical-ly. "Imagine my telling that solemn little donkey anything he can't find in a textbook! Modern psychology is a brand new science that's helping a lot of unbalanced people. But it's still rudimentary, crude and frightened of the vast unknown within us. Yes, it is! These psychologists and psychiatrists are little boys gingerly testing its depths with their toes, scared to death of really getting wet!"

"Come now, Helen." Turner looked frightened by her relapse into this realm of metaphysical nonsense.

"All right. Let's look at it!" She cut him short and continued. "I had a sudden awakening that I tried to tell you about several times. You wouldn't listen any more than that stuffy Dr. Gottman would listen. You still wouldn't try to understand if I tried to tell you. You think I'm going crazy. But I know I have found myself at last. And this is the way it must be."

Turner's gaze lowered, then his face. He sat picking at the edge of a towel with his lean brown hands like a reprimanded, lovable little boy. But still too much of a man, she thought proudly, to wound her with a bitter look, a harsh word.

She wanted to fling herself upon him to soften their parting with a last embrace. Yet she restrained herself from even taking his hands. Standing up, she looked down at him with quiet tenderness. "Look! It's Christmas Eve! You're not going to miss it with me, anyway! . . . Now hurry up! I'll wait for you in the lobby!"

Facundo's little piñon fires were already half burned away and reddening the snowbanks when they crossed the bridge. Luis and Maria had lit the candles inside. Young Dr. Gaylord had happened to be passing by, and had been persuaded to stay. Emily and he were smoking up the room with fragrant cedar. All of them were still waiting dinner with an overcooked turkey.

Turner was embarrassed; he imagined he looked as badly as he felt. "I've already had too much Christmas spirit!" he informed them defiantly.

"Not for a man who's had the frightening car wreck you've had!" said Helen consolingly. He did not answer, but she saw his eyes film over with an inexpressible sadness. An unfathomable chasm had opened between them, she thought somberly, but like a weak and dizzy tightrope walker, he was still doing his mortal best to bridge it.

9.

With her final break with Turner, the person she loved most, the Woman at Otowi Crossing felt freed again from the clinging entanglements of the world of Helen Chalmers. Guilt and care dropped from her; her spirits soared. Every simple task took on a new meaning. Each mesa, mountain and canyon, the storms and the shadows that cloaked them, stood out as with preternatural clarity in an effulgent blaze of twilight. There began now her finest year: that last quiet interregnum before events and acclaim caught up with her. Her annual letter for that year, known to collectors as the "Four Seasons Letter," reflected in all in a few simple pages.

"My friends," she began, "this New Year must surely bear blossom from the rich fullness of the last. Jack hardly had packed up and left right after our Christmas Eve gathering before it began to snow" . . .

Only Facundo could remember when it had piled so deep. Every morning she awakened to stare entranced at the white-robed mesas and mountains. Breaking trail to her mailbox, she saw every weed, stalk and branch coated with silver. When the sun did come out the whole visible world sparkled like one huge, rough-cut diamond.

With snow came intense cold. At night the temperature dropped to twenty degrees below zero. The river was an unbroken ribbon of ice till noon. Then it cracked, and gnawing with sharp edges at the banks, sluggishly unwound through the canyon. At four o'clock its movement stopped; by dark it was frozen over again.

Hundreds of birds came for the feed Helen put on their tray. Wild animals left strange tracks in the yard. One daybreak she glimpsed a gray fox scurrying away like a puff of smoke. At night she heard the frightened-child-scream of a cougar.

"I catch him this trap!" boasted Facundo in the morning.

"You won't try any such a thing!" Helen protested. "Do what

133

you want in the mountains; it's none of my business. But not here. Whatever comes here is my friend!"

She did not rebel against the difficult trips to the pueblo or to town for supplies. She took Facundo with her to help dig out the jalopy when it got stuck. All day long as she worked in the kitchen, she could hear the ring of his axe at the woodpile. How wonderful after years of aloneness to feel someone around! Yet Facundo never intruded on her essential privacy; they were both too busy. Only at night after the Xs had gone did they visit.

"Them dishes clean," he would announce cheerfully. "I go home now!"

"You'll freeze in that old hut, Facundo!" she would protest. "Why don't you go out and stoke up the fire in your stove and then come back till it warms up?"

For a little while then they would sit quietly before her fire. Facundo would tap on the small drum in his lap, and sing the songs she loved to hear over and over again. "The Eagle Song, Facundo! Yes! The Corn Dance Song! I know it now!" Often he would tell her stories—simple little folk tales whose subtle morals she might not catch until later. Sometimes he would merely sit sunken into himself, the flamelight playing over his anthropoidal, prehistoric face. She had never known how sensitive and fluid it could be when watched carefully for its reflection of changing moods.

Abruptly he would say something about the ancient people who had lived in the ruins above, or allude to a detail of their rituals which he still faithfully followed. At that instant he dropped his guise of an old man who did her chores, and became again the personification of the intense racial vision which, deep in their unconscious, compelled his people's belief and behavior. Always his remark so casually made with an averted face opened for her the secret door to the inner meaning of the whole ceremonial, always so hidden by its intricate ritualism of mask, dance and song. A tingle raced up her spine; her life took on a sudden richness, a new depth of understanding. And going to bed, she gave herself in sleep to the slow wheeling of the constellations across the midnight sky.

Spring came late. The melting snow rushed down canyon, barranca and arroyo in cataracts. The river, gorged with debris, swept past in a muddy flood. She could hear the Indians singing as they

134

cleaned out the irrigation ditches and made ready for spring planting. Sere, tawny vegas turned green overnight. Gaunt cattle fattened on the lush grass. Up the arroyo she found three mariposa lilies whose seeds had waited patiently to germinate through years of drought.

Emily, she observed, had never looked so happy. She had taken up fishing, and came in every evening flushed and excited.

"But no fish! Emily, why don't you ever catch anything?" Helen asked her pointedly. "Is it because you never put any bait the hook?"

Emily looked guiltily at her expensive and unused tackle, and flushed redder still. "I don't care! I like to get out!" A few minutes later she managed to mumble, "I just happened to run into Dr. Gaylord. It's rather late I know, but I suggested he eat here. He's a little sensitive about—you know, not having any reservation—"

"So that's the fish you're still angling for! Emily, for goodness sakes! Set up a card table in my room, and you two can eat in there in peace."

The Xs came regularly five nights a week, mostly the same, self-selected small groups. Was it because many of them were foreigners in a strange land, or because their responsibilities were so great, that they had need of the warmth and simplicity they found here? Helen did not care any more than she cared what they were doing up on the Project. It was enough for her that they came to Otowi Crossing to find an essence of life they lacked upon the Hill. Often she glanced up at the ancient pottery bowl on the mantel. More than ever it became a symbol under which she fought to preserve an unchanged core of life in a changing world.

Summer brought a stifling heat that drove her every few minutes to the kitchen door for a breath of air. A haze of dust lay over the valley. The river shrank to a slow brown stream in whose shallows the two herons stood one-legged hour after hour. A hawk hung motionless in the sky. A blue bottlefly buzzed on the screen . . . And she loved every moment of it too: its mellow ripeness and slow pulse, the corn-stalks stretching out their arms for rain, the changing patterns of the stars. The garden did very well. There was everything she needed for the table; all the jars on the root cellar shelves were filled; and twice a week she sent vegetables up the Hill, adding to her small savings

Then again the corn turned yellow and a chill wind rattled the dry stalks. Cottonwood and aspen burst into conflagration. Over them the wild geese flew south, honking, circling, and reforming their silver V along the immemorial skyway. The fire was lit again every evening. Newspapers came with the ever horrible war news There were magazines and books. Most of them unread. The demands for human contact made upon her were more important. Maria and Luis depended upon her for advice; the new baby needed attention. Other babies she once had held on her lap returned from war, wounded or embittered, needing consolation and cheer. An old man at the pueblo had died. She went to the adobe where he was laid out for burial in his best blanket. From under it protruded his feet. She noticed that the soles of his moccasins were worn through. He had not spared his steps in dancing nor trudging to help people. No, nor would she spare hers.

The leaves fell. The willows glowed red. The river ran a clear soap-green, frothing into white suds at the rapids. It was winter again.

Helen had never been so happy! Her life had taken on a new fullness and richness. The lacy pattern of veins on the underside of a leaf, the cold touch of a wounded grosbeak's feet in her hand, the faint smells and sounds she now sensed in very breeze—every detail seemed significant. A casual remark from a friend bared a whole life and character. Every incident carried seeds of the past and future. Each day was different. Her preternatural awareness of it all was pitched to an intensity that wore her out. She went to bed exhausted but replete. And so quickly did she drop off to sleep she hardly had time to fold her hands on her breast, like a swimmer resting on a tide, knowing that in the next moment the other mysterious half of her life would bear her into a still different and richly significant existence separated from her conscious awareness only by the blink of a heavy eyelid.

This, of course, was merely the outward shell of her life. For the inner substance which gave it shape and meaning she could no find words. Yet she began to feel she owed it to Turner to help him understand somehow, sometime, the intangible thing that had happened to her.

How? He seldom wrote, and she didn't know if he would ever

136

return. Perhaps it would be best if he didn't. Something always came up between them. No, it was difficult for her to talk with people. For their communication was not restricted to conversation. Eyes, hands, the movement or posture of their bodies—even the faint aura of their personality and the invisible vibration to which their character was pitched carried on a communication often at variance with their words. Only when she sat down alone to write, difficult as it was for her to translate her thoughts and feelings, did she feel free to express herself.

So one night she began a secret journal in an unused household expense ledger, striving in it to give him some comprehension of the incomprehensible. It was like trying to measure a rainbow with a dressmaker's tape, or illustrating the majesty of the sea with a drop of water in her palm.

"I'm going to write down here everything as it happened from the first so you'll have a complete record," she began. "Then you'll understand that what is happening to me is simply an awakening to my true Self, the real ME. Not the physical body, the conscious mind, the personality with which I'd always identified myself. But the ME behind all these. What it is I can't explain because it isn't a separate thing. It's a totality of everything, an infinite world that embraces all time and space, a consciousness that pervades all forms of life in some degree. In it you lose yourself like a drop of water in the ocean, and yet you find yourself.

"You see how hard it is to put it into words! Maybe because I want to tell it all in one breath, and I can't. It's an experience that has to be lived through, step by step. That's why I'm putting it down day by day in this Dime-Store ledger labelled Secret because it's as precious as the classified documents on the Hill."

The night wind had come up. Out the window Helen could see it whip the last sparks from the chimney of the hut in back and fling them like red stars across the sky. She could almost hear Facundo snoring, like an old man snores, as she envisioned his thin old body knotted up in his blankets.

What made all of us do what we do when we were ready to do it? Not the humblest of us knows our high destiny. Had a chunk of graphite imbedded deep in the rocky core of the earth ever suspected then that in the lead pencil in her hand now it would be striving—

so hard!—to mirror the supernormal brilliance of a light that had not yet reached the blackness of its subterranean kingdom?

THE WOMAN AT OTOWI CROSSING

Part Three

1

Emily had finished the first draft of her dissertation, but before sending it in she asked her mother to go through it carefully, making detailed notes on every point that could be clarified and expanded with knowledge Helen had gained from Facundo. "It's terribly important," she insisted. "I want this *Inquiry* published as an original source book on the subject!"

Helen weakly assented and for nights on end struggled through the long manuscript. The result was disastrous. Early one Sunday morning Emily returned to discuss with her the manuscript and the notes on it Helen had written. Her face was stiff and pale.

The premise of Emily's bulky tome was simple enough. The origin legend of the Aztecs stated that they came from seven womb-caverns to the north, but no one could establish by historical facts that they originated in New Mexico and migrated south. So by parallels between ancient Aztec and modern Pueblo rituals Emily was attempting to prove it.

Helen refuted the premise on the grounds that Emily had missed the real meaning of Pueblo ceremonialism. She insisted that the seven womb-caverns weren't geographical locations and that the migration didn't take place over an actual route of a few hundred miles. The whole thing was really a profound myth or parable outlining in ritual terms the evolutionary journey of all mankind from an ancestral home deep in the womb-caverns of our own unconscious.

"You see, dear, as I tried to explain in my notes—"

Emily blew up like a firecracker. "Hazy generalities, every one! Can't you get it into your head I'm dealing in scientific specifics? You're trying to write off me and my whole work, and I won't have it!" Grabbing up Helen's notes with her own manuscript, she rushed out in a huff.

Emily explained her reaction more clearly in a letter she wrote

141

a few years later to a publisher who had asked her to write a biography of her mother:

"I must decline your kind invitation to prepare for your publication a biography of my mother. As you are aware, I knew her only for a few years before her death. Any material I could offer would not add substantially to Mr. Turner's *Intimate Sketches of Helen Chalmers,* for which I supplied the necessary facts about her family background.

"You will appreciate my disinclination to contribute to the controversial myth of the 'Woman at Otowi Crossing' grown up about her. I cannot comment on the fact that she was seen conducting an Indian rite alone at midnight in her home. I feel it my duty, however, to remark on her use of Pueblo Indian symbolism to express many of her beliefs.

"My mother received only a high school education: one of the reasons why my paternal grandparents objected to my father's marriage to her. She read very little. She was not a member of any church. Her closest friends were the Indians at the nearby pueblo—particularly Facundo, the Cacique or 'medicine man,' who worked for her as gardener and dishwasher. Through her constant association with them for many years, many persons believed she 'thought like an Indian.' Certainly much of their mythology, kiva symbolism, and ritualism was familiar to her. It was natural that she used them to express her rather abstract ideas. They superseded for her the religious teachings of orthodox creeds; they replaced the intellectual dissertations of our more academic philosophies; and they eliminated her need for wordy explanations.

"My *Inquiry* publicly acknowledges the help I derived from her. I do not minimize this. Yet as an anthropologist and ethnologist, I must frankly state that I adopted from her suggestions only the material I could substantiate by factual research and which contributed to my premise.

"We scientists who work with materials of the past for the benefit of posterity must be so constricted. We must deal with observable facts, not with imaginary conjectures. It is one thing to regard a prehistoric myth as a valuable anthropological record of a primitive people's life-pattern. It is quite another to adopt the same myth as an esoteric experience common to people of all times and races, a blueprint for life today. No. I find it almost absurd to believe that we could live now by the tenets of an almost primitive tribe.

"My mother's death has not mitigated this difference of opinion between us. Yet sometimes I confess to an uneasy feeling when I recall that she who so firmly believed in myth as a living experience is today the subject of a living myth herself."

The allusion in it to the Indian rite which Helen was seen conducting alone at midnight in her house Helen described in her *Journal* as one of the incidents of her friendship with Tranquilino.

Tranquilino had come back from war unable to resume his former life. A tall young Indian with a maimed arm and a tortured face, he lived suspiciously alone in a squalid adobe along the river. Not only did he refuse to work the land allotted him. He rebelled against demands to do his share of community work, and ignored his ceremonial duties. All day he sat drinking rotgut whiskey or cheap wine. Then staggering drunk, he lurched down the road venting his hate on everything he met, clubbing dogs and a stray horse, throwing stones at children. The sight of a group of young girls giggling beside an irrigation ditch infuriated him most. He would rise suddenly out of the bushes, shaking his penis at them, and cursing them as they fled in terror.

"That boy no good," said one of his uncles gravely. "Maybe better if he die that time than to shame us all."

This shocking verdict aroused Helen's pity for the condemned. Tranquilino had been such a lovely little boy, shy and sensitive, with big brown eyes. One of those children the world over who saw faces in flowers, in pebbles, in the jutting cliffs. Often he had brought her a stone picked up along the road. "My friend," he would say of it. "I hear him call."

Then one day, still young and proud and innocent, he had gone down to Albuquerque for the first time. The Government had cut his hair short, stuffed him into an Army uniform, and shipped him to a strange land across the water. Here he marched for miles, dug a hole in the ground with a few companions, and lived like a gopher. Why? He did not understand. Early one morning it happened. A blinding, blasting explosion. Blood and guts spewing all over him, dirt pouring down upon him. The salty taste of his own blood, and then darkness. All for no reason at all.

Soon he was home again. His own people shunned him. Spanish boys beat him up. The Anglos put him in jail whenever he went to town. Still for no reason. So now with his maimed arm, his slight deafness and his limp, he nursed his hate for everybody and everything.

One Saturday morning Helen met him on the road to the pueblo. He had already begun drinking and his grimy shirt was splotched with vomit. As she walked toward him his face contorted into a grimace of anger. His right hand crept down to his unbuttoned trousers.

"Stop it, Tranquilino!" Helen commanded, resolutely walking up to him. "What is that you would show to the sun in front of me? Is it the manhood you left behind on the trail of war? A warrior so ashamed of his wounds he must show this thing to make children believe he is a man! Ai!"

The look in his eyes was a terrible thing to see, but remorselessly she went on. "Put down that bottle! That is your manhood now. Put it down!"

Tranquilino dropped the half-filled bottle in the weeds. His face was still frozen in a mask of hate, but he turned it away a little with his best ear toward her.

"Your clothes are dirty, Tranquilino. Your breath smells like a coyote's. The flowers, the stones and the mountains, all your old friends hide their faces from you. They do not see their friend. You do not see them. Tranquilino has not come back from the road of war. Listen then to one who has the power to bring him back. Listen, I say!"

His eyes were wild in their red sockets, but he did not move.

"Go to the river. Wash yourself, your clothes, your hair. Wash the whiskey out of your belly too. Then come to me before the sun has gone into his house-mountain. It is the power in me that says it. Go!"

She clapped her hands three times quickly and softly. Then the fourth time loudly, sharply. With a little cry Tranquilino fled in his sloppy boots.

At sunset he came to her pale and weak, his hair and clothes still damp. She had set the table with her best silver and china. There was a chafing dish full of Spanish rice and chicken, a casserole of beans baked in brown sugar, bread and sauce and butter, a small sweet pudding. Tranquilino ate like a famished dog; she could not bear to watch him. When he was through, he looked up at her with shame and fright.

"Good!" she said sharply, taking down the ancient prayer bowl she had found in the cliffs above, and setting it in front of him. "You know it? From the Old Ones it came. It has power. Facundo would not touch it. No hands have touched it but mine. Pick it up."

Tranquilino stood and lifted it with trembling fingers. Into it Helen poured some cornmeal from a paper sack. "See? My fingers have not touched it either. It has been ground with the proper songs and prayers."

The sun was setting. In its last flicker Helen could see a tiny bead of sweat standing out on his forehead.

"Go now. You will sleep, but you will not dream. I will be making medicine for you. When the moon stands high you will awake as I say," she told him. "You will climb up to those cliffs where the Old Ones lived. There, when Our Father Sun comes out standing, you will greet him with pinches of this prayer meal. To him, to all the directions, to the birds of the air, the fish of the waters, to all the children of the earth, you will empty this bowl. You will empty your heart. Then, because your thoughts are right, you will know that they have heard you. They will know that their old friend, Tranquilino, has come back to them again. I say it! Now go!"

Shortly before midnight she awakened stiff with fright. It was as if a vast, imponderable and implacable black sea of evil was rolling toward her, beating against the house. As she sat up in bed trembling, she seemed to see, with eyes other than her own, a figure riding on the crest. It was crouching as if ready to pounce, holding a pottery bowl high for a weapon. It was Tranquilino, eyes blazing with resentment against her.

She fought to stop him with all her strength of will. Still the black wave kept carrying him toward her. She was wide awake and deathly calm now. This was not the way to do it, she realized sud-

145

denly. She was trying to force her will upon him instead of helping him his own way.

Jumping out of bed, Helen lit the lamp and swiftly marked out on the floor with lines of cornmeal the pattern of the four directions. At each corner she molded a little sacred mountain and in it stuck a prayer-feather of eagle-down that Facundo had given her. Through the center of the enclosure she laid with more cornmeal a line of life running from east to west, corresponding to the path of the sun overhead. On this she sat down quietly, head bent.

Almost immediately she felt better, immured within this symbolic pattern of Tranquilino's own world. Her thoughts and feelings cleared. It was as if both of them, Tranquilino and herself, were now embodied within one magnetic thought-field, swept by the same invisible currents of life. Without conscious thought she gave herself to it fully, eyes closed.

How long she sat there, Helen did not know. But when the time came, she got up stiffly, blew out the lamp, and went back to bed.

For a week Helen did not see nor hear anything of Tranquilino. Then one morning on her doorstep she found the old bowl. In it was a small stone. She set them both on top the mantel. Late that night the stone happened to catch her eye. The lamplight brought out for just an instant the face upon it, then vanished as she went to examine it.

Later, when she saw Tranquilino dancing in the pueblo, his maimed arm covered with twigs of spruce, Helen knew he was on the way back. He still got drunk occasionally and fought with his Spanish neighbors, but he had resumed his ceremonial duties. As he passed her on the turn, she smiled and lifted a finger to him in greeting. Tranquilino did not smile back, perhaps because she was sitting with Facundo and the other old men.

The women sitting around them noticed this sign from the Woman at Otowi Crossing to him she had brought back to life with her power. "*Ai. La hechicera. Cómo no?*" they whispered. So her fame kept spreading among those who recognized her growing power.

2.

They were meeting often now. Emily might be reading in the

146

Public Library in Santa Fe when Gaylord came in. A couple of weeks later they occupied adjoining seats in a Spanish movie house. More often Emily would be casting a hook into a lonely stretch of the Rio Grande when Gaylord came strolling along the bank.

"Well, look who's here!"

"Gay! Imagine seeing you!"

They would break out into a peal of laughter. Then they would untangle her line, lie down on a blanket spread under a giant cottonwood, and stare at a sign painted on the bright blue sky: THOU SHALT NOT ESTABLISH OR MAINTAIN SOCIAL RELATIONS WITH RESIDENTS OF NEARBY COMMUNITIES.

"Gay! Can't you ever forget that damned Project for a single minute once a week? That's all we ever have. I won't have it spoiled. I won't!"

She would fling herself upon him with a kiss that called up a mindless desire from depths they had never known in themselves. It frightened them both a little. They would roll apart and lie clasping hands, fighting for breath and calm.

That's the way it always began. An exciting, breathless acknowledgment of the magnetism that drew them together, and then an hour or two of companionship during which they both acted like adolescents. What made these meetings doubly precious, and lent an exciting filip to each rendezvous, was the air of secrecy surrounding them. Neither of them questioned the restrictions that kept them from normal visits together, for they were in a period when it would have been impossible to endure the presence of a third person. But it was Emily who took the initiative in contriving means to circumvent detection. It was a procedure she enjoyed: picking each rendezvous; waiting an hour in nervous anticipation; then, like a spider who had spun her web, pouncing upon him with a voracity that would have swallowed him whole.

Gaylord was sometimes uncomfortably aware of her relentless conspiracies. But did he ever subtly withdraw, or push upon her too fast, she slid away from him like a cake of soap. It was a game to them both: a game they were not aware of playing, whose rules they did not know but which they instinctively obeyed, and of whose outcome each was deathly certain.

They were so alike! It was a delight to learn that they both liked

147

dill pickles, disliked parties, read in bed at night. But gradually they began to be aware of the appalling differences.

One spring day, just after they had met in the gorge below Otowi Crossing, it began to rain. At the first drops Gaylord crowded against the trunk of a cottonwood, gazing apprehensively up through the spreading branches.

"Silly! We can't stay here. It's going to pour!" laughed Emily. Grabbing the lunch basket with one hand, and hitching up the loose skirt of her squaw dress with the other, she started toward the river. A few yards out she stopped. Gaylord, shoes and socks under his arm, was still hesitating on the bank. "The water's not hip high and there's no quicksand. Here!" She went back, thrust the basket at him, and took him by the hand.

Across the river she found a shallow cave. It was wonderful! High and dry, where they could sit and watch the rain unravel in slanting silver threads against the black, basaltic cliffs. Gaylord, however, would not sit down until he was satisfied there were no snakes. Then the ground was too cold. He kept standing, trying to dry his head with a handkerchief lest he catch cold. A little exasperated, Emily darted out for some scraps of driftwood and built a fire at the entrance to the cave.

"But what if the wind changes and blows the smoke in here?" he asked. "Won't it suffocate us or at least smell up our clothes?"

"Why, no," she said calmly. "We can always go out and get soaked." Then she began to laugh. "Really, Gay! You're worse than any tenderfoot I ever saw! Didn't you have a country home or ever get out of the city?"

"No, I didn't," he answered with one of the dry, matter-of-fact statements she was growing used to.

In the next hour Emily learned all the basic facts about his life. That's what they were: basic facts, stripped of all feeling and embroidery. There were no Paters nor Maters in his family. His father had been a mechanic's helper in a small town in upper New York who had met Gay's mother in Brooklyn and settled down. Successively a garage mechanic, a plumber's helper, and a furnace caretaker, he finally had got a job on the Elevated in Manhattan. They lived in one of those horrible brownstone cliffs in the upper East Side eighties that stretch from Central Park to the river. A downstairs flat, with a big trash can standing beside the door, and a sign above it: NO LOITERING. Emily shuddered; his mother was still living there. His father had died soon after Gay had entered college. There was a small pension for his mother, Gaylord added.

"He must have been a fine man to stand up under all those difficulties of finding work," blurted Emily, embarrassed by the stark recital.

"Why?" asked Gaylord. "What else was there for him to do?"

"You must have loved him, Gay!"

"I guess so. But I never admired him or wanted to be like him. He was never methodical enough to be a success at anything nor careless enough to be fun. Just dull—or too tired all the time."

"And your mother—"

She was busy working too; a chocolate dipper in the days when chocolates were dipped by hand. Gaylord used to watch her pour the hot chocolate from the kettle on a cold marble slab, then in a single dexterous movement cover a piece of fondant with a thin coating marked on the top with a scroll to designate its flavor. Now that her trade was outmoded, she was a candy maker in a small shop on upper Broadway. "I'll send for a box sometime," Gaylord said with mild enthusiasm. "They're pretty good. She doesn't use much glucose in their best grade stuff."

"I'm glad you write her regularly," said Emily. "She might be worried about you."

"I do. But I never saw much of her there. I had a pretty stiff course at Columbia—which I liked, and of course I was doing odd jobs like everybody else."

Emily listened to him with an uncomfortable feeling. It was not so much his sparse remarks as the details he left out that worked on her imagination. She could see the whole picture. A dull, tired, inept father who stayed at home with his shoes off all day Sunday, as in the comic pictures of her childhood. A mother who wore her hair in a bun to keep stray hairs out of her chocolate, and who always wore heavy-soled shoes to protect her feet against the cold, stiff, concrete floor. All three of them in a four-room flat, where Gay slept on a couch in the dreary parlor.

For Emily, reared in Pater and Mater Chalmers' fourteen-room house, with a private dormitory room at college, Pater's suite in

New York to occupy at will, and frequent summer trips to Central America, there was nothing romantic nor ennobling about this poverty. It was just plain distressing, middleclass drabness. Gay apparently had not resented it. Cut off from the neighborhood's juvenile gang warfare and boy's games by a studious disposition, he had had no boyhood at all. In high school he was recognized as having an intellect far beyond his age, and encouraged to study still more. At the university he was brilliant; this meant scholarships and laboratory work to pay for his tuition and incidental fees. He had few friends and they all were like himself.

Emily realized exactly what he must have been: one of those studious, shy grinds she had glimpsed on her own campus. Threadbare clothes, straphanging on the subway, the last one out of the library at night, working in the laboratory all day Saturday. No parties, no dates. Not quite sure who won the last football game. Cold leftovers at home, the sixty-five-cent Blue Plate Special at the drugstore counter. But a favorite with all the professors .... Brilliant and unbalanced, knowing everything about graphs, statistics, mathematics, the theory of probabilities, and all abstractions in physics, but hardly knowing that there existed such things as green grass, wild animals and queer birds, a yellow moon, the taste of Scotch whiskey. Why, he'd never even had breakfast at Rumplemayer's or danced at the St. Regis roof!

"I know it was difficult," Emily said sympathetically. "You must have lived with a lot of Jews in that neighborhood too."

"My mother is Jewish," he said somberly, without looking up. "I thought you knew. . . . But how could you? It doesn't show in my name at least. My father wasn't."

A brittle Jewish intellectual? He couldn't be! He looked like a Greek god! "What difference does it make?" Emily said quickly. Gaylord, sitting on the floor of the cave in his gray flannel slacks and checkered sport shirt, betrayed nothing of the inferiority complex demanded by his background. In fact, there was something about Dr. Edmund Gaylord that frightened her a little. Perhaps it was that blunt honesty devoid of all feeling. Or his extraordinarily quick mind.

"Oh Gay!" she said, moving closer and putting her arms around him. "Are you sure you're not getting tired of me? Hold me close

150

then, and don't let's talk. The afternoon's gone already and it'll be a week before I see you again. Please, Gay, kiss me just once more so I won't forget!"

Gaylord was relieved to drive back on the Hill after every rendezvous. There were now more than five thousand people in Los Alamos and more were arriving daily. A far cry from the hundred scientists first estimated as sufficient for the Project! The place was a madhouse of round-the-clock activity punctuated by explosions on South Mesa. The very air seemed imbued with a feverish excitement and driving urgency. Yet behind this facade of haphazard haste he knew the strict organization and orderly procedure that controlled every hour of the day and the movement of each person. No one was allowed here who did not have a job to do; all were bound together into an intangible whole isolated from the confusion and competition of the world below by a barrier of strict secrecy.

Gaylord knew how lucky he was to be one of them. He could not forget how he had been an unknown student devouring hamburgers sandwiched between books, studying the mysteries of unpopular science in order to become a threadbare professor eking out a dignified existence in a jerkwater college. Then suddenly an incomprehensible destiny had transformed him overnight into a veritable young Jupiter upon a New Mexican Olympus. Not for a moment did he fail to appreciate that he had got in on the ground floor of a very good thing. The restrictions of secrecy that at first had cramped and frightened him he now rather enjoyed. They emphasized the preciousness of the knowledge which he shared, making him feel like an initiate in an esoteric cult not to be profaned by the vulgar eyes and ears of the common laity.

A half-mile past the Lodge, Gaylord stopped in front of a long wooden dormitory for single men. His room was on the second floor. The minute he stepped inside, he felt pleased as always at its cramped barrenness. His narrow bed was freshly made. His few clothes were hung up on hangers; shoe trees were in every unused pair. On the small table were neatly laid his slide rule, sharpened pencils, and writing pad before a short row of scientific books. There was nothing unusable, unneeded, or decorative in the room.

Downstairs at the end of the hall he took a quick bath in the shower room. Then he dressed and hurried out to the Tech Area.

151

It lay along the south rim of the mesa; a jumble of gaunt wooden shops and laboratories separated from the living area by a seven-foot-high hurricane fence already flooded by spotlights. A few gates provided the only access, each attended by Security guards who demanded inspection of a second identification badge required to be worn in plain sight by each person inside. The site to which Gaylord went was in the gloomy, narrow canyon below, a large wooden building backed against the fifty-foot rampart of cliffs. A blaze of light outlined the shaggy pines around it, the seamed rock wall behind.

"Hello Gaylord," the Group Leader said as he entered. "Don't you get enough of this place in the daytime without coming back at night?"

"Had a day off and thought I'd better see if the place was still here!" Gaylord replied cheerfully.

"A day off. What's that? You fellows have it mighty soft, anyway. Wish I had nothing to do but push a pencil over paper all day long. I just hope you've got your decimal points in the right place again!"

Gaylord laughed; the reference to decimal points was an old joke among them all. That Spring they had been constructing another "pile," a low power reactor which they familiarly called the "Water Boiler" and for which Dr. Breslau had made the theoretical studies and mathematical calculations. As it had neared completion, the tension increased. The reactor if it worked would be the first to use enriched fuel, one part of the fissionable U-235 isotope to six parts of non-fissionable U-238, instead of ordinary uranium.

The uranium-235 arrived from Oak Ridge, Tennessee. Too precious to be entrusted to ordinary shipment, it had been brought by two special armed couriers, secreted in ordinary scuffed suitcases that held the special gold-plated stainless steel boxes inside.

All was ready for the reactor to become critical. Dr. Breslau assured the crew that his estimates of the amount of fissionable material required and of the correct settings for the control and safety rods were exact.

"We believe you, Doctor!" said one of his colleagues jokingly. "We're willing to set the control rods at the very points you say, and to pour the exact amount of the fissionable solution directly into the reactor—if you'll sit on top of it until it begins to operate."

"Ja!" Dr. Breslau's blue eyes did not twinkle. "My figures are correct. You will see. But we must not set the precedent of ignoring any possibility of human error. No?"

So the reactor was started with extreme caution, the control rods being carefully adjusted and the fuel container being gradually filled. When the critical point was reached, Dr. Breslau was proved correct. The amount of fuel and the control rod settings were exactly as he had foretold.

Now they were finishing construction of the high power unit. A squat cement cube fifteen feet square and eleven feet high surmounted by instrument panels; and in whose working face was the "glory hole," a square tunnel into its critical heart where would be inserted the precious U-235.

It did not look imposing. Gaylord knew it was but a research reactor being built to give his colleagues experience in the operation and control of a chain-reacting asembly; a tool for further work. Yet this Los Alamos Water Boiler would be the first homogenous reactor, the first to use enriched uranium fuel, and the most economical reactor thus far constructed. With the great electrostatic accelerators and cyclotrons around him, those "atom smashers" which could hurl thunderbolts of millions of volts, it gave Gaylord a sense of the great power being harnessed for work. Power undreamed of, power to remake the world in a new image!

Gaylord went home late in the darkness, already eager to be up at work next morning, feeling a sense of guilt for having spent the day with Emily in violation of Security rules. He was in love with her, but at the same time he resented her hold upon him. This conflict between the emotional and rational demands upon him was new to him. It confused and worried him, and he could not determine how to resolve it.

"Why do we have to keep meeting in secret all the time?" Emily had asked at their last meeting.

"You know perfectly well the restrictions I'm under!" he protested.

"But there's no restriction against your coming down to the Tea Room for dinner once in awhile. All the other Xs do. Even Mother has noticed it, vague as she is."

153

There was no answering this common sense. But just the same he felt an apprehension of something he could not name.

3.

One rainy evening Helen opened the kitchen door to his hesitant knock.

"Miss Chalmers, I've come for dinner!" To qualify the boldness of this extraordinary declaration, he broke into an apologetic laugh. "Everybody does. Come here for dinner, I mean!"

"Of course, Dr. Gaylord. How nice of you!" Ignoring his curious bashfulness, Helen helped him take off his slicker, and cut him a hot sliver of the roast. "Emily hasn't showed up yet, but I think you'll like this."

He nodded with a dejected air and sat down at the kitchen table. When Emily still did not come, Helen said forthrightly, "Drat that Emily! I've been hoping she'd come in time to fix a place in my room where you could have dinner by yourselves. You see, all my few tables are reserved long in advance. I can't possibly take anyone who drops by. There's just no place for them to sit down."

Gaylord's mouth sagged; she could not face his disappointment. Fortunately Facundo came in. Helen snapped at him hurriedly. "All right, Facundo. *Ándale!* We can't keep hungry people waiting. Are those two new men still waiting? Good!"

She turned back to Gaylord. "Emily will be coming along sooner or later. You might just as well wait, but there's no use going hungry for her. It's just so happened I've had a cancellation and I'll give the table to you and two young men who each wandered in like yourself if you'll share it. How about it?"

The two men were both Xs. As Helen showed them to their table it was evident to her that Gaylord was casually acquainted with one of them, Emil Salzburg by name. The other one, Klaus Fuchs, was obviously a recent arrival but well thought of, from the slight deference shown him by his table companions.

Busy serving with Facundo, Helen could not help gradually noticing the difference between them and the familiar "regulars" like Dr.

Breslau. These of course were older, mature men; they knew how to relax from the tension of whatever they were doing up on the Hill.

The three younger men were too tense. Gaylord of course was keyed up to seeing Emily walk in the door at any minute and like most young men betrayed his nervousness.

Salzburg ate quietly, head down. Occasionally his olive-colored face would light up, his communicative hands would flash like his black eyes. Then again he would sink deep in introspection. There was a great deal of the artist in Salzburg, she thought; in whatever he did there would be a faint consciousness of how it would appear to others.

"More butter? Of course, Mr. Fuchs! And another hot muffin, they're awfully small . . . Facundo, fill up the baskets. Be sure and put the napkin over them so they'll keep hot."

"You are so kind, Miss Chalmers. And may I compliment you. They are delicious. Everything is!"

Klaus Fuchs was perhaps the most attractive man who had ever entered the Tea Room. Slim, pale, with dark hair and a small round face, his horn-rimmed glasses gave him a studious look without detracting from his charm. His good manners were easy and natural. He was smooth without being suave, friendly without being intimate. Yet in serving him, Helen noticed a trivial peculiarity. He had the habit of absent-mindedly dividing his servings into two portions on his plate: a slice of roast, half of his potato, a few stalks of asparagus to each side.

This peculiarity fascinated her throughout dinner. Salzburg, when she set his slice of chocolate cake in front of him, tasted the icing immediately as a test. Gaylord dug his fork into the bottom layer, saving the frosted top layer for the last like a small boy. But Fuchs, again, neatly divided his piece into two equal halves, pushing each slightly to one side before beginning to eat.

Helen was annoyed at herself for unconsciously spying upon her dinner guests so closely, especially these three nice young men who had not been here for dinner before. Yet it was such little things about her guests who could not talk of their life and work that supplied her only connection with them as persons.

"Ah, Facundo! I have done it again!" growled Dr. Breslau. He crossed his knife and fork on his empty plate, leaned back and scowled. "Don't bring me a bite of dessert!"

The old Indian shuffled noiselessly to the table, his hairless eyebrows lifting as he saw the empty plate. "That good! I eat him!"

"Of course he wants his cake and coffee, Facundo!" remonstrated Helen, fortunately looking around. There was no doubt Facundo would have taken him at his word. The amount of food that fine trencherman could put away was always a joke between him and Facundo. Breslau bantered with extravagant statements. The old Indian, with a more quiet humor, always affected to take them seriously. Helen remembered that when Facundo first began to help her serve, Breslau one evening in mock impatience had exclaimed, "Facundo, don't bother to wait for that old meat to cook in the kitchen! Just lead the horse in here and I'll slice a piece off him!" Facundo had quietly shuffled out of the room. A moment later, while she was still standing and talking to Breslau at his table, they heard the front door open and a strange sound in the hall. Both looked up to see Facundo leading in one of the burros that he sometimes brought for gathering pine knots.

"All right, Facundo," now grumbled Breslau. "If she won't let you eat it for me, I suppose I ought to." He turned toward the table across the aisle. "How was the cake anyway, Mr. Fuchs? What about it, Emil? Gaylord, did you manage to get it down?"

"Yes sir. Very good. We—"

The sentence stuck in Gaylord's throat. Starting to rise, he remained frozen in a cramped posture of ludicrous surprise, and then sank down to stare fixedly before him.

Helen flung around like Breslau to see Emily standing in the doorway. A Red-Riding-Hood shrouded in a transparent, pink raincape, her cheeks glowing from the cold rain, she held her fishing rod in one hand.

Breslau let out a peal of quick-witted laughter. "Our little anthropologist! It is time you returned. The fishing is better here. Yes?"

"No! It isn't!" Her cheeks redder still, Emily held up the end of her line. From it dangled a tiny trout scarcely four inches long.

From every table in the dining room came shouts of good-natured laughter.

"Thank you, everybody!" Emily indignantly flounced down the hall into the kitchen.

Still laughing, Helen tried to restore order. "Dr. Gaylord, will you be so kind as to go out and take that poor little thing off the hook for my daughter? Now Facundo, get Dr. Breslau's cake before you forget it. And hot coffee for everybody."

"Hey, Gaylord!" Breslau's shout stopped him a moment at the door. "Be sure and tell Miss Emily to put that fish on ice until tomorrow. I'll have a filet off it for dinner!"

The incident at least had got Gaylord out into the kitchen with Emily, thought Helen. They were still there when all the guests departed, and she and Facundo had cleared the tables. Emily had helped herself to some dinner and had given Gaylord more cake and coffee to keep her company.

"It's my second piece, Miss Chalmers. I hope you don't mind," he said quietly.

"For goodness sake, Dr. Gaylord! Make yourself at home!"

"Him in there have two!" recalled Facundo, still impressed by the way Dr. Breslau's appetite had belied his words.

Helen laughed. "He always has two pieces when it's chocolate. Never mind, Facundo. I put away a big piece in the cupboard for you with lots of icing. Sit down and eat it." Wearily she made herself a cup of tea and sat down. There was nothing shy about Gaylord now. He was friendly and relaxed. He and Emily even helped Facundo with the dishes. Then leaving him to scrub the pots and pans, the three of them went into her room for a while.

This was the first time Helen had visited with Gaylord, and she was impressed by him. He knew where he was going. Yet the feeling struck her that even as a small boy he had never been able to wring joy and fun out of a vacation day for anxiously preparing for the school day ahead. He still could not live today for anticipating tomorrow, a preoccupation with the future that was an occupational disease afflicting most ambitious men.

Resolutely she dismissed the thought. Always these windows opening upon people's characters as if enticing her to follow their lives, forgetting her own! The ache in her arm and shoulder recalled her own limitations; she was glad when Gaylord and Emily left.

Facundo came in before going out to his hut. His dark face was somber. "Mebbe you go bed now. Too much talkin'."

A tingle of comforting surprise shot through her. In her absorption with other people's problems she had forgotten there might be someone who could divine her own.

4.

His name was Kaminsky, Karenski—something like that. He was a frail little man who looked rather seedy in his shiny coat and frayed sleeves, and his tiny bookshop was somewhere down on lower Third Avenue in New York. He specialized in books on mysticism and the occult: Vedanta, esoteric Buddhism and Yoga; Plotinus, Jacob Boehme, Meister Eckhart, William Blake; books on crystal gazing, the Tarot cards, numerology and astrology; Blavatsky, Ouspensky and Guerdjieff;—everything old and new, spurious and authentic. A long shelf above him was filled with books about the Woman at Otowi Crossing.

"Yes," he began, "the demand for them keeps growing. I thought it was the usual new fad when the first ones came out. But when my regular customers kept coming back for more I knew there was something worth looking into. . . . You know the people I mean. A lady whose chauffeur drives her down from Park Avenue, a bricklayer up in the Bronx, men and women in all walks of life, from everywhere in the world—my mailing list goes to seventeen countries, you know. All forming without knowing each other a kind of secret brotherhood. They know that this dark age of materialism is in such an advanced stage of decadence it can't last much longer before the boards are cleared for the new age."

He stopped to polish his glasses with a dirty handkerchief. "Of course we don't have her own authentic message yet; her *Secret Journal* has never been released. Still it's surprising how much of her is coming through." He flipped his handkerchief toward the shelf. "A revealing remark here, an illuminating incident there, as if everything she said and did made an effect upon someone. And when you put them all together, they make a piece. Yes, there's no doubt about it. She had it all right, a glimpse of the universal whole.

158

"What a spot she was in to receive it! At the birthplace of the oldest civilization in America and the newest. Probably in no other area in the world were juxtaposed so closely the Indian drum and the atom-smasher, all the values of the prehistoric past and the atomic future. A lonely woman in a remote spot with few friends, she felt herself at the hub of time."

He paused to take down a book and thumb through its pages. " 'Every moment, every incident contains all the seeds of the past and of the future,' " he read slowly. "That's our key to the Woman of Otowi Crossing. Her apperception of each moment of time as a capsule of eternity. It's amazing how often the past was laid open to her—as on that day she found an ancient pottery bowl. I prefer myself those revealing precognitions of the future. Especially that miraculous Mushroom Incident! It started her talking to others about her experience for the first time. It was the beginning of her fame. And of course it led to that F. B. I. investigation which was hushed up so quickly.

"Perhaps only I know why. The agent who was sent to interview her holds a responsible position with the Security force over at the United Nations now. A well-dressed, inconspicuous man you'd never notice except for a small feather he wears in the band of his Homburg. He came in here the other day. In fact, he comes quite often. . . . Yes, he's one of them, you might say. He said talking with her was the greatest experience he's ever had. A strange coincidence, perhaps. . . . Yet I prefer to believe that is only the word we use to designate those inexplicable moves by which an irrevocable destiny achieves its appointed ends."

A cold fall rain had begun outside; one could hear the whoosh of tires on the pavement, the empty shop was so quiet. Mr. Kaminsky hitched his chair closer . . .

That summer was proving too much for Helen. The heat, the unrelenting task of feeding the Xs every night, her loss of weight, and the pain in her shoulder and arm—these worried her as only physical shortcomings. It was simply that her slender, nervous body, like a candle, was burning with too intense a flame. Impulsively she closed the Tea Room for a week.

Turner had just returned. Helen insisted that he and Facundo take her on a camping trip. They didn't go too far, for they travelled behind Facundo's scrawny team in the old box wagon filled with equipment and supplies. But it was lovely, just as she had known it would be. A quiet spot downriver. A small valley threaded by a narrow stream rushing down from the mountains. The still, tepid, brown Rio Grande below. The cool, blue pine forest above.

The first night Helen slept in a little pup tent before a fire to keep away stray mosquitos. Turner slept silently outside in his bedroll. On the other side of the fire snored Facundo. The next night Helen moved outside with them so she could see the stars and the new moon shining over the pine tips.

"Facundo!" she protested almost as soon as she was settled. "Stop that awful snoring!"

The old Indian, tightly wrapped in his blanket as a tamale, went on snoring. Helen moved her bedroll to the other side of the fire near Turner. "I just can't stand the screech of that rusty buck-saw cutting through a pine knot," she said goodnaturedly. "Besides, it's scared away the rabbit."

Turner rolled over. "Rabbit? This time of night?"

"The rabbit standing on the new moon, I mean! Remember the decorative motif of the old Fred Harvey demi-tasse saucers? Emily says it came from the fifth sign of the Aztec calendar. She saw it in the Codex Borgia. So every new moon I always look for the rabbit and I never see one. What do you think's happened to it?"

"I don't think anything!" Turner zipped out of his bedroll and yanked it farther away. "All this crazy talk keeps me from sleeping more than Facundo's snoring!"

Turner's bark was worse than his bite; he was just trying to show his independence of her. He had come back looking a little older, with some new lines in his face and splotches of gray on his temples. He'd had a difficult time, she knew, since they had parted. But he had won through. He was so gentle, so kind; his whole manner showed not a touch of the bitterness that would have tinged the character of a lesser man. She was proud of him.

From then on they all slept apart, three spokes of a wheel evenly radiating from a glowing hub. Facundo kept busy all day long— cutting wood, trailing his hobbled horses, splicing their old harness with buckskin thongs, picking whiskers from his chin with a rusty pair of pliers. When he fished it was in the little stream above, in the cold still trout pool where the deer drank deep at dawn. Indian fashion: lying down on the bank above a still pool, and lowering into it a loop of fine horse-hair. Then, after an hour's wait perhaps, dexterously flipping up a snared trout. Only Facundo could have such patience.

Turner fished in the river below. A broad shouldered dwarf cut off at the thighs by the brown flood; casting his Royal Coachman or Rio Grande Special, reeling his line back, casting again. His inexhaustible energy tired her to watch him.

With delicious abandon, Helen gave herself to every mood. Early mornings she climbed into the pine slopes hunting columbines and mariposa lilies. At high noon she bathed in a quiet pool, dried shiveringly on a flat rock. The afternoons were no good, really; they never were in New Mexico. The white, glaring light removed all color from the land; shapes were sharply outlined without perspective; everything went stale. Helen felt her mind and emotions go dead; life coagulated within her. There was nothing to do but give in to the sun. She stretched out naked, with closed eyes. Little by little now she could feel the radiant power penetrating and diffusing within her. Facundo was right. The Sun-Father was the noumenal source of all the earth's energy; nothing could exist without his invisible radiation. Day by day as her skin grew brown, she could feel the ache ebbing from her shoulder and arm, and a new strength and life rising within her. But the sun made her drowsy; she knew when she had enough, and crawled into the shade to sleep.

Late afternoon she awoke a different woman. It had been so good to be alone and lazy all day; now she wanted company and talk. One of the horses had broken its hobble. She helped Facundo to catch it. Then she went down to the river. Color had come back to the bold escarpment in glowing red and glossy black. The river was tawny silk. Turner, through fishing for the day, had stripped and was noisily splashing in the rapids. She slid down the bank just as he came wading out, ludicrously holding his right hand in front of his crotch.

"Jack Turner!" she accused him with laughing eyes. "I can't believe it! *You* ashamed of having *me* see you naked! Of all things!"

He laughed low and easily without self-consciousness as he pulled

161

on his shorts. "Well, I'll tell you," he said. "When I was a kid and first started to go swimming with the boys from the pueblo, I noticed that when they came out of the water every blasted one of them held his hand in front of his penis. I thought it was the funniest thing I ever saw! Indian kids being shy and ashamed when we were out there all alone!" He paused to dry his mop of hair.

"Then one day when we all came romping out of the water, I saw an old fellow like Facundo sitting on the bank. Just as wrinkled and dark, maybe even older. Fact is, he was the Cacique. He called me over. 'White boy better learn purty quick,' he said. 'Him cover up himself so Sun don't see. That power it come from Sun. Boy better learn not to brag of his power or Sun take it back!' " Turner grinned. "Funny how a kid picks up little things like that. I reckon I just got into the habit without noticin' it."

The quick warmth of a truth reaffirmed shot through her. "It's true! These Indians know!" She stopped and looked at him squarely. "We can talk about things now, can't we, about us?"

"Why sure, Helen. What's troubling you?" His clear eyes showed no hurt nor resentment.

"Nothing's troubling me. Something just popped into my mind I want to say. You remember that moonlight night when we first went swimming together—and went to bed togethe afterward for the first time too? And how wonderful it was, the evening and the night and the next morning!" She knelt and slowly took off her shoes and stockings. When she stood up again her eyes were wet and shiny. "I just wanted you to know that having sex and going swimming were the best things we had together. Oh, we're here on this little earth of ours such a short time! Things happen, there's no planning, and the time flies and then we're gone. . . . That's what I mean!"

She stood quietly facing him, her hand resting lightly on his wet brown arm. "Someday I'll write you all I want to say. But promise me something now, will you?"

He nodded.

"That when I die, no matter what you think of me then, you'll remember that I didn't want to be different!"

"Hell, this talk of dying is morbid! Come on!"

It was over—this sudden gust of deathly seriousness that chilled both their hearts. She hitched up her skirt to the thighs and stepped into the river. "Oh, I want so much to go swimming, but I just don't feel up to it," she called plaintively. "Come on, I'll go wading with you instead. Is the current strong?"

He looked somberly at her thin, emaciated legs, then waded out and took her firmly by the hand. The water foamed around their legs, splashed back from a rock in a fine mist; the strong current sucked the sand from under their feet so fast Helen could hardly stand. Abruptly Turner picked her up and carried her back to the bank.

It had been so long since she had seen him! There was so much to talk about: Emily, Gaylord, Facundo, friends in town and at the pueblo, his work, where he had been and why. . . . The late afternoons were not long enough. Wound up like a clock after the day's restful aloneness, she talked while cooking Facundo's and Turner's hearty supper, and seldom ran down till they were in their bedrolls. How wonderful every day was! She had forgotten the Tea Room, the Xs, the chores of everyday life, even the war. Even Facundo's persistent snoring echoed in sleep the inaudible and invincible pulse of the earth beneath her.

Early on the morning of the day they returned home, Helen took Turner on her walk. At the entrance to a narrow box canyon they came upon a growth of tiny wild mushrooms in a tangle of rotting logs. She knelt before them with a little cry of delight.

"Don't pick any," cautioned Turner. "They might be toadstools instead of mushrooms."

"There's no difference! It's just an old wives' belief that the edible ones are mushrooms and the poisonous ones are toadstools, and that mushrooms are converted into toadstools when a venemous snake breathes upon them. Almost all of them are good to eat—horse mushrooms, meadow mushrooms, all kinds." Helen picked one and held it up. "But if you ever see one with a little frill around the upper part of the stem—about here—and a bag at the bottom of the stem, look out! It's a Destroying Angel—the *Amanita Virosa*—the most poisonous mushroom known. But so beautiful! Tall and stately, with the satiny whiteness of absolute innocence."

"*Amanita Virosa*," muttered Turner. "The devil with them all! To me they're all putrid excrescences! Parasites living on other plants and dead matter, manure! They're abnormal! They give me the creeps!"

His vehement abhorrence amazed Helen. She suddenly realized that he, as whole races of people throughout the world, was a mycophobe—one who instinctively feared these fungal growths. Helen herself was a mycophile who had always known and loved them, as had all Indian America. There was really something strange about them to have caused this great cleavage between peoples. So many of her rational Anglo neighbors hated them. Yet something about their naked, pale, curious shapes, their earthy smell and musty charred taste, made the Spanish folk and Indians about her ascribe to them an attribute of the mysterious, as had the Aztecs and Mayas long before them. "They got power," Facundo had told her once, but would say no more.

Whatever their strange properties, thought Helen as she walked along in silence, their shapes were repeated by tall rocky buttes and mesas everywhere. Soft sandstone stems eroded away from their hard basaltic caps and softly rounded mesa tops, they stood against the sky like huge mushrooms of bare rock, a primordial motif of this weird and ancient America.

Helen paused suddenly near the upper end of the canyon where the walls narrowed. Before her on the meadow was a large circle of mushrooms. Begun years ago when the spores of a fungus had started the growth of a spawn mycelium, it had spread outward year after year until it now embraced the width of the little valley.

"A Fairy Ring! Jack, look! Have you ever seen one this big before?"

Utterly charmed, Helen jumped into the magic circle and was skipping across the meadow when she was brought up sharply with repulsion and amazement. At the far edge of the ring stood the most monstrous mushroom she had ever seen. The fungus stood nearly two feet high, its cap more than a foot in diameter. Its coarse skin was turning a putrid yellow, splotched with brown; withered gills hung down from the underside of the cap. Bloated, aged, and repulsive, the thing gave Helen a feeling of such overwhelming malignancy that that she stood staring at it as if hypnotized.

Turner, a few steps behind her, let out a snort of disgust. He passed her in a flash, running toward it with measured strides. She saw him reach the edge of the clearing, all his weight and momentum thrust forward as he pivoted on his left leg like a football player about to make a drop kick. She saw his right leg go back, his heavy boot swing forward in an arc—and hang there as if fixed in a time whose movement had suddenly ceased.

"Don't! Jack! Oh no!" she screamed, clenching both hands at her breast.

At that instant it happened. With all the minutely registered detail of a slow-motion camera, and in a preternatural silence, she saw the huge and ugly mushroom cap rise slowly in the air. Unfolding gently apart, its torn and crumpled blades opening like the gills of a fish, the fragmented pieces revolved as if in a slow boil revealing a glimpse of chlorine yellow, a splotch of brown and delicate pink. Deliberately it rose straight into the air above the walls of the canyon, its amorphous parts ballooning into a huge mass of porous gray. The stem below seemed to rise to rejoin it; then, shattered and splintered, it settled slowly back to earth.

Not until then, strangely enough, did Helen's sensory consciousness record the impact of Turner's boot tip when he had kicked it apart. She felt rather than heard the slight thud; the slushy rent of senile, decayed tissue; the sharp, suction-like plop when the cap was torn from its stem. The sudden disturbance, still in slow-motion, travelled toward her in a vibratory wave through the earth, shot up her legs and seemed to tap her sharply behind her knees.

When she straightened, the cancerous gray cap was still rising and expanding like a mushroom-shaped cloud in the sky. As she watched, an upper current of air pulled it slightly apart.

Now again she screamed. Crouching down in terror, she vainly covered her head with her arms against the rain of its malignant spores. Countless millions, billions of spores invisibly small as bacteria radiated down around her. They whitened the blades of grass, shrivelled the pine needles, contaminated the clear stream, sank into the earth. Nor was this the end of the destruction and death they spread. For this malignant downport of spores was also a rain of venemous sperm which rooted itself in still living seed cells to distort and pervert their natural, inherent life forms. There was no escape, now nor ever, save by the miracle of a touch.

165

Abruptly she felt it upon her. It was Turner, lifting her to her feet.

"Helen! For God's sake! What's happened?"

It was over. The meadow, the far pines, the canyon walls and clear blue sky rushed back into focus. Time released the natural flow of movement. The chirp of a bird broke the preternatural silence.

Helen shuddered, wiping her damp face. "I—I don't know exactly what happened. It was just like a bad dream, a nightmare, that hit me suddenly for a few seconds. That's all. It's gone."

"Are you sure you're all right?"

"Quite, Jack. But just go off for a half-hour. Take a dip in the stream or something. I want to stretch out and relax."

He looked at her with a worried frown. "I don't want to be nosey, Helen. But I don't want to worry about you."

"Don't!" she said as lightly as she could, and with a smile. "There is nothing wrong with me. Really!"

No! Stretched out in the sun, feeling its radiant warmth and life, she kept telling herself there was nothing wrong with her, with mushrooms, the whole world.

5.

Just the same, the vision or fantasy ended Helen's long period of tranquility. If such a thing had happened within her, it must in some way, sometime, happen in the world outside, she told her few friends.

Gossip travelled fast in that news-hungry area, and the result of the incident soon reached Turner in a roundabout way. Shortly after returning to La Oreja, he had received a letter from the American Newswire Service. His columns were good but their field was restricted. Why not enlarge his coverage to current economic and political developments in a column for ANS? They also might work out something in the way of special feature assignments if he were interested.

In the newspaper game it was something to be a by-line reporter for a national wire service like ANS; better yet to have a regular column. The offer was too good to refuse. So Turner had obtained a release from Greenleaf, flown to New York, and committed himself to a troublesome future on a very nice contract indeed. Stopping at Otowi Crossing on his way back home, he told Helen the good news.

"What are you going to cover here, Jack?"

"I'm going to break the news about that damned Project on the Hill! All its secrecy, code names and aliases—this cloak-and-dagger stuff is silly!"

Helen knew that at first he had felt the frustration of a small boy fenced out of a World Series game without a single knothole to peek through. Then she had watched his resentment increase through the proprietory interest in the area he felt, like most people in the valley. He had picnicked, fished, shot wild turkey on Los Alamos Mesa. Now his old camping spots had been closed off and his curiosity was denied the right of knowing why.

"No, Goddamn it! This is America's war, the whole Free World's war. What right has the Project to adopt the high-handed methods of totalitarian countries? It's high time for somebody to squeeze behind the curtain and break the story of what's going on up there!"

A shiver of apprehension shook Helen. "But be careful, Jack. Don't let it blow up in your face."

"Like your mushroom did?" He laughed heartlessly. "Don't worry! It's facts I'm chasing, not fancies!"

There were few to find. Luis couldn't tell him anything. Every morning a truck picked him up at the pueblo and took him to the Hill. He worked on a road gang. It was hard work; they were always in a hurry. But every so often there would be a big bang, and he would look up from his pick to see a little puff of cloud rising across the canyon. That was all he knew.

Maria told him how the bus carried her back and forth. Free! Nobody paid nothing for that nice ride! She worked as a maid. Alone in the house with the radio playing. Music all day! Imagine that! But she didn't work for anybody in particular. That wasn't allowed. The bus stopped at that place where every maid was given her assignment, and the next day she was sent somewhere else.

Turner was aghast. The place was so damned secret that even

an Indian housemaid was hired by the Manhattan Engineering Project and assigned the home she was to work in for the day! Big bangs. Many peoples . . . That was all he found out.

Scarcely a week later he got a lead when he turned on the radio just in time to hear a commentator ending a newscast story on Los Alamos. Apparently the statement had been written for him by a conscientous objector who knew a man at Illinois Tech whose roommate worked on the Project. The radio commentator's name was George Dale. Turner immediately wired the network for a transcript of the full broadcast.

Exactly what beans had been spilled about the Project Turner was not sure: something about a new explosive force derived from the atom or something. Knowing nothing about an atom, Turner drove to the public library in Santa Fe and plagued the librarian for literature on the subject. The books were too technical to understand but an early article speculated on the possibility of unlocking an atomic force greater than any power yet known.

Elated with this little information, Turner had a drink and a chat with the bartender in La Fonda, and hurried home to bang out on his typewriter a background piece which he mailed to New York that night:

> Of two things only are we sure about Project Y, the hush-hush scientific outpost hidden on a high mesa north of Santa Fe in the mountains of northern New Mexico.
>
> Many peoples. Big bangs.
>
> It is a top-secret installation overflowing with people, but each person, even an Indian housemaid, is carefully cleared into the area. Not even a construction worker knows the purpose of the big bangs that take place on Thursdays at "Project Why."
>
> Still, one might venture a conjecture . . .

Two mornings later at breakfast Turner was interrupted by a pleasant but firm individual who identified himself as an F. B. I. agent. What he had to ask was brief and specific. For what reason had Turner been making a study of a specific subject of scientific research? Just why had he discussed the activities of a classified Government project in a public place? Turner felt a chill run up

168

his spine; the only persons he had talked with were the librarian and the bartender at La Fonda.

"Now I must ask you pointedly, Mr. Turner, what is your connection with the Miss Helen Chalmers who operates the tea room at Otowi Crossing? What information have you elicited from her regarding the Project and its personnel?"

"Goddamn it! Leave her out of this!" protested Turner. "I've never discussed anything about her customers with her, ever!" He jumped up and thrust a carbon copy of his piece in the agent's hands. "Here. I sent it off yesterday. It doesn't say a thing!"

The unpleasant interview was followed by a wire from ANS ordering him back again, this time with a plane priority. When he arrived in New York it was to find that his chief, McAndrews, had been caught in a squeeze. An Army G-2 officer upon hearing the Dale broadcast had notified the Manhattan Engineer District. Consequently the broadcasting company had turned over Turner's request for the transcription to the F. B. I. without answering. Almost concurrently the Albuquerque F. B. I. office had notified the New York office of its interview with Turner, advising that his article had been sent to ANS. So here they were, a half-dozen men beating the bushes about a remote mesa in far-off New Mexico.

"I'll be frank with you," the impeccably dressed Scotchman said at last. "We consider ourselves fortunate in having found Mr. Turner to cover such a remote but evidently significant area. I agree that he has been too diligent in this case—not knowing, of course, what he was running into. But I think we can all trust to his discretion in the future. Can't we, Jack? We never allow our valid interest in news of any kind to conflict with our country's best interests. You may rest assured of that."

As McAndrews accompanied his visitors to the door, Turner walked to the window and stared down miserably into the steel and concrete canyons far below.

"Well, it's been a boon-doggle!" he said abruptly when McAndrews came back. "Now if you want to draw a cancellation of my contract I'll sign it."

"You're quitting already?" asked his Chief quietly. Then he laughed. Turner turned around. McAndrews had changed. He was no longer an impeccably dressed, urbane executive. He was a down-at-the-heels reporter with a sharp nose, a native Scotch shrewdness, and indomitable stubbornness, who had fought his way up from the streets to his present eminence.

"Something's going on out there in your neck of the woods, Jack, that's going to hit every front page in the country. I can smell it from here! ANS is going to break that story when it's ready. Keep an eye on it. Just don't get into trouble. That's all."

Turner stiffened. That reportorial instinct which nothing could quench! It had bred a strange fraternity of men with a loyalty to a creed that no one else understood.

"O.K.," grinned Turner. "I'm not fired then! But if you hear of anything about to break on it, give me the chance, will you?"

"That's what you're there for," said McAndrews. "But if I were you, I'd steer clear of that woman's tea room at the bottom of the Hill."

Wondering how Helen had happened to be involved, Turner stopped off at the Crossing on his way back home. Emily was there, angrily asking her the same question.

"You must have said something to somebody, Mother! Gay told me that he had been questioned about coming down here to dinner and what he talked about. Very nicely, of course, for they know he never talks about his work."

"I've never said anything about any of the Xs or what they talk about here!" protested Helen. "I only mentioned that mushroom thing."

"I told Gay about that," went on Emily. "He wouldn't discuss it. But he won't be coming down here very often, I'll tell you that!"

"What are you worried about?" asked Helen. "Nice Dr. Breslau telephoned me that customary questioning of some Project members was going on—where they dined off the Hill and all that. But not to worry if an F. B. I. agent happened to stop by for a talk with me, too. Just be completely honest."

"Did one come?" Turner asked sharply.

"You mean that nice man in a very neat gray suit? Oh yes," she said in a vague, innocent manner that annoyed Turner. "He ate three pieces of berry pie and we had a lovely talk."

"That was him all right!"

"I had a good feeling about him immediately," went on Helen.

170

"We talked about the tremendous life energy locked up within all matter, within ourselves. He agreed that it should be such a boon to mankind if it could be released."

"Mother!" cried Emily. "Why did you have to force all that on a perfect stranger—on an F. B. I. agent of all persons?"

"Because he understood perfectly that the inner and outer universes of man are synonymous; and that whatever happens subjectively in one happens objectively in the other. Of course he said he didn't quite understand how I knew its approach was so imminent from merely feeling it in the air. That is, until I described to him that mushroom thing. It made him most thoughtful, I must say. For the first time he took out a little notebook and wrote down all the details as I remembered them. Finally he got up, telling me that few people understood these things, and suggested it might be best not to talk about them.

"As he left, I noticed a feather that had fallen just outside the door while we were talking. It was from the wing tip of one of those small hawks which shoot up so straight and fast into the sky. 'Sun hawks' the Indians call them. It was such a good omen I gave it to him to put in his hat band. He was afraid it would fall out, and asked me if I would mind fastening it with a few stitches of thread. It was while I was doing this he ate his third piece of berry pie."

Turner shrugged helpfessly. What trouble would her obsession cause next?

6.

Early that fall Maria, on her day off, brought her baby over to the Crossing. A cute little thing with big black eyes and plump brown cheeks, he was crawling around in the afternoon sun while Helen and Maria watched from the kitchen door.

A car drove up. From it stepped a young man and an older one impeccably dressed and wearing a Homburg hat. Helen caught a glimpse of his pallid white face and frozen features as he suddenly stopped. The baby had fallen in front of him and was spread out wailing. The man knelt, picked the child up with a tender hug, and set him on his knee. The younger man, annoyed at the interruption, called sharply, "Mr. Throckmorton! Please!"

Throckmorton! So this was he, thought Helen who had never seen him before. His porcelain face had broken into a smile. He was chuckling and bouncing the baby up and down. This was not the caricature that Turner had described. This was a warm and lonely man, repressed and terrified at what his world had done to him. A childless man who loved children because he was a little childish too. And one who wanted only to treat all others with the same magnanimous paternalism with which he was now stuffing pennies into the baby's little mocassins.

"Mr. Throckmorton!" his companion called again sharply.

Throckmorton put down the child carefully and stood up, adjusting his hat and tie. His face froze again into its usual immobility. He walked up to them sedately.

"Miss Helen Chalmers, I take it," the young man said glibly. "I'm Milton P. Jasper, lately public relations consultant for the Sunshine Empire Tourist Agency, now directing the campaign for Mr. Throckmorton here."

"A darling baby! I could see she liked you immediately, Mr. Throckmorton. Won't you both come in?"

Throckmorton smiled at her. Sitting down at the kitchen table with Jasper, he cleared his throat. "Ahem! Miss Chalmers. As you know, I am endeavoring to be elected by my constituency as State Senator. Perhaps you can help me."

Helen could see the effort it cost him to speak. But having officially opened the subject, he had done his part and now looked helplessly at Jasper.

Jasper rubbed his hands together, leaned forward. "Let me speak plainly, Miss Chalmers. We can't afford to be formal in politics. Here's the deal. All the cards on the table. Throcky here is doing all right. But he's got to cinch the vote in our remote provinces. That's where you come in."

"Perhaps not, Mr. Jasper," Helen said quietly. "I have no interest in politics whatever. But I do want you to taste the cookies I made this noon. Some hot coffee too?"

"I'm not accustomed to coffee at this hour, Miss Chalmers," protested Throckmorton.

"Milk then for you, and coffee for Mr. Jasper." Helen served them and sat down again.

Jasper wolfed down his cookies, took a sip of coffee. "Yes, that's where you come in, Miss Chalmers. The news is going around that you're a real witch and seer—able to see the future and all that. So you take a day off and go to one village and then another. You don't say a word about politics, you don't do a thing. But when people drop in for a peek at the future, why you can see it plain as the nose on your face! You can see Throcky in office and everybody who voted for him riding to a big factory in a new automobile. How about that?"

"Precisely!" said Throckmorton.

Helen looked at him without answering. A new light was shining in his eyes. He was the same man she had seen a few moments before, but he was looking at a different image of himself cast by his same compulsive need.

Jasper was double-talking now. "You might drop a good word to anybody who stops in here, too. Every vote you swing is worth a dollar to us if Throcky here is elected, Miss Chalmers. That's how practical politics is nowadays." Letting this sink in, he added quickly, "Of course we can't pay you! We wouldn't even suggest it! But still, as a token of our appreciation, Throcky I know would—well, install a new gas stove for you, put in a big refrigerator, straighten you up a bit here."

"Exactly!" murmured Mr. Throckmorton. "For helping me to help the people."

"Listen!" Helen said, tilting up one ear. "You can hear the trumpeting and thrashing of a hundred wild elephants, the braying and crashing of a thousand burros. But their sound isn't as loud as the voice of a single blade of grass they trample underfoot."

Throckmorton squirmed uneasily. But Jasper leaned back and gave his thigh a resounding whack. "Talk about political double-talking! Jesus, Throcky, don't you savvy that parable or whatnot of hers? Those elephants are Republicans and the burros are Democrats! Miss Chalmers, don't ever let anybody tell you you're a starry-eyed dreamer! You've got the wit of a born *politico*!"

She stood up, prim and stiff. "I've told you I cannot participate in politics in any way whatever. Is that plain?"

"Just so." Throckmorton looked sad as he walked to the door. But outside Jasper cheerfully took his camera out of its case. "Well anyway you don't mind if I take a snap of you, do you? Here, stand next to Throcky."

"Why not? Let me take your arm, Mr. Throckmorton."

He brightened up immediately, warm and lonely man that he was. Yet as the two men walked off to their car, she could not help calling out, "Watch your step, Mr. Throckmorton, or the grass will trip you!"

He lifted his feet quickly. Jasper looked down and let out a puzzled laugh. They were on the gravelled driveway; there wasn't a blade of grass in sight.

Turner was covering Throckmorton's campaign for ANS which thought it might have a significant bearing on the development of the secret project at Los Alamos. It seemed at once frightening and ludicrously funny. Fastidious, reactionary, wealthy Cyril Throckmorton III of Philadelphia, a Protestant Anglo, was making his pitch to poor Catholic-Spanish country people on a platform of industrialization. There had never been a railroad in the whole region. There were no coal deposits, no water for power plants, no other natural resources; no reason nor means of developing the area industrially. Yet to every poor *paisano* in his corn *milpa* Throckmorton was holding out the dream of great smoking factories to which he could drive to work in a shiny new *máquina* for a weekly wage exceeding his present yearly pittance.

Throckmorton, in short, was not only militantly rousing all the religious, racial, and economic issues to which the region was prone; he had hit upon the exact note to which the ears of a people exploited for centuries were attuned.

New Mexico politics, as Turner knew, were probably the most devious of any state in the country, and in these upriver counties they were the worst. The poor Spanish people, isolated and remote, had existed in a peonage system from earliest times. First as actual peons under the whip of Spanish grandees and rich *hacendados*, then succumbing under American domination to the reign of *politicos* who exploited their racial inferiority to combat the ever encroaching Anglo aggressiveness. Each little village had its *jefe politico*. He

174

bought votes, helped the people to mark their crosses on their ballots, distributed patronage. It was an economic system rather than a political system, really. A hot-blooded Democrat might stick a neighbor Republican with his knife, but next year he was a Republican and just as rabid. Politics was only an exciting game played with Spanish pride and fervor.

This was different. For the first time an Anglo—a *rico* and publisher of *El Porvenir*—was endeavoring to give them equal wealth. *Madre de Dios! Que hombre!* When had it happened before?

The morning came when Turner was almost blown out of the house by a loud basso voice shrieking, "*Viva El Tercero!*" He ran out into the patio, looked over the wall. Across the road stood a sound truck grinding out full blast the strains of *La Cucaracha*. From adobe huts and fields people came running to crowd around this wonderful *máquina de música*. When the record ran out, the loud basso resumed it shout of "*Viva! El Tercero! Vota Vd. para El Tercero!*," following it with a long political spiel.

Its force and aptness struck Turner as unbelievably funny.

"Cyril Throckmorton III" was painted all over the sound truck, as for days it had emblazoned every handout and advertisement. Of course no Spanish tongue could achieve such a name as "Cyril Throckmorton," but the "III" had caught the people's eyes, ears, and fancy. "*El Tercero*," The Third! *Si! Cómo no?* And as the wheeling *máquina de música* shrieked across milpas and mesas, Cyril Throckmorton III, Champion of the People, became to everyone El Tercero. Just like Il Deuce, thought Turner. A little back-pasture Fuehrer on the make!

Even this did not prepare him for what he saw in the front window of *El Porvenir* one afternoon as he was walking by. No! It couldn't be! But it was. An enlarged photograph of Throckmorton and Helen Chalmers standing arm in arm. It was the only thing in the window and it had no caption. But it was enough.

Throckmorton's campaign was doing well enough, but he needed a gimmick; something or someone to help him cinch the vote. This was it. Indians held a respect for Helen that bordered on awe. Spanish villagers kept endowing her with unusual powers. Even Anglos were now talking about her. Much as Turner hated to admit it, she was beginning to exert an influence. In politics now? To put Throckmorton in office?

175

Turner's face flushed with anger. Didn't she know that this mere photograph of them together gave her tacit approval of Throckmorton? And if she hadn't permitted it . . . No, by God! It was too much!

He strode inside, jerked the photograph out of the window, tore it in pieces, and flung them on the floor. "Don't ever let me see a photo like that again!" he shouted, almost incoherent with rage. "You keep her out of his dirty rotten campaign! Or by God—" Unable to finish, he shook his fist and burst out of the room.

His outburst did no good. On election night he and his photographer went with a gathering crowd to the Throckmorton house in the fashionable suburb of Carson. Spanish style, it sat back from an immense courtyard jammed with Spanish laborers, farmers, and villagers from miles around. There they stood, gazing fixedly and silently as if at a sacred shrine, waiting for a miracle to manifest itself to their patient faith. A tingle ran up Turner's spine as suddenly, instantly, the whole packed mass erupted into wild shouts and cheers of frenzied acclaim.

El Tercero had stepped out upon the portál. He was dressed in the charro costume of a Spanish *ranchero* of the Colonial period: tight fitting riding trousers and short leather vest, both heavily embroidered and decorated with silver. He stood straight and silent as if oblivious of the tumultous roar that kept up unceasing, minute after minute. El Tercero, Spanish grandee, benevolent dictator, protector of the poor: the undying image of a master still stamped upon their hearts.

Graciously he took off his sombrero, held it at his breast. The roar died to gasping silence. "Come in, my good friends, and drink a glass of wine with me."

With a shout, the crowd lunged forward for free beer. *Viva El Tercero!* State Senator, Bestower of Gifts, Giver of the Word, Maker of Laws!

"The bastard!" growled Turner. "I'll get even with him yet!"

7.

That winter brought Emily and Gaylord to an impasse that neither knew how to break. Meetings outside were no longer possible,

176

holding hands in a movie unbearable. Only occasionally did Gaylord come down to the Tea Room for dinner, and a short drive afterward gave them their only chance to be alone together. Forced into a state of increasing irritability, they always wound up in a quarrel — as tonight, a Sunday evening when Gaylord was driving Emily back home.

Abruptly he slammed on the brakes, grabbed her roughly, both hands around her breasts, and kissed her so passionately that it bruised her lips. Then excited and contrite, he drove on slowly to El Mirasol. It was a clear night in February, and in the pale light of a new moon the dark guest ranch loomed up monstrously exaggerated in size.

"Why do you have to stay here?" he grumbled. "It's so expensive!"

"Oh, I'm extravagant!" she boasted. "Spoiled rotten by knowing that on the first of every month dear old Chase National will have a check deposited to my account from Pater Chalmers' estate. Why shouldn't I be comfortable at least? You never take me anyplace!"

All their differences in background and temperament were coming out, and now the underlying male-and-female antagonism between them was accentuated by the first signs of early spring which made them restless with an urge they could no longer deny.

Gaylord snapped out the headlights and Emily lunged into his arms. "You cut my lip back there! Oh Gay, what makes us fuss at each other like this?"

They both knew, giving in again to the same urgent intimacy. Only to be recalled, unsatisfied and frustrated by the smallness and coldness of the car.

Emily reared back, smoothing down her skirt over her legs. " Quit mawling me! This petting in a cold car's no good!" she said savagely. "What are we, a couple of adolescent kids? Why don't you come up to my room?"

"And have Saunders find us in the morning?"

"There's other hotels, aren't there?"

It was out at last. Yet even under the drive of urgent necessity there rose a practical problem. Gaylord, with his horror of being observed, wanted to go to some obscure motel within the limits of the area prescribed by the Security restrictions placed upon him.

Emily balked. "I'm not a floosie to be taken to any drive-in and registered under a false name! I'm going to spend the weekend at La Fonda, the kind of hotel I've always been accustomed to stay in. I'll be there in my room Saturday afternoon. Just walk in. What could be more simple?"

Yet that Saturday when Gaylord drove down the Hill, he was oppressed by fear. Security restrictions were tighter than ever. What would happen should he be found out? Just now when . . . He drove slowly past El Mirasol, hoping against hope that Emily's car would be in the driveway. It was gone. She was actually in Santa Fe . . .

Weak with nervousness, he staggered toward the bar of La Fonda for a drink to give him courage. Abruptly he turned back, remembering that he'd heard a bartender was planted there by the F.B.I. to keep tab on all Project personnel. With shaking hand he lifted the receiver of the room telephone and asked for Miss Emily Chalmers.

"Why hello, Gay!" she answered. "I'm just having a sandwich and some tea. Why don't you come up?"

He felt like a fool, her voice sounded so casual. Yet he crept upstairs and down the hall hunting for her room as if expecting every moment to feel clapped on his shoulder the heavy hand of a house detective.

She answered his knock with a muffled, "Come in." For a moment he could not see her clearly in the shade-drawn dusk. She was in bed, huddled under the covers and crying. The sandwich on the table was untouched; the tea had been cold an hour. "I waited and waited," she sobbed. "I thought you weren't coming and I was mad and ashamed. And then the telephone rang and it made me cry, I don't know why."

As he threw the catch on the door and walked toward her, she flung back the covers. She had on a sheer flesh-pink nightgown with a lace bodice that revealed the darker pink of the nipples on her full breasts. A narrow ribbon tied over her hair had slipped off and was hanging over her right ear. Gaylord lunged down beside her and quickly, awkwardly, jerked her gown up over her head.

"Your hands are ice cold!" she protested, and then swiftly, "I don't care! Gay!"

They were so flagrantly virginal, in such a savage hurry; everything about their lying nakedly entwined together was so rapturously

178

new; and yet it was as if somewhere, sometime, they had known all this before. It was not very satisfactory, this first time, but it improved as they lost their haste and shyness. And now there was no more antagonism between them, no more irritableness. They were like they had been at first, with all the tremulous ecstasy and the mystery and the promise of a long forever.

Their sexual relationship reassured Gaylord. Each time he now saw Emily he noticed how poised and confident she looked. She had lost her lingering girlishness with its faint air of anxiety. He felt different himself: relaxed, invigorated, cheerful.

Then it happened. He was sent off the Hill with still another group of scientists and technicians under strict Security orders not to reveal where they were going nor the purpose of their mission. He was gone nearly a month. He did not write Emily, of course, knowing she would take it for granted that something unusual and important prevented him from getting in touch with her.

A break came the first of June when he was sent back home. He had barely enough free time next day to meet her for a few hours in Santa Fe.

Emily was sitting in the lobby of La Fonda when he entered, huddled on the end of a couch as if pathetically trying to escape notice. Her face, usually glowing with vitality beneath her tan, was pale and drawn. She was wearing a white sumer dress, and the short cotton gloves to match it she was nervously twisting into limp strings in her lap.

On seeing him, Emily jumped to her feet. With a gesture that would have appeared ludicrously melodramatic had he not seen the boundless relief filling her wild, troubled eyes, she dropped her gloves on the floor and clasped her hands at her breast. "Gay!" she gasped hoarsely. "You came!"

He snatched up her gloves, took both her hands. "Emily! What's wrong?"

"They wouldn't give me a room. They're full. But I've got to talk to you somewhere. I've got to talk to you," she kept repeating.

"Let's get out of here!" Gaylord guided her out of the lobby into the street. He could feel her acute nervous tension lessen as they walked east on San Francisco and turned south in front of the Cathedral. Her stiff arm through his relaxed. They clasped hands.

179

"Emily, you knew that only something very important which I could not foresee nor mention could have kept me away and prevented me from writing. I shouldn't be here now. I don't have much time as it is."

Her voice was clearer, steadier now. "It's not that, Gay. It's—oh, where can we talk?"

They had come to the Alameda running beside the little Santa Fe River. The stream was no more than a wide ditch, but its deep banks were green with grass and shaded with trees. They sat down near the Castillo Street bridge where there was some privacy from occasional cars passing along the road above.

"Look!" Gaylord broke the silence abruptly. "I believe that's— yes it is! Dr. Klaus Fuchs. The man who sat at the table with Dr. Salzburg and me at your mother's that night when you came in with the fish."

Fuchs was driving slowly along the Alameda in an old Chevy coupe, peering out of the open window at the Castillo Street bridge just ahead.

"Must be looking for somebody," mused Gaylord. "That's funny. I didn't know he was in town."

They saw the Chevy come to a stop when it reached the bridge. A pudgy little man dressed in a shabby suit stepped forth. He and Fuchs said something to each other, then the man got in the car and Fuchs drove on.

It was Saturday, June 2nd: a date, time and incident whose every detail—the splash of dried mud on the left front fender of the Chevy, Fuch's anxiously searching glance, the wistful face and shabby suit of the man he met—was impressed upon Gaylord's memory as an inalienable part of his and Emily's own meeting.

Emily seemed not to have noticed the casual occurrence on the bridge. She drew a deep breath and said abruptly, "Gay, I'm pregnant."

Everything inside him seemed to drop silently and heavily into a bottomless pit in his belly, leaving him devoid of all sensation. "Emily! Why—how in the world could that have happened!"

She gave a short and embarrassed laugh. "I guess the way it usually happens." This was the first time she had put her fear into words. Now it was a burden shared; she looked immensely relieved.

180

"It's all right, Emily. Don't worry. You know I love you and we're going to get married. You know that!" He was excited now and vehement. "The thing is let's don't worry now. Not *now*! We can't now, of all times!"

Frowning slightly, she bit through a blade of grass and spit it out. "It's never happened to me before, but I think it must be a thing a woman just knows regardless of the signs. . . . Oh, you have no idea what I've been through! Every week going by and not a word from you. I kept wondering how you'd take it, if you'd be angry, or not love me any more because it happened so soon."

"I do love you! I couldn't be angry!" he angrily insisted. "And you mustn't worry. Not *now*!"

"It's about time to worry a little, Gay. We've got to decide what to do about it."

"Not yet. It's impossible!" he went on swiftly. "I shouldn't be here now, I told you. I have to be back up on the Hill in just three hours. I'm leaving Los Alamos again right away. Don't ask me where I'm going, how long I'll be gone, why. It's the most horribly secret and important—and don't tell anyone I told you even that, understand! My God! There's nothing I can do about it now, Emily."

She bent her head, covered her face with her hands, and broke into dry, brittle sobs that wracked his body more than hers. "We can't wait. We can't," she mumbled over and over.

He held her closely, covered her head with wild kisses, but his soft reassurring voice was indomitably stubborn. "Just till I get back. Please . . . Emily, please!"

At last he put her in her car, and watched her drive off with one last, stricken and abandoned look back that still carried the element of indestructible trust. Then, full of panic, he ran to his own car.

Late that night he left the Hill in a funereal procession that crept slowly down the tortuous mountain grade. In the middle rumbled two military prime movers whose loads were swathed in tarpaulins. In front and behind were cars full of scientists, engineers and technicians. Preceding and following these were armed detachments from the military post, accompanied by Security officers.

Gaylord, crowded in one of the rear cars, could not see the Crossing at the bottom of the canyon as the convoy turned north upon the newly paved road. Not a light twinkled among the lumpy sand

181

hills. Even Espanola was dark. They crossed the big bridge over the Rio Grande and turned south. Silently, darkly, they slipped through Santa Fe and headed south again.

One of his companions nudged him. "Since when have you become a chain smoker? Relax! What are you trying to do, asphixiate all of us in our sleep?"

Gaylord ground out his cigarette, leaned back, and stared sleeplessly at the rushing darkness. Emily couldn't be pregnant! She'd been mistaken. But what if she were?

A vast sense of impersonality overwhelmed him for the first time. He felt like an actor trapped in a role he was incapable to interpret. A stern sense of duty conflicting with personal feelings offered alternate postures which he was too frozen to act out. He felt possessed by the disenchanting illusion of his freedom of choice; as if he were an instrument reacting to a gravitational field set up by powers beyond his comprehension. A man decisive in his work, he resented his indecisiveness for the very reason that he was confronted not with a rational choice between clear-cut issues, but between the two poles of his own nature: the over-riding dictates of rationality with its degrees of calculated probability which till now had constituted his one frame of reference, and that vast realm of instinct, impulse and private emotion which he believed he had disinherited.

He loved Emily; he wanted to marry her. But not now! She would not settle down for one minute in one of the ramshackle living units on the Hill assigned to married couples. She could not abide the Security restrictions, with limitations on her shopping trips, travel, maid service, correspondence, and everything else. But even if she would, how could he take time out now? Requesting to be excused from duty at the very moment when two years of secret and urgent work were to be put to the ultimate test! His secret meetings with her expressly against Security regulations, everything would come out! Why, he'd be arrested and confined in prison for the duration; he knew too much classified information to be simply fired.

No, no, no! he protested with every sane thought he could command. They could not allow themselves to panic. They would have to see it through just a few weeks. Then . . .

Then again all these agonizing possibilities parted to reveal Emily's face with its fright and helplessness. He controlled a wild desire to fling himself out of the car and rush back to her, regardless of what happened. Instead, bound in the straight-jacket of incalculable providence, he wiped off his sweaty face and leaned back exhausted. The car rushed on to a destiny he was powerless to foresee or control.

8.

Something was coming to a verge. The Woman at Otowi Crossing could feel it bottled up within her, gathering force, crying and straining to be freed. What it could be, she did not know. No apperception revealed its shape or meaning. Not a dream broke her strange and increasing tension.

In the peculiar lull around her she sensed the same ominous interregnum. The loud and frequent explosions up on the Hill had ceased. The steady stream of traffic dwindled to a trickle. Her regular Xs stopped coming to dinner. Only the wives drove down for fresh vegetables.

Alone and apprehensive, she waited for something to happen. But nothing did.

One noon Turner stopped by to find her lying on the couch behind drawn shades. "Under the weather, Helen?" he asked cheerfully.

Wearily she clasped her head, her breasts, her belly. "I feel tight all over. Like I'm about to burst."

"I'm on my way to Albuquerque. Come on. Let's see a doctor."

"It's not that, Jack." She paused, then blurted out, "I feel just like I did before *it* happened that time."

"Oh. Another spell, you mean." He gave her a look of compassionate pity.

"Not a 'spell' as you call it," she protested. "Simply a feeling in me something's going to happen." She got up, flung back the shades, and stared out the window. "Maybe it's Emily I'm worried about. She doesn't come over any more."

"I'll find out what's happened to her when I get back. Stop worrying. About her—everything!" He went out and got into his car.

183

It was almost three o'clock when Turner arrived in Albuquerque. The overgrown, crowded city was stifling hot on its barren plain. Striding along Central Avenue, coat off and sleeves rolled up, he suddenly stopped in surprise. There was Emily standing on the corner at Fourth Street.

She was all dressed up, cool as a cucumber, in a pale green dress and floppy picture hat made of the same green cheesecloth or something. What struck him instantly though was her look of a trapped animal. She stood staring vacantly out at the traffic as if waiting only for time to pass. Turner walked over quickly and took her by the arm.

Emily flung around with a surprised, frightened face, threw herself against his chest, and burst into tears.

"O.K., O.K. if you have to have a crying jag!" He patted her clumsily on the back. "But does it have to be on the busiest street corner in town?"

A movie down the street had just opened its doors. He led her inside to a dark and empty section in back. The raucous dialogue of a cheap Western muffled the sounds of Emily's sobs, but in the flickering light of the screen Turner could see the intensity of her outbreak. She sat humped down beside him, stuffing a handkerchief into her mouth, her kness drawing up at every paroxyism of frightened weeping.

He put his arm around her, drew her against him. "That's right, baby," he whispered. "Let it all out while you're at it."

Emily finally lay limp and exhausted against him, clutching his hand with trembling fingers. He let her rest a while, then led her out. "Where are you staying—El Alvarado?"

She nodded, swabbing her face with a powder puff. The comfortable, old-fashioned Fred Harvey hotel was only a few blocks down Central. Emily's room was on the second floor, overlooking the station platform and railroad tracks. Turner settled down in the only chair, propping his feet on the foot of the bed. Emily took off her picture hat, crouched down on the bed against the propped up pillows, and kept staring at her watch as if waiting for the hour of execution. Turner said casually as he could, "You're scared, honey. When does it happen and why—if you want to tell me?"

"Five o'clock!" she whispered hoarsely. "And I'm frightened—

I am, I am! I don't know what she'll do to me!" She rolled sideways, burying her face in the pillows.

"And what do you think *she'll* do—if I don't stop her?" he asked quietly.

Emily reared up, threw back her head defiantly. "She's going to give me an abortion, that's what! And you're not going to stop her. Nobody is!" she hissed.

Turner stared out the window at a goat bucking a string of empty boxcars down the tracks. Of course it was that Goddamned, supercilious Gaylord on the Hill!

"Somebody told me horseback riding would help." Emily was quietly, desperately candid now. "But it didn't. Nothing did . . . I tried all the medicines in the drug stores . . . Maria went out in the full of the moon and gathered a herb she knew, and I drank the tea like she said. I told her it was for a Spanish girl who was in trouble. But it was me. And the time kept passing all the time—"

Turner lit a cigarette with nervous fingers.

"Then I asked the Spanish maid at El Mirasol, telling her it was an Anglo girl friend of mine, and I gave her twenty dollars not to tell. She arranged it. She said it was simple; her aunt in Albuquerque did lots of them for her friends." Emily looked at her watch again. "She works at a bakery, but she'll be home at five. She lives off Broadway, on the south edge of town, and if I take a taxi—"

"Emily, Emily," he said tenderly. "Things like this just happen. All you can do is to make the best of them . . . both of you."

"Leave him out of this!" she screamed. "I haven't said where he is or what he's doing or anything! Anything!"

"I know you haven't. We won't get upset over anything right now. We'll keep it a secret till you have the child."

Emily jerked her hands away. "A child? Now? Like this?" Her look of horrified amazement betrayed her. It was the inconvenience, the ill-timing, the thought of her mother's disapprobation and the public disgrace that was her main concern. Turner stiffened with resentment. The ignorant, selfish little fool! Hundreds of women far younger than she were maturely facing life with large families. With her leisure, education and money, it was nothing but that deep-rooted selfishness and willfulness to have her own way in everything that had finally caught up with her. At the same time Turner felt keenly her anguish. She was at the point of hysteria; he dared not antagonize her.

"Sure," he said consolingly. "You've been reading too many books of etiquette and old-fashioned novels. But this is 1945, baby! You can go to the best doctor in the best hospital anywhere. And you'll always be proud—"

"Proud of my bastard child as you are of yours!" she spat at him from a tense and bitter face. "You Goddamned hypocrite! Still trying to keep your own daughter a secret! As if I didn't learn about her my first day in La Oreja!" She stopped for breath, then broke out again. "Did you give this sentimental spiel to that Indian girl you seduced? And what about that child now? Why, you're so damned scared to face them both you never go to the pueblo! That's why you never have anything to do with Indians any more! Oh, you stinking, cowardly hypocrite!"

Turner felt trapped under the blinding spotlight turned upon him. What she said was true, but it was not the whole truth.

"I've put her in a good school, Emily. Her mother married long ago and has several more children. I see her husband often. Indians take these things more naturally—as you should." He met her angry, accusing stare without flinching. "What I think I'll do now," he added calmly, "is just run out there on South Broadway and cancel your date. I'll slip the woman a bill for her trouble. Then we'll have a good dinner and ride back home together."

Before the words were out of his mouth Emily had jumped off the bed to stand in front of the door with arms outstretched. "You won't!" she screeched. "If you take one step I'll scream the roof off. I'll get everybody up here and have you put out of my room for molesting me! Try it! I dare you!"

Turner stifled the impulse to jump and clamp a hand over her mouth; she was yelling already loud enough to be heard in the hall. "Go ahead!" he said quietly. "The manager of this hotel has known me for twenty years. I'll tell him exactly who you are and what you intend to do. We'll report your woman to the police and have her arrested. I'll also report your maid at El Mirasol as an accessory. Abortions are illegal in this state, young lady! Now scream if you think *I'm* fooling."

Emily was suddenly, desperately quiet. "In five minutes I'm going down and get a taxi. If you interfere or make any trouble I'll kill myself—with a quinine capsule I filled with that ant poison so hard to get. Don't think I haven't thought it all out."

"That'll be nice for your mother to think about!" Turner tried to sound sarcastic.

"About your driving me to it, you mean?"

Turner felt suddenly defeated. "O.K. Emily. I'm going to let you go. But I'm going to tell you exactly where you're going and exactly what for."

Frankly, brutally, he described her imperiously riding in a taxi across the hot sand flats to a squalid adobe on the outskirts of town. A fat, tired Mexican woman let her in, locking the door against a husband home from work and clamoring for a can of beer. Drawing the blinds, she built a fire in the kitchen stove, boiled a greasy pan full of ditch water. Now in the closed up room, too stifling hot to breathe . . .

Emily's face grew pale and damp. Her fastidious horror of squalor, all her fright, started her to trembling again.

"What she's got to do to you won't be easy. You're too far along." Ruthlessly he went on—until suddenly she let out a low moan and covered her face with her hands.

"I can't! I can't!" she murmured piteously. "God, what am I going to do?"

Turner rose. "All right. I'll cancel this impossible date. Then I'll find a first-rate doctor in town with a modern surgery and a nurse in attendance, so you'll have nothing to fear. I'll go with you and stay by you afterward. O.K.?"

Without a word Emily stumbled into his arms. He held her closely until she stopped trembling. "Give me the woman's name and address now. . . . I'll be back shortly. Then we'll face this thing together."

The next afternoon it was Turner who kept nervously glancing at his watch as he sat in the waiting room of the doctor's office. Evidently there were no insurmountable ethical, professional nor legal barriers to the practice of illegal operations for one who could afford payoffs, protection and such an attractive suite in a downtown office building. No wonder it cost so damned much! Cash on the barrelhead, of course!

He studied the original French Impressionist paintings on the wall, thumbed through the fashionable magazines on the tea table, and then leaned back on his comfortable couch to light another cigarette.

Christ, it was taking a long time! He began to worry about Emily behind the closed door to his left. What if anything should go wrong? What if Helen ever found out?

It was over. The door opened. Emily and the doctor came out. She looked pale but calm, and gave him a shy smile.

"Are you all right, Emily?"

"She'll be quite all right," said the doctor. "You have my telephone numbers here and at home, in case you want to call me."

A sharp, quick look passed between them: the professionally friendly look of an illegal practitioner that did not quite mask a slight contempt for the middle-aged man who had brought such a young girl to him; and a look of gratefulness from a member of the helpless laity who still paradoxically held a hidden contempt for the man beneath the white coat.

"Will you call a taxi, please?" Turner asked the secretary.

"There's one waiting for you," she said sweetly. " 'Bye now!"

At the hotel, Turner stopped at the desk. "My niece is a little under the weather. Will you please plug her telephone on your switchboard? I'll take any chance calls for her in my room."

They walked slowly up to Emily's room. Turner drew the window blinds to shut out the late afternoon sun. "How're you feeling?"

"I'm all right, Jack. You don't have to worry about me any more."

"Why don't you go in the bathroom, put on your nightie, and then pile into bed where you can be comfortable? I'll just stick around for a few minutes in case you want a drink or something."

She was asleep by the time he had finished his cigarette. Her face was faintly flushed like a child's; her breathing was regular. Turner unbuttoned his shirt collar and slumped down in his stiff chair beside her.

Emily awoke about eight that evening. He switched on the desk lamp. "How're you feeling?" he asked again. "Hungry? Want a glass of milk, a sandwich?"

"I've had a rest," she said petulantly in a blurred voice. "Now I guess I'm sleepy."

She rolled over, flung out one bare arm, and swung off again on the tide of sleep.

Spoiled brat! Completely tuckered out. No wonder! Switching off the lamp again, he tiptoed out of the room. "What I need now," he thought with profound relief, "is a good doctor myself or a double-Scotch and a thick steak!"

9.

This is it, thought Gaylord working in the blinding brilliance of the July sun. Trinity, when he first had heard it, was only a Top-Secret operational code name. Then, when more and more men began to leave Los Alamos and he himself accompanied them, it became a place: Trinity Site. A desolate desert in southern New Mexico known as the *Jornada del Muerto* littered with men and equipment closely guarded by a detachment of armed MPs. Finally, as the pace of the work stepped up, it took on the nature of a vast and mounting endeavor: Operation Trinity.

Its pattern was deceptively simple. All activities revolved about a vertical steel needle. A fragile, slender, steel tower one hundred feet high, it thrust into the brassy sky like the spire of a medieval church, the phallic symbol of man's challenging dominance of the flat, mute, and unresisting earth below.

From its foot, crews of men were stringing wires to instrument bunkers out on the desert, and to the control point 10,000 feet to the south, in which were installed the timing and firing devices. Inside these "dreadnoughts," massively timbered bulkheads reinforced with earth, more men were mounting panels of instruments, the scientific eyes and ears that would record the result of the operation. Most of the personnel with their mere human faculties, Gaylord knew, would be stationed at the time at an observation point 17,000 feet south from ground zero. Still another observation point lay seven miles away, where the special engineering detachment was stationed.

Gaylord's own work was not physically arduous, but it was tedious. Complex circuitry, electronic measuring devices and hundreds of instruments to be calibrated and tested to scientific precision. Concentration and long hours. A constant urgency broken only by a few hours sleep in the barracks.

Yet often when he suddenly awakened after restless sleep, or straightened up from his work in the blinding sun, Emily's face appeared before him more poignant, more accusing than ever. Instantly all that part of him which owed secret allegiance to the midnight stars, to the ebb and tide of the mysterious instinctive, the dark unconscious, flung him headlong against a rampart of piercing pain and torturing guilt. It was more than he could stand! With all his effort he thrust it from him, as he had to do, and hurried back to his work.

Time was pressing now. As the tension inside him was increasing to the breaking point, so too was it mounting around him. This was the night of July 12th and the unit had been moved into the right front room of a deserted ranchhouse for final assembly of its complicated components and gadgetry. Gaylord chewed his lip as he stood waiting in the crowd of men around it.

Before him lay the final product of $2,000,000,000 and two and a half years of crash effort spent under the tightest secrecy impositions in history. The end result of the team-thinking of the best scientific brains from Europe and America. This, with a small amount of matter from the Belgian Congo, had been designed to release the energy of the universe locked up within the atom from the beginning of time. Gaylord looked at it with trepidation—a thing so secret that still he feared his own knowledge of its size and shape and weight, its very admitted existence.

The full significance of it was also apparent on the faces of all the men around him. They too wondered if it would work at all— or work so well that it would blast them all into eternity. Still, in sweating silence, no one moved nor spoke.

In a few minutes the vital and irreplaceable nuclear material was formally transferred from the custody of the civilian scientists to the Army. The officials went out. Then the insertion was made and the basic assembly completed.

About ten o'clock next morning the device was fully armed and hoisted to the top of the hundred-foot steel tower. Yet Gaylord still faced another sleepless day and night. For in addition to the apparatus necessary to cause the detonation, complete instrumentation to determine the pulse beat and all reactions of the device had to be rigged on the tower. Would it be a dud or blast them into kingdom come? In this vast range of speculation as to what the yield of the device would be, somebody proposed a pool.

"Chip in a dollar, make your guess, and the winner takes all the money. What do you say, Gaylord?"

Gaylord threw in his dollar. "Ten k.t. I'll string along on that." An explosive force equivalent to 10,000 tons of T.N.T. It was a figure that meant nothing at all.

By Sunday night, July 15, all was ready. Posted throughout New Mexico were agents of the Counter Intelligence Corps to investigate any excitement or undue interest after the shot. A special evacuation outfit of 150 men left the site, prepared to clear ranches and isolated communities if the radioactive fallout level became too high, or even the small towns of Socorro and San Antonio if the wind changed. All the access roads were now blocked, and a final check by name was made of every person in the restricted area. The secret time of the test had been set at four a.m.

Worry about the weather now set in. Lightning flashes and peals of thunder made aerial observations of the test impossible. It was undecided whether to postpone or go ahead with the test. Every man stayed at his post waiting for the storm to break or clear.

About four o'clock the decision was made to fire at five-thirty; the rain had stopped although the sky was still heavily overcast. Gaylord with most of the men left for the main observation point, 17,000 feet from ground zero, where they were massed on a bit of high ground.

Waiting became intolerable. A deathly silence settled over the crowd in the darkness. It was suddenly broken by a voice over the radio loudspeaker announcing minus twenty minutes.

Every five minutes the voice came on. Gaylord began to tremble. Curiously all thought of his work was drained out of him. He thought only of Emily.

At minus two minutes the order came for every person to lie face down on the ground with his feet pointing toward the explosion.

Gaylord stretched out flat on the damp earth, one hand clutching a pair of high density goggles and the other digging into the ground. He did not know who was lying on each side of him, but he could hear their hoarse breathing in the awesome silence. He closed his eyes to see Emily's face looking at him with all the agony of her own waiting and indecision.

At minus forty-five seconds the robot sequence timer took over. From now on, he thought hazily, the whole complicated mass of intricate mechanism that he himself had worked on was in operation without human control. And now came the countdown.

"Minus ten seconds."

"Minus nine seconds."

"Eight seconds."

Gaylord had trouble breathing. He lifted his face an inch, spit out the dirt in his mouth.

"Five."

"Four."

His fingers released their hold on his dark goggles and dug into the ground for support.

"One."

"Fire!"

At this instant a blind girl seated at her window in Albuquerque, 120 miles away, spoke quickly to a companion. "What is that bright flash in the sky?"

Gaylord, face down on the ground with his eyes closed, felt the same sudden sensation of light on his eyelids. He cautiously opened his eyes. The ground underneath him was so brilliantly lit he could distinguish its tiny grains of sand. He turned his head slightly. The whole area was clear as if seen in the brightest daylight; a mountain range stood out in bold relief. He rolled over, mutely counting seconds with a dry mouth, and grabbed for his dark glasses.

What he saw through them was at once beautiful and terrifying. A huge, searing ball of fire brighter than the midday sun. It was boiling violently, swiftly expanding in size, and slowly, majestically rising straight into the sky. Changing in color from livid red to yellow, gray, blue and purple.

Gaylord jerked off his dark glasses. Abruptly now came the shock wave which seemed to strike him sharply in back of his knees, and

192

the awesome roar of the detonation followed by a dull, prolonged rumbling as the sound was reflected by a range of desert mountains.

The fireball clouded over to an ash gray. As it rose swiftly into the substratosphere, it sucked up from the ground a long, vertical stem of dust. Finally it changed into a mushroom-shaped cloud sheared off from the stem by upper level winds. Still Gaylord watched it climb—20,000, 30,000 feet or more, and drift lazily away.

He was suddenly aware of the commotion around him. Trucks and jeeps arriving. Men rushing about, slapping each other on the back. Shouts and scraps of conversation. The tower, except for the concrete stump of one leg, had been completely vaporized . . . Fermi, he heard, already had made the first estimate of the yield—20 kilotons.

This is it, thought Gaylord dazedly and finally. Trinity, with the awesome power of 20,000 equivalent tons of T.N.T., had blasted open the Atomic Age.

Curiously, he felt little elation. Like most explorers who had found what they believed they had sought, he wanted only to go home—home to Otowi Crossing, to the great red river curving into night and rest and sleep, to the big branched cottonwood and the picnic basket between its serpentine roots, and to her who waited there timelessly and forever in a dream of peace. Emily! Oh, Emily!

All that week Helen had endured the continuing, ominous interregnum, waiting for something to happen. There was no use thinking about it. One's rational mind, geared by habit to its little objective world, was shut off from the greater subjective whole that encompassed it. One had to break through in order to see its true reality. But she couldn't break through at will. And when it happened suddenly and unpredictably, and only for an instant as it always did, she couldn't hang on to it. No, there was no use thinking about it. She could only obey her compulsion to keep alone and accept whatever might come.

No one intruded on her privacy. Her business had come to a standstill. Emily, abruptly and unaccountably, went back East without saying goodbye. Turner did not come down. Not even Facundo disturbed her. Every morning when she went outside she could glimpse him on the flat roof of his little hut reverently waiting for sunrise with his prayer-bowl of cornmeal. Engrossed in the same mystery, each ignored the other.

Still she could not find peace. Everything seemed bottled up within her, and the pressure still made her uncomfortable.

One night she awakened screaming. It was as if everything, house, mountains, the world, the heavens, was enveloped in one brilliant apocalyptic burst of fire. She was still screaming, crouching in bed and fighting off the tongues of flame with her arms, when Facundo rushed in.

"The candle! That did it! Put out the candle!" she kept screaming.

Facundo struck a match in the darkness, lit a lamp. "No candle. You dreamin'," he said quietly. "All over now."

Bathed in sweat and trembling, she lay trying to erase the nightmare from her mind while Facundo made a pot of tea. But its sensations were too vivid to be banished. How horrible it was! Facundo made her drink some tea, then dozed the rest of the night in a chair beside the lighted lamp. Still she could not go back to sleep.

For two weeks afterward Helen felt ill. It had been more than a nightmare, but not another break-through like the first one she'd had so long ago. That had opened to her the one creative wholeness with all its peace and plentitude. This one, for all s similar overpowering brilliance, was impacted with something negative, destructive, evil. What did it mean?

Towards the end of the month Turner stopped in on his way to Santa Fe, the first time since she had talked to him about Emily. A curious restraint kept them apart the few minutes he stayed. Bad as she felt, Helen could not bring herself to tell him of her nightmare —another "spell" as he would call it. Turner too felt tongue-tied. He had avoided her since Emily's abortion lest he let something slip about it. Nor could he tell the purpose of his trip to Santa Fe.

The whole damned thing annoyed him, anyway. Two weeks ago Monday he had heard rumors of a mysterious explosion that had occurred at dawn. Windows had been rattled in Silver City and Gallup. In Albuquerque a flash had "lighted up the sky like a sun," Passengers on a Santa Fe train reported that they had seen a plane explode in the sky to the south. Then a Forest Service lookout gave what Turner considered the best clue: a flash followed by an explosion in the direction of Alamogordo.

Turner had promptly telephoned the commanding officer of the Alamogordo Army Air Base for a brief statement to release to American Newswire Service. What he got was the terse information that a remote ammunition magazine had exploded, causing no loss of life or injury to anyone, and little property damage.

A fine run-around! There were rumors in Santa Fe that the incident had been something related to Los Alamos. The Hill was still swathed in its everlasting secrecy, and Turner had not been able to run down the rumors. Now, disgruntled, he was going to Santa Fe for a last try before giving up the chase.

So they sat there like two strangers, with nothing to say. Turner got up. "Well, I've got to be running along. You're still not looking well, Helen. The least you can do is stop worrying. Emily's all right. Take my word for it!" He patted her clumsily on the back and hurried out.

Helen watched his car rumble across the bridge with a feeling of intolerable sadness. It was all her fault. Everything was so bottled up inside her she couldn't come out to anyone.

Early in August one night the queer bodily pressure within her finally broke, and with it her mental tension. Whatever it had been, it was over now. With great relief she got up only to discover she had passed blood. This did not frighten her; it added to her relief to believe that all this period of mental anguish, her nightmare itself, had been caused only by a physical disturbance.

It was dawn by the time she had heated water and taken a bath. How life keeps repeating itself, she thought as she dried herself, remembering how frightened she had been a few years ago by the swelling between her breast and shoulder blade. But she had forgotten it and there was no sign of it now though perhaps the muscles seemed not as flexible as they had been. This too was a similar disturbance that would pass away.

Still a curious lassitude possessed her and low spirits such as she had not known for a long time. By noon she was always depleted and spent the afternoons on her couch, listless and lonely.

That Monday afternoon, when she was sitting forlornly on her couch, Helen heard a car stop outside. Looking out the window, she saw it was crowded with women from the Hill. Laughing and talking excitedly, they jumped out and trooped through the door.

"Helen! It's happened! Look! Have you seen it yet?" shouted one of them, flinging out a newspaper in front of her with the banner headlines:

ATOMIC BOMB DROPS ON JAPAN
LOS ALAMOS SECRET DISCLOSED BY TRUMAN

"You haven't heard it yet? Don't you ever turn on your radio?" shouted another, throwing the switch.

" . . . The bomb was dropped 16 hours ago on Hiroshima, located on Honshu Island, Japan. The announcement was made in a statement by President Truman released by the White House today. It is an atomic bomb, a harnessing of the basic power of the universe. It packed a punch equivalent to that normally delivered by 2,000 B-29's . . ."

Helen's head began to whirl. She felt dizzy. Still the voice on the radio filled the room.

"The atomic bomb dropped on Hiroshima today, as disclosed by President Truman, was developed in secret facilities at Oak Ridge, Tennessee, at Richland, Washington, and at an unnamed laboratory near Santa Fe, New Mexico. Mr. Truman said the work was so secret that most of the employees did not know the character of it . . .

"Concurrent with President Truman's announcement, an official War Department news release made today reveals that mankind's successful transition to a new age, the Atomic Age, was ushered in July 16, 1945, in a remote section of the Alamogordo Air Base, 120 miles southeast of Albuquerque, New Mexico . . ."

She could stand no more, and put her hands over her ears. Still the local radio station kept up its din.

"Santa Fe learned officially today of a city of 6,000 in its own front yard. The reverberating anouncement of the Los Alamos bomb also lifted the secret of the community on the Pajarito Plateau, whose presence Santa Fe has ignored, except in whispers, for more than two years . . ."

10

"I'll never forget that day if I live to be a hundred!" exclaimed Alice Person. "Los Alamos was our one big adventure and that was its successful climax. Yet it's Helen Chalmers who sticks out clearest in my mind."

Waiting for the tea to steep in its lovely old Japanese porcelain, she glanced casually around her ultramodern apartment on Chicago's North Shore.

"Fred's first job as a chemist was there on the Hill," she explained. "We'd just been married and our first home was one of those chicken-coop prefabs. We were Little Shots, no Bathtub Row for us. But life was so exciting we didn't mind the makeshifts. Men never talked to their wives about their work, it was so highly classified, but that summer when they began to leave the Hill on a secret mission we knew it was coming to a head.

"We were almost as excited over Helen's queer predictions. Little chills ran up my back whenever I thought of them. As quiet and gentle as she was, I couldn't help believing the talk about her was true. I mean that she had extrasensory perceptions and all that. I told this to Fred when we wanted to resume going down for fresh vegetables which we used ourselves and also peddled to neighbors for her. Dear old Facundo always tied up the bunches so neatly!

"But Fred hit the roof. 'You keep away from that woman with her hypnagogic attachment!' as he called it. 'You know she's in a sensitive spot, feeding all the Big Shots every night! Do you want us tagged by the F. B. I.?'

" 'But Fred, you know you haven't told me anything I could pass on to her!'

" 'Can you prove that in court?' he yelled back. 'You stay away from her while I'm gone!'

"So for weeks I didn't see her. Poor thing, Helen needed that extra money too." Mrs. Person paused to look at the tea. "Oh dear! Let me add a little hot water. It's far too strong for such a delicate leaf. . . . But with Hiroshima the lid was blown off everything. I ran down the street. Men were pouring from their labs. Women were buzzing on every corner. I met our group of wives in the community center and our first thought was Helen. She'd been right! Did she know? We piled in a car and drove down to tell her.

"I must admit she had let her appearance go. Nothing to speak of, just the little things a woman notices—her hair not groomed, a spot on her dress, a run up her stocking. She looked seedy. Well, we burst in upon her to find she hadn't read the papers or even turned on the radio.

" 'That's OUR GADGET, Helen! An atomic bomb! We've won our race against the Nazis!'

" 'You were right about that mushroom cloud, Helen!' shouted Joy Perkins. 'It was exactly as you described! Listen! It'll make you happy too!'

"Helen only put her hands over her ears and let out a low moan. 'It shouldn't have happened this way! Oh no!' She covered her face with her hands as if trying to shut out something which none of us could see.

"What it could have been I couldn't imagine. This was the end of the greatest scientific experiment in history, the end of the war. I couldn't understand why, if one were a mystic and could foresee something in the future, one should be so upset about it when it came to pass.

" 'But it did happen, Helen!' I said to her a little crossly I'm afraid. 'It's wonderful and it's all over and you ought to be glad!'

"Then it came. She reared up with a wild, hysterical face, shouting, 'No, it's not all over! This is just the beginning! I'll tell you why! I'll tell you what I saw!'

"It was her nightmare. That terrible, livid vision of what was yet to come that resulted in the Security investigation Fred had warned me about. Fred is always right. I knew then I shouldn't have come. One of the women in our crowd blabbed, of course. I never did find out who it was."

The Security meeting held a few days later emphatically was not an official investigation nor formal inquiry. Security officers didn't work that way. For one thing, a prophetic dream was not a subject they were prepared to cope with. And for another, they agreed that the quieter it was kept the better. The meeting, in fact, resembled a gathering of friends. Still there was a certain grimness about it, an air of embarrassment, that made them all feel uncomfortable.

It was conducted one afternoon in the Tea Room by common consent of all parties. The armed Security guards, pretending interest in the shrubbery, were posted outside to prevent intrusion. Helen had made coffee, laid out cups and saucers on the kitchen table. Now she sat on the living room couch looking frightened and defeated. Around her were grouped the F.B.I. investigator who had previously called upon her, a Security classification officer, a colonel from the Army Manhattan Engineer District, several scientists including Breslau and Gaylord who were known to have seen her frequently, and Turner who obviously had been included to give the meeting an unofficial air but who had agreed not to give it any public notice.

"Don't you want some coffee?" Helen asked nervously.

No one spoke or moved.

Then the F.B.I. investigator, who took the initiative of acting as chairman, said quietly, "Now Miss Chalmers, don't be nervous. We're here just to get things straight. That's all. I've already talked to everyone here and many other people on the Hill. We're quite prepared to accept the fact that no one has revealed to you any information at all about the atomic blasts, either before or after they took place. Is that true, Miss Chalmers?"

"Of course! No one has ever said anything in this house about his work on the Project."

"And did you know anything about the blasts in advance, Mr. Turner?" asked the Security officer.

"Nothing! I haven't heard anything yet about Miss Chalmers' dream or whatever prompted this meeting!"

The men nodded, and the F.B.I. man turned to Helen with a smile. "I must assure you too, Miss Chalmers, that your mushroom vision, prediction, or precognition of the nuclear bomb detonation was not entirely unusual. We have on file at least twenty-three other authenticated cases of persons throughout the country who also accurately predicted the same occurrence far in advance. Some of them are so uneducated and uninformed that they are still completely ignorant of the meaning of their predictions. So tell us simply just how it happened you made the statements attributed to you."

Helen wrung her hands. She could not keep her mind off Hiroshima with its 66,000 people killed, 69,000 injured, and its 60,000 buildings destroyed. What was Nagasaki now, with 14,000 buildings in smoking ruins, 39,000 persons killed, and 25,000 injured? Lovely Nagasaki with its sacred shrine, its pine and camphor trees, the Genoa of Japan. No! One cannot use the incalculable life-giving power of the sun for death and destruction. It must not be evoked from a machine-made bomb or gadget. "No! It shouldn't have happened this way. It shouldn't!" She covered her face with her hands.

"Miss Chalmers! Please! It did happen this way. But this is not what we are here to discuss. You predicted something worse to come. That is what you must tell us about."

"Yes, Helen," Breslau said kindly but firmly. "Just start at the beginning."

Helen collected her strength. "The beginning, I guess, was the queer thing that happened when Jack here kicked that mushroom and I saw it rise into the sky just like you say the mushroom cloud of the atomic bomb does."

"Yes, many of your friends interpreted it as a precognition or prediction of the Alamogordo and Japan bombs," the F.B.I. investigator said quietly. "We discussed it at the time. The incident is past and over. Let us try not to be confused. You asserted much later— just a short time ago—that something else was to follow these first atomic bombs, even though the war is over. How did you come to make that statement, Miss Chalmers? This is what we must get straight."

Turner moved over on the couch to sit beside her. The presence of his big body gave her courage. "It was that horrible nightmare. Something like that mushroom thing and yet nothing like it at all. There was the long stem of the mushroom growing up into the sky, up to a little mushroom cloud on top. What made it different was that the stem was so long and thin, and the cloud so small. Like a long narrow candle with a tiny radiance about the wick on top. Then suddenly it happened. Oh, how terrible it was! I still can't forget it!"

"What happened?" asked the Security officer tersely.

"I can't describe it. The wick suddenly sputtered into flame and touched off all the earth and sky into one monstrous explosion that enveloped the whole world in a fiery flame. Yes! Your atomic bomb, terrible as it is, was small and puny compared to this!"

"And you felt in your dream it was this candle that touched it off?" asked Breslau.

Helen faced him defiantly. "Yes! The candle, your atomic bomb if that's what it was, was what fired it! Oh, I know you're good men up there, Dr. Breslau! But look what you've done! Set the world on fire!"

Gaylord, drawing a deep breath, looked covertly at Breslau to discover that Breslau was looking covertly at him.

"The world hasn't been set on fire, Miss Chalmers," the F.B.I. man said quietly. "It was just a dream and the war is over. You're allowed one prediction that won't come true, you know!"

Everybody smiled with relief.

"No harm's been done," he said at last, glancing at the Security officer. "We just wanted to learn from you yourself exactly what you based your statement on. A dream. Only a dream! That satisfies me. How about you?" He looked at each man in the group around him, his gaze finally resting on Helen.

"I must warn you again, Miss Chalmers, about talking too readily about your predictions. I remember once talking to a chicken raiser who predicted the world was going to crack open like an egg because all his eggs were cracking. You don't want to be put in the same category by public opinion, do you?"

Turner frowned. "Of course she doesn't! And she'll be more careful from now on! Now who else wants some coffee?"

11.

Shortly after Gaylord had returned home from Trinity he had learned, of course, that Emily had left for the East without leaving a forwarding address. The only information Helen could give him was the address of the Chalmers apartment in New York, and that of the office handling the Chalmers estate. He now received a telegram that his mother was seriously ill. Hurriedly he packed his bags and caught the first plane to New York.

201

The trip was miserable and futile. His mother was in a hospital, dying. No one answered the doorbell of the Chalmers apartment in Gramercy Square, and at the office of the Chalmers estate he was told that Emily had been in New York but had left for Mexico. "If you'd like to write her a note, I'll be glad to forward it when we receive her address," offered the office manager.

Emily's frantic predicament was quite plain to Gaylord now. He had no doubt that she was really pregnant and had fled New Mexico to have the child in New York. Yet even this monstrous city had not offered the anonymity she sought. So now she had fled to a foreign country—to Mexico of all places! Frantic with worry himself, Gaylord could not hold back the compassion he felt for her. Yet all he could do was to scribble a telegram to her and rush back to the hospital to see his mother for the last time.

Then it was necessary to arrange for her funeral and a reception for her old neighbors in the dreary flat. The Escobars, the Clausowitz, the Rubensteins—they were all there as he remembered them and would always remember them, speaking in a dozen idioms and accents the language of their intimate neighborliness his mother had always known and loved.

Gaylord had not spared the meats and sweets, the sour cream and the thick sweet cream, the multitudinous pickles and pastries, the smoking coffee, cold and spiced liquors necessary to honor her who had held this last worldly fortress against adversity with so much courage. He could envision her smiling approvingly behind her little hacking cough as she watched her neighbors eat and drink, smack their lips, and recall another incident of her and Papa. Occasionally someone let out a keening cry. It was followed by a chorus of moans and sobs. Then again they resumed eating and talking.

Always they had regarded him as aloof, a little cold and superior, his nose always in a book. That made no difference now. Because he was her boy, the perpetually strange child about whom she had gossiped across back stoops and front steps for years on end, they acknowledged him as an inalienable member of their strange tribal group. A man clapped him familiarly on the back, put a glass into his hand. A woman pressed him to her steamy bosom and cried into his hair. They knew he was going to give away the tawdry furniture in the old flat before he left. So Gaylord could see them also furtively appraising the stuffed sofa, the size of the table, the quality of the silver they were using, a Maxfield Parish print on the wall.

The whole thing upset him. What manner of woman had his mother been behind that drab exterior trudging interminably from a dreary flat to a sweaty candy kitchen? These people were telling him now with their appetites for the food and jokes she loved, with their memories of the lifelong battle she fought beside them. They loved her. She was one of them, a member of their tribal body who had been amputated from their life by the God of all hosts, and with all the passion of their great vitality they were proclaiming for the last time the mystery of her being.

A great and nameless longing for Emily possessed Gaylord as he listened to them. He wanted her here now, quickly, before it was all gone forever: this flat, these neighbors, that picture on the wall, all this richness and warmth and vitality that had been his only home. He wanted her to feel herself this strange tribal unity to whose perpetuation they had committed in turn a child of their own. He owed it to his mother, to Mama who . . . and suddenly, he could not help it, a wracking sob caught in his throat. Across the room a sharp, keening cry jerked it out, and with it his tears. A new outburst of weeping began. Not for her, this time. But for him, her boy, who now for the first time, and at the very last, had acknowledged with his own open tears the bonds that made him one of them.

The fall rains began. Gaylord finished his last chores in the downpour, trudging the length of upper Broadway with its gray weathered cliffs hemming the gray leaden river. He had forgotten the reeking smell of wet clothes in the crowded subway, how gray and desolate, lifeless and unreal the towers of Manhattan looked wrapped in mist. He seemed caught in a torturing interlude between the death of his mother and the birth of his child. The world wept with him, etching upon his soul a deepening sadness. Emily had not answered his wire. His leave from work expired. Worn out, he returned to Los Alamos.

That Forbidden City of Atomic Research, the Hush-Hush Bastion of the Future, and the Most Important Small Town in America, as Turner variously called it, was changing too. Many of Gaylord's colleagues felt guilty about the Frankenstein monster they had created. Others wanted to get back to normal life on a quiet university or college campus. Women were tired of living in makeshift quarters and having their babies born in a post office box—that stale old joke; they demanded homes of their own. Everyone chafed against the secrecy and military restrictions.

As the exodus of scientists and their families continued, there was talk that the Laboratory itself might be abandoned. Only Dr. Norris Bradbury, who had been appointed Oppenheimer's successor, still fought to hold it together. Gaylord himself thought of leaving. What held him was something so secret and appallingly significant for the future that he hardly dared to admit it to himself; something to which only Helen Chalmers, unknowingly, had given shape with her strange and frightening nightmare.

Still terribly lonesome and worrying about Emily, he began to drive down to Otowi Crossing to visit with Helen during the long evenings.

"No, no news," she would say. "Just that telegram from Mexico City wishing us all a Merry Christmas but giving no address. Don't worry. She'll be coming back soon!"

Gaylord frowned. May, June, July. . . . It would be late in January. And then? Still something kept him from telling her what had happened between him and Emily. Was it deference to Emily? Fear of hurting Helen? Or his own cowardice? He didn't know, and kept suffering from his own silence.

Helen slowly regained her peace and equanimity. She had learned by now to accept her dreams, visions, and fantasies as a part of her own unique truth, however they were regarded by other people. If their meanings were not always plain, they still served to connect her to an inner life which she had found could be as brutal and cruel as it could be sublime.

In January Facundo invited her to the Buffalo Dance as usual. A needless courtesy. Helen had been going for years; anybody could go. But as the old Indian left, he repeated the invitation with sharp, mandatory instructions.

"You go plaza. Before day come. *Muy temprano!* They wait for you at my house. They take you." His rheumy eyes probed her deeply.

In the morning before daybreak? Though the public dance was

not held until evening? Who were "they"? And where would they take her? For what? Helen knew better than to ask questions. She nodded quietly. "I'll be there, Facundo."

It was so bitter cold at four o'clock in the morning! Even in the house her hands stung; her teeth chattered against her cup of tea. As she walked outside to pour hot water into the radiator of her jalopy, the cold struck her like a blow. It seemed to embody the freezing darkness of the canyons, the faintly visible snow cap on Tsichoma Peak above, the spectral luminosity of the frozen river. Shivering in boots, coat and mittens, she managed to start the car and drive across the snowy *vega* to the pueblo.

Out of darkness the massed adobe walls loomed even darker. Fresh snow had fallen during the night. There was not a footprint nor a hoofprint, no wheeltrack of wagon nor car. No light gleamed in the adobes. They seemed to squat there, heavy, lifeless and withdrawn, like Indians themselves, compressed to earth by dark and cold. But as she left the car and trudged around the corner into the plaza, she saw a light.

A little fire of piñon sticks was blazing in front of the house in which Facundo's nephews lived. Around it, wrapped in blankets and shawls, huddled three women and two men. Helen could not see their faces; they were swathed to the eyes. No one spoke. They simply, grudgingly, drew apart to let her stand humped over the flames.

It didn't do any good. The little blaze simply stuck out a few red tongues at the steadily inrushing cold, and then snapped back as if bitten by frost. Why didn't they go inside the house to wait? Build a fire in the fireplace? Have a cup of strong black coffee sweetened with too much sugar? Anything to fortify her against this steadily encroaching, bitter cold! But no. They had to get up in a cold, dark house, fling on a thin blanket, and wait freezing outside in the naked dawn.

A mangy, whimpering dog crept tremblingly between her legs, sucking the warm air of the fire with frosty jaws. Helen let it be. Men and women drew closer in a smaller circle. On one side Helen could feel the hard thigh of a man, tense with cold, pressed against her. On the other side she felt the flabby buttocks of a fat woman shaking through her thin blanket. Still no one spoke or moved. They stood like Indians stand around a fire, close and humped over, to soak up all its warmth. One of the women's eyes were closed. A man stared vacantly, unseeingly, into the cold darkness. This interminable Indian patience that could outlast the hours, the rigors of all weather. For what?

The cold was increasing. It was like an acid eating through her thick coat and woolen underwear, into her flesh, the marrow of her bones. But the darkness was lessening. Helen could see the mountains beginning to outline the horizon, the gritty stars paling in the sky, even the great cottonwood taking shape across the plaza.

The big man in the striped Pendleton blanket spoke in a deep, quiet voice. "We go now. I say it."

The younger, smaller man followed him. Then the women: the scrawny old one, the big fat one, the thin one. Helen fell in behind. Single file, they unhurriedly crossed the plaza, drew away from the pueblo. Breathing hard they plodded up a wagon road, then climbed into a defile betwen the lumpy, round, bare hills on each side. At its foot they paused, drawing together into a group that now seemed brightly colored as the blankets they wore.

Day was breaking. Down below Helen could see smoke rising from the chimneys, and felt a premonitory tingle of excitement as she realized where she was. It was down this passage in the hills they came once each year. Out of darkness into day. Out of the mountains into the land of men. All the great, invisible forces of mountain and plain, of the darkness where the spirit dwells, but masked for this day in the visible and primordial beast shapes of buffalo and deer, elk and antelope. The potent energies of nature transmuted into mass, still inviolate, but evoked for the good of all.

All at once sound and smell smote her. She stared up the gulch. Revealed by the lifting mist, two men jerked back the blankets from a small fire they had been smothering. Instantly, in a great soundless explosion, the bluish smoke puffed out. As if materialized from its cloud, the great heads and curving horns and shaggy humps burst forth, tossing with power . . . Power! This is the power, something sang within her. The immemorial power of the medicine buffalo whose thunderous hooves had shaken the earth, whose genitals, horns, beards, hides and even dust had been held sacred. The immense thunder-power of the buffalo which brought snow and carried away sickness. Power evoked by a flip of the wrist, out of a puff of smoke, out of the mountain mist, out of the cloud of dust that had followed their lumbering herds . . . Still they kept coming. Shaking their heads with their old-man beards, tossing their in-curving horns. And following close behind them the stately, powerful elk, the quick-stepping deer, and the sinewy, graceful antelope. All walking down the slope toward her, slowly now, proudly con-scious of their impacted meaning. Bent over, their front feet of thin sticks and branches prodding for footing in the snow. Yes! She could see now the tiny puffs of eagledown tied to their horns, the bits of red yarn fastened to the ceremonial kirtles worn underneath the masked heads and robes. And she heard the tinkle of little bells and deer-hoof rattles worn around the men's legs just below the knee.

The stately procession was now almost abreast of the small group of watchers. The three women stepped back and Helen with them. But the two men walked up behind them lest they cringe back too far. As the procession advanced, the old wrinkled woman at the head of the line reached out a scrawny hand from her blanket and gently touched one of the masks. It was enough! She drew it back with a look of esctatic wonder on her face. The second woman put out her hand, timidly then resolutely. Then the third.

The buffalo leader was opposite Helen now. She shrank back—but against the man behind her. "Ai, ai, ai. It is the time now," he said softly in his low, strong voice. She pulled off her mitten and stretched out her naked hand, blue and numb with the cold.

She did not think this is Facundo I touch, the wrinkled old Indian who chops my wood and scrubs my pots and pans. Nor did she think this is old Facundo, the Buffalo Leader for perhaps the last time in his aging life; nor how difficult it must be for him to walk, bent double, under the heavy head and robe. She did not think at all. For as she touched that great head with its coarse hair and little black beard and curving horns, she felt the sudden release of power. It seemed to spark the gap with a bluish, electric glow even before her finger made quick, firm contact, and the power flowed into her full and strong.

And now with all the ecstatic wonder and mystery at the touch, the thought struck her: This is the only real power and the way it should come! Stored up until it could be released under full control.

Inviolate, not to be alienated by the individual, but spent for the good of all.

The stately procession passed down the hill, across the plaza, and into the kiva to remain until the public dance that afternoon. Helen looked at the women around her. Their shawls were down now, and the rising sun shone on their smooth, black hair. Their faces no longer were the faces of ordinary women who had got up too early, and were pinched with cold. They were the faces of women who had been granted the touch of power and consecrated to something far greater than their humble daily tasks. How beautiful they really were! She walked with them back into the plaza proudly and humbly, and wondering why she had been privileged to accompany them.

As they passed a group of people, a small boy drew back, clutching his mother's skirt. *"Es la hechicera?* The white woman?"

The woman answered, *"Cómo no?"* as she smiled at Helen, showing her gleaming teeth.

The women with Helen stopped. It was over; their thoughts were turning to other things; they acted just like women. The big fat one turned to Helen. "Ai ai. We eat now! Meat and chile, fresh bread. Good hot coffee to warm our cold insides . . . Ai, ai. Everybody. You come too, no?"

The little scrawny woman spoke up. "We got store cake too. Pink!"

Helen no longer felt the cold. A new, joyful aliveness was gushing up inside her, eager to flow out and merge with all the warm friendliness about her. She laughed. *"Cómo no?* I'm hungry!"

THE WOMAN AT OTOWI CROSSING

Part Four

1.

As the spring solstice approached, Facundo persuaded Helen to drive him to visit a friend living in another pueblo. Not until she had committed herself did she find out that it was a remote pueblo downriver. Remonstrating at the distance and the time the trip would take, she finally learned that Facundo's friend was a kiva chief whose turn had come "to work for the sun" during this important time.

Now she saw in proper perspective the reason for his visit. Facundo's friend, with his kiva members, was immured in the underground kiva for forty days and nights. He wore only handmade moccasins and a blanket of handwoven native wool, without color or decoration; he ate no canned goods nor any prepared foods; he was not allowed to see nor talk to anyone without permission. His full thought and energy was consecrated with ceremonial prayer, song and recital to the task of strengthening Our Father Sun at this crucial time of the spring solstice when his power was weak, so that he could continue his unremitting daily journeys across the sky. Praying too that his radiant, life-giving energy would continue to be infused in everything that lived—the tall wild grasses and corn plants, the tiny insects, the fish that leapt to the surface of the waters, the myriad birds of the sky, all the beasts of field and forest, and finally man—that they too might continue on their Road.

"It is permitted to take something," Facundo suggested gravely.

"Of course." She laid out a couple of heads of lettuce, a large firm head of cabbage.

She could see Facundo's mouth water. Green leaves! For one stuck down in the kiva, without sunlight and the touch of earth underfoot, what could be better than these crisp green leaves that tasted of both! He had known on many such occasions himself how they felt on the tongue and inside his shrunken bowels.

Helen added some fruit, then paused. "What do you think, Facundo?"

The old man did not know how to say it, even to her. "That which a man takes to do what he must do when he has forgotten how to do it. That medicine in a bottle. Sí, mebbe so."

"Of course! I should have thought of it myself!" If there was one thing those men needed, confined without exercise or proper food, it was a good laxative. She put a bottle of a safe physic in the paper sack. "Now we're ready!"

Facundo delayed. "Mebbe that Governor smoke."

Facundo never forgot anything! Helen threw in a sack of Bull Durham and a package of Wheatstraws, and fled out to the car.

They drove steadily on the paved highway down the slope of the plateau, dipped into the wide plain, and turned off on a dirt road that led westward to the mountains. They stopped for a sandwich where the river poured out of the gorge in a wide bend. Then they crossed the rickety bridge and started climbing the foothills through a growth of sage and piñon.

It was nearly noon when they came to the pueblo, almost hidden in the hills. It was as if they had entered a world that no one knew existed. The drab adobes clustered close together for companionship in loneliness. The hard beaten earth of the little plaza. The absence of color, movement, sound. And over all, the wan, tepid light . . . A little eerie, really.

It was then Helen became aware of the drum beat. The low, muffled sound seemed to come from inside the earth. The vibration traveled up her legs to the pit of her stomach even before her ears caught the echo of its sound. Off in the corner of the plaza, a solitary, naked little boy was dancing slowly in the thick dust, as if his feet too were moved by the vibratory rhythm in the earth rather than by the audible sound.

Facundo walked to a house across the plaza and knocked. A woman appeared, looked them over, and left without a word. They kept waiting at the door. Finally she reappeared, beckoned and vanished. They went inside.

The Governor was waiting to greet them. He had had time to put on a colored shirt, tail out over his baggy pants, and to take down his staff of office from a nail on the smooth adobe wall. He and Facundo shook hands, white fashion. They all sat down. The Governor was a sparse little man, his thin black hair drawn back from his weathered

212

face and tied into a chignon in back with a white rag. He sat stiffly erect, holding the polished mahogany cane with a gold top and tied with a cluster of colored ribbons—one of the canes presented to each pueblo by Abraham Lincoln as a token of their local sovereignty.

After a time Facundo respectfully requested permission to visit with his friend. The Governor stood up. "It is permitted, as you know," he said gravely, and went out.

In a little while he came back from the kiva with Facundo's friend, and sat down in the corner to monitor their conversation as prescribed by tradition. The Cacique was old, but not as old as Facundo. He wore only a pair of moccasins made of deerskin, and a coarse, black wool blanket. His unbound hair fell to his shoulders. He and Facundo nodded silently at each other, and sat down on opposite sides of the room.

"This my good friend," Facundo said in English, inclining his head toward Helen sitting on the third side of the room.

She got up with the paper bag holding her gifts of cabbage, lettuce, fruit and physic. The Cacique made no effort to take them, merely flipping his hand toward the Governor who got up and took the bag from her. But he gave her one direct look: the blank, open look of an owl; a look that was still withdrawn, inturned, and not focused on the outer world. Yet curiously she felt that he saw into and through her from those subterranean depths whence came the muffled, vibrant drum beats.

Immediately he lowered his eyes, looking at the floor in silence as he sat hunched in his blanket. Facundo also sat staring at the floor in silence. This was their visit. It lasted almost thirty minutes.

The Governor was silent too, but Helen heard him scratching at his back, watched him keep spitting into a little box of sand near the corner fireplace. Then suddenly she forgot his presence as there rushed out to her something that entwined and composed the two old men before her. Two great waves of pure, mindless feeling that gushed out, mingled, and subsided into an intangible flood that filled the whole room, engulfing her completely.

This was the essence of prayer, she thought as it caught her up. A powerful, intangible force, unweakened by any reservation whatever, unconstricted by the illusions of time and spatial limits, that reached out to the tiniest insect, the humblest rodent, all the birds of the air, the fish of the waters, the beasts of plain and forest, and man. Not only themselves, but men of all races and colors and beliefs, even the white men who had shattered their tribes and were ignorant and contemptuous of their faith. She sat head bowed, bathed in its flow.

The kiva chief finally raised his head. His time was up. He and Facundo rose, their "visit" over. They shook hands.

"That good work you doin'," said Facundo.

"My friend. We give thanks to you."

He went out slowly, carrying the paper sack to the kiva. Facundo shook hands formally with the Governor, gave him the sack of Bull Durham and packet of papers. Helen fumbled in her purse, and gave him a new silver dollar. Then they went back to the car.

The sun was shining palely on the sand hills when they stopped at the turn of the road so Facundo could go into the bushes. The red river glowed far below. A strange, timeless peace held everything in its calm. Facundo came back and stood beside her without talking. A blue bottlefly buzzed around, settling on his arm. He slowly stuck up his forefinger, and Helen watched the fly crawl upon it. Then suddenly Facundo flipped it joyfully away on the breeze.

"Got long road to travel to the sun, that horsefly!" He laughed low and deep. "Him better get goin'!"

One afternoon late in May Gaylord drove to another kind of kiva on the Hill. The sky was clear turquoise. Birds sang in the pines. Emily presumably had had her child; he had stopped worrying and was engrossed in his work again. It was on another novel reactor: the first "fast" reactor ever built, utilizing fast neutrons to maintain its chain reaction, whereas all previous reactors had used thermal neutrons slowed down by water or graphite. It would be unique also in that it would be the first reactor to use plutonium for fuel instead of normal uranium, and liquid mercury for cooling.

Gaylord always smiled when he heard the nickname for it that had grown out of Dr. Breslau's sly humor. Breslau, who had helped to design it, had left Los Alamos on a short trip. Worrying how its construction was going during his absence, he had sent a telegram carefully worded to avoid any breach of Security. The wire read:

"In a cavern, in a canyon, extrapolating
    must be fine. Since you're the miners,
    Forty-Niners, tell me, how is Clementine?"

As the reactor was being built in a deep canyon, and Forty Nine
was the code name for plutonium, the crew had no difficulty trans-
lating his query. Roaring with laughter, the men promptly named
the fast reactor "Clementine."

Gaylord was out of the canyon now, driving across the wide
mesa to the south. Ahead of him stretched what still seemed an un-
tamed wilderness of pine and piñon seamed by rocky arroyos. Yet
he glimpsed a shop building here, a lab there, a storage facility. What
a laboratory! Hundreds of buildings, mere shacks though they might
be, scattered throughout seventy-seven square miles of remote mountain wilderness so thoroughly isolated by Security that not even a
plane was allowed to fly over the area.

The road snaked down past ancient Indian picture writing on
the black volcanic rock to a secluded clump of wooden buildings in
a clearing. Up the canyon from them was a small laboratory that
was popularly called a "kiva" after the isolated and well-guarded
room in a pueblo where the Indians conducted their secret ceremonies.
It was appropriately nicknamed, thought Gaylord, for in it was conducted highly classified and dangerous experiments to test the nuclear
properties of fissionable material. It was one of these that Gaylord
had been asked to attend.

He showed his badge and was cleared into the area. Parking his
car, he walked swiftly to the kiva.

"Good!" said Dr. Breslau sharply, closing the door behind Gaylord as he entered. "We have been waiting for you!"

Dr. Breslau's impatience betrayed his known dislike of these experiments and the way they were conducted. A methodical scientist
and a stickler for observing the utmost safety precautions, he had re-
peatedly declared them too dangerous to be performed in what he
regarded as a perfunctory manner. The time would come, he said,
when these critical assembly experiments would be conducted in an
empty laboratory by remote control and viewed by television from
the control board in a blockhouse a half mile away.

Gaylord smiled at him. "Why the hurry?" he asked cheerfully.
"I'm two minutes early."

The large room, its bare walls painted white, was furnished only with a desk and a table bearing the apparatus for the experiment. Dr. Emil Salzburg who was to conduct it, and the five other scientists, laboratory assistants, and technicians who were to witness it with Breslau and Gaylord, stood talking in the corner. As was customary, they had dressed as they pleased—sweat shirts, sweaters, sport shirts, odd trousers. Salzburg had on a sports shirt and khaki trousers tucked into a pair of fancy cowboy boots. Only the thick lenses of his horn-rimmed spectacles identified him as a scientist and bookworm. He nodded at his companions and walked to the desk. The group followed him.

"Right here behind me, please," he said to Gaylord.

Gaylord obediently moved up to stand immediately behind and a little to one side of him, the others grouping around them—two about six feet in front of the desk, the other four standing some eight feet behind it.

The apparatus before them was appallingly simple: essentially no more than two half-globes of greasy, silver-gray metal; a counter to register the radiation of the metallic globes with audible clicks like a metronome; and an instrument to permanently record the radiation intensity on a roll of paper.

Salzburg began to explain it. Despite its simple appearance, this critical assembly, stripped to the barest essentials, constituted the heart of a great nuclear reactor or an atomic bomb. For when the rare, precious, fissionable material contained in these greasy, silver-gray lumps was slowly brought together into one mass, a nuclear chain reaction was instigated which could be sustained at a certain intensity by strict control, as in a reactor. But if they were brought together suddenly, provided they had been constricted by an outside force under certain other proper conditions, the instantaneous fissioning would result in the searing blast of an atomic bomb. A reactor was merely a critical system; a bomb simply a supercritical system.

Below certain limits of size, weight and geometry, a mass of fissionable material was not dangerous. But just how big a mass was required for it to reach a critical configuration? That was the purpose of these experiments.

The components were slowly manipulated together. If the critical dimensions were not attained, the chain reaction would soon die out.

If the critical size were exceeded, a chain reaction, when started even by a single neutron, would increase exponentially, as shown on the chart. In this manner the amount of fissionable material required to form a critical mass could be determined by actual test.

There was no danger of an explosion; but if the chain reaction was permitted to get under way, the critical mass became intensely, dangerously radioactive. The trick was to bring the assembly just to criticality—just!

Dr. Emil Salzburg talked well. As he turned around, Gaylord could see the serious look on his deeply tanned face, his lower lip protruding slightly beyond the upper. Behind his thick glasses his eyes sparkled. His short, slender body was alertly alive. Yet Gaylord seemed to feel about him a curious, nervous excitement and a faint sense of almost dramatic expectancy—the same peculiar quality that Helen had sensed in him that evening when they and Klaus Fuchs had shared a table in her Tea Room.

Gaylord had seen Salzburg often since that evening, but he did not know him well. No one did; Salzburg kept to himself. Older than Gaylord and extremely competent, he yet was always in the forefront when anything promised to be exciting or dangerous. It was he who had tested the criticality of the world's first atomic bomb exploded at Alamogordo.

He turned around, and manipulated the two half-globes into position. The counter clicked slowly in the silent room. The pen of the recording instrument flicked up to mark the paper.

"The dragon has been awakened," said Salzburg. "See, we have tickled its tail!"

Salzburg loved to tickle the dragon's tail. He had a feeling for the experiment, and he had done it competently, assuredly, over and over again. He bent down, carefully manipulating the two pieces of fissionable material closer together. The counter began to click steadily, faster, with the increased radioactivity. The red line on the recorder began to climb across the roll of paper.

Gaylord moved closer, putting his hand on Salzburg's shoulder and bending down to see better. The other observers were intent and silent.

Deliberately Salzburg continued his slow manipulations. As the two pieces of metal were drawn closer and closer, the click of the

217

counter increased to a rapid rate, and the red exponential line on the paper climbed upward.

Salzburg paused. Gaylord drew a deep breath, his ears cocked to the clicking counter, his gaze fastened on the two lumps of greasy, silver-gray. The point of criticality was almost reached. One last, deft manipulation . . .

Suddenly, without warning, as he peered over Salzburg's shoulder, Gaylord saw it happen. The strange, quick blue glow known as the Cherenkov effect. The pen of the recorder leaping crazily off its red line, off scale entirely, and with it the sudden, insane clicking of the counter before it stopped dead.

Almost before he consciously realized that Salzburg's hand had slipped and that the two half-globes of metal had plunged together into a single mass, Salzburg threw himself forward and tore them apart with his bare hands. Then he stepped back and turned around, his dark brown face a sickly yellow. In his sports shirt and cowboy boots, he looked suddenly to Gaylord like a pathetic, terrified boy.

Perhaps the other observers, like Gaylord, felt on their tongues the dry, sour sensation of excessive radiation, and a quick fear gripping their bowels. But they were all scientists, and men, and they did quickly what had to be done. They noted on a slip of paper the exact positions and distances of each of the men in the room. They observed the time. It was exactly 3:20. Then they hurriedly left the laboratory, got into cars, and drove off.

2

They had not gone very far before Salzburg vomited. A few miles farther, he vomited again. No one spoke.

They reached the hospital and sent for doctors and authorities on radioactivity. It involved many types of radiation: positively charged alpha particles, negatively charged beta particles, deeply penetrating uncharged gamma rays, neutrons, and X-rays. Radiation itself was measured in *roentgens*: a roentgen being the amount of X or gamma radiation which produced a specific electrostatic unit of charge. What was the lethal dosage? It was not known exactly, but it was believed that the median lethal dosage was from 200 to 400 roentgens—that is, the amount that would be lethal to half the people exposed to it, although 25 roentgens would cause temporary blood changes.

What dosage, then, had each of the eight persons received? It depended on many factors: the power of the radiation source, the critical mass, the time of exposure, and the shielding each might have had. Salzburg of course had received the full dosage; moreover, his bare hands had come into physical contact with the fissionable material at the very instant of the chain reaction. But by lunging forward and breaking the chain reaction, he had reduced both the dosage and the time of the exposure of the others. Closest to him was Gaylord who had been standing only three feet from the assembly and partially shielded by Salzburg, with only his head, shoulders and one arm exposed. Next closest was Breslau, standing about six feet in front of the desk . . . So many factors to be taken into consideration. So many complicated computations to make. It was impossible to determine the dosage and probable extent of injury right away.

A wave of nausea caught up Gaylord. He too now retched violently.

Salzburg said quietly, "I'm sorry I got you into this. I'm afraid I have less than a fifty-fifty chance of living. I hope you have better than that."

That night Gaylord in his hospital bed felt no pain, but the nausea persisted. Between attacks he estimated his own chances to be a little better than fifty-fifty. He could not be sure, and rather hazily he wondered at times if he already had begun to die. So soon? It was a queer thought, he thought hazily as he thought about it as if he could think about such a queer thought he had never thought of thinking about before . . .

Slowly the effects of the radiation on his cell tissue caught up with him. His temperature rose. Under the fever his face flushed, constipation and anorexia set in, drowsiness overcame him. An itching rash broke out on his body. Lesions appeared on his knees, elbows and hands.

Doctors and nurses came in every three hours to give him intromuscular injections of penicillin. His fluid intake was increased. He was given lyophilized plasma, then two blood transfusions.

The dosage computations had been completed. He had received a median lethal dose of 390 roentgen of 80-kv X-rays and 26 roentgens of gamma rays.

Doctors and nurses kept coming in. A few friends appeared for a moment. Gaylord was too drowsy to care. He lay there with a puzzled look on his face, listening to the birds singing outside, watching the stars ...

When he awoke, a nurse was standing by the bed.

"How are the rest of them coming along?" he asked.

"Fine, Dr. Gaylord. Just fine!"

Two of the laboratory assistants and technicians, both in their early twenties, had received up to 140 r. Dr. Breslau had received 187 r. All were recovering nicely.

"And Dr. Salzburg?"

The nurse said quickly, "We are doing everything possible for him."

Salzburg lay dying down the hall. He had received a full body dose of 1,930 r of 80-kv X-rays and 114 r of gamma rays; and 15,000 rem in his hands. He might have been standing fully exposed to an atomic bomb, completely protected from its blinding light, searing heat, and terrific blast, yet helpless before the lethal power of a radioactivity that could not be seen, heard, smelled, nor felt.

His hands and arms, blistered, blood red, swollen and still bloating, were packed in ice to reduce the pain. His lower abdomen was red and the pain spreading. His tongue was sore from touching a gold inlay that had become radioactive; a dentist was called in to cap it. His temperature and pulse rate were rising abruptly, and now the leukocyte count was falling; his white blood cells were failing to reproduce. His red marrow was turning liquid. Mental confusion was setting in ...

On the morning of the ninth day Dr. Emil Salzburg died. Nothing could have saved him.

Next day prompt cauterization stopped the bleeding from Gaylord's nose. The occult blood in his stools disappeared. He began to feel better. Five days later he was discharged from the hospital. He felt all right, though he still had a dryness in his mouth, on his forehead and left hand, and in his groin. Tired and weak, he lay in bed the clock around, staring with a puzzled expression at an old, strange world that seemed far newer than the New World he had helped to build.

When the first wild rumors of the accident had reached Turner, he telephoned at once for full information. None could be given him; the details were classified. He banged down the receiver. Those damned Xs were still conspiring to withhold public information from the press!

Helen Chalmers was more discreet. She merely requested to see Gaylord at the first opportunity. Two weeks later when he returned home from the hospital Helen received notice that a visitor's pass was waiting for her at the gate. Los Alamos was no longer a closed Secret City. Permission was granted anyone to visit a resident in the living area although the technical area was still closed.

As she drove through town that afternoon, Helen could find few of the old landmarks she had known. The Big House in its meadow had been torn down; the meadow itself was gone. In place of the other log buildings of the school stood row on row of apartments, hutments, prefabs of all kinds. She kept driving westward on Trinity Drive toward the forested slope of the mountains on which stood newer, more permanent buildings than the temporary wartime structures below. Here Gaylord had moved into a comfortable flat allocated him because of his salary and long employment.

He was alone when she entered at his call, lying stiffly propped up on the couch.

"Gay!" she said cheerfully. "How wonderful that you're home!"

As he turned his head slightly to greet her, a flicker of pain passed over his stiff, calm face. It had begun just a few days after he left the hospital, he told her. The skin on his left temple was so sensitive that just a touch of the hair aroused a spasm of intense pain. Now gradually the hair was coming out, and the beard on the left side of his face had stopped growing. Perhaps it was her imagination, but his left eye seemed duller than the right.

"I saw Dr. Breslau," Helen said casually. "He's feeling fit as a fiddle again, though a little tired . . . Not his appetite. He still insisted on two pieces of cake!"

Gaylord grinned slightly.

"You'll be able to come down to dinner soon too," she went on. "In the meantime I'm arranging for Maria to come here every day to look after you until you return to work. You remember the Indian girl who used to take care of me?"

221

He nodded gratefully.

Chattering lightly, Helen recalled the amusing evening he had shared a table in her Tea Room with Salzburg and Fuchs. "What ever became of Dr. Klaus Fuchs?"

"Oh, he went back to England. The big atomic energy project at Harwell. He's head of the theoretical division."

There wasn't much to talk about but as she stood up to leave, Gaylord raised his hand. "Helen, there's something I must tell you. Perhaps I should have told you long before this."

She sat down again. Then bluntly, without excuses, he said he had made Emily pregnant — the reason she had run away.

"Don't blame yourself, Gay," Helen said calmly. "And don't blame Emily for running away and refusing to let you know where she is. Things like this happen, and we must accept them. Perhaps the child will bring you together again."

"I'll never regret our having a child, however it happened," he said in a flat, expressionless voice. "It's one of the most important things that has ever happened to me. You see, it probably will never happen to me again."

The edge of the pillowslip brushed across his left temple, causing another spasm of pain. Gaylord waited for it to pass. Then, coldly objective, he stated that while he was suffering only a passing illness due to radiation exposure, sperm counts and testicular biopsies had disclosed he was undergoing a state of sterility. It was hoped that this might be as transient as other temporary effects. Still, who knew?

Helen said nothing. What could one say?

"I believe Emily ought to know this," he said quietly. "Neither of us can afford any illusions now. Will you write her, Helen? I can't."

"Tonight, Gay. And I'll wire the office of the Chalmers estate to forward my letter to her immediately, wherever she is."

3.

The shock came one Sunday evening a couple of weeks later. Turner had caught a fine mess of trout upriver and brought them to

Helen to cook for dinner. His boots were muddy, his shirt sleeve torn, his face red and glowing from the sun and several drinks he had taken. He pushed back his plate, filled his pipe, and slid the pouch over to Facundo. "Roll a cigarette with this new tobacco, Facundo. *Qué bueno! Muy delicado!*"

Then he began a long tirade against the Xs on the Hill because the details of Gaylord's accident were still withheld from him. This was the new and monstrous problem now forced on the world—Security! Ever since the days of the cave man, security had implied merely physical protection from enemy attack. But castle moats, fortified towers and walled cities were no protection against an A-bomb. Security now implied the secrecy with which one nation could guard its scientific discoveries and technological skills from all others. A national security involving all the police mechanisms of investigation, clearance, and compartmentalization of knowledge.

"Nothing is immune from it!" he declaimed. "Not even your dreams escaped investigation! Why, we're getting as secretive about our science as Facundo here with all his kiva stuff!"

Facundo was offended. "I not talkin' about them things! I don't say nothin'!" He got up to sulk at the window and in a moment slid noiselessly out of the room.

"It's no good!" went on Turner. "It's breeding a tribe of secretive, intellectual robots like Gaylord who's never had a real emotion!"

"You're wrong, Jack!" She told him quietly and briefly about Emily and Gaylord. "You can't blame either one of them. Emily was foolish to run away and have the child in Mexico. Gaylord really loves her and he's so glad for the child." She paused. "You see, he's undergoing sterility from the radiation exposure he received in that accident and—"

"No! The poor bastard! . . . Oh, the poor son of a bitch!"

"He's not either! Imagine what he's gone through!" Helen pleaded with an excess of compassion. "And Emily too!"

"Stop it!" he yelled, jumping up.

"It's true, Jack! Please! There's nothing to be angry about!"

"Shut up! For God's sake stop that drivelling sentimental nonsense! Emily had an abortion before she left here. I helped her get it!"

Helen reared back as if he had struck her. "She didn't! Oh,

223

no!" she wailed piteously, sinking back down in her chair as Turner advanced to stand over her.

"Christ no!" he roared. "It's just something I dreamed up for a soap-box opera. Who in the hell could believe such a corny situation? A poor son of a bitch looking forward to a bastard child that had been aborted. God Almighty! What a preposterous fantasy!"

She stared at him with unbelieving eyes.

"What did he do about it?" demanded Turner. "He was in New York. Why didn't he force the manager of the Chalmers estate to give him Emily's address? He knew the man sent her a monthly allowance. Do you think for one minute I'd have sat here on my tail mooning about it? I'd have gone to Mexico City, hired a detective, found out her address from the passport authorities—something!"

"But Gay's not practical about such things like you are, Jack. He didn't know what to do!" Helen pleaded.

Turner flung away to stalk around the room. Then like a man impelled by a force he could not resist, he came back to confront her again. "And what about you all this time? Didn't you suspect something strange was up, the way Emily went off without a word? You saw Gaylord all along. Didn't you notice anything peculiar about his manner?"

She put her hands over her face, unable to face his accusing stare.

"No! You didn't! You've been too damned busy nursing your psychosis to have any concern for anybody! Come off your perch, Helen," he went on. "You're living on this corrupt and rotten earth same's the rest of us. We're not noble souls puffed up with divine morality. We're weak and afraid like Gaylord. We're selfish and headstrong as Emily. But by God, we're human!"

The angry intensity of his outburst revealed a Turner who was all too human himself. For too long he had bottled up his resentment of Helen for breaking off relations with him. Now it was all coming out at last!

Helen put her head down and burst into tears. Turner shuffled awkwardly around the table. "I don't mean to be hard on you, Helen. But this is a practical world. Abortions are dime-a-dozen nowadays. And Emily was in a bind!" He paused. "You say you wrote Emily about Gaylord?"

"I mailed it that night," Helen sobbed.

"Jesus Christ! I told her she'd be sorry! You better write her again, tonight!"

Turner suddenly strode across the room toward the door. "I never liked Gaylord! At least the looks of the poor son of a bitch. And now he's going to think I not only helped to double-cross him, but enjoy telling him about it . . . Not you! Goddamn it! It would be me, after all, who's got to drive up there now and tell him he's no more got a bastard child than the man in the moon!"

As he grabbed up his fishing coat, Helen could see a bottle of whiskey sticking out from the pocket.

Turner was upset by the prospect confronting him. As he drove up the Hill, he kept stopping the car to uncork the bottle and take a big swig. By the time he parked his car in front of Gaylord's flat he was already tight. Grasping the bottle, he walked to the door. The light was still on and through the window he could see Gaylord in a dressing robe sitting forlornly in a big chair, dozing over a book. Turner took another swig, and rang the bell.

The door opened. He could see the surprise in Gaylord's eyes as his glance took in his own muddy boots and fishing garb. Raising the bottle in his left hand, he said cheerfully, "Yep, it's me! Just came from a fishin' trip. How about a drink?"

Gaylord quickly latched the screen. "I can't discuss the accident with you, Turner. You'll have to go to our Information people."

"I don't want to interview you!" yelled Turner, yanking at the screen. It would not open; and fearful that Gaylord would close the door in his face, Turner lowered his voice to a confidential whisper. "Not about the accident. Something more secret, more important. Personal . . . . Emily, old boy!"

Gaylord looked suddenly old and tired and sick. He unlatched the door and stepped back in his slippers.

Turner strode in, holding up the bottle. "How about one first? It'll make bad news easier to swallow."

Gaylord's eyes narrowed. Coldly polite, he went into the kitchen and brought back a glass and a pitcher of water. "I've been too ill to join you."

Ignoring the glass and water, Turner took a big drink out of the bottle and spread his legs. "Gaylord," he said in a thickening voice, "you're going to hate me and I can't help it and I'm sorry. I wish

225

it didn't have to be me who had to come up here but it was and I'm here and—"

"What is it you came up here to tell me about Emily?" demanded Gaylord sharply. He was still standing and did not offer Turner a chair.

Turner took another gulp of whiskey, seeking desperately for an excuse to delay the inevitable. Gaylord's silence and set face closed all means of escape. Turner spread his legs still wider and resolutely blurted out, "Emily didn't have a child. She couldn't. She had an abortion last summer before she went to New York. I helped her go through with it."

For one quick moment, foggy as he was, Turner saw the swift pain, the spreading anguish, and the undying regret that leapt into Gaylord's eyes before the invisible shutters closed over them. "My God, man! I'm sorry! Believe me!" Impelled by a burst of real compassion, he staggered forward and grasped Gaylord by both shoulders.

Gaylord steadied him, then quietly drew himself away.

"I know how it was with you and Emily, Gaylord. I've been through this myself. What can I say, man?"

Gaylord drew his robe closer about him as if trying to conceal the hurt and sorrow wracking him inside. "There's nothing for either of us to say, is there?"

His dignified composure, set face and steady gaze aroused in Turner a measure of admiration. They stood looking at each other without speaking.

"I've got to get up early and I'm awfully tired. Do you mind?" Gaylord said in a flat, empty voice. "Thank you for letting me know."

Turner set down his whiskey bottle on the table and lumbered unsteadily out the door.

4.

Emily awakened at sunup in her charming old house in Cuernavaca feeling as if she were locked up in a prison. Throwing on a dressing robe, she fled out to the long garden in back to sit by the tiled pool. An ancient *ahuelhuete* tree still dreamed of Guatemozin and Zapata in the bright sunlight. Crimson and magenta blossoms painted the garden wall. Old Popo's snowy head stood out in the clear sky. But there on the gate, sunning itself in a stench of carrion, perched a rusty black *zopilote*.

How horribly repulsive this huge buzzard was! She fled back to the house. But the French door had snapped fast behind her, and the massive iron catch on the portal door was bolted shut from the inside. Emily let out a shout of anger, then another. "Isabel! I-SA-BEL!"

Isabel, the maid, came with the house. She was a scrawny little thing, honest and dependable. But like most Indians, she was mortally afraid of the *aires de la noche,* and every nightfall shuttered and bolted the house against every breath of air. In a moment she came running to let Emily in.

Seething with resentment, Emily paraded her through the house to fling windows and doors open. "I've told you before! Why do you have to keep locking me in!"

"Señora! *Los aires de la noche!*" protested Isabel, as if the lurking airs of night still might jump down her throat and attack her from within.

"*Señorita!*" Emily corrected her haughtily. "*No hay hombre!*"

"*No hay hombre! Qué lástima, Señora!*" wailed Isabel. A woman without a man. What a pity!

It was ridiculous!

Their daily fuss over, Emily dressed, ate a *papaya,* and hurried to the street corner. It was *el dia del turismo,* the day she went to Mexico City for mail and shopping. The *turismo* was an old limousine provided with extra jump seats to crowd in eight passengers. When it came, Emily squeezed in and settled down to enjoy the hour's trip over the mountains and down into the Valley of Mexico. Yet a shadow, like that of the *zopilote,* followed her as it had from the Sangre de Cristos and Central Park.

In New York, whence she first had fled, Emily found that she had carried her troubles with her. She had not only got herself knocked up higher than a kite, but she had permitted an illegal operation to be performed on her. Her own compliance was abetted by Gaylord's desertion of her at her crucial hour of need. To abandon her without a word, to walk off leaving her no address, was unforgivable! When news of the atomic detonations broke, and she realized why it had been impossible for him to stay with her or write her, she felt worse. She pounded her pillows with her fists, then soaked them with her tears.

The Chalmers apartment in Gramercy Square with its brocaded drapes and silver candlesticks gave her no peace. She dined out alone and sought escape in shopping sprees. She was lectured for her extravagance by the legal guardian of the Chalmers estate, and for three whole days cooked all her meals in the apartment. It was all a farce! She fled to Mexico City.

The Regis was too much like any big New York hotel. Emily moved into a smaller one and began to prowl around her favorite city. *Viva Mexico!* It was Mexico all right, but the *viva* was gone. The lawns of Chapultepec were crowded as those of Central Park; the floating gardens of Xochimilco were worse than Coney Island on the Fourth of July. Even the *mole de guajalote* at Prendes had lost its flavor, perhaps because the cafe was crowded with a convention of American automobile salesmen.

Learning that Gaylord had arrived in New York just after she had left, Emily tore up his telegram and fled to Cuernavaca. People throughout the world travel on the same routes and in the same strata like schools of fish; and here the same school of fish that swam through Santa Fe on its way between Albuquerque and La Oreja now eddied leisurely through Cuernavaca on its way between Mexico City and Acapulco. All day they filled the plazas, the markets, the churches, even the familiar Bella Vista hotel where she stayed.

Emily drove out into the *tierra caliente,* and the brilliant sun beating down on the sugar cane fields blinded her. At Cuatla the wind had come up; the dust was like a thick dun fog; she could not even glimpse the snow-covered summit of old Popo. At Yautepec she stopped before the most gorgeous display of beans she had ever seen: brown, yellow, purple, green, red, and speckled, just like Indian corn at home. But she was irritated because she couldn't find any of the fine hand-woven cloth she wanted.

A few days later came another minor earthquake. "Goddamn it!" she screamed as her vase of flowers crashed on the floor. "I hate it all! Everything! Everybody!"

It was then she found a charming old house on the side of the barranca. Ruthlessly she plunked down all her quarterly income for its lease, imperiously wiring New York for an advance on her next. For a while she was content to stay home. Then it too became a prison with iron-barred windows, iron-studded doors and gates which her jailer bolted shut each night. Her only paroles were these weekly trips to the ultramodern center of ancient Aztec Tenochtitlan.

Today, after lunching and shopping, Emily found a big bundle of mail waiting for her at the American Express office. She stuffed it into a bright-colored hemp *bolsa* and hailed a taxi.

"Tostón! Tostòn?"

"O.K., O.K.," the driver grumbled, opening the door.

She drove to the bus station where she was to catch the *turísmo* home. It stood at the corner of 5 Calle de Nezahualcoyotl and 20 de Noviembre, in an old and tawdry part of the city that always depressed her. To take her eyes and mind off the drab surroundings, it was her habit to read her mail during the long wait between reserving her seat and boarding the bus. The little waiting room was more crowded than usual. She bought her ticket; and unable to find a seat, went out on the sidewalk to read her letters. There were two from Helen.

There was hardly room to stand among the crowd of Indios squatting on their bare feet, wrapped in *serape* and *rebozo*, mindlessly waiting as they had waited through centuries already. Nervous and impatient, Emily squeezed between an old woman holding a parrot in a wicker cage, and a man sucking a section of sugar cane, and began reading Helen's letters . . .

How strange it was that this run-down *barrio* so long ignored now leapt out at her with a vividness of detail that imprinted itself indelibly upon her memory. She stood staring at the coarse, brownish stone facade of the building across the street, at the gargoyle faces carven upon the lintels of the doorway. A juke box was playing in the corner *cantina*. Three bars of the music kept repeating themselves in her brain. There was no escaping any of it, anything. She had fled as far as she could, and now on this tawdry street corner she was brought to bay . . . It was impossible! All this time believing she had carried and given birth to his child without letting him know! And now he had been made sterile by an accident!

The *turísmo* came up; she got on. As it drove off, she could see the gargoyle faces leering at her and hear the three bars of music biting deeper into her brain.

Arriving home, Emily shut herself up in her bedroom. She had reached a dead end.

Verna Taylor was her only friend. Small, trim and not unattractive, she sat on the porch of the Bella Vista drinking tequila from late afternoon until midnight. She owned a small shop specializing in custom-made Mexican silver, and made it her business to know everyone of note in Cuernavaca. Forty and unmarried, she was respected for her business acumen and feared for her cutting gossip.

"Emily Chalmers? Of course I knew her then!" Miss Taylor clapped her hands to signal a waiter for another *copita,* and leaned back with a smile. "I was trying to eke out an existence here with a tourist bookstall when she took that huge De Vaca house across the *barranca.* She'd send her maid for a dozen American books at a time; finally I went out to collect something on her account. There she was, alone in that *hacienda* big enough to quarter a troop of Federal cavalry—as it did during the Zapata revolution. Shut up in one dark bedroom. Packages of books all over, not one opened. Unable to eat or sleep, and crying her eyes out.

"I felt sorry for her and went to see her every day. She was too proud to tell me at first, but I guessed her trouble. She'd got screwed and got left. Who hasn't? That—or vice versa—is Chapter One in Everyman's autobiography, the universal theme of love.

"She didn't get any better and I got worried. Something was really eating her. Finally she broke down and told me. She'd had an abortion and run away from the man, whoever he was; I never knew. This put a different light on things. Don't ask me what having an abortion does to a woman. Only a woman knows and she can't tell exactly what herself. She may ignore it, bluff it out, or anything else. But knowing she's been impregnated with another life besides her own and then having her insides scraped out does something to her. It does to a woman like Dr. Emily Chalmers anyway.

"Something had to be done, so I started taking her out to the pyramid of Teopanzolco near the old railroad station here, to Xochilcalco, and then to the pyramids of the sun and moon at San Juan

Teotihuacan. That did it. She had a fixation on pyramids, you know, and began to snap out of it."

Once again Miss Taylor reared back, raised both hands, and began the noisy clapping that embarrassed everybody on the portál and brought two waiters on the run.

"*Sorda hija de tal!* Don't tell me her mother was the famous Woman at Otowi Crossing. Our little blossom was never born from a human womb! She was sired by the Chase National Bank out of the Pyramid of Xochicalco. The man doesn't exist who can thwart her ambition. Every poor bastard who tries to sleep with her she emasculates. She goes to bed with her *Inquiry*. It's her only love.

"That's Doctor Emily Chalmers please! One must never forget that sanctimonious title of academic ignorance . . . Or her stinking Book of Revelations - - that sacred *Inquiry!* I attended one of her lectures this winter at the National University where she occupies a chair of anthropology. Someone in the audience asked her a question. 'Why, I don't know,' she answered. 'Let's see what the *Inquiry* has to say about it.' Jesus H. Christ! As if it was an immortal pillar of wisdom she hadn't whittled out herself! A frigidly orthodox academician pukey jealous of her mother's greater fame. God, what a tragic joke!"

It was getting late. In the pale moonlight the white-clad Indians, vendors and beggars were emptying the plaza and going home. As they straggled past the porch each one paused to bid Miss Taylor goodnight. Their faces were grave, their voices low. She too answered them in the mother tongue of the hills, slurring her "Adios" to a soft "Adios'n."

"I don't mean to be nasty. I'm just trying to explain the change I felt come over her. Or maybe she was born selfish and ambitious. Anyway she didn't let her broken heart interfere with her plans for the future. She meant to get her *Inquiry* published, return to New Mexico for some teaching experience, and then come back here to 'occupy the chair' she's plunked down in now. So she sent out letters, pulled the proper strings, and early in September boarded a plane for Albuquerque."

She put out a hand to steady herself, then reached for her empty glass.

From the moment she saw it, Emily was delighted with Sandia School. It stood on the eastern outskirts of Albuquerque, fronting Sandia Mountain. All the buildings were Spanish in design and name; Bienvenida, the administration building; La Jornada with its classrooms; La Mirla, the older girls' student house; and Yerba Buena, the young girls' dormitory, which also contained the "Very Little Theater." It was all so peaceful and gracious, with its lawn, patios and portales, its spacious rooms and quiet corridors, its tiled floors and murals. A preparatory, residential and day school for girls, it seemed the counterpart of the former Los Alamos Ranch School for boys that she had seen before it was taken over by Project Y.

It even had an art director whom Emily met one afternoon: Michael Dillon, a really fine artist. She immediately stuck out her hand. "So nice to find you here, Mr. Dillon! I've seen your paintings on 57th Street in New York."

He shrugged. "Who the hell gives a damn about art these days? Everything's science and engineering, or stocks, bonds and big business . . . Well, I've still got a paint brush in my hand, and a pot of beans on the stove. What more could I ask?"

Emily laughed. "Oh come, Mr. Dillon! It's not every artist who can be flattered with the adulation of so many charming young ladies in such a beautiful, secluded retreat as this!"

"A secluded oasis of culture?" he asked ironically. "Do you by chance know what lies behind that cloud of dust? Sandia Laboratory, a small branch of the Los Alamos Scientific Laboratory located on Sandia Base, ballooning into the headquarters of the Armed Forces Special Weapons Project! There, young lady, is where they're turning out the missile cases of the atomic bombs dreamed up on the Hill." He turned swiftly to point toward the south. "I don't suppose you know what's right over there, either! Nothing more than Kirkland Air Base, the Air Force's Special Weapons Center which provides the bombers to carry these 'special weapons' and drop them on target. Secluded, hell! This little culture academy is a dead duck sitting squarely between two of the biggest military installations in the whole damned atomic energy complex!"

What he said irritated Emily, but she shrugged it off. She was happy here. All her girls were from good families, young, alert and enthusiastic. Their respect restored her self-confidence, their youth

232

gave her a new vitality. They worked hard in school. She took them on picnics to nearby pueblos. They all had fun.

Too, Emily like the place she had found to live. It was a little adobe house in the former Spanish village of Los Griegos that had been annexed by swiftly growing Albuquerque. Emily furnished it very simply with a few good Indian and Mexican things, and began cooking her own dinners to avoid driving into town. Hidden behind horn-rimmed spectacles that gave her the appearance of a bookish owl engraven on an *Ex-Libris* plate, she spent the evenings making hurried revisions in her *Inquiry* that had been accepted for publication.

Eventually it came out with quite a respectable splash. Too heavy for popular reading of course. But warmly accepted by museums, libraries, academic institutions and professional readers as a standard source book. Emily squared her shoulders. She had become an authority in her field.

Only then did she buy a new car and drive up to Otowi Crossing.

5.

"Mother! Facundo!" she cried, jumping out of the car. "Nothing has changed!"

"Same," affirmed Facundo stoutly.

"Oh, Emily! Of course we're the same. All of us!"

Yet the change in all of them was apparent as they walked in the door. Emily had lost the last trace of immaturity. There was an angularity, a self-assurance about her that her effusiveness could not dispel. She was conscious of this herself as she kept squaring her shoulders in recognition of her success. A success whose slight prominence permitted her to look down with new objectivity upon this thin and wasting woman, this old and wrinkled Indian, still trying to hold together a pitiful little adobe being gnawed away by time and weather.

She felt its full impact, although she could not understand its hidden meaning, as she watched her mother making tea. All her childhood and youth she had nursed the sweet and sentimental fantasy of a story-book mother she had never known. Only to be brought up

233

short by the terrifying aspect of this strange fey woman with her in-scrutable notions and unpredictable attitudes. It was impossible to believe them the same, however hard she had tried. So she had con-tinued her search through archaeology, anthropology, and ethnology for the mother she had never known, would never know. And now — there in the car, here in her lap, accompanying her wherever she went! — was the mother of her long and impassioned search. The hoary mother of us all, ancient America, recreated in her own image: the *Inquiry* itself. "The breathing, living image of our continental earthmother" as her colleagues had praised it; or as Verna Taylor had unkindly reviewed it, "The most magnificently dull reiteration of aca-demic incertitudes imposed upon us since the dictates of the Inqui-sition!" Its success had freed her at last from her compulsive search and had cut all the bonds that sentimentally held her to Helen. Se-cure and self-assured, she settled down to drink her tea and listen to Helen talk about the more obvious changes around them.

A great deal had happened since Emily had left, Helen was saying. Congress had created an Atomic Energy Commission to take over the national program. Things were humming up on the Hill. New and modern laboratories were being built on South Mesa, and the com-munity was being rebuilt into a modern, up-to-date town. But of course with new restaurants the Xs seldom came down to the Tea Room any more.

Emily hesitated, then asked abruptly, "He's all right now, I sup-pose?"

"He looks fine, Emily. So busy though, I've seen very little of him lately."

Of course she had loved him, but what would he be like now and how would she feel if she ever saw him again? Would he be changed as much as the woman before her? Try as she might, Emily could not recognize the old childhood image of her mother so discounten-anced by this strange frail woman facing her. She looked like the projection of her own imagination, a faded caricature of an unsub-stantial wraith with her untidy hair and wrinkled dress.

"And Jack?"

He had been away for a month visiting the big atomic energy plants in Tennessee, Kentucky and Ohio. His articles on these had been followed by others on the large plutonium plants on the Columbia, Savannah and Mississippi rivers. A gigantic new industry, he reported, that equalled a dozen of the largest other industrial empires in the country.

Opening her purse, Emily took out a snapshot and handed it to Helen. "Give this to him, will you? Tell him I've found Throckmorton's sheep ranch."

Throckmorton had not been re-elected as State Senator; his platform of industrializing a remote ranching area naturally had been futile. But he had moved to Albuquerque and announced his candidacy for the national Congress over a radio station he had bought. Most of its programs were in Spanish, directed to the Spanish vote. Throckmorton's new appeal was remarkably simple. As an influential sheepman, he proposed that New Mexico return to its basic sheep economy. Just how a swiftly growing urban population could return in the Atomic Age to an outmoded grazing economy, he did not explain. But to thousands of native sons frightened by the influx of Anglos, the platform held great appeal. Throckmorton was elected and moved to Washington.

A Capital newspaper pictured his arrival. He was sitting astride the hood of a limousine. A large pair of curving ram's horns was mounted on the radiator cap, and he was wearing a big Stetson hat.

Turner then had been requested by ANS to build up a background story on him in case his views might sometime make front page news. But Turner had been unable to find a record of any ranch properties that Throckmorton had bought or leased. He owned only his newspaper and house in La Oreja, and the radio station and a house he had bought in Albuquerque. So soon after Emily's arrival, Turner had written her a note asking her to tell him of any sheep ranch she heard about that Throckmorton owned.

"This is it," ended Emily. "A nice ranch-style house with a two-acre lawn in front. In the Corrales section just north of where I live. I passed it on one of my evening walks and snapped it with my camera."

Helen looked at the print more closely. There was Mr. Throckmorton sitting out on the lawn in a rocking chair looking at a few sheep grazing around him.

"Twelve sheep. The whole flock," said Emily. "That will interest Jack."

235

Emily got up, declining the invitation to stay for supper. Helen walked out with her to the large and impressive new car. Its color matched perfectly the robin's egg blue of Emily's gloves and the ribboned spot in her hair. What a picture she made as she got in and settled behind the wheel! She had joined the multitude of those who had compromised with life and the marks of her success sat gracefully upon her. "Take care of yourself and Facundo too, now," she said with a smile.

"Emily dear—" Helen blurted out in a tremulous voice whose rising pitch seemed to sound at once an impassioned plea and a strange warning.

"Yes, Mother?"

Helen did not finish. She stood staring fixedly up into the sky with a concentration that seemed to be drawing the color from her cheeks and lips.

Emily swung open the door, jumped out, and flung her arms around her mother. A wave of nervous expectancy washed over her as she felt its dragging weight.

"Mother! Lie down a minute! Here now!"

Kneeling on the ground, she slipped an arm under Helen's head, brushed back a wisp of hair from her eyes. They were open, still staring upward with a look of wonder curiously tinctured with bemused concern. "Balloons . . . A universe of ballooning worlds . . . Don't you see them, Emily?"

Despite herself, Emily flung a glance upward toward the empty sky. "Of course, Mother!" Emily was shaken; this was the first of Helen's spells she had seen. For an instant she had the wild desire to rush off in her car for help. But what could one do for a woman who hadn't fainted or wasn't frothing at the mouth or anything like that? She was simply lying on the ground, watching imaginary balloons! As Emily hesitated, Helen sat up. Color was coming back into her face. She managed a smile.

"How strange to get so giddy, Emily! Just from remembering some balloons I once saw when I was little. Here. Give me your hand."

Emily walked back to the house with her. Then, anxious to keep a dinner appointment, she drove away quickly.

Shortly afterward Helen described her vision to Gaylord who had started coming down again.

236

"Was it a fantasy or simply a childhood memory that suddenly popped into my mind so clearly that it made me dizzy?" she asked as they sat alone together in her big room.

It was herself she asked; Gaylord remained quiet.

"I'm inclined now to think it must have been a forgotten incident," she continued. "Still it had the consistency of a dream although I was wide awake. I was strolling through Washington Square, possibly on the day of a parade, when I came to an Italian standing beside his hand-organ. A monkey was crouched on top, holding out a tin cup for pennies. He had a wrinkled, naked face whose sly expression repulsed me and he was dressed in a suit held together with some big brass buttons that made him look like a caricature of an official of some kind. Then I noticed a great bunch of colored balloons tethered to a corner of the hand-organ, straining in the breeze to be free. Each one of them was imprinted with words in an unknown language like ancient Greek or Arabic. Strangely enough, I divined their meaning instantly, but I can't remember it now. See what I mean when I say it had the consistency of a dream although I was wide awake?

"Well anyway, the monkey leaned toward me in his officious little brass-buttoned suit, his face grimacing in a sly smile, and insolently thrust his tin cup toward me. I backed away in refusal. Then suddenly, with a little squeal, he jerked the bunch of balloons free from their tether.

"Oh, those wonderful balloons rising in the air! A kaleidoscopic jumble of tossing, whirling balloons of all colors, colliding, impenetrating, merging into one great pattern! It made me dizzy to watch them. Then it happened; I don't know how, maybe they snagged on the protruding branch of a tree. But they exploded all at once in a burst of color that swiftly faded into the pale blue sky. My dizziness stopped, my eyes cleared. It was over that quick!"

What it meant, Helen didn't know. Nor could she find a rational meaning in several other visions, fantasies, and dreams she related to him during that period. Yet she was convinced that each one was in some way a message to her from that vast inner world in which she was searching for her own real self. Something in her knew things she did not know, and spoke to her in a language she had not yet learned.

It was of these things they talked, evening after evening, during that year when Gaylord came to know her best. Never of Emily. Nor about Fuchs who, it was now known, had passed the secret of the A-bomb to Harry Gold at the Castillo Street bridge in Santa Fe just before Trinity. What drew them together, neither questioned. It did not seem strange to Gaylord that Helen trusted and confided to him her psychic adventures, for neither Turner nor Emily was interested in such things. Just what compelled his own acute and sympathetic interest he did not know. Perhaps it was Helen herself more than what she said, the strange inner glow that lit up her eyes, gave life to her words. There are people who make one feel small and unsure; others who enlarge us in their presence. And in Helen there was a fey quality that untied knots within him, awakened his imagination, and opened up a vast world, nebulous and unreal as it seemed, which he had never dreamed might possibly exist.

Gaylord talked little. He was content to sit quietly, staring into the fire through the growing cloudiness of his bad eye. Yet he listened closely, his sharp mind registering unspoken questions and answers, a new yeast beginning to foment within him. What finally resulted, of course, was his series of papers on psychic phenomena related to the myth of the Woman at Otowi Crossing, published after her death. Permission has been granted to include here the following excerpt:

"If my scientific colleagues find anything strange in an atomic physicist stumbling into the unfamiliar realm of psychic phenomena, they will perhaps not regard it too amiss that he is a man indulging a hobby. Other men play chess; I am interested in trying to discover if the gambits of the supernormal are controlled by any natural laws of universal science. It is a broad field, and in these brief papers I have restricted my remarks to that area embraced by the myth of the so-called 'Woman at Otowi Crossing.'

"Like most scientists, I prefer conclusions that can be reached independently by different observers using the same explicit methods. This approach is not possible here. Everything factually known about Helen Chalmers constitutes one vast paradox. The myth about her is itself controversial. Hence I have confined myself to inquiries as to what is the essential basis of the myth about her; how does it relate, in its broader aspects, to the specific field of atomic physics; and what bearing upon it have those dynamic events and curious incidents which I personally experienced during my too brief friendship with her.

"What then, essentially, is the basis of the myth of the Woman at Otowi Crossing?

"It rests on the strange simultaneity of two events that took place in the vicinity of Otowi Crossing little more than a decade ago; the development and experimental detonation of the first atomic bomb, and the psychic phenomenon experienced by Helen Chalmers. Is there a definable parallel between the objective process accomplished in atomic fission and the subjective process she underwent?

"Nowadays every schoolboy knows the basic principle of the first crude A-bomb. It was explained publicly several years ago when the *New York Times* published a *Description of Atom Sabotage Devices* which had been approved by President Eisenhower, the National Security Council and Atomic Energy Commission, with a supplemental letter by J. Edgar Hoover, Director of the Federal Bureau of Investigation. The article briefly defined an 'implosion' as a bursting inward, contrasted with the bursting outward of an 'explosion.' It then explained:

'The scientists who worked on the first atomic bomb needed an implosion in order to compress nuclear material enough to get an atomic 'explosion.' They solved their problem by forming a large sphere of explosive material. In a hole in the center of this sphere they placed the fissionable material they wanted to squeeze.

'Then instead of using one detonator to ignite the explosive sphere, they placed many detonators around it. These detonators were connected electrically in such a way that they could be fired simultaneously . . .

'When this fast-burning imploding wave reaches

239

the sphere of fissionable material, this mass has no place to be pushed except in upon itself and is thus compressed.

'We have now explained very simply the basic ideas which govern atomic bomb design . . .'

"The similarity of this implosive-explosive process objectively in the A-bomb and subjectively as it happened to Helen Chalmers is at once casually apparent. Fear, worry, guilt, dread, shame, financial failure — all this psychological dynamite accumulated within her, recalled with pain and anguish, and brooded upon, seemed suddenly on a quiet day to be detonated from all directions; to be driven in upon her, implosively, with immense psychological force.

"What happened? We may refer to any description of the explosion of an atomic bomb. The same sensation of blinding brightness, of a great fissioning within her, a sudden fusion of all her faculties; and then an unbroken stillness in which her essential inner self, as if vaporized and transformed into new elements from its old atomic structure, rose slowly in a new spiritual entity to a new height of comprehension.

"If each of these events was preceded by a long period of secrecy and preparation, they were followed by an indefinitely long period during which their effects occasioned frenetic public excitement and controversy. I refer in one case, of course, to the invisible radioactive fallout from the atomic cloud slowly encircling the earth. Helen Chalmers' experience also resulted in a psychological fallout, if we may be permitted to so term it here. What precisely was the nature of the effects engendered by the remarkable psychic energy she released? And to what extent have they affected others?

"The cryptic answers are expressed in the media of all the psychic phenomena with which I was then totally unfamiliar. During my work I also happened to undergo a rather strange experience. It was enough to awaken my interest in an aspect of human nature I had not dreamed existed. With these incidents I began my probing. And with an account of them I begin these brief papers . . ."

240

6

Their peaceful evenings at the Crossing were broken by momentous events: the detonation of Soviet Russia's first A-bomb, a decade before most American scientists expected it; the arrest of Dr. Klaus Fuchs which explained it; and the beginning of another war when North Korean troops crossed the 38th parallel. America's reaction was reflected in a burst of activity on the Hill. A new site for testing improved A-bombs was established in Nevada. President Truman gave the order to proceed all-out on the development of a new bomb rumored to be so powerful that an A-bomb would be required to ignite it: a Hydrogen Bomb, or Hell Bomb as the papers reported it, which would release power measured in millions of tons instead of the thousands of tons released by the A-bomb.

Gaylord and a large corps of scientists left for Nevada. Turner, greatly excited, followed shortly afterward. It had been some years since he had been in Las Vegas and he was dumbfounded by its change. That former little frontier town had mushroomed into the rootin'est, tootin'est honky-tonk in America, the lushiest, plushiest gambling center of the world. Along the Strip now stood great resort hotels, bars, casinos, restaurants and electrically lighted swimming pools in front of every motel. A Twentieth-Century, Technicolor, Arabian Night whose munificence would have shamed the wildest dreams of an Oriental potentate. Riding high on an expense account, Turner registered at an Aladdin's Palace and walked back across nineteen acres of velvet lawn surrounded by tropical palms to his luxurious room.

Next morning with other members of the national press corps he drove out to see the obverse side of the ironic paradox that had selected the vicinity of Las Vegas for the site of the nuclear test operations which they had been sent to cover. Forty miles north across the desert they passed Indian Springs. The straggle of cottonwoods, a hamburger stand and a filling station were still there as Turner had described them in one of his early Chile Line columns. Now behind them loomed Indian Springs Air Force Base, a complex of new barracks, hangars and runways established to lend air support to the upcoming atomic test operations. Twenty miles farther west they came to a vast and squalid disarray of tents, makeshift barracks and rubber water tanks: Camp Desert Rock, just established by the Army to quarter troops which would participate in military maneuvers connected with the tests.

A few miles off the highway the reporters were stopped. The road to the test site was barred to unauthorized visitors by a pass gate. Armed security officers in jeeps patrolled the near boundary. The entire perimeter was patrolled by a plane to keep out stray hunters and prospectors. Even air traffic over the area was controlled.

Turner swore. "Just like the Hill! How are we expected to see anything?"

There was only one available vantage point. A rutted mountain road snaked up 12,000-foot Mount Charleston to an open ridge on Angel's Peak. Here, fifty-three miles away, they could look northward into that remote desert valley hemmed in by the landmarks of an almost forgotten era: Specter Range and Skull Mountain, Emigrant Valley, Pahranagat Valley, Arrow Canyon. Pint Water and Papoose Range, and the Sheep Mountains. A tingle of excitement raced up Turner's spine. Down there glistened the ancient lake beds of Yucca Flat, Frenchman Flat and Jackass Flat. There too protruded the foundations of the old ghost mining camp of Wahmoni that had been one of his Whistle Stops. What was going on down there now? The whole world wanted to know.

So every midnight these pioneer press members of the Atom Bomb Watchers Society, as they called themselves, left the plushy confines of Aladdin's Palace, their bars and casinos, and drove through darkness and bitter cold to the snow drifts on Angel's Peak. The test shots would be held on undisclosed days at dawn. Camera men braced their tripods against the howling wind, opened their shutters as the time neared. Swathed in blankets, huddled in coats and gloves, the reporters kept waiting.

Then one morning, just before dawn, it finally came. A flash of blinding light that lit up the crinkled desert mountains, the rocks at their feet. A livid red fireball dangled suspended before them. Murkily changing into a monstrous, convoluting doughnut fried in the satanic fat of blast and heat. Swiftly expanding into a giant mushroom cloud shearing off from its dust stem and slowly rising into the stratosphere like a genie out of an uncorked bottle. It was then the shock wave reached them, gently shaking the rooted mountain.

"Christ Almighty God!" Were there no translators of Government gobbledegook, no fission poets to sing hallelujah to these spectral fungi born of a poisonous age? They flung into their cars and roared down the mountainside to file their feverish announcements at the first telephone. "VEGANS ATOMIZED!" The continental atomic test series had begun.

However the detonations affected the various members of the press corps, their reportage varied greatly. One wire service reporter seemed hell-bent on unearthing statistical and scientific details. Another featured background summaries. Turner ignored all these approaches. In his daily column for ANS, he strove to reflect the effect of the detonations upon people. To find out, he interviewed the owner of the Cactus Springs lunch counter whose door had been blown open by the blast, a garage mechanic, the waitress at a hamburger stand where he was having coffee. He observed that the Land of the Hard-Way Eight was being flooded with tourists come to see the blasts . . . Watched the crap shooters in the Golden Nugget who did not look up when a shot went off . . . Talked with businessmen in North Las Vegas where all the burglar alarms had been set off by the explosion . . . Described the new "Atomic Hair-Do" advertised by a beauty parlor.

Hearing of a school being conducted in a converted supply room on the Indian Springs Air Force Base for the benefit of the children on the base and those of the construction workers living in a large trailer camp nearby, he drove out to see it. One woman teacher was teaching a group of children in the first grades how to spell. Carefully they followed her pointer on the blackboard and repeated, " 'A is for Atom', 'B is for Bomb', 'C is for Careful' " . . . "Yes," she explained, "they learn to spell Atom before they learn to spell Mother.

"The children aren't afraid at all when the shock hits us on the first bounce off the troposphere and the cloud rises practically over our heads," continued the teacher. "They're getting the same psychological indoctrination as our combat troops."

What were the indelible symbols impressed upon the minds of these Atomic Age Kids, the first generation of mankind to live on the shaking threshold of the new age? Yes, he reported, there was growing up here a new Western Americana more fabulous than the Indian stockades, gold camps and ghost towns of the vanishing past.

From the roof of a downtown building Turner watched the gorgeous annual parade of Helldorado week. Nine Sheriffs' posses on matched Palominos with silver mounted gear, resort hotel floats swarming with chorus girls, a band of Paiute Indians, bathing beauties, covered wagons, surries and buckboards, a miniature Boulder Dam, and finally the prize entry—the Twenty Mule Team Borax Wagon that had hauled borax out of Death Valley, and which was driven by the last, aging mule skinner. Over it now swept a squadron of new jets. At the exact moment it roared overhead there burst from the horizon another mushroom cloud. The camera man beside him caught it all in a single frame—the past and future of that gigantic and fabulous paradox which was America itself.

Turner was a good reporter. He was no longer confined to his Western Americana. Also he had got over his rather old-fashioned and sentimental feeling about women. Nature had taken its course. He was sleeping with a chorus girl at one of the resort hotels—a chirpy, gorgeous redhead with little in it, and did not hesitate to slap her familiarly on her luscious behind whenever he met her at the bar. Their affair did not affect his relationship with Helen. He loved her still, and he was worried about her. So between shots and test series he shuttled back to New Mexico to see her almost as monotonously as the scientists. Also he had his house in La Oreja to keep up, and other assignments to cover. Then in winter cold or summer heat he returned to stare down from Angel's Peak into that remote Valley Where the Giant Mushrooms Grew, remembering that other little valley where with Helen he had seen the Fairy Ring.

One test series followed another with strange code names: Ranger, Buster-Jangle, Tumbler-Snapper, Upshot-Knothole. The number of shots increased. So did their intensity. Photos of the Los Angeles City Hall lit up by the flash no longer made the front pages. The flash was reported seen as far away as Kalispel, Montana. Blast waves reflected from the troposphere had broken store windows in Las Vegas; bouncing back from the higher ozonosphere layer, they were now recorded as far as Albuquerque. Giving a "bigger bang for a buck," the detonations were increasing to a power twenty-five times that of the nominal 20,000 tons TNT equivalent of the initial Trinity shot.

The tests by now, even for the press corps, were losing their nebulous quality and taking on a practical aspect. As much information as possible was declassified for their use, but still it was not enough.

"To hell with all this paper stuff!" exploded Turner, speaking for the group. "When are we going to be allowed to see a Big Bang itself?"

There was no denying their demands. So one day in March came an announcement from Washington that an inspection tour and an "Open Shot" would be held for the press.

7.

Early on the morning of D-day minus one they left Las Vegas in Security-escorted buses, and this time the pass gate opened to let them through—the first eyes of the outside world permitted to see the Valley Where the Giant Mushrooms Grew.

Turner stared with amazement at the vast array of barracks, mess halls, warehouses and shops that constituted Camp Mercury, the base camp housing the scientists and workers. Twenty miles north, after entering another guard gate to the Forward Area, the buses climbed up the familiar rocky pass separating Frenchman's Flat and Yucca Flat. On it now stood a huge, doubly-reinforced concrete blockhouse without windows save for inch-thick glass portholes. This was Control Point, the electronic nerve center of the test site. Turner got out and with the other correspondents silently paraded through its labyrinth of rooms to the control room. Everything possible had been declassified for their inspection: arrays of electronic equipment, instrument panels, frequency control indicators and gadgetry beyond their comprehension.

"What's the idea of always shooting so early in the morning?" a reporter asked boldly.

Patiently a scientist explained. Darkness was needed to obtain the best possible photography of the second's lifetime of an explosion. For this the fastest high-speed camera in the world had been developed at Los Alamos. It could take successive pictures at the rate of fifteen million frames a second, supplementing other devices that registered impressions every one-hundred-millionth of a second, the standard of measurement called a "shake." But also light was needed for the maneuvering of planes immediately after the detonation. So the shot was scheduled for a predawn moment to meet both conditions.

Downstairs Turner saw the windowless stuffy room with its tiers of bunks for the scientists during their confinement. A placard on one marked "E. Gaylord" aroused a guilty feeling in him. He had not seen Gaylord since the night he'd informed him of Emily's abortion.

The buses now rolled northward over barren Yucca Flat, stopping at a firing area marked by a steel tower rising above the grotesque clumps of cacti. A short distance away lay an underground, lead-lined instrument bunker with a reinforced steel bulkhead door facing away from ground zero. Here, when Turner strolled up, a scientist was explaining its function to gathering newsmen. It was Gaylord, dressed in khaki trousers and sports shirt, with an aloof and lonely air that enhanced his prematurely thin hair, fading eyebrows, and an eye on which a cataract was beginning to form.

From the little cab that housed the bomb on top of the tower, he explained, a coaxial cable was run to this instrumentation bunker. At the instant of detonation the cable, like the whole tower, would be completely vaporized—but not before the electric signals had raced to the hundreds of oscilloscopes, cameras, instruments, gadgets, gauges and monitors that would record their precious information. Hours later when the radiation had died down enough to permit reentrance to the bunker, their readings could be taken.

Christ, what a dull life for a man! Living months in the dreary barracks at Camp Mercury; immured for days in the Control Point blockhouse and in this underground catacomb!

Like most of the other reporters, Turner was always more interested in the human rather than the mechanical equation, and his boredom was shaken off the moment the buses took off for the *pièce de résistance* of the whole show. They leapt at him out of the wide, sandy plain with all the human frailty and tragic intensity that forever bespeaks our faults of comprehension, the weakness of our flesh, and the brief tenure of our days; that appeal to the heart of man rather than to his intellect. They were two modern, six-room, frame houses, completely furnished, which might have stood on the corner of Main and Elm Street in any of a thousand little towns in America. A town which suddenly and unknowingly at dawn tomorrow was doomed to be blasted forever off the face of the earth. Doom Town, U.S.A.

The house Turner entered, only 3,500 feet from the tower, was occupied by a large family of plaster dummies, completely dressed, with their lifelike faces painted and powdered. All the Mannequins were oblivious of their impending doom. In the living room Mr. Mannequin lounged in his easy chair, watching the TV. On the floor beside him sprawled two staring children; a smaller one was bellied out before a book of comics.

Mr. Mannequin was not a man to bother about those queer and complicated atom doings in far off Nevada, nor to worry about the world situation in general. "I'm just too doggone tired when I get home from work," Turner seemed to hear him say. "Taxes, rising prices, all that's enough worry for me. With all the kids we got, it's too expensive to go to the movies too often. Besides, a fellow likes to loaf around his own home."

In the dining room the table was already set. Mrs. Mannequin was out in the kitchen cooking dinner. The refrigerator door was open, showing fresh vegetables, milk, eggs, and the remains of a roast waiting to be made into hash. The pantry shelves were stocked with canned gods, packaged cereals, glasses of jelly and preserves. "Yes, we're getting along right fine now that Mr. Mannequin got a little raise," she seemed to say. "We've paid for the car. Now we can start to set a bit aside for a rainy day. It's a little town that'll never be famous for anything, but we like it. A good place to raise kids. They can ride their bicycles to school."

Upstairs a teen-age daughter was primping for her boy friend; she wanted to look like Mimi de Vere in her latest movie . . . Yes, a nice homey family, these Mannequins, but not without a heartache too. An older boy, Hank Mannequin, had run away from home and they had not heard from him.

Turner crept out feeling like an interloper. A car was pulled up in the driveway with its door open, and on the ground lay a doll. Turner picked it up and placed it carefully on the seat so the car would not run over it. Somebody in the crowd let out a raucous laugh. For over the Mannequins, over all Doom Town, hung a threat that not even a doll could escape.

Riding back to Las Vegas, Turner heard a correspondent talking in the seat behind. "Now who the hell would steal one of those dummies? And how—out of that house, out of a firing area in the most carefully guarded spot in the whole country! And for what? It beats me!"

That night Turner rolled and tossed in his pink sheets in Aladdin's Palace. He dreamed of Helen Chalmers. Dressed in a white nightgown, she was sitting in an armchair on Angel's Peak and looking down on a simple, homey family that would never see the sun rise.

"Why does it have to be us?" they pleaded. "We've never hurt anybody! Can't you find a better way?"

The telephone rang. It was 2:00 a.m., D-day, and time to get up . . .

Again in cold and darkness the buses rushed through the desert night. Past Camp Desert Rock where boy-troops were being loaded into trucks and half-tracks. Past Camp Mercury. Past Control Point ablaze with lights. To unload finally at an abrupt rise of jagged volcanic rock on the shore of the ancient Yucca Lake where an enterprising newsman had stuck up a sign: News Knob.

In the flicker of lights Turner saw rows of benches and tables at which the reporters could pound out their copy. Signal Corps vans providing radio-teletype circuits over which they could file it for transmittal to the nation's waiting press. TV and radio transmitters. A coffee stand. Loud-speaker. A couple of latrines. And stretching out in front of him a dark and naked immensity in which glowed a single light—a 100-watt lamp in the tower cab seven miles away. Doom Town was dark. In their white, two-story house at Main and Elm the Mannequins were peacefully sleeping. Mr. Mannequin faced a hard day at the office. Mrs. Mannequin's face wore a pleasant smile; she had hidden away in the cookie jar $2.80 for her weekly bridge game that afternoon.

The agonizing wait began. Cameramen scurried up News Knob, wedging their tripods between rocks. Reporters got out typewriters with fumbling fingers. The loud-speaker commentary began.

"H-hour minus 15 minutes! Attention please! High density goggles are being issued at the foot of this stand. Last call for dark glasses! Repeat . . ."

Longer and longer lines formed in front of the latrines. "What the hell you doing here again, Turner? You no sooner get to the head of the line till you're back at the foot!"

Shivering with cold and nervousness, Turner buttoned up his coat and stared at the desert mountains beginning to take outline against the sky. Above them he could see the dim vapor trails of the planes boring in on their prescribed flight patterns.

The minutes dragged by, each doled out from a dwindling measure. He was before his typewriter on the table now, stiff with cold but feeling a drop of sweat running down his cheek.

"H minus one minute. Put on your high density goggles or face away from the blast. Repeat. Do not face the flash without high density goggles."

Turner flung a quick look around. Men were crouched at tables or backed against rocks, all braced for the shock. The lights went off. In the wan dawn the flat shone like a tranquil sea. Beyond it a Joshua tree bristled weirdly against the horizon.

The count-down began.

"Ten seconds!"

"Five."

Turner leaned forward, gripping the edge of the table. The goggles over his eyes were so dark he could see nothing. It was as if he were shrouded in a blackness that nothing could ever penetrate.

"One!"

He lowered his head, closed his eyes . . . The abrupt, brilliant, and blinding flash of a hundred suns struck his eyeballs. Men, mountains, everything around him stood out insubstantial and without shadow in that silent gush of clear, cold and pitiless white light. He stared transfixed at its focal point. It was ballooning now into what might have been a monstrous, flaming planet suspended in space before him.

A draft of hot air struck his shivering body. Turner did not notice it. For as he jerked off his goggles, he saw the swiftly expanding fireball beginning to boil in writhing convolutions of purple, orange and iodine.

The blast wave rolled in with a jarring shock; simultaneously he heard a sharp crack whose thunderous roar kept echoing from the surrounding desert mountains. Turner could not tear his gaze from the rising fireball. It was clouding over into a giant puff ball, and sucking up from the ground a stem of dust and debris.

From deep in his memory the image leapt immediately from his mind to his fingers. He knew it now! The monstrous *Amanita Virosa*, the Destroying Angel, the most poisonous fungus of its species. There was the frill around the upper stem, the discolored bag at the bottom, the wrinkled blades of the gill hanging down from the underside of the cap. Bigger, higher, it still kept climbing. An ice sheet formed on top of its rounded cap, its glossy whiteness reflecting the first rays of the sun. The Destroying Angel was full formed now. Tall, stately, shimmering with the satiny whiteness of absolute innocence; yet raining down its invisible, poisonous spores upon the earth, the cacti and the lizard in the sand, the rattlesnake and the skittering bird . . . This was the image Turner's mind saw, the head to the story his fingers pecked out on the typewriter. This was the unconscious way a man worked, cold and nervous in the dawn, facing an indescribable reality; as a man must work or not at all.

By the time the mushroom cloud had ascended to 40,000 feet and began its slow drift around the planet, Turner had filed his copy. Now the wait began anew, this time in the blazing sun. The flames of burning Joshua trees died down, but across the barren lake bed clouds of dust still rolled. Not until mid-afternoon did the buses load and take off toward the site of Doom Town.

A few miles out they were stopped by a radiation monitor. He was dressed in his booties, gloves and protective clothing, wearing his oxygen mask, and carrying his detection instrument. In the barren immensity he looked as a man may someday look when he stands for the first time on the barren surface of a new planet in outer space.

"I'm sorry," he said. "The radiation level is too high for you to proceed farther."

Clouds of radioactive dust still hung above the sandy plain. Turner could not see where Doom Town had been. Nor was he disappointed at not being able to view the wreckage on the corner of Main and Elm. Doom Town, like Wahmoni on Jackass Flat, like all the other vanished ghost towns, belonged to the past. All the Mannequins had perished save Hank, the Outcast of Yucca Flat, the boy who had run away from home. Turner wondered what had become of him as he rode back to Las Vegas.

Two weeks later he found out. ANS released a news item datelined Portland, Oregon, stating that Hank Mannequin's headless body had been found in the Willamette River by the Harbor Patrol. A glass jar was tied around his waist. In it was a note which read:

> "They took my Mom and Pop,
> my brothers and sisters, to
> use in the atom bomb test.
> That's not for me. Goodby
> cruel world."

8.

There was a lull in work after the Open Shot, an ebb tide that sucked Gaylord down into the maelstrom of complete boredom. Other scientists rushed gaily into Las Vegas for a fling of gambling, dinner shows, and cautious flirtations with chorus girls. Still others brought out their families from Los Alamos for a brief vacation. For Gaylord all of this had grown stale—the perpetual round of drinks, the rich food, the gaudy shows, the constant crowds of people with flushed faces desperately searching for pleasure that had no joy in it.

Or was it he who had gone stale? Gaylord did not question his own work, but now it seemed to him that he was too close to its trees of fact to see the forest of its implications. He caught himself wondering about this great, rationally founded, precisely calculated scientific complex in which there was not allowed any factor of chance, luck, or miscalculation. To read the newspapers one would think nuclear physics had become man's newest religion for all practical purposes. Everybody professed to believe that its discoveries would cure all the world's ills and unlock the secret of life. More and more neophytes were being trained in its complex rituals, spoke its apostolical language, and guarded its esoteric knowledge from the profane laity. What trash! It sounded like Turner! Yet Gaylord was disturbed by a growing uneasiness. He needed to get away for a new perspective. Unable to face Las Vegas, he found an excuse to fly back to the Hill, to the nebulous inner world of the Woman at Otowi Crossing which alone might answer his curious need. It was an escape, of course.

Helen was glad to see him and they resumed their evening visits as if he had never been away. She and her tea room showed the marks of adversity. Her clothes were shabby and her roof leaked. She was too poor to afford a new roof and Facundo too old to patch the cracks in the old one. So she simply placed a stewpan under each leak, casually referring to a light shower as a one-pot rain, or to a heavy downpour as a six-pot rain.

Helen herself looked worn and thin: the planes in her oval face were more pronounced, the bow of her lips straighter, her hair graying. To make up for this physical deterioration an indefinable psychic energy suffused her whole body with warmth and richness; the inner glow that was slowly burning away its gross sheath. She was like a slender candle in that big, dusky room.

Gaylord could see at once she had made the turn. Despite her outward adjustment to temporal circumstances, she was now wholly immersed in that twilit zone which sheathed her inner world. How differently she saw everything in that translucent light filtered from the enduring brilliance within and shadowed by the material shells without! A medium that muted sound to peace and stillness, allowing every entity about her to speak in its own voice.

"It isn't difficult for most of us to establish a connection with the animal world, it's so close to us," she explained. "Nor for some of us to break through to the plant kingdom. My own first revelation made me realize that the earth itself, the breathing mountains, every pulsing stone is alive too. Have you ever held a stone, knowing that sometime it would throb with a beat like the pulse in your hand? Sometime, Gay, maybe a century, because its life-cycle is so immeasurably longer than ours. But you know this better than I, handling uranium like you do. Oh, how can we imagine we live among great hulks of inanimate matter? That would be too depressing! For these great shapes, solid and lifeless as they look, aren't mere gross mass; they're living bulks of undifferentiated spirit waiting to be freed. That's why mountains have always been sacred. One feels the vibrations they give off. And each is pitched to a different key."

Wound up, she walked to the window. It was too dark to see the two great mountains above, but Gaylord could remember their shapes from the way she now described them. One of them was softly rounded, feminine, and benign. The other, a jagged escarpment of bare rock, was distinctly masculine and malign. Helen knew them well. From here at the window she would watch for days the emanations each gave off. Periodically the tension between them snapped. Storm clouds gathered round their summits, lightning flashed, thunder pealed. These outbreaks came at rhythmic intervals whose duration she had learned to predict.

"That's all storms are," she assured Gaylord. "Restoration of balance between the psychic forces embodied in nature as in ourselves. If we understood them better we could check our own tempers, prevent our crime waves, and perhaps control the weather, for we affect the weather as powerfully as the weather affects us."

If Helen's dreams, visions, and compulsive efforts to re-establish her true identity had confused Gaylord at first, her current evening talks at least outlined to his imagination the appalling secret self she sought—that indefinable absolute which would find room within her breast for the greatest constellations and farthest galaxies; that within her mind would turn all time into one immortal moment with one eternal thought; and which would give to her heart the boundless compassion to embrace every living entity. It seemed at once a mammoth absurdity and a triumphant assertion of the human mammal which alone had the courage to proclaim its eventual emancipation from all matter. Gaylord washed it down with a cup of tea, then stumbled out into the darkness of his own timid doubts.

One other evening highlighted his visits with her. When he came in, Helen was re-reading some clippings of Turner's reportage. "They're good, aren't they?"

"Very competent."

She looked at him a long time and so intently that Gaylord felt himself being drawn into the abysmal depths of her dark eyes. "Jack keeps saying you conduct some of these 'diagnostic experiments' as he calls them."

Gaylord fidgited. "It's a big, team project, but that's my work."

"Now look, Gay!" she said sharply. "We've never discussed your work in the slightest manner, and we're not going to now. So don't be nervous. But there's something I must tell you. I don't know quite how."

"It isn't psychically classified?"

She ignored his attempt to joke. "Everybody, all these reports, keep mentioning a 'field' in physics. A field of force or magnetic field,

253

like that aura about my two mountains . . . No! Don't try to explain it! We won't go into your technical side of it at all. I simply want to tell you there's another field included in every scientific experiment. A field of human spirit.

"I can't explain it," she went on slowly. "All I can say is that it's created by the unconscious or psychological state of the man conducting the experiment. Do you know what I mean?" she asked desperately. "That this field, or whatever you want to call it, affects the experiment just as much as the field of physical force around those instruments and gadgets."

Gaylord didn't understand it, but he got the idea. A synchronic result of the forces of matter and spirit. Simple as it sounded, he couldn't relate it to the vast complex of precisely calculated experimental procedure he was familiar with in Nevada; to the awesome burst of an atomic bomb. He could only shrug and wait silently while she brewed a pot of tea.

When she came back she said simply, "Some of us, you know, are accident-prone and inclined to failure because of the negative field we create around us. By changing it we not only help ourselves but affect the cause that has created the whole world's unrest."

"Just how?" he asked sharply, once again the cold and rational physicist.

"Gay, I don't know," she said, the warmth and compassion flowing out of her. "I don't know why and how I was lifted out of my own rut, but when we need it most it happens."

Gaylord saw Helen once more after that evening. She was cheerful and casual, but he flew back to Las Vegas with a curious feeling of apprehension.

Checking into Aladdin's Palace, Gaylord went out to lie alone on the lawn beside its heart-shaped swimming pool. A movie star was posing on the diving board, nakedly revealed by a white silk Bikini. Cameras clicked. People clapped under their striped umbrellas. Waiters rushed out with more cocktails.

He fled to his room. After a shower, he lay on the bed staring out at the tropical palms etched against the desert hills. At twilight he got up and dressed carefully, putting on a bright red waistcoat. It was in fashion now, and it symbolized for him all the sophomoric haber-dashery denied a theadbare, penniless youth.

Walking to the casino, he stood awkwardly at the bar, drawing his coat back to expose the merest glimpse of his gaudy waistcoat. Other men more confident and purposeful strolled past to the roulette wheel and crap tables. Women minced by in dainty slippers over the thick carpet. At every stride he could see the shapes of their full thighs, the movement of their rounded buttocks underneath their sheer gowns. Two women waiting to be asked for a drink smiled at him expectantly. Gaylord averted his gaze. They were all forbidden fruit in a garden to which he had lost his passport on a Saturday in June.

His last physical examination had showed that the indistinct hazi-ness in the posterior cortex of the lens of his left eye had developed into a radiation cataract, diminishing visual acuity of the eye. No other abnormal physical or laboratory finding was noted. There was some atrophy of both testes, but sperm counts and testicular biopsies disclosed that he was recovering from the sterility caused by his radia-tion dosage of some 400 roentgens.

Gaylord believed it only at the moment he thanked the doctors, then continued to feel growing upon him not only sterility, but im-potence, frustration and despair.

He dined alone, watching the dinner show, then had a nightcap at the bar. A plainly dressed man edged up. "A big crowd, sir. May I help you find a taxi home?" The agent was evidently new or he would have waited to make certain Gaylord was drunk and beginning to talk about his work, but Gaylord shrugged without offense. "No thanks. I'm staying here." He went submissively to his room and crawled into bed.

Fitfully he slept, dreaming hazily of a betrayal that had occurred on Saturday, June 2nd, at the Castillo Street bridge in Santa Fe. Harry Gold had been caught in Philadelphia. Scotland Yard had picked up Klaus Fuchs. But where was that other arch betrayer, Edmund Gaylord?

He woke up sweating, blindly resentful of the F.B.I. agent whom he had allowed to send him to bed like a child. Behind the agent stood a father who had stormed up and down a dreary flat because his son would not go out in the streets and romp like other boys. And behind this tyrant father stood still more authorities—the neighborhood policeman on his beat, a schoolteacher, the Prexy of the university, and Security officers. What had he done that they should plague him so? He dropped off to sleep again, knowing they somehow had sentenced him to a radiation accident and lifelong frustration, impotence and sterility. There was no way out.

He awoke worn out. Dressing in khaki shirt and trousers, he neatly packed the little red waistcoat with his dress clothes, checked out of Aladdin's Palace, and drove back to the test site.

He still resented the fact that Washington had let in a crowd of gawking newsmen for an Open Shot. Like Turner, they all seemed to think that every situation was expressly created for them to stick their noses into. When they couldn't satisfy their individual curiosity, they growled to high Heaven that the sacred right of their Free Press was being violated. And the stuff they wrote! Inaccurate cliches—like the Alamogordo bomb, which wasn't fired near Alamogordo at all; it was closer to Socorro or San Antonio. Pure emotionalism. Mere sensory reactions to things too technical for them to take the trouble to understand.

Now the three-ring circus was over. The test site was buttoned up as usual. Once more Gaylord was in a cold, impersonal world run with mathematical precision, where nothing could go wrong. Gaylord felt better. He repressed his sense of frustration and surrendered himself to the mounting pressure of work.

It was D-day minus five again. The test was to be another tower shot and a most important one. Tied into it were an unusual number of diagnostic experiments. Innumerable circuits to be checksd, thousands of relays and gauges, a hundred special gadgets and high-speed cameras.

By D-1 all the experiments were ready. The execute order was issued. That evening at H-hour minus eleven Security began checking every person in the area by name, number and assignment. In the Control Point blockhouse Gaylord lay resting on his cot, listening to the loud-speaker—"Big Brother" as someone had dubbed it—blaring out the time, orders, and developments. He heard his name called and went out. The Advisory Panel's last weather evaluation meeting was over. The Test Manager had given the final go-ahead. It was midnight, H-hour minus five. Gaylord joined the firing party in the control room, unlocked the master switch box with the only existing

256

key, and made sure there was no power on the line to the firing area. Then they drove out into the night, ascended the 300-foot tower by its elevator hoist, and armed the device.

Back at Control Point, Gaylord could not restrain the tenseness and the anxiety now building up inside him. Sitting at his post in the control room, he could feel the terrifying deliberateness, the mathematical precision of the events now happening in ordered sequence.

"Who's using that electric razor!" the loudspeaker blared out. "You're jamming radio communications. Desist! Cease! Stop it!"

Planes began taking off from Indian Springs. Troops from Desert Rock were positioned in their trenches.

His eye on the clock, Gaylord turned to the control board. The first section of the complex instrument panel was used for air bursts, when it received signals from the bombing plane that the device had been released, and then recorded the detonation. The second and third sections contained the frequency control equipment for tower and surface tests. Here Gaylord pressed the button setting in motion the sequence timer. It was H-hour minus 15 minutes. Now the electronic robot took over, the cams, the switches, the levers pulsing their signals in faultless, inhuman sequence.

In the instrumentation bunker under the lee of the tower a ventilator closed. Electronic tubes began to warm up. The shield over a high-speed camera folded back. Near to the tower hundreds of mice were waiting. Also eight 35-pound pigs, each of which had been shaved and dressed in tailored Army uniforms. There was nothing odd about this to Gaylord. The pigs had been shaved so that their hides would be more comparable to human skin, and so test more accurately the protection against atomic burns given by uniforms of various materials.

"H-5 minutes!" Three miles north of the tower were positioned a hundred rabbits, haltered and corseted in cages so that one eye would face the brilliant flash. Their eyes would be open, Gaylord knew. One hundred alarm clocks set to awaken them were now going off out there in the chill darkness and silence.

Gaylord shivered in the small control room as he and the other men in the firing team watched the green lights flash to red before them. Nothing could stop that relentless march to detonation.

"Minus ten seconds!"

257

The final count-down had begun.

"Nine . . . eight . . . seven . . ."

All the green lights were red now. Gaylord stiffened.

"Two . . . one . . . ZERO!"

The instrument lights still glowed steadily. Black needles still stood immobile against white dials. Gaylord flung a quick agonizing look of disbelief through the porthole. On top the tower, the light in the cab still showed like a pin-prick in the darkness. No! A nameless fear gutted Gaylord of all feeling. No voice spoke in the silent room. Gaylord jumped to his feet. It couldn't happen! It couldn't!

But it had.

At that same moment the high bare ridge on Angel's Peak, shrouded in freezing darkness, seemed as crowded as Grand Central station. About Turner shivered not only the numerous members of the press corps, but tourists from Los Angeles, a crowd of Civil Defense spectators, and Delicious Dolly.

Delicious Dolly was the most curvacious chorus girl in the line at Aladdin's Palace. Attired only in skimpy dance tights and jersey, her face and limbs blue with the cold, Dolly poised on the edge of the cliff. Her consecrated task was to interpret in dance postures the greatest drama of the era. Against the very fireball and mushroom cloud itself she would strike the poses of "Apprehension," "Impact," "Awe" and "Survival" which the publicity camera behind her would record for posterity.

The press corps had been advised to be in position five minutes ago. Cameramen had opened their shutters; reporters stared down into the darkness; Delicious Dolly struck her first pose. Still the shot did not go off.

Turner was annoyed. Not only at the large crowd which had come to see what was rumored to be an unusually big bang. But because the shot had been delayed and postponed so many times that it had taken on for the newsmen an obdurate, derisive character of its own. The "Jinx Bomb" they called it.

Dawn lighted the sky. "What the hell's wrong now?" a man grumbled. Camera men closed their shutters. Correspondents took off their dark glasses. Dolly lit a cigarette. "This is the last time I'm going to lose sleep over this baby!"

A car came roaring up the mountain grade. Another reporter jumped out. "She's a jinx, all right!" he yelled to the crowd. "They pushed the button but she didn't go. A misfire! Got it over the radio."

"A misfire?" Men stared at him unbelievably. "Jesus! What they goin' to do?"

"Somebody's got to climb up the tower and pull its stinger before the rest can go into the area. You know—lift out its guts, tinker with the trigger, disarm it . . . They're starting right away . . . That Gaylord's one of 'em."

"But what if"—

Gaylord again! For Christ's sake! Turner jumped into his car and hurtled down the mountain.

9.

In compliance with Turner's formal request, an interview with Gaylord was arranged that afternoon. Seated at opposite ends of the table in the closed room, they sat facing each other. Between them sat a classification officer to make sure that no classified information would be inadvertently divulged.

"You had no idea what had gone wrong?" asked Turner.

Gaylord shook his head. "We checked all the circuits from Control Point and found nothing wrong."

"How did you feel about it?"

Gaylord's tired face stiffened. "It wasn't my business to feel anything. Our job was to find out."

Turner frowned. "The other two men are being interviewed by somebody else. Please forget the 'we.' It's your personal story I want, and I deeply appreciate your granting me an interview."

"It wasn't a one-man job," insisted Gaylord. "Every check had to be witnessed by two other members before it could be crossed off the list. Also at every step we reported back to CP by radio telephone."

"So if the thing exploded they'd know just how far you'd got?"

Gaylord nodded.

"All right then," pressed Turner. "H plus one hour. The master switch controlling power to the tower was locked open with a special padlock to which you carried the only key. You got into a car and drove toward the tower. What did you do then?"

"We took off our high density goggles," Gaylord said lamely. Patiently he explained that the road to the tower passed through several danger zones. Within eight miles from ground zero the flash could blind every eye exposed to it. At five miles the heat would scorch exposed flesh. Within the three-mile zone the shock waves could bowl over an auto, and within two miles the chances of survival from flying debris were small. At one mile lay the domain of lethal radiation, of total danger. "The point of no return," added Gaylord in his flat voice. "There was no need to protect our eyes."

He wet his dry lips with his tongue. For a minute he was silent. It was during his ride then, it had happened: that strange feeling of disassociation he later described in his series of papers. It was as if he had been suddenly separated to float, nebulous and detached, directly above and behind the figures of his two companions and his own body in the car. He could see himself driving like an automaton, obeying the habitual reflexes of his muscles. Such an illusion or actual experience of disassociation was not uncommon; most of us have known it, very briefly, in times of high emotion. Gaylord's experience was more complete. He felt freed from that instinctual pattern of behavior which had constituted his emotional or psychological field; suddenly released not only from all fear of immediate catastrophy, but from all that field of fear and guilt that had enveloped his narrow, ordered life. Whatever happened was of no consequence to himself as he was now, impersonal and detached, without will or decision, content to accept the dictate of a destiny beyond his wish or power to command.

Turner broke the silence. "What did you do then?"

At 3,500 yards the three men reached the switch station with its eighteen-inch-thick concrete walls and a steel door facing away from the tower. They unlocked the door, opened the master switch. Nothing happened.

Next, Gaylord went on monotonously, they drove to the underground recorder vault 3,000 feet from the tower. Slowly and methodically they checked interlocks, impulse recorders, the really delicate gadgetry, while above them, like a held breath, a fiery gust waited to be expelled from the mouth of hell.

"Never mind every damned detail!" interrupted Turner. "Hell! Weren't you in a hurry?"

"The procedure couldn't be hurried," Gaylord said gently.

Then they walked to the foot of the tower. A ten-ton elevator had lifted the device to the cab on top, but its hoist, power unit and cable drum had been removed the night before—to save the taxpayers the $25,000 cost of a new elevator, added Gaylord. "So we had to climb the ladder. It had 300 rungs, one foot apart."

They began climbing. Breathing hard. Sweating. Resting. Then climbing again.

The sun came up. The rimrocked desert below spread out flat and empty as the sky above. Gaylord could see himself gritting his teeth, hanging on against the wind while he unslung his hacksaw.

"A hacksaw! For what?"

The trap door into the floor of the cab had been wired shut to keep it from banging. Now the wires had to be sawed through. Turner could hear in Gaylord's voice the rasping hack, the nerve-jangling vibration.

The wires parted. They pulled themselves into the lofty cab. Stealthily, to avoid the slightest jarring, they tip-toed to the armed bomb.

"A 'device,' not a 'bomb,'" interrupted the classification officer. "We don't shoot off bombs like firecrackers. We detonate experimental devices for diagnostic purposes."

Two cables tied the firing rack receptacle to the firing mechanism.

"We can omit the details," cautioned the classification officer again.

Turner was past the point of caring about mechanical details. He sat staring at Gaylord as if he were seeing in him for the first time a man whose intellectual integrity constituted a courage beyond any physical or emotional weakness.

Gaylord cleared his throat. He had knelt on the floor of the cab. A muscle in his forearm twitched as he loosed the collar of the first cable. It could happen now if it were going to . . . He yanked it free . . .

The second cable was ready. If it doesn't happen now, he thought mechanically, it won't . . . Now! . . . There was a shattering silence as the cable jerked free.

261

At the same instant his curiously detached self rushed back into his body as instantaneously and effortlessly as it had separated long before. It was as if he had dreamed the whole phenomenal objectiveness, save that deep within himself he knew he was somehow still free of something which had long oppressed him. But he had no thought for anything now. He and his two companions simply looked at each other without speaking, feeling the sweat break out on their faces and hands. The device lay disarmed and harmless before them.

"Later we found the trouble," Gaylord explained, wiping his sweaty face with a soiled handkerchief. "One of the crucial measuring devices had failed to function, causing an interlock and preventing the detonation. Just as it was supposed to. For without that important measurement, the test would have expended three million dollars worth of fissionable material, gear and gadgets, and would have been scientifically valueless."

Impulsively Turner jumped to his feet, threw his arms around Gaylord. "God Almighty! You're a better man than I am!"

A slow, warm smile crept over Gaylord's drawn face. "I hope you don't play it up too much. Remember one of the others has a wife and kids he doesn't want scared."

"I'll let you look over my copy late this afternoon. Guy Alvord wants to see me first. Then maybe we could have a drink together. What about it?

Gaylord nodded. "I'm going to take a nap. When you finish your chat drop by . . . Yes, do!"

Late that afternoon Gaylord left his room in Aladdin's Palace and came walking across the lawn with swinging strides. His head was up, his shoulders squared. He had left his jacket unbuttoned, and one could see an open expanse of bright red waistcoat and the shine of its large brass buttons. Turner was sitting in the lobby with a dejected droop to his shoulders and a disconsolate air about him.

Gaylord flung open the swing doors and whacked Turner on the back. "Jack, you old roustabout! Have I kept you waiting?"

Turner rose and stared at him with amazement. "For Christ's sake! If a nap will do that for a man, I'd better have one. Come on. I need a drink!"

Guy Alvord, with whom he had just had a stormy session, was a

262

big-framed man, somewhat bloated from the Scotch he drank. His by-line was internationally famous. He covered United Nations assemblies, World Series, race riots in South Africa, a Presidential election and a Hollywood premiere with equal facility. Whenever and wherever anything special happened, Alvord made good his boast of arriving there firstest and fastest and getting the mostest. But he never stayed, never wrote a follow-up. It was as if every new situation was an oyster for him to pry open, flip out the pearl of publicity, and leave the meat of the story untouched. He was a ruthless, overbearing, and brilliant reporter.

"Of course I was the Guy who broke the story of the Woman at Otowi Crossing!" he boasted later. "It'd have been another scoop too, but I made a deal with Jack Turner. Still it was I who turned the trick."

Lying on the bed, shoes off, he poured himself a stiff drink of Scotch. "Here's the whole story. I first heard about her during a preliminary Atoms for Peace conference in Geneva. A lot of the scientists had been at Los Alamos and they were swapping stories about a woman near there. She was evidently a strange duck, but they're a dime a dozen anywhere so I didn't pay too much attention. Yet something must have stuck in my mind, for that spring when I was flying out to Nevada to see a big bang, I stopped off at Los Alamos to see Breslau. It was a Saturday, and he and a lot of his staff had gone down to the bottom of the Hill to put a new roof on a Miss Helen Chalmers' house.

"Something clicked. It was that strange woman I'd heard about. And for Breslau himself and a lot of other top men to take time out to fix up her leaky roof was even stranger. So I drove down there. Not only they were sweating it out with hot tar, but a visiting Nobel Prize winner from Europe whose name I was asked to withhold. Right then I knew I had something! An undiscovered Twentieth Century mystic hidden right in the shadow of the Atom Bomb!

"Sure I got the story—her visions, dreams, Tea Room and everything else. All I had to do was ruin a pair of pants helping to spread that damned tar while I talked with everyone on the roof. I even met her, but she wouldn't talk. That convinced me; the phonies in every line can't stop talking. I soon figured why. A reporter friend of hers, Jack Turner, was sitting on her story.

"So when I got to Vegas, I sent for him. Now don't get me wrong! Jack Turner and I are good friends now. I saw him the other night in that plush New York apartment where he lives with that good looking daughter of his. He's top man in ANS. But when he came to see me at Vegas that afternoon, he was still the Great American Boy on the make with his head still full of the Romance of the Wild West."

He took another quick snort and held up the bottle. "Here. Have one. Well, to make it short, he blew up like a firecracker when I asked him for the low-down on this Chalmers woman. He even threatened to beat me up if I released a word about her. Yes, by God! It was so funny I could have cried. They'd had some sort of an affair and she'd broken it off. Now he was sitting on the biggest story of his life, still in love with her and trying to protect her 'reputation'!

"Turner's a big outdoorsy fellow and might have made things rough for me. But I had him where it hurt. 'Tell me all you know about her quick, or I'll blast the whole story open right now,' I told him. 'I'll give plenty of wordage to how an ANS reporter's tried to keep it under cover, too, Turner!'

"Well, he turned pea green and stood there wondering whether to jump me or cry on my shoulder. Right away I made a quick deal. If he'd give me the dope, I'd hold it till he could release something simultaneously in his own column about her.

"That's what we did. I broke the story and splashed the Woman of Otowi Crossing on the cover of every Sunday Magazine section in the country. On the same day Turner began the columns about her personal background that formed the basis of his later book. But by then she had gone up to Heaven, or wherever mystics go, in a pillar of fire, and the smoke of it, like a mushroom cloud, is still going round the world."

10.

A disgruntled Emily arrived at Otowi Crossing with all her bags and suitcases. "It's finished!" she told Helen as she got out of her car. "They've done to Sandia School just what they did to Los Alamos Ranch School. The AEC has taken it over too! Oh, this damned atom business! Can't anything be done to stop it from swallowing the whole country?"

"Emily! How good to have you home again!" cried Helen. "It doesn't matter! You know it doesn't!"

It really didn't. Dr. Emily Chalmers, successful author and distinguished anthropologist, and endowed with ample funds from the Chalmers estate, could well afford to pout at the loss of a minor teaching job that already had served its purpose. Emily herself was well aware of this; her vociferous annoyance served only to cover up her reason for returning to the Crossing.

Moving back into El Mirasol, she came every day to visit Helen and every night she went home more conscience-stricken. As Turner had written her, that bright candle of a woman was burning low. No wind would ever make it flicker, but Emily was terrified lest it suddenly snuff out.

Facundo worried her too as she watched him valiantly tending the dwindling little vegetable patch and chopping wood for the stove. An aging Indian and a sick woman holding a crumbling adobe fort against the assault of time. It was ghastly, pitiful!

"Goddamn it, Mother!" she blew up one morning. "You cooked that truck driver a hamburger! Why didn't you send him on? Has this finally come to be nothing but a hamburger joint for truck drivers? There's no need for that!"

If only Turner would come, who alone could do something with her! But still she pleaded with Helen to take a vacation with her.

Helen laughed. "What would I do in the Canadian Rockies or in Mexico, dear? Do be sensible!"

"But you're so thin, Mother! You need a rest. We've never taken a trip together. Please! Just a short one, anywhere."

Helen finally agreed, provided Facundo went with them. For years the old Indian had cherished an ambition to visit the Hopis in Arizona, those people whose power was so strong. It would be so generous of Emily to give him this trip before his life was over.

Such a simple, humble request! The tone of her voice shamed Emily.

Long before sunup a dozen old men came from the pueblo to see them off. They brought gifts to take: a few "Mothers," those sacred ears of perfect corn; some matched parrot feathers to be worn at ceremonial dances; a little buckskin bag containing "medicine." They squatted down in front of Facundo's hut, and their voices in the paling darkness sounded soft and insistent. "Them Hopis. No people have stronger power. Ai! Take them our prayers. Be sure to get theirs for us. And take care to bring back spruce from the *kachinas* so that we may plant it in our own fields. Ai! Ai! What a shiny, big car! You will travel like rich people!"

They all had to be fed, of course. It was eight o'clock before the shiny big car drove off. Emily in blouse and Levis. Helen in a hat and shabby suit beside her. Facundo in back, wearing a clean shirt and his best moccasins, with a red headband to keep back his straggly gray hair.

Mile by mile westward this strange hegira indelibly etched upon Emily's contrite heart its triumph and its pathos, its glory and its sadness. What could one do for a woman who lived only on tea and Post Toasties, and an old man who constantly and delightedly chewed on rare hamburgers and slices of raw onion? Facundo's kidneys in fact were in no better shape than his teeth. Emily kept stopping the car and staring stonily ahead while he got out to water beside the road, oblivious of passing cars. Oh, it was so horrible! Horrible because she could give them so little, and they were so great-hearted and simple that their extravagant pleasure wrung her heart, and she could not bear to face the fear that this trip might be their last.

Emily turned into the vast, unmarked sage and saw it rise at last out of the empty and arid desert, out of the wilderness heart and hinterland of America itself. The first of the three Hopi mesas. Carefully she drove up the steep, rocky slope of Second Mesa to the ancient pueblo of Shongopovi perched on the cliff-edge of a far spur. The summer sun blazed mercilessly down upon its flat dirt roofs. Waves of wind, rolling in from an ocean of sand, flung dust at its rock walls. There was no sign of water, not a tree, no speck of green as far as she could see. Yet old and desolate as it appeared, Shongopovi somehow gave her the same feeling as Facundo and her mother, the same soft aliveness and curious awareness.

Nine remote little villages clinging to three rocky mesas in the heart of a desert wilderness, the oldest inhabited settlements in America. Resisting for centuries succeeding waves of conquest, still keeping at bay the technological civilization swirling about them, without the need to fight. For these Hopis were literally a "People of Peace," armored only by the protective power of which all other tribes were so respectfully aware. A spiritual force they stubbornly affirmed with their daily lives. For this they had given up the temporal illusion of power and unrestrained freedom. All their strength and thought they poured into their great religious ceremonies whose one object was to help maintain the harmony of the universe, to insure the continuation of life through all its forms, mineral, plant, animal and man. It was all there in Shongopovi, in every face—the same soft aliveness and curious awareness.

They stayed with a family that Facundo knew. The house was cool, bare and clean, with a piece of linoleum on the mud floor. Facundo got out his "Mothers," feathers and medicine bag, and went with the father to the kiva. The mother accepted their big box of groceries gratefully and went on beating out *piki*, the wafer-thin Hopi bread she was preparing for the coming ceremony. The children too restrained their curiosity with a quiet courtesy.

Helen and Emily wandered outside. A big golden eagle was tethered to a little platform on the roof by one leg. He sat staring out across the illimitable, sunlit desert with fierce, proud eyes. In a little while he regally spread his great pinions, hopped up in the air to soar away, only to be yanked down. He was too proud to pick and claw at his tether with his curved talons. He sat patiently looking out into freedom. Then again he lunged away only to be jerked back.

"They will kill you, big proud bird!" thought Emily sadly. "You have been master of the air. No living thing has climbed so high above this free and naked land. But now you have been captured, your head has been washed to make you one of them. And soon they will bloodlessly snuff out your life and bury you. They will kill you, big proud bird!"

Late that afternoon the kiva priests returned from their pilgrimage to the mountains after the sacred spruce. At midnight Helen and Emily watched them plant the two trees in the plaza. The male spruce to the right of the shrine, then the female to the left. Those strange masked figures, like nothing seen on earth! How eerie it was in the moonlight!

They were *kachinas*, spirits from other worlds, Helen told her as they went to bed. This was the eighth night of *Niman Kachina,* and tomorrow they were going home.

Next day they danced in the plaza from sunup till sundown. Nothing she had ever seen had prepared Emily for their pure, stylistic abstraction. A long row of anthropomorphic figures in their strange *kachina* masks, gargoyle faces topped with terraced *tablitas* painted with cloud and rainbow, and hung with eagle down. A ruff of spruce around the throat. Bare bodies darkly painted. The inevitable Hopi kirtle, and a fox pelt dangling behind. Dancing in the stifling heat, the thick dust. Shaking their gourd rattles. Singing with deep male voices. While a gnarled old man flipped drops of water over them with an eagle feather; sprinkled them with pinches of sacred corn meal.

They danced as men have never danced anywhere else, and never will. With one body, one mind, one spirit, in a rhythm that shook the cliff-rock beneath them and the dome of sky above. These were not solely men to whom this power and grace and precision had been a stylistic and superlative art for a thousand years. They were men temporarily embodied by the spirits of mineral, plant, animal and human entities, all the invisible, spiritual forces of life which had come to bring fecundity to field and flock and people, manifesting their divine powers for the good of all. Now they were going home and this was simply their "Home Dance."

Once again they filed back to the kiva to rest. Helen went into the house to her cot. Emily sat staring into a mystery not explained in her *Inquiry.* The crowd of dark-faced Hopis patiently waited. And down upon them all the eagle stared unblinking with his fierce, proud look.

"Tonight they will kill you, big proud bird! Because freedom must give way to the sun of life for all," thought Emily. "I don't understand it at all!"

Soon the *kachinas* came back into the plaza, the old priest sprinkling corn meal before them. Their right hands lifted; the gourds rattled. Their feet came down, shaking the earth. And from deep underground, up through their powerful chests, welled forth the low voice of the chant, soughing like wind through the spruce. They wheeled, parted, came together again; and their strange gargoyle heads lifted fiercely and proudly toward their brother on the roof top. The current of their vibrations shook Emily like a tangible force. She shivered in the stifling heat, not knowing what it meant.

Then suddenly at sunset the silence rushed in. It was over. Standing in the crowd, Emily, Helen and Facundo watched them leave. Silently alone they filed down the rocky trail toward the setting sun, a weirdly beautiful procession of unearthly figures struck by a strange enchantment beyond the touch of man. Only for an instant they paused at the far point of the mesa where they would leave behind their nonessential outer forms. Then they vanished at last, as the *kachina* component of all living things must also vanish, into the enduring home of the spirit.

"It's getting time for us to go too, Facundo," said Helen softly, with a look turned deeply inward.

"Pretty soon mebbe," Facundo said quietly without looking at her.

But when neither moved to leave, the fearful meaning of their words struck Emily. For the first time she knew that her mother also knew what was wrong with her.

Next morning she drove them to Grand Canyon for a few days' rest in more comfortable quarters. Still she could not understand how this stricken woman and aged man could be so happy here on the tourist-crowded South Rim.

Nothing seemed to bother Helen. She napped in her room in El Tovar, dressed primly for dinner, and stared for hours into that canyon of unfathomable mystery. Everything to her seemed as fresh, wonderful and luxurious as it had been years ago when the park was first opened.

Facundo was magnificent. A little Napoleon in a red headband, he kept bellboys on the run for ice-water and postage stamps. He asked solemn questions of the train crew, offered sage advice to the cowpokes down at the corral, obligingly posed for a snapshot in front of a group of tourists for fifty cents. At curio stands and coffee shop he took what he wanted with sublime assurance. "My friend she pay!" The plunder on his dresser top kept mounting. To the medicine objects and the twig of spruce he had been instructed to bring back home, gifts of *piki* and a flour sack full of little Hopi melons and peaches, he now added machine-made bows and arrows, gaudy silk handkerchiefs, gee-gaws and colored postcards for his horde of "nephews" ranging from four to forty years.

Yet none of these extracurricular interests detracted from the engrossing meaning of that gigantic Upside-Down-Mountain lying at his feet. All his ceremonial life he had sat before the little hole in the floor of his kiva: the *sipapu*, the place of Emergence whence came man from the dark underworlds, the Place of Beginning. It was only the symbol, as the kiva itself was the universe in miniature. Now before him was the reality, the monstrous chasm, the abysmal mile-deep hole which extended down through the nebulous past to the rock bottom core of a world that had existed unchanged millions of years before his forefathers had made their Emergence here in human form to begin their life upon its surface. At sunrise and at sunset Facundo stood on the rim to cast pinches of prayer meal into the great *sipapu*, the womb of Our Mother Earth, the revered Place of Beginning whence came man.

Alone in her room, Emily wept. "They are going to die!" she knew. "Just like that big proud bird of Shongopovi, they are going to die. Too soon! And they've never had a vacation but this!" She pounded her pillows with both fists. "Why doesn't Jack come back and do something about it!" Finally she rose, washed her face in cold water, powdered, and put on a cheerful smile. It was time to join Helen on the terrace.

The Woman at Otowi Crossing sat watching the Canyon in the setting sun. Spires and pinnacles lengthened, clefts and chasms deepened, buttes, mesas, whole mountains contracted and expanded in its abysmal depths. Clouds of pink and violet, green and orange ebbed in and out of its gorges like frothy tides. With all these infinite variations of color, these mutations of form and permutations of substance, it was a realm of the fantastic unreal, a world of illusion.

Helen never grew tired of watching it. For if it was to Facundo the revered Place of Beginning, it also seemed to her to embody the illusory depths into which all worlds and civilizations faded, and all temporal times vanished like discarded *kachina* masks when the spirit left the flesh. Over the edge where the cliff-swallows skittered in the fading light, she peered down past all those successive layers of rock that geologists equated so curiously with eras of time, into the Archeozoic Era at the bottom. Who could comprehend their relative time spans—one million years, 1500 million years! What was the need for it, really? For as she gazed deeper, she saw Archeozoic Time merge into Azoic Time, and it into a Cosmic Time that merged with the Psychozoic Time to come; in a whirling wheel, the past linked with the future, and all moving time stood still in eternity . . .

She looked so primly dressed for the cocktail hour, so pensive and lonely, that Emily hesitated in front of her.

"I've been thinking," said the Woman at Otowi Crossing quietly.

"Yes, Mother."

"I've been thinking we ought to take this Grand Canyon back home with us. It's the only thing big enough to hold all that junk Facundo's been buying! What in the world's he up to now?" She let out a little peal of laughter. "Come on, let's have a cocktail! One of those pink ones!"

They were so happy Emily could not bear to take them home. Imperiously she loaded them into the car. "We're going over the bridge so you can see the North Rim for the first time. Then we're going to drive through Zion National Park and meet Jack in St. George. I telephoned him last night. Let's have a real vacation!"

The strange enchantment lasted all the way through northern Arizona and into the southern province of the old Mormon Empire, the Land of the Honey Bee, the heart of Utah's Dixie. Apricots were already ripe. New alfalfa filled the early morning air with a fresh green fragrance. Little barefoot boys were selling lemonade at home-made stands along the dusty road. About it all clung an air of quiet gentility that nothing could disturb.

Yet suddenly, shortly before nine o'clock, the music from the car radio was cut off.

"We interrupt this program to make an important announcement," stated a grave voice. "The radioactive cloud from this morning's atomic detonation in Nevada is reported to be moving east southeast toward southern Utah, northern Arizona, and Grand Canyon. Motorists are advised to close their car windows and air intakes while driving through the area. Keep tuned to this station for further announcements."

A wave of unreasonable fear shook Emily at the wheel. She slammed on the brakes, closed up the car, and flung a look upward. The sky was clear and cloudless. She could not see the invisible, inaudible, tasteless and odorless rain beginning to fall upon them, and this terrified her still more. There was no escaping it. They could not flee from it; it would pursue them home.

She started the car again and hurtled into St. George as another announcement came over the radio.

"All residents of St. George, Utah, and vicinity are advised to go indoors and remain until further notice. There is no cause for undue alarm. However, all precautions should be taken to avoid exposure to radioactive fallout as the mushroom cloud passes overhead. Close all doors and windows. Do not drink water exposed to the air. Do not eat food that has been left exposed . . ."

Stores were closing. People were hurrying down the wide shady streets to their high gabled houses. A caretaker was locking the door of the old red stone Stake Tabernacle. A gardener was running across the lawn of the Great White Temple.

Was there no sanctuary at all from that pitiless rain? "What'll we do? Where'll we go?" wailed Emily.

"Why, perhaps to a motel," suggested Helen quietly.

There were two standing across the street from each other. Emily whirled into one; and without bothering to check in at the office, yanked Helen and Facundo into the first open door.

It seemed impossible that they could be trapped so helplessly in a motel room bestrewn with dirty towels, its bed not yet made. Emily locked the door, threw the catch on the closed windows, and peered outside. All traffic had stopped and the street was almost cleared of cars. The few last people visible were running home. Somebody was whistling and frantically calling to a dog. "Nephi! Here, boy!" A woman next door ducked out as if into a heavy downpour, apron up-flung over her head, to grab up a saucer of milk on the doorstep. Then there was nothing more to see; she was looking at a town empty and dead as a ghost town.

Facundo wandered into the bathroom to get a drink of water.

"Don't drink that!" ordered Emily. "It might be poisoned!"

Facundo scowled and walked toward the door. "No breakfast. I hungry!"

Emily barred the door with outstretched arms. "You can't cross the court! Remember what happened to Gay!"

It was fantastic! The drive-in was in plain sight, yet they could not get to it. There was no radio to tell them how long they might be imprisoned. "What'll we do?" Emily cried.

"Why don't you ask Jack?" asked Helen. She sat quietly on the unmade bed, hands folded primly in her lap. "Isn't that him driving into the motel across the street?"

Emily rushed to the window again to watch Turner grab his bag out of the car and duck inside the building.

"We've got to let him know we're here! But how?" asked Emily helplessly. He was so close, yet separated from them by an invisible barrier no one could cross.

"I should think, Emily, you could call him by telephone. There's one here in the room, you know."

11.

Turner felt as helplessly trapped in his own room.

After agreeing to meet Helen, Emily and Facundo in St. George for a short vacation, he had driven from Las Vegas up to the little village of Alamo in the lonely Pahranagat hills to attend a public meeting in the schoolhouse. Here several A.E.C. officials had come to calm a crowd of ranchers apprehensive that bunches of stock were being made ill by radioactivity from the atomic tests. Turner listened carefully. Throughout the tests he had become casually acquainted with three of its effects. The brilliant flash, a hundred times brighter than the noonday sun. The searing heat of the fireball with temperatures approaching one million degrees Centigrade. And the tremendous blast whose shock waves had been recorded as far as Albuquerque. The fourth effect, radiation, he knew nothing about; nor did the ranchers gathered around him.

The spokesmen carefully explained, pointing out that its effects were neglible off the test site. Yucca Flat had been selected largely because the prevailing westerly winds would blow the mushroom cloud eastward across the least populated area of the United States where its fallout would descend upon barren range and desert. By the time it reached more populated areas, the cloud would have climbed to tremendous heights and its fallout would be neglible. Aside from

273

these considerations, precautions were taken to postpone test shots if the wind direction indicated a path over any community, or if the weather predictions indicated snow or rain which would increase the fallout. There was no cause for alarm, the spokesmen assured them. No stock could be possibly harmed.

Reassured as were the ranchers, Turner drove off to meet Emily, Helen and Facundo. The road followed up the course of the Virgin River to Riverside, a clump of cabins occupied by fifteen people who had come to fish, then to the old Mormon village of Bunkerville. A few miles past it he heard the announcement over his car radio.

The news stunned him. Despite all the rational, administrative precautions that had just been explained to him, something had gone haywire. The Destroying Angel, that great poisonous fungi of the atomic species, was passing overhead and letting fall its rain of deadly spores. Worse! It was following his course up the Virgin, over the Riverside cabins in the tules, and old Bunkerville.

Like Emily, he raced for St. George only to find it buttoned up. Where in the hell could they be—an impractical girl, a hazy woman, and an ignorant old Indian? Idling along, gawking at the scenery? But there was no hunting for them now. He dashed into the first motel and gave himself up to his own claustrophobia.

The ring of the telephone aroused him. It was Emily. "It's me, Jack! I've been trying to get you for an hour, but the lines have been so busy and we're right across the street if you'll only look out the window and see Mother and Facundo waving, but we can't come . . ."

He brushed aside the curtain, and saw in the opposite window a figure waving. Then Helen's quiet voice interrupted Emily's excited jabber. "We're quite all right, and I know you are too. But I don't want to take too much of your time now. With so many people everywhere upset and worried, I know you have your work to do. We'll see you when this is over."

Her reassuring voice put his feet on solid ground. Of course he had work to do! Securing a telephone line on an emergency basis, he called the Chief of Police, the principal of the school, then picked random numbers out of the telephone book. Finally his call to ANS in New York came through.

"Yes!" he shouted. "It's on U.S. Highway 91 to Salt Lake. Mormon . . . Farming . . . Population 4,545 . . . . It's been buttoned up more than an hour now. The cloud is passing overhead. Volunteer units were formed to notify residents by house-to-house canvas. Then the radio station broadcast the warning . . . The 815 kids in school are being confined without recess. No, no panic. People seem to be taking it pretty well so far, but cars are backing up at the roadblocks. . . . . No! How in the hell would I know what the radiation intensity is, cooped up in here? Sure! I'll give you a rundown just as soon as I can."

Just past noon he saw two radiation monitors strolling down the street with detection instruments, taking readings. An hour later he flung open the door and drew a full breath of air. Then he rushed across the street to join Helen, Emily and Facundo. "It's over! Come on out!"

"We eatin' breakfast now?" asked Facundo.

"Yes, and lunch too! Come on!"

But it wasn't over yet. The trouble was just beginning. He received an urgent call from Orderville, Utah; it was necessary for him to leave at once. "Look, Emily. This is no place for a vacation now. You'd better go on home. Orderville is on the way. I'll drive that far with you."

They had trouble getting out of town. The cloud passing overhead had crossed both Highway 91 and 93, and roadblocks had been set up to stop traffic for contamination checks. Cars were lined up a block ahead of them. A large Greyhound bus had been found contaminated. It had to be driven off the road for a thorough cleaning and washing, and the passengers sent on in other cars.

Finally they got away and drove through the monolithic scenery of Zion National Park to the turnoff. Emily with Helen and Facundo continued on home. Turner swung off to the tiny hamlet of Orderville to investigate the trouble.

Ten employees in a mine nearby had come to town ill and vomiting with "radiation sickness" from the test fallout. Test site officials had been notified immediately, and there arrived behind Turner a group of officials, doctors and a radiation monitor. Readings taken in town, at the mining camp and elsewhere showed that the radiation levels were insignificant and could not possibly have caused any radiation illness. One of the miners drove to Kanab to be examined. The doctor reported that his patient's white and differential blood counts were normal and that he was not suffering any illness. Behind him came other miners, wives and children, some of them vomiting, others with bodies broken out into a red rash. It was the final consensus that there had been no hazardous fallout, that the people had not been contaminated. Their illness, however, was real. They were suffering from fear.

Turner rushed back to Las Vegas.

The whole population seemed to have gone crazy with excitement. Both of the town's newspapers and all four of its radio stations were assuring the aroused public that the fallout had not been hazardous to people, animals, water, or crops. Yet that afternoon two prospectors drove into town with a truckload of ore which their Geiger counters showed to have suddenly become hot. Immediate tests made by radiation monitors from the test site revealed that not only the men's truck and ore bags, but their own clothing was contaminated by fallout; and they were rushed to a hotel, washed thoroughly, and dressed in a complete outfit of new clothes. On the heels of this came rumors that the fifteen fishermen at Riverside had received excessive radiation, but had checked out of their cabins and could not be located for treatment.

Turner stormed into the AEC office. "What the hell do you mean giving out all this hokum that neither people nor animals, water and crops, have been contaminated? Just wait'll I report the FACTS! What a mess of trouble you've stirred up!"

Still it kept up as more reports of the "invisible pall" kept pouring in. Of pigeons falling dead out of the sky at Yuma, Arizona. Of radioactive "blue snow" falling in California and New Mexico. Of bands of horses on Nevada and Utah ranges found blinded, suffering lesions, and with patches of hair on the backs turned white from excessive fallout.

Turner did not accompany the radiation monitors, test site and public health officials to check out these rumors. Congressman Throckmorton had just arrived in Las Vegas to "investigate" all the trouble the tests were causing. It was a junket, of course; and Turner, loaded for bear, went to the press conference Throckmorton had called in his hotel.

Throckmorton did not create the best impression. He was dressed in the striped trousers and severe black coat he thought proper, which made him look sleek and pompous. His appearance justified his reputation for riding high on the seas of a troubled world. Already he had become the leading spokesman for a group of rabid reactionaries, greedy pressure groups, and shouting warmongers.

After a few minutes of innocuous talk Turner asked the first leading question. "What did you think of the test shot this morning, Sir?"

The shot had been a whackeroo, as the reporters dubbed it: a dawn air drop at high altitude whose awesome flash had lighted the Western sky from Canada to Mexico, and from the Golden Gate to Colorado. Press speculation maintained that the explosion was the biggest ever set off on the continent, and that it was somehow related to H-bomb development. This speculation could not be confirmed, the whole thermonuclear development was so highly classified.

Throckmorton fell into the trap with his answer. "Impressive, I might say. An impressive indication of what the far more powerful bombs we are about to set off will do. Yes, gentlemen! You have seen how this fair land of Nevada has been laid waste by our puny A-bombs. But with the great H-bombs we are developing, we shall devastate whole countries and destroy our enemies before they can destroy us!"

A tremor of uneasiness rippled through the group of correspondents. For if what the Congressman said were true, it would confirm speculation that the thermonuclear program was progressing rapidly and successfully, and that the rumored H-bomb would soon be a reality. There was some reason to believe Throckmorton. Security could lock the lips of Q-cleared personnel, double-lock safes, erect fences around facilities, post armed guards. But it was a truism in the newspaper profession that sooner or later some Congressman, with Congressional immunity, would spill the beans.

Most of the reporters began to slip away. Fully accredited representatives of reputable papers, they could not put themselves or their papers on the spot by featuring such a statement from a fledgling new Congressman without having it confirmed by official A.E.C. spokesmen. They were to find that it could not be confirmed, of course. But by that time it was too late. Turner had cornered the Congressman alone with two pages he had typed up from Throckmorton's remarks.

"Mr. Throckmorton, you are representing the United States government. I am representing the American Newswire Service. I believe we can avoid personalities in light of this astounding proposal you have just expounded for the benefit of the entire world. Tomorrow every newspaper in the country will carry your name on the front page. Every radio will broadcast the text of your remarks. I assure you the Throckmorton Proposal will create a stir greater than the Marshall Plan, greater even than the Monroe Doctrine!"

A fatuous smile flitted over Throckmorton's pallid face. He cleared his throat pompously. "A-hem . . . Perhaps so . . . You think so, eh?"

"If you will authorize me to release it," answered Turner quietly. "Read it over, please. And sign both pages."

"The Throckmorton Proposal, eh? Well!" He pulled out his pen and with a flourish signed both pages.

Turner slipped back to his room to telephone New York at once. After all these years he had cooked Throckmorton's goose at last!

Perhaps only Milton P. Jasper, now Executive Vice President of the Throckmorton Endowment Fund, knew how thoroughly browned it was. The offices of the Fund were housed in the huge mansion on Connecticut Avenue in Washington, D.C., and the sitting room in which Turner had taken tea had been converted into Jasper's private office.

"That so-called Throckmorton Proposal?" Mr. Jasper slapped the table with the flat of his hand. "An apt phrase and a damnable trick played upon a simple, generous man by an unscrupulous reporter impelled by personal spite! But I am letting myself be carried away by memories of that dreadful time. I was stunned by Mr. Turner's magnificent impudence. It was the sort of trick, I must confess, I might have been proud of accomplishing myself in those days.

"As you know, I was a brash youngster showing off as a Public Relations Consultant for the Sunshine Empire Tourist Agency when I undertook to manage Mr. Throckmorton's first political campaign in New Mexico. I put him into office using all the P.R. tricks of the trade, including cashing in on the name of Miss Helen Chalmers by indirection. I didn't know then that she was to become the now-famous Woman at Otowi Crossing, and that Turner was in love with her. But Turner never forgave Mr. Throckmorton for that. His revenge was the Throckmorton Proposal."

A shadow of regret, perhaps of embarrassment, flitted over his oily, heavy-jowled face. "Why Mr. Throckmorton fell for such a trick I don't know. Perhaps it was natural. He was an abnormally simple man, perhaps mentally retarded somewhat or seriously repressed by his extravagantly wealthy, ambitious, and historic family. He was uneducated in the ways of the world; he was helpless in politics. And so as a fledgling Congressman anxious to make an impression, he was the prey of flattery from every quarter. I was his private secretary then, but I did not accompany him on the trip to Nevada. Perhaps if I had, that disastrous interview would never have happened."

He paused to light a cigar. "Well, there's no need to detail what happened. Public announcement of the Throckmorton Proposal hit the front pages with a splash that spattered the whole country. The ink had no time to dry before officials and citizens rose in angry protest. Government spokesmen refused to comment on Throckmorton's statement relative to the thermonuclear development program, and refuted his proposal to destroy enemy nations as contrary to the peaceful objectives of the United States, in violation of the charter of the United Nations, and a betrayal of the hopes and aspirations of all humanity. Newspaper editors, preachers in their pulpits, and housewives over their back fences shouted protestations. Women's clubs and luncheon clubs mustered speakers to do battle. Even the most rabid reactionary groups who had used him betrayed him with the whisper, 'Throckmorton has gone too far.'

"Then, timed perfectly, there appeared in Turner's columns a biographical sketch of Throckmorton's political career. A masterpiece of journalistic innuendo! Superficially written straight, without editorial bias and with correct facts and statistics, it nevertheless posed as a documented history of a demogogue's bid for power.

"Accompanying this was a leading picture magazine's full spread on 'the distinguished author of the Throckmorton Proposal.' It presented intimate photographic glimpses of him dressed in the costume of a Spanish *hacendado*, sitting astride his limousine under a ten-gallon Stetson, and at home gazing at his flock of twelve sheep. There was finally a full-page photostatic reproduction of one of his poems as it had been sent in his own handwriting to the former editor of his *El Porvenir*.

"I tell you it was catastrophic! It transformed Mr. Throckmorton overnight from a dangerous demagogue to a harmless buffoon. It ruined him and it killed him.

"You could see the mortal blow to his blue-blood Philadelphia pride in the way he walked down the street: arms hung down at his side, fingers dangling; head down, face expressionless, eyes staring straight ahead. He looked like a zombie. His wife left him of course; they were as ill-matched as a long rainy morning and short ugly bride. Then he moved into this old mansion to live alone. A misunderstood philanthropist, my kind and generous benefactor. Yes, only I stuck with him, knowing the true heart beneath that frigid facade."

Mr. Jasper paused, his soft-fleshed body sinking back into his executive armchair, a fatuous smile of self-satisfaction flitting over his chubby face. He looked for a moment completely feminine. Like a patient woman who had endured the foibles of her exacting master to achieve at last a long cherished and amply rewarded widowhood. Yes, his faithfulness had paid him well.

He sighed. "The end came slowly—two years it took. He spent most of the day in bed. All morning going over his financial affairs with his lawyers and stock brokers. He was not illiterate as Turner claimed. It was simply that he never read anything but financial statements, stock quotations and market reports. What a keen grasp of finances he had! It always seemed to me that he had possessed that faculty from birth; the self-protective instinct of the wealthy. After the session was over, he had a light lunch in bed and took up his embroidery. Those slender, delicate, white fingers! The small exquisite stitches he took! I can see them yet. And all the while his mind was formulating plans for this munificent Throckmorton Endowment Fund which I have the honor to administer as its Executive Vice President.

"One afternoon he looked up, needle poised, and inquired sharply why I did not address him as I used to. 'But Mr. Throckmorton, sir!' I stammered with embarrassment. A distinctly mischievous smile spread over his patrician face. 'Hand Throcky that skein of scarlet yarn. Yes, that will do very well,' he said. But I could never bring myself to utter that brash nickname again.

"Only one thing worried him. He believed that his downfall had been foretold on the day we had called on Miss Helen Chalmers to enlist her aid in his first campaign. Over and over toward the end he murmured, 'A remarkable woman. She warned me that the green grass would trip me.' It was in memory of his high regard for her that our Fund lately underwrote the expenses of some research into psychic phenomena undertaken by a certain Mr. Meru. Do you know him? Let me give you his address. Perhaps he can partially explain how the inexplicable influence of that strange woman at Otowi Crossing somehow extended, in some measure, into the lives of all who knew her."

12.

The test series in Nevada ended. Gaylord and his fellow scientists returned to the Hill where they began working longer hours than ever before in preparation for another mission. Turner was back home for a rest between assignments. Emily too was still at El Mirasol, waiting for her chair of anthropology to be dusted off at the National University in Mexico. It was all as it had been before, but only on the surface. Something was coming to a verge—in each of them, in the greater world outside.

That Helen herself was approaching a crisis of some kind was obvious to both Emily and Turner. Whenever they met at the Crossing, Emily contrived to draw Turner aside. "You've got to do something, Jack! You've got to!"

"Your mother's not a woman who can be pushed into anything, Emily," he answered patiently. "If she won't go to a doctor, what can I do?"

"Make her! I know the finest diagnostician in New York. My apartment will be all ready for her!"

"Make her go yourself! She's your mother, not mine!" Turner's patience was exhausted. "Quit nagging at me!"

Helen was quite aware of the intent of their consultations, but did nothing to ease their concern for her welfare. The curious sense of her own anonymity kept increasing, and with it she felt herself beginning to lose interest in the temporal identities of those around her. She saw them now as she saw herself and the A-bomb: *kachina* forces garbed in material forms and masked by outward circumstances, but slowly and inexorably moving toward a common end. What tremendous physical energy inside the atom was unlocked when in a fraction of a second it burst forth from its confinement in matter! Yet it was but a material reflection of that still greater psychical power captive within herself that would be released soon. It must!

Inevitably Emily and Gaylord met for the first time since they had parted so tragically just before Trinity. Helen, Turner, and Emily were visiting at the Crossing one afternoon when Gaylord drove up in his small, mud-splattered coupe and parked it beside Emily's great, chromium and robin's egg blue sedan. They watched him get out and walk toward them in a suit that needed pressing: tall and prematurely gray, with one filmed eye. There was no denying his warm friendliness as he greeted Helen and Turner, then strode up to Emily.

"Emily! How good to find you here and looking so well!"

"Hello Gay!" Emily smiled and gripped his hand firmly, yet neither her voice nor manner carried the conviction of inner warmth. Her smartly tailored fox-gray suit, with matching gloves and slippers, themselves reflected the brittle severity of her own maturity. Still standing, they now faced in each other the meaning of time and love. Two strangers who once, mind to mind, lip to lip, belly to belly, had been driven together by the force of a mysterious synchronicity that having accomplished its purpose, whatever it was, had then ebbed completely, leaving them stranded on separate islands floating ever farther apart in the gulfstream of time and love. It was over, all over.

"My congratulations on the success of your *Inquiry*," Gaylord said as they sat down.

"It seems adequate," answered Emily, launching into a long discussion of its reported merits.

Her manner puzzled Helen. It was as if Emily now somehow saw Gaylord as a rival whom it was necessary to impress. Gaylord indeed looked impressed; he listened intently, nodding his head from time to time.

Turner finally interrupted. "And what's going on with you up on the Hill?"

Gaylord shrugged. "It's been announced there'll be a test in the Pacific soon."

"A thermonuclear test?" asked Turner quickly.

"That wasn't announced," Gaylord answered, grinning at him.

A few minutes later he got up and Helen walked out to the car with him. "You're going out to the Pacific?" He nodded. "Be careful, Gay."

"I've been more interested than you know in your psychical experiences," he said abruptly. Then with a smile, "Tell me. Do you really fly on a broomstick to consort with spirits on Black Mesa?"

Helen smiled back. "You'll find out for yourself someday, Gay."

He stooped, kissed her lightly on the forehead, and drove away without looking back.

When Helen returned to the house, Facundo had come in and was playing dominos with Emily and Turner. She lay down on the couch and watched them. They finished the game in silence, then Emily and Turner stood up "We're going to do something about you, Mother," said Emily firmly.

"We'll see," she said quietly, walking with them to the door.

Facundo still remained, carefully packing away the little wooden blocks. Helen watched his gnarled hands, his dark wrinkled face.

"They want me to go to that doctor in New York," she said.

"Mebbe you go."

"It won't do any good."

"No good." The old Indian's face was bent down to the table. His voice was low, soft and without feeling. He simply stated a fact that could not be walked around or away from, which could not be softened by regret or pity. Helen knew it herself, yet to hear him confirm it so remorselessly jerked her back for an instant into the role of a lonely, failing woman. A flash of apprehension lighted up her eyes.

At this instant Facundo looked up. Like most Indians, he kept the hairs plucked out of his eyebrows; and beneath their ledges of dark smooth flesh, his eyes lay nakedly exposed. Their look stripped her of her worldly role and fear.

"I go clean up kitchen now," he said in the same soft, flat voice.

Helen laughed. Trust Facundo! He never wasted effort nor words.

A couple of mornings later Turner returned. Warming up the coffee, he abruptly spoke what was in her own mind. "You might as well go to New York and get it over with, Helen."

"I suppose you'll all feel better if I do," Helen agreed listlessly. "I only dread the long train ride and the needless expense."

"Nobody rides the train that far. I've made reservations for us on the plane. Friday morning." He hesitated. "Got to go on business myself, and I might as well have company."

Relief and gratitude engulfed her; she ignored the lie. "I just wouldn't feel right staying in the Chalmers apartment. I couldn't! But there's a small hotel for women. It's quiet, respectable, and inexpensive. Perhaps—"

"To hell with that! I've reserved rooms for us at the Plaza. We might as well make it a honeymoon—sort of!"

It was so queer! She felt like a mere woman again, and she was in his arms and tears were running down her cheeks, and all her mortal dread of the trip was gone.

They were airborne now. The roar of the motors hushed. The vibrations ceased. The great airliner, spacious and comfortable as a hotel lobby, hung suspended in empty space. Far below there slid past a land without perspective, an earth without touch or meaning. Helen had never been in a plane before. It was difficult to believe that it was moving.

She glanced up and down the aisle at the other passengers. None of them were hanging out their windows, breathlessly watching enchanting new canyons and meadows swinging round the bends of the river. Nobody rushed across the aisle to yell at a fisherman squatting under a cottonwood. All were nonchalantly searched out reading or napping in an oppressive stillness devoid of all adventure and excitement. She listened futilely for the mournful, lonely wail of the whistle from the quill, for the clickety-clack of the wheels on the rail joints . . . . It all rushed back to her poignantly bittersweet, and with a beauty gone forever. Trembling as if with cold, she began to weep. "It's not like the Chile Line, Jack . . . The fun's all gone!"

Turner rang for the stewardess. "My grandmother here is cold."

The girl stared at him with cold politeness. "The temperature is normal, sir." She took down a blanket and neatly wrapped it around Helen.

When the stewardess had gone, Helen rolled over toward him. "Your grandmother! How dare you!" She let out another sob.

Turner stretched out complacently. "I'm always hearing about the interesting people who travel by air. But me, I always seem to get stuck with some woman on a crying jag."

They arrived in New York in time for dinner. Turner ordered it brought up to the little sitting room between their bedrooms at the Plaza. Helen was embarrassed at the obvious expense of the suite and at sharing it with him. What would people think? Next morning she was even more embarrassed when he walked into her room and casually thrust a wad of bills into her purse.

"You're a big girl in a big city now. Why don't you ditch that old rag you're wearing and buy some fancy duds?"

Helen whirled on him indignantly, but he went out whistling before she could say a word. She sat down on the bed, amazed at her angry reactions. She thought of the comfortable plane trip he had given her, this lovely suite, and money for new clothes—of his years of care and devotion. He loved her! This stricken, middle-aged woman she saw in the mirror, with a dark pinched face and gray hair, and a shabby suit hanging on her shrunken frame. Yet something within her had rebelled against accepting these material tokens of a love that so long had been her only bulwark against loneliness. Why? What had forced these conventionally circumspect and falsely moral values of a young Helen Chalmers upon the anonymous selfhood she had become?

She walked to the window and stared out at the tall, proud towers thrusting into the sky. At the labyrinth of deep canyons honey-combed with cliff-dwellings. The sleek limousines slinking like cougars down the avenue. The hordes of hunters swarming out of the sidestreets. The ships of seven seas bringing all the treasures of the five continents. The wealth, the power, the glory—all of it was there in every ligament and integument of this monstrous city. It was The City as no other city ever had been or will be again. The magnificent megalopolis of the world, the greatest monument built by mortal man to the pride of his unspent youth and the passions of his flesh . . . And something of it was still rooted in her own. Suddenly she realized why she had really come to New York. Just as suddenly it all vanished—her conventional vexations, the seed of The City implanted in the flesh of Helen Chalmers, and The City itself.

Taking up her purse, she went out and bought a suit, shoes, a new hat, and then a simple dinner gown.

"Madame is perhaps a trifle underweight. It will take a little time to make proper adjustments."

"It's not important. Just take up some quick tucks where they'll be least noticed, and deliver it by special messenger before five o'clock."

"But Madame!"

Madame's gratuity was convincing; it could be done.

Helen hurried home to rest. She was still in bed, surrounded by a litter of packages, when Turner came in.

"Well! Did your money hold out?"

"Of course not! There was a pearl necklace I needed at Cartier's that was only $19,000. Oh Jack, you're so stingy!"

They both broke out into laughter.

Their "honeymoon" spree began. Breakfast at Rumplemayer's. Dinner at Chambord's. An evening at the St. Regis. Helen picked at her food, napped, went out again.

They went to a musical with delightful scores and gorgeous sets, produced with such sleek precision that it had no meaning whatever. They went to the theater. The characters were homosexuals, perverts, nymphomaniacs, lymphomoniacs, neurotics and criminals, all cursing terribly and shouting quite too loudly. They reminded Helen of the creatures one finds under a rotting log in the forest, yet nothing in the play intimated that they too would be helped along the Road by an infinite grace and compassion.

"Don't be a dope!" growled Turner. "Normal people aren't dramatic, and no play's any good if it isn't an immediate hit. Now behave yourself! These tickets cost me $22 apiece!"

Everything was crazy! Everything was fun! Helen went to bed exhausted afternoon and night. Finally the strain of waiting began to show on Turner.

"Is there anyplace left you want to go?" he asked late one night.

"I wonder—" she hesitated a long time. "Do people still walk across Brooklyn Bridge?"

They walked slowly over the bridge, the old and great and beautiful bridge, to Helen the only bridge in all the world. It was nearly midnight when they stopped on the high arch as Helen had stood nights on end on the creaky little span over the Rio Grande at Otowi

Crossing. In greenish moonlight the river flowed beneath her empty and still. Out of abysmal darkness the massive cliff walls and tall towers of Manhattan rose before her, held in a strange greenish enchantment untouched by time. This was The City as men in a space ship from another planet might glimpse it millenia hence: the deserted city of a forgotten race of ancient cliff-dwellers whose spires and stellae jutting up from an abandoned earth attested at once to something magnificent and futile, heroic and pathetic, mortal as the crumbling stones yet imperishable as the spirit which had discarded it.

Helen shivered and limped on. Only to stop exhausted at the far end. "I can't go back."

Turner put his arms around her and whistled for a taxi.

Two days later Helen kept the appointment Emily had made for her with the doctor. She would not let Turner come in, not that day nor those afterward. Nor did she discuss with him the details of the diagnostic examination, the pokings and proddings, the endless questions, the smear tests and laboratory analyses. Finally it was over.

Turner could read it in her eyes late that afternoon when he met her downstairs and helped her into a taxi. It stopped in front of the hotel. Turner tugged at her arm, put her into one of the waiting carriages. The old coachman doffed his stovepipe hat, buttoned up his long frock coat, and flicked his whip over his nag. Clippety-clop, they drove slowly, clippety-clop through Central Park.

How beautiful it was—just as it had been when she was a little girl, before gasoline buggies had come into vogue. Lovers were strolling by, arm in arm. Birds were singing. She could hear shouts of children at play.

"We can go home now," she said quietly. "There's nothing anybody can do."

Turner put his arm around her, and she leaned her head on his shoulder. "He was such a nice doctor, Jack. He was telling me about these new radio-isotopes that will do so much for cases like mine in the future. He said the doctors at a little place called Los Alamos in New Mexico were pioneering their application. Isn't that funny?"

Far off there sounded a loud coughing roar. "The seals and sealions at the zoo," said Turner quietly.

They kept driving on, clippety-clop, through the fading afternoon. "How much time did he give you?" Turner asked steadily.

"Oh—enough. It doesn't matter." She suddenly stared up at him. "Jack. Don't let me worry about you. I don't about anybody else."

He drew her closer without replying.

"G'wan! Kiss her!" yelled a schoolboy from the walk. The carriage rolled sedately on, and finally stopped in front of the hotel. The old coachman helped them out and lifted his stovepipe hat. "Thank you, sir! I hope you will both be happy."

Turner's face stiffened, but Helen quickly put her hand on the old gentleman's rusty sleeve. "We have been—for many years! A long and happy life to you too!"

They went in and had dinner upstairs. It was no good. Neither could think of anything to say. They parted and went to bed.

Turner could not sleep. He kept twisting and turning in a futile effort to squirm free of the inescapable fact glaring at him from the darkness. Neither could he fight it. Nor could he resign himself to the unimaginable barrenness of life without her. The bottle of Scotch on the dresser was empty; his cigarettes were gone. Worn out, he lay listening to the muffled, barking coughs of the sea-lions sounding faintly from Central Park.

Her bare feet running through the sitting room made no sound. There was simply the click of the latch on his door and the sudden impact of her thin, wasted body as it flung down beside him.

"Jack! You've let me worry about you! Please! Don't be sad about me! Ever!"

The clasp of her arms about him and the comforting solace of her voice did not unloosen the knot of pain within him. He could only hold her still closer to shut out the mournful barking coughs coming from a far off, desolate and misty shore.

"Listen!" she said. "We've had everything wonderful that a man and a woman could have together. Everything! Now let me go free! Don't spoil it with pain and regret!"

He drew up the covers about her; dawn was near and it was cold. Cold as a distant shore on whose wave-washed rocks the sea-lions were barking at a ship putting out in the gray mist. He kept thinking of another dawn when they had lain together, listening to the palm fronds rustling in the wind and the mission bells tinkling in the patio below.

"We won't talk about it," she said softly. "I've written all I could say and more besides in a little journal just for you. Promise me you'll read it all. Then you'll understand."

Still he held her as if he could never let her go without him . . . But now the ship stood out from shore, shrouded in a wet gray mist, and with a little shudder gave herself to the boundless sea. The sea-lions stopped barking on their wave-washed rocks. And he saw that the woman from Otowi Crossing was asleep beside him.

13.

Home again at her ancient crossing, Helen stared at the familiar shapes around her: at steep-walled Tunyo where the spirits met, at To-tavi, T'omo and Shumo, and Tsichoma already touched with snow. Fall was coming early that year. Cottonwoods and chamisa were yellowing; aspens glowed on the high ridges. Still the blue herons stood one-legged in the shallows of the river.

She tried to fight off the feeling of anonymity possessing her more each day. There was so much to do! She wrote her last Christmas Letter, telling of her trip and thanking everyone for their devotion. She boxed up her few belongings, marking them for various friends. With her last savings she ordered from the Montgomery Ward catalogue the clothes that Facundo would need for the little time he had left. She did not want people to see him as just another destitute old Indian in a thin shirt and ragged trousers squatting against a sunny wall.

These simple preparations gave her a curious feeling. As if she were helping someone whom she had long known to get ready for a long journey. "It's that curious feeling of disassociation from her—me!—and everybody else, that's getting stronger all the time," she scribbled shakily to Turner in her secret journal. "I'm beginning to have it about you when you're here during the day. But the real me still wants you to have a complete record of this whole, strange and wonderful Emergence from its start to its beginning . . ."

Days later she wrote another paragraph. "I'm beginning to feel imprisoned now. Fluttering around like a bird in a big, gloomy edifice and no way to get out. Every once in awhile the foundations give way, a wall cracks, some stones fall in—'bowl obstructions,' you know. That nasty business Emily goes into such a tither about! Does this sound morbid? I just can't tell you how remote it all is to me—"

And again: "The tenacious hold of the flesh on one is appalling! It's got a life of its own that hangs on with teeth of steel. I've got nothing more to do with it at all. But I should be more grateful, I know, I've used it so long."

Turner and Emily drove her to the new hospital on the Hill, but within a few days Helen began to mutter insistently that she be taken home. She did not want to be stupefied by drugs and injections which would abort the necessary process she was going through; to be completely deadened to that strange and wonderful moment of release and transfiguration when it came.

Emily protested of course, but Turner cut her short. "She's always been crazy as a hoot-owl! Why force her to be different now? Go down and sign the release. I'll take care of everything else."

So they moved her back down home again where she could lie listening to the scrape of a leaf on the flagstones outside and the river hurrying by. A full-time nurse moved in. Maria came to cook and do the chores. Turner took a room at El Mirasol with Emily.

The nasty business got worse. Yet she would take but an occasional light opiate or mild sedative; in her lucid moments she was terrified lest they give her too much. Emily and the nurse were shocked and frightened at her stubbornness. But Turner growled back, "God-damn it! Let her be. It's all you can do for her now."

Facundo had put up a sign that the tea room was closed, and tried to keep out visitors. Yet day after day more people came to inquire about her. Old residents on the Hill, neighbors to whom she had sold vegetables, former patrons of her tea room, valley folk from all the river towns between Santa Fe and La Oreja, an old gentleman from Albuquerque who had been a locomotive engineer on the Chile Line, groups of Spanish people—withered *parteras* and *curanderas* shrouded in rusty black *rebozos,* whole families with children and dogs—came with picnic lunches to squat patiently on the ground outside the fence, staring steadily at the house in which lay the *hechicera.* "An earth woman. A sky woman," they wailed. "*Una Señora que no ha pecado!*" They frightened Emily a little. What could they possibly want, squatting there so stubbornly all day long?

The mail also increased. Emily found it impossible to acknowledge the letters that poured in from everywhere: from scientists, truck drivers and cattle buyers, artists and people she had never heard of, all of whom wrote with equal intimacy; letters on embossed stationery and ruled tablet paper, "Get Well" cards, and an envelope containing only a sprig of sage. Their number and diversity frightened Emily a little too. It seemed impossible for her mother, an unsociable woman isolated for most of her life at an obscure river crossing, to have known so many people.

The old Indian men at the pueblo came every evening. None of them ever entered the house. They sat with Facundo in the courtyard around a small fire to keep off the frosty chill of night. For hours Emily could hear the throb of their little drum, the weird and wavering sound of their low, soft voices as they sang.

With colder weather the birds were coming back. Myriads of wings fluttering around the house and beaks chirping to be fed, so they too could take up vigil in long rows on the fences and telephone wires.

Late one night after the old men had gone back to the pueblo, Emily went outside for a breath of air. Faintly visible beyond the fence stood a band of deer. Seven of them. Quietly waiting. For what? Emily flung up her hand, stamped her foot. The big petals of their ears bent forward, but the animals did not move. Cold chills racing up Emily's spine froze her on the spot. Suddenly she was startled by Facundo's voice behind her.

"They here!" he said complacently. "They her deer." He nodded casually at their seven celestial counterparts in the Pleiades.

It was all too strange! The circle of dark, staring faces by day, the blanketed figures singing around the fire by night. The waiting birds and beasts. All gathered about the woman inside, a queer woman Emily had never known. An unreasoning fear of something intangible and unknown swept over her. She stumbled inside to Turner.

"I can't stand it any more! I know she's always been a little off. But why do they keep calling her a *hechicera* as if she were a witch? And Facundo and his crazy superstitions! It all gives me the creeps. It's unnatural. Everything! I tell you I can't stand it!"

Turner gave her a steadying look from sleepless eyes in a bearded face. "Of course you can! You're just letting your imagination run away with you. Now go to bed and get some sleep!"

He warmed up the coffee on the stove, took down from the shelf a bottle of cognac, and went out to the courtyard. Facundo, wrapped in his blanket, was still squatting before the red coals. Turner poured each of them a cup of coffee with a spot of liquor in it. "It won't be long now," he said tiredly, sitting down.

The old Indian took a greedy swallow and smacked his lips. "Ai, ai, ai! Mebbe soon. Mebbe no. They knowin'!" He inclined his head toward the seven gray ghostly figures still standing behind him. The faint and ruddy glow of the coals shone on his ancient, dark and weathered face—on the timeless and sexless visage of an old man who soon would sing his own death-song and take up his own Road with a clear mind untroubled by fear. One of his withered red-brown hands reached out and softly tapped the little drum between his legs. He threw back his head with its straggly gray hair, and his soft but high-pitched voice soared shakily over the pine tips.

The deer bounded away to stand quivering on the slope. Then slowly they turned about, and with quick delicate steps came back to wait at the fence.

14.

Time and the sea now were also running out on another remote spot halfway round the little planet Earth.

Gaylord closed the switch at ground zero and climbed into the waiting helicopter. As it rose he looked back down at the tiny spit of land on which he had finished his last chore. It was the last sight that he or any man would ever have of Elugelab in the Marshall Islands, midway in the Pacific between Hawaii and the Philippines.

Gaylord could not get it out of his mind when the whirlybird landed him neatly on its mother ship, nor later that evening when he stood on deck looking out into that dark watery expanse which occupied the major part of the earth's surface just as it comprised the major constituent of the body of man.

Elugelab was the focal point of a vast network of work and anxiety that stretched from Eniwetok to Bikini across two hundred miles of sea. Each island and atoll had become as familiar to Gaylord as the mesas at home; and each was as littered with base and outpost camps, instrumentation bunkers, shops, laboratories and utility buildings. Trucks, jeeps and bulldozers crawled over snow-white beaches. Whirlybirds shuttled across blue lagoons ringed by coral reefs. A reconnaissance plane roared down a landing strip cut through coconut palms and pandanuses. Big four-motored planes flew in to the base camp of Eniwetok, and back to Honolulu. Offshore lay a fleet of ships. Land, sea and clouds swarmed with men: scientists, technicians, engineers, construction crews, doctors, government officials, Air Force and Navy crews, Marine and Army GIs. Ten thousand men brought five thousand miles to achieve a venture that would be consummated in a fraction of a millionth of a second—if it were successful.

Gaylord shivered in the clammy heat, glancing at the luminous face of his wrist watch which had been synchronized with WWV, the world-wide time station. That crucial second was not far off—if the weather held. It was H minus seven. Instrument stations had been placed on all the islands, even the tiny mile-long sandpits that made up Bikini Atoll. Military weather group technicians were stationed on Rongerik, Rongelap and Utirik Atolls. More crews were standing by at their ship-instrumentation stations. The command ship stood forty miles out at sea, in radio communication with all groups. Aircraft were making search flights for ships in the surrounding waters that had been closed for security reasons in accordance with the provisions of the trusteeship agreement between the United States and the Security Council of the United Nations. Everywhere—on the islands, in the air, and on the ships at sea—every man was at his duty station. On Rongelap Atoll native islanders were going to bed in their palm-thatched huts. A gull flapped by overhead. A fish broke surface, sliding swiftly down again into the dark water, leaving a phosporescent wake. They were waiting too.

Over the loud speaker sounded an imperative voice: "Dr. Gaylord! Calling Dr. Edmund Gaylord!"

He turned and went below . . .

Ever since he had been in the Pacific, that watery plain billowing endlessly around him had kept reminding Gaylord of the vast empty deserts of the New World and its scientific landmarks: the develop-

293

ment of the first atomic bomb at Los Alamos, its historic explosion at Trinity Site, then the rapid series of more nuclear tests in Nevada which had increased the 20-kiloton power of that first crude bomb more than twenty-five times.

Yet underneath all this work on nuclear fission had been running another deeper tide. As far back as 1942 the possibility had been recognized that far greater energy could be released by instantaneous fusion of atoms of a light element like hydrogen than by fission of atoms in a heavy element like uranium. Up on the Hill during the very time of Operation Trinity one of the basic ideas for achieving such a thermonuclear reaction was proposed and discussed. Then, upon Presidential order, development of an H-bomb got under way.

A Top Secret program of basic research so carefully controlled that even many scientists on the Hill did not know of its existence until Helen Chalmers' strange dream flashed a warning to proper quarters. This, Gaylord knew at the time, was what had occasioned the inquiry so quickly hushed up. But it had made him sweat with apprehension, and Breslau too, as the work proceeded.

A great electronic brain, the mathematical analyzer, numerical indicator and computer nicknamed the MANIAC, was built to make the calculations. The Nevada test site would not be able to meet public safety requirements for the field test of the new H-bomb. Men and machinery began moving to the mandated Marshall Islands. The secrecy held. The tension grew. Gaylord began to realize that if the thermonuclear or fusion bomb were successful, it would take its place with the nuclear or fission bomb as one of the two great scientific achievements of the age. And then what?

"Yes. What then? That was what troubled me when I came up on deck again about midnight," he recalled later. "The briefing was over. For hundreds of miles in every direction the sea had been cleared of ships. The weather would hold. The shot would be made. Its predicted yield was a thousand times that of a nominal nuclear blast. Of course it couldn't set fire to the ocean's hydrogen and turn the Earth into a short-lived star! That was scientifically impossible! Yet all my forebodings on the eve of Trinity returned a thousandfold, as if in direct ratio. And that strange nightmare of Helen Chalmers kept coming back to mind.

"I forgot I'd given up smoking in Nevada after running through a couple or more packs every shot night, and I kept reaching for a cigarette. I remember that intense craving vividly and I wonder why I didn't ask somebody for one. But everyone else was pacing up and down the gently listing deck, sweating it out like I was.

"We all felt the thing would go, but for some strange reason I kept wondering what then? The principal fuel, as you know now, was deuterium or heavy hydrogen; and the ocean contained enough to supply the power demands of future world civilizations for millions of years if the thermonuclear reaction, like the fission reaction, could eventually be slowed down. But this would require sustaining millions of degrees of temperature, equivalent to that on the sun itself. The program now known as Project Sherwood with its experimental, controlled fusion machine, Columbus II, is trying to do just that. An achievement to which a man might well devote a lifetime.

"Yet still another prospect pushed this out of my mind—the one now known as Project Rover. Experimental three-stage rockets were being designed to place small instrument-carrying satellites in orbits around the Earth. But it was already admitted that they would be incapable of carrying a pay load large enough to send a manned rocket ship to the moon. Indeed, development of a nuclear propulsion system for this purpose was to be my next field of effort.

"You understand I've been accustomed to working on secret projects far in advance of any publicly releasable news about them. Also that I've never been troubled by any philosophical generalizations about the specific tasks assigned to me. Yet these rational projections of scientific plausibility fetched up short against the black curtain of night. We might achieve control of the illimitable power contained in the earth and the seas. We might project ourselves to another planet. But what then?

"I can't explain why this rather naive questioning gripped me then, so suddenly and intensely. Perhaps because every little detail of my work had been made so vastly important, they dwarfed the big things in significance, and this was just a reaction. But I was so keyed up my mind kept jumping forward from one thing to another so fast it seemed I had already sold short my own earth and time but couldn't see anything ahead.

"Maybe that's why I couldn't get her out of my mind. Yes, that strange woman I had left slowly dying at Otowi Crossing. With her fey intuitions, that unfounded, confounded dream! . . . Somehow she embodied the answer to all my questions. But what was it? Something too intangible to be put into words, yet with a meaning I could almost grasp.

"It's funny what a man thinks of at a time like that. One of the men in my task group confessed to me later that the only thing he kept thinking of was the gas he had left burning under his coffee pot when he left the Hill. Imagine a man worrying about an explosion on his kitchen range five thousand miles away when he was facing the explosion of the equivalent of twenty million tons or more of T.N.T.!

"But just as he was bracing himself for the eruption of his coffee pot, I was waiting for Helen Chalmers' death . . . What did I expect to happen? I don't know. But in some strange way her dream and death and the test shot seemed indissolubly connected . . . I'm not explaining this very well. It wasn't a matter of fact and logic, but of mood—which is a fact beyond logic. It all made sense and it didn't, even at the time. I was so nervously wrought up I went below for more coffee.

"The inexorable rush of time had stopped. The clock on the wall looked like the one Teller had sketched with its hands pointing five minutes to midnight. The coffee mugs on the counter, men's sunburnt and sweaty faces, their low voices—everything seemed suspended in an ominous interregnum before that black curtain of the future I could not pierce. I don't know how long I sat there until a hand shook me and a voice shouted, 'Come on! Let's go!'

"I got up and went to my post. Once there with things to do I felt better; you know how it is. Everything leapt back into focus. Time took up its march, then rushed at me with H-hour and the countdown. The needles on the instrument panel flicked over. I twisted around and stared out the porthole through high-density goggles . . ."

He gave a helpless shrug. "Who can describe a thing like that? There wasn't any black curtain between me and night and the future. There just wasn't anything but that sudden, silent gush of pitiless white light before whose blinding brilliance vanished sea and sky, all consciousness of space and time. Then out of it, like an immense planet which had hurtled out of its orbit toward us and suddenly burst into flame, appeared a monstrous ball of fire. Still it seemed to hang there motionless in dissolution, a livid red fireball more than three miles in diameter in a blinding white light, though it was swiftly rising from the impetus of a blast force more than twice its predicted yield. Then gradually changing into a gigantic cloud soaring aloft so high that it would encircle our planet three times. Beneath it now the tumultuous, upflung walls of water collapsed. The waves rushed in to fill a crater gouged 175 feet deep in the ocean floor, and the great Pacific swept over where once had been the tiny island of Elugelab."

He paused. "A terrible, compelling sight. Like the one Helen must have seen in her dream. One a man needs to see but once to know that he has been granted in his mortal lifetime a vision of that apocalypse in which each planetary body in time bursts into dissolution and vanishes into eternity. Yes! 'If the radiance of a thousand suns were to burst at once into the sky, that would be like the splendor of the Mighty One . . . I am become death, the shatterer of worlds.'

"I'll admit it. The fear was in me as in everyone else. I know that now. But at the moment I didn't feel it because of that strange, indissoluble connection between Helen Chalmers and the shot. I felt instead an overpowering surge of relief and gladness as if I were witnessing, far off in the Pacific, the death and transfiguration of that strange and lonely woman at Otowi Crossing whom I had never understood till then. The supernatural brilliance of that light, blinding as the radiance of a thousand suns; that tremendous release of the universal energy confined so long within her mortal frame; the final asssertion of spirit over matter;—they seemed to me then, and they have in some measure persisted ever since, the triumphant affirmation of her conviction of that enduring mystery which having no beginning could have no end, being the light and the life eternal, and not only the destroyer but the maker of worlds without end . . ."

He was an old, old man with a hairless brown head and a piercing stare. High in a New York skyscraper, he sat at a desk in an otherwise empty room whose door was lettered simply "M. Meru." The desk was bare save for a cheap household ledger labelled "Secret Journal."

For forty-three years he had been investigating psychic phenomena, and as an authority in his peculiar field he was consulted by large foundations, universities, the courts, theatrical agencies, doctors, psychiatrists, and an increasing number of persons compelled to learn of his existence.

"Most of the cases called to my attention are quickly detectable as conscious or unconscious deceptions—outright frauds, professional tricks, spurious age regressions, psychopathic disorders," he began in a gentle voice. "Those remaining take most of my time; they are of growing concern to a large number of my clients. The Throckmorton Endowment Fund, as you know, has supported some of my research. The time is coming when we shall have a National Institute of Parapsychology to take over what some people call my curious hobby. Telepathy, clairvoyance, fragmentary memories of prenatal existence, precognition—such things are no longer rare nor unusual. Even authenticated instances of the experience of creative totality commonly known as 'enlightenment' are occurring at an ever increasing rate. It is a component of our nature derided and repressed so long, I suppose, that under the increasing stresses and strains of our materialistic age it is suddenly breaking forth . . . Or perhaps man is indeed reaching a new phase in his development."

He opened his folded, withered brown hands and gently tapped the household ledger before him.

"To get back to Helen Chalmers . . . Mr. Turner brought me her *Secret Journal* here; he was thinking of destroying it as the product of an unbalanced mind. I found it, on the contrary, to be the most complete and courageous record of a valid mystical experience in modern times ever called to my attention. I urged him to publish it. Mr. Turner was unable to comply with my request. How could he reverse his beliefs of a lifetime and admit that his view of Miss Chalmers had been wrong? No; we must understand these things too. But he placed it in my care, with the understanding it would be published after my death."

Mr. Meru paused. "Mr. Turner also kindly persuaded Dr. Emily Chalmers to allow me to peruse her mother's notes on her *Inquiry*. They compliment the *Journal* in an extraordinary way, restating Helen Chalmers' own personal experience in the ritual terms of a primitive people. I was not surprised although I know nothing of the latter. Granting the universality of such an experience, it can be stated in any media of expression, ancient or modern. I was, however, unable to secure the Doctor's assent to make them public. For a woman so established in her field, she could hardly be blamed for refusing . . . No, one must accept both the static and dynamic points of view."

Mr. Meru's gentle voice broke off as he glanced at his watch. He pulled out a desk drawer, removed a little tin whistle and a bulky paper sack, and strolled to the open window. A thin whistle sounded, followed by a sudden whir of wings. In an instant the air was filled with pigeons fluttering around the grain he spread on the sill and flying inside to perch on his bald head and shoulders. A little man in blue serge enhaloed by white birds, Mr. Meru smiled quietly.

"Suppose that Helen Chalmers' *Journal* and her notes to her daughter's *Inquiry* are never released. Does it matter, really? Do they tell us anything more than the existing literature of many centuries? The myth of the Woman at Otowi Crossing, preposterous as it seems to many, is an ageless myth of deep import."

He erased his winged halo with a slight wave of his arm and sat down at the desk again. Reaching into a drawer once more, he brought out a thermos of hot tea, a cup, and a packet of brown wheat crackers. "My lunch time now. You and my inadequate teeth must permit me to dunk."

Chewing the end of a wet cracker, he went on. "In this day of over-rationalization we are inclined to disparage myths. We depend on science which is a record of observable facts. We treat even theology as a body of historical facts which outweighs its essential metaphysical meaning. Yet myth expresses as no other medium the deepest truths of life. No one consciously creates a myth. It wells up spontaneously within us in the same involuntary processes which shape the mind, the foetus within the womb, the atomic structure of the elements. So it is with the myth of the Woman at Otowi Crossing. We ourselves created it—we of a new age, desperately crying for a new faith or merely a new form that will model old truths to useful purpose. Helen Chalmers affirms our mistrust of the neuter and negative materialism of our time. In the image of a warm and pulsing human being, she embodies the everlasting Beauty combatting the Beast, the spirit versus the flesh, the conscience of man opposed to the will of man. Helen Chalmers is dead and will be forgotten, but the myth of the Woman at Otowi Crossing is woven of a texture impervious to time. We ourselves, each one of us in turn, simply tailor it anew for successive generations."

He opened the *Journal* and pushed it across the desk. A stray pigeon flew in, lighting on his shoulder. Mr. Meru began feeding it crumbs from his cracker, some of them falling on the excerpt he had pointed out:

So all these scribbled pages, Jack, are to help you understand that an awakening or Emergence, as the Indians call it, is more than a single momentary experience. It requires a slow painful process of realization and orientation. Just like a new-born child, you get it all and instantaneously in the blinding flash of that first break-through —the shattering impact of light after darkness, of freedom after confinement. Then the rub comes. The learning how to live in this vast new world of awareness. The old rules of our cramped little world of appearances won't work. You have to learn the new ones. The hard way too, because everything you've known takes on new dimensions and meanings. This process of awakening with new awareness, a new perspective on everything about you, of perceiving the "spherical geometry of the complete rounded moment" as Gaylord once called it—this is the wonderful experience I've been going through.

How many thousands of obscure people like me all the world over are having the same experience right now? And for no apparent reason, like me. Keeping quiet about it too, because they can't quite understand it at first or their friends might believe them mentally unbalanced. That's why some day you'll get this Dime-Store ledger. To reassure you it's a normal, natural experience that eventually comes to every one of us. So when your turn comes, Jack, don't be afraid. Be glad! It's our greatest experience, our mysterious voyage of discovery into the last unknown, man's only true adventure . . .

300